To Lee-Ann Ahlstrom

Fantastical wishes!

Benjamin

Wingheart

LUMINOUS ROCK

BOOK ONE IN THE WINGHEART TRILOGY

BENJAMIN GABBAY

ARKANE BOOKS

TORONTO, CANADA

Published by Arkane Books
Toronto, Canada
www.arkanebooks.com

Library and Archives Canada Cataloguing in Publication
Gabbay, Benjamin
    Wingheart : luminous rock / Benjamin Gabbay.
(Wingheart ; 1)
ISBN 978-0-9880543-0-1
    I. Title. II. Title: Luminous rock. III. Series: Gabbay,
Benjamin. Wingheart ; 1.
PS8613.A23W56 2012   jC813'.6   C2012-902964-5

Cover art and design by Tomasz Maronski
http://tomaszmaronski.carbonmade.com/
Internal art by Benjamin Gabbay
Author photos by Jeff Bloom

Printed in Canada

Preserving our environment
Arkane Books chose Legacy TB Natural
100% post-consumer recycled paper for
the pages of this book printed by Webcom Inc.

MIX
Paper from
responsible sources
FSC FSC® C004071
www.fsc.org

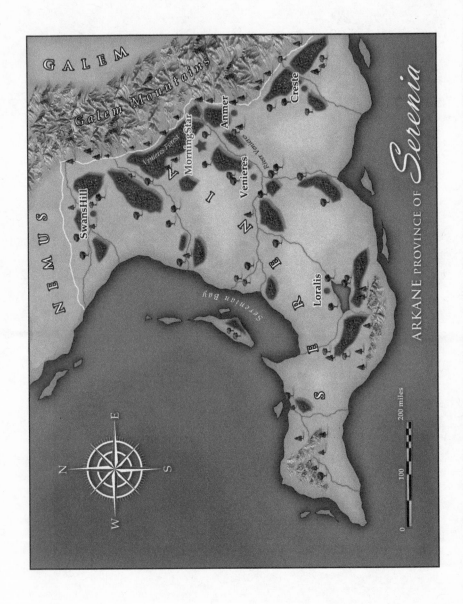

ARKANE PROVINCE OF *Serenia*

TABLE OF CONTENTS

Table of Contents

Table of Contents

The Burial

THE COLD, UNBLINKING EYE of a full moon cast its glare upon the forest floor. Its pallid light gave form to the mist that coursed like a river of smoke over the damp earth, breaking against the stagnant, spectral columns of ancient oak and cedar. There was a wind, too faint to disturb more than the frailest of leaves, yet enough to instill the air with a nearly imperceptible whisper. But the stillness was torn by a rustle of footsteps, signaling the arrival of two men as they approached an open glade within the deepest reaches of the forest.

The men were draped in identical dark cloaks, complete with hoods that shadowed their features. Their steps slowed as they entered the clearing. Before them stood an empty grave—a monolithic headstone artfully sculpted of slate-gray granite, with a freshly dug hole nested at its base, the earth and mud piled neatly nearby.

"Here it is." One of the men drew toward the headstone and shook his sleeve off his black leather gauntlet to palm the stone's surface. "Lay the coffin next to it."

Another four men clad in the same sinister garments emerged from the darkness of the trees. Together, they bore the weight of an august wooden coffin, elaborately carved as if it belonged to a king. One of them lugged a thickly braided rope with which to lower the coffin into the grave. When the men reached the clearing, they set the coffin down next to the headstone.

"The rest of the troop will arrive shortly," said one of the two who had first entered the glade. The six men kneeled around the coffin, hands on their laps, observing the ethereal rays of the moon shimmer upon the casket's ornate façade.

"Our master is dead," the first man proclaimed in a tone of deep sorrow. "The greatest power ever known to this world has departed...and our invincible empire falls to rubble."

A silence passed before the next man spoke, burying his face in his palms. "I do not understand..." he muttered, his voice dampened by his gauntlets' leather. "He was a lich. You cannot kill the immortal!"

The man who sat at the farthest end of the circle grimaced despondently. His eyes fell from his companions and came to rest on the coffin. "There were powers afoot within that temple that we cannot begin to comprehend," he said. "Our master was dabbling in forces beyond even his control. Too often did we witness their danger; it must have been no less than those forces that cost him his life."

Only seconds passed before another wave of footsteps descended on the glade. An even larger gathering of cloaked men began making their way through the pall of tangled branches, advancing stalwartly toward the clearing in which their master's coffin rested. They were trailed by the last three of the men—bearers of tall, murky-gold candles that were etched with a skein of glyphs smothered in hardened beeswax. Marching with even pace, the entire party entered the glade and dispersed across it.

The candles were set down and positioned meticulously, one at the casket's head and one at each side of its base. As the men came to kneel around the coffin, one raised his hand and, as if by magic, with nary a touch to the wicks, the candles vigorously flared alight.

The assembly bowed low to the coffin, their hoods wilting until their eyes were obscured by the black cloth. They beheld the fateful silence and, with folded hands, commenced their solemn requiem beneath the watchful gape of the moon.

"Master," one of the men began to speak, "we are eternally indebted to you for ushering us into a new era of power and glory. Under your indomitable rule, our empire rose to conquer the mightiest kingdoms and dethrone the insolent monarchies that plague this world. You brought death and terror to our enemies; you rendered us powerful and feared by all. You always remained loyal to us, just as we remained loyal to you. You embodied the very essence of the Treus Aetherae, and the boundless powers in death, which you once conquered and wielded as your almighty weapon, but which ultimately turned against you in their untameable ways. Now, as we lay you down into this sacred earthen bed, we ask you, if you wish to show us—speak to us—one last time before you sleep. For even to the grave, we will always remain loyal to you, our Lord, Master, and one true leader."

With shut eyes and fallen heads, the men awaited their master's response. Time stood still as no sound was heard, nor was any word spoken, until, finally, a vicious burst of wind slashed through the trees. Like a serpent, the airstream coiled and slithered around the followers, sending shivers up their spines. Smiles spread across the men's faces as they opened their eyes, believing they could sense the very presence of their master.

With that sudden boast of wind, the topmost candle was knocked onto the edge of the casket. Its flame began to lick along the coffin, scoring its way up to the lid, where it stopped and remained still in a single place, burning the wood where it rested.

The men bored their gazes raptly into the flickering ember as if in anticipation of something to occur. And at last, the flame moved. It drifted across the coffin, etching a faltering cursive strain of symbols into the wood. After it came still again, ashes settled within the black groove of its trail; and indeed, the symbols were letters, forming words:

I am not dead

The followers were astounded. "I do not believe it..." said one man, gaping in amazement. "He truly is a lich!"

Shifting from his kneeling posture, the next man laid a quivering hand upon the lid of the coffin before posing his question: "But, Master, we ask you, what fate has befallen you, if you say you are not dead?"

The flame was mute at first; it appeared as if the force that had driven it were waning, unable to deliver its response. But within seconds, it moved again, drawing across the wood to leave a trembling inscription in its wake:

I am alive
But my soul is trapped

"Trapped!" one follower exclaimed as the sentence eased to a close under the flame. "How is that possible?"

"Wait," interjected another man, raising a hand in silence, then lowering it onto the peak of the casket lid. "You say, Master, that you are not dead, and that your soul is trapped. Will you ever live among us again? And if so, when?"

The coffin's flame shot up fiercely, sending sparks of the fire flying. This time without delay, it scrawled a promising reply:

When I regain my power

For a lingering moment, the followers were left to study their master's script, unsure of what to speak next. Likewise, the flame burned in staunch wait. "How?" was all that one man asked.

Though the flame first appeared to wither, it rose again to engrave, as if in a whisper, their master's final response:

**My future followers
will lend their power to me**

Instantly, the flame vanished from the coffin's surface. The followers were awestruck, bound still to their places on the forest floor by their master's portentous message. Said one of the men in a hoarse murmur, an irrestrainable grin curling about his lips:

"Our master, Drakathel, is alive."

Morning Star

UNSET BURNED AWAY THE sky like flames set to a canvas of blue silk. The autumn air was crisp and still, disturbed only by the occasional drone of a passing vehicle or the fleeting whip of the wind. One young man, Magnus Wingheart, trod solitarily along the sidewalk, one hand coiled around the strap of the empty messenger bag that was slung over his shoulder.

Tall and well built, Magnus appeared older than his sixteen years. He sported a long-sleeved shirt layered over a pair of bleached denim jeans. His thick brown hair fell slovenly past his forehead, resting on fair eyebrows set above dark-hazel eyes.

Magnus was returning to the bookshop owned by his older brother, Drake, where Magnus often spent his afternoons assisting with a variety of chores. One of the tasks he commonly assumed was sending out deliveries through a shipping depot just down the road. The shop frequently received orders, mainly for the rarity of the books that it sold—many dating back more than a century.

Inattentively, Magnus gazed over the familiar, irenic setting. The roadside was lined with a variety of quaint storefronts, most of which were base to an upper level of apartments. As if swathed in translucent gold silk, their rooftops caught the diminishing glow of the sun in the final minutes of its descent below the horizon.

The boy turned a corner and made his way down a crescent road. He didn't need to travel far from the mouth of the street before arriving beneath the forest-green awning of his brother's shop. Magnus clumsily shifted his bag onto the opposite shoulder, allowing him to retrieve a set of keys from his jeans pocket. He unlocked the door, and the rattle of the chimes above it announced his entrance. He lobbed the empty bag onto the floor as he stepped in, closing the shop door behind him.

Magnus scanned the soundless bookstore for his brother. Row upon row of wooden shelves extended across his view, brimming with innumerable tomes devoted to an endless array of topics. With no sign of Drake, Magnus presumed his brother to be out, or upstairs in the apartment where they lived. His eye caught sight of a scrap of paper taped to the cash register on the front desk, which sat by the display window at the left of the entrance. He paced up to the register and tore off the slip; bored disappointment trickled over his face as he read the note his brother had left him:

I've gone out to run a few errands. Please check the notebook in the top right drawer for another list of book orders.
Thanks,
Drake

Magnus twitched his lip, forcing a dry smirk. Though he was always willing to assist his brother, he often tired of the repetitious chores. He wrenched the drawer open and extracted his brother's notebook. Glancing at the scrawled column of book titles, he dragged an empty cardboard box out from underneath the desk and hauled it to the nearest aisle of shelves.

Tackling the task with little enthusiasm, Magnus found himself placing more attention on the haunting orange glow that loomed over the street outside the shop window than to locating the books that his brother had marked on the list. He idled as he became gripped by his musings, his mind cast adrift as clouds carried by wind.

Magnus had been helping his brother in the shop for close to six years now. Drake had started the business when he was nineteen, with the support of their then-guardian, Cecil Handel. Having raised the brothers for nearly a decade, Cecil was the closest that Magnus ever had to a father—his true parents, Brendan and Myra, had drowned in a sinking tour boat shortly after Magnus' birth. At least that was what Cecil and Drake had always told him. For Magnus, his parents' past was so vague that they would, at times, seem no less than imaginary.

Not even a photograph existed of them, and each time Magnus would try to question his brother about their parents' tragic demise, the issue was brushed aside for the reason that it was too dreadful to discuss.

Magnus was jarred from his daydream by the obnoxious roar of a motorbike streaking past the bookshop. His lackluster stare trailed the bike down the road and into the fading sunset, before falling back on the crate beside him, reminding him of his task.

Since Magnus was familiar with the stock of the shop, it didn't take him long to locate the books on Drake's list and pile them trimly inside the box. Seeing his work complete, Magnus heaved the crate up to his chest. He lumbered toward the back of the store to arrive at the open doorway of the shop basement, where his brother stowed the books for delivery. After steadying his balance with the load in his arms, he began his descent down the basement's sheer flight of stairs.

The air here was dank and musty, like that of a long-abandoned cellar. The basement was the one part of the bookshop that was rarely ever cleaned. Magnus had many times offered to do the task, but his brother was firm to refuse, insisting that he'd eventually take care of it. It was apparent, however, that Drake's workload prevented him from doing a thorough job. In hopeless disarray, books and crates were stacked about the basement floor, smothered in a weeks-thick, undisturbed coat of dust. A beige rug mottled with inerasable filth was sprawled over the center of the room. There was no light aside from the few pale rays that managed to penetrate the grimy panes of the windows on the western wall, and after sundown, it quickly grew dark here.

With the unwieldy crate obstructing his view, Magnus placed his step too far over a stair and stumbled. His heart lurched as his surroundings churned and he plummeted down the incline. He lost his grip of the crate, which hurtled to the ground, casting its books in twenty directions across the hardwood floor.

Magnus groaned from the pain of his impact with the ground. He pulled himself to a kneel and began to collect the tomes that lay scattered from the foot of the stairs all the way to the farthest ends of the room. After gathering the lot, he took count of the pile he had recovered. He was one book short. Magnus recounted, feeling certain he had scoured the entire basement. Of course, he could have easily overlooked something in such dim light. He had always disagreed with his brother over his refusal to install a lamp in the room. Drake had insisted that because the room was rarely used, it wasn't worth spending the money.

The missing book was nowhere to be found. Magnus snatched a flashlight from one of the decrepit wooden shelves, flicked on its switch, and resumed his search. He was close to giving up when he saw the flashlight's beam fall on a mysterious bulk underneath one of the shelving units. He kneeled over, his head nearly touching the floor, and shone his light directly beneath the unit—there, the book lay.

Magnus set aside the flashlight and extended an arm

into the awkwardly narrow slot between the floor and the base of the shelves to retrieve the book. To his surprise, his fingertips made contact with ice-cold metal. His arm jolted in surprise, leading his hand to collide with another, duller object. This time, Magnus withdrew the item, pleased to find the book secured beneath his palm. He placed the tome back inside the box after brushing it free of the dust that clung to its cover, then reached for the flashlight again.

He flooded the light under the shelves to examine the cold piece of metal he had knocked his hand against. On closer inspection, the slot beneath the unit was surprisingly clean for an area of a room that saw so little attention. Near the base of the wall, under the gleam of the light, he spotted a thin metal rod that appeared as if it had been tossed there quite like the book.

Magnus tried to draw the rod out from under the shelves, but was only able to extract it halfway, as if it were snagged. When he tugged at the metal again, now with greater force, he managed to pull it free. It was, in fact, a short, blunt-ended steel rod; stranger yet, it was welded to the link of a heavy chain that appeared to lead under the shelving and along into the floor. When Magnus attempted to haul out the entire length of the chain, a clatter resounded from beneath the basement rug—like that of a key being turned in a lock.

Magnus lowered the rod and watched it mysteriously retract to its original position under the shelf with the sound of sharply clicking steel. Intrigued, he peeled back the rim of the rug to bare the hardwood slats beneath. What

Magnus saw there stunned him: a trapdoor had opened where the carpet once was, its fallen wood panel suspended from a hinge on its lip. A ladder was nailed to the rim of the opening, ushering the way into a pitch-dark shaft.

Magnus was rooted to his place by utter shock. This was the stuff of fiction—a trapdoor concealed so inconspicuously in the basement of his own brother's bookshop. Though he knew he ought to wait for Drake to return, he could not resist the lure of his curiosity. He had to explore the shaft.

Magnus seized the flashlight, flicked it on, and turned its head down into the stark blackness. Nothing more could be seen than the dull shine of hardwood about seven feet below. With a clammy grip and a hammering heart, he lowered himself into the shaft and descended the coarse wooden ladder. The room above faded while the gloom below devoured him. As he arrived at the bottom of the shaft, he immediately swept up his light.

An unremarkable table, mounded with at least a dozen books, and a matching chair stood in the room's center. The premises were confined, and made even more so by the hoard of books and wooden crates piled across the walls, spanning from the floor to the low ceiling.

Magnus drifted past the slovenly heaps of tomes. He cast the beam of his flashlight onto a particularly hefty volume—*The Markus Eal 3784 Herbology Encyclopaedia*. There wasn't anything too unusual about an encyclopedia, aside from the fact that this one was in astoundingly good condition for a book that didn't appear to be very modern.

Magnus would have been quick to consider this place no more than a storage chamber left behind by the building's previous owners, but the lived-in appearance of the room suggested otherwise.

He directed his beam onto the face of another, somewhat smaller book—*Conjuring the Secondary Elements: The Fundamentals of Advanced Spellcasting*. Magnus was taken aback by the puzzling title. He was left to presume it to be some form of occult book or fantasy novel, before turning his attention to the table behind him.

Of the many books stacked here, only one drew Magnus' attention. Enfolded in a jacketless crimson hardcover, it lay at the edge of the table, in front of the chair. Magnus took it into his hands to examine its title, set in shimmering gold letters: *MorningStar*. But as his eyes moved further down on the cover, he felt as if his heart had stopped from shock—the author was Brendan Wingheart, his father.

Magnus had barely another moment to think before he heard the entrance door's chimes ring faintly from high above him. "Magnus?" he heard Drake call out.

It took Magnus several seconds to reply. "I'm downstairs," he hollered back warily. "In...the basement."

Magnus didn't quite know how to describe where he was, or if his brother would understand. But when he looked up through the trapdoor, he received his answer. There Drake stood at the peak of the shaft, a half-lit silhouette against the basement ceiling. His face revealed no surprise, only an expression heavy with despondence, darkened by the shag of his brown hair.

Magnus tried to speak, but Drake stopped him, uttering the first words after their bout of silence: "How did you find this?"

A bitter anger settled inside Magnus upon hearing his brother's question. It was obvious from Drake's vacant response that he had known about this place. The boy laid the book back down onto the table and clambered up the ladder to face Drake. "I came down into the basement to store the books you told me to gather," answered Magnus in a frigid monotone, "when I tripped on the stairs. I fell, and one of the books slid under a shelf..." He shone the flashlight back under the unit where he had discovered the steel rod and chain. "...where I found this."

But Drake didn't even bother to look. Instead, his eyes fell shut under a wretched sigh.

"Did you know about that trapdoor?" Magnus questioned suspiciously, almost certain of his brother's reply.

Drake opened his eyes and reluctantly answered, "Yes. I did." And before Magnus could respond, his brother guided him back to the trapdoor. "Come," was all that Drake said before heading into the shaft.

Magnus descended the ladder without taking his eyes off his brother. Even the veins of his hands pulsed with ire against the splintered wooden rungs. Once both he and Drake had reached the bottom, Magnus used his flashlight to steer Drake's attention to the crimson book on the table.

"This book..." Magnus said sternly, "...did our father really write this book? What is this place, and how come you never told me about it?" The further that Magnus drilled his brother for answers, the more his fury seethed inside him. He couldn't fathom why Drake would have wanted to cover up something as important as a book that may have been written by one of their parents.

A thin lining of remorse pressed on Drake's face. He stepped past his brother and took a seat at the table. Straightening himself, he grasped the book firmly. "This book *was* written by our father," he said with audible guilt. "This place is my study. Sometimes I come here to read when you're out with your friends or running an errand."

"But what's so special about this place that you'd want to hide it from me?" Magnus' voice rose in frustration. "And these books..." he stole one of the volumes from the table at random and read its title aloud: "*Chronicles of the Archmages.* Why in the world would you stash all these... bizarre books down here? And what about the one our father wrote?"

Drake did not lift his vision from *MorningStar*'s resplendent cover, appearing absorbed and almost troubled in his pondering. "I hid these books from you for your own good, Magnus."

"What's so good about hiding our own father's past from me?" Magnus snapped, infuriated. "My whole life I knew practically nothing about our parents! Why didn't you ever tell me about that book?"

Drake rose from his seat and passed Brendan Wingheart's book back into Magnus' hands. "First, read this," he said. "Then, we can talk. Then, you can ask as many questions as you please."

Magnus silently considered his brother's offer. With an icy glower affixed on Drake, he delivered a slow nod in response. Drake smiled thinly, unease still heavy on his expression, then turned to ascend the ladder, leaving Magnus behind in the study with his father's book in his hold.

Magnus was paralyzed by the disarray of emotions that flooded him—anger, toward Drake, for having kept from him the true history of their father; frustration, for not understanding why he did; and fear, in wondering whether there was truth to the suggestion that the study had been concealed for his own good.

He pulled up the chair and sat down at the table, just as his brother had done. He took note of what appeared to be a lantern perched at the table's edge, but failed to see any obvious way of igniting it. Its construction was more like a birdcage, with a clouded pane of glass encircling an obscure, glimmering mechanism inside it.

Magnus set down his flashlight so that its beam was aligned with the pages of Brendan's book as he opened the volume on the table. He swept his fingertips through the dimly lit sheets, bringing them to rest on a page near the end of the book, where he skimmed over the text with voracious eyes:

> *After the war, exceptionally few of Recett's followers were found to remain loyal, or even alive, at last allowing Serenia a much-needed opportunity to recuperate after its gruesome battle.*

As for Recett himself, although many claimed to have seen him dead, some even declaring to have been his slayer, no evidence has, of yet, been brought forth to council that would offer proof of the warlord's death. Though the possibility of his survival must be seriously considered, it is not likely that Recett will ever again pose a threat with his forces in such a crippled state.

Magnus was endlessly perplexed by the mere paragraph he had read. Once he'd finish the book, he wouldn't know where to start questioning his brother. *I'll start*, he decided, *from the beginning*. So, as he reopened the book at its first page, taking his flashlight in a hand aquiver, he began, ardently, to read his father's words.

2

In Shade and Shadow

T WAS NEARLY TWO HOURS past midnight when the blackout struck Northvalley Crescent. The sudden collapse of an electrical pole had downed the power to some three dozen stately properties that branched off the narrow main road. Sunken in the pit of an overgrown vale, the street was an unlit void darker than the sky itself.

The houses here were perched on vast grounds sprawled across tree-strewn slopes and hillocks. Despite their mansion-like size, none were extravagant in appearance. The area's wealth of streetlamps served as an effective deterrent against all forms of unsavory activity, but circumstances were changed in a blackout. One particular home, nestled unobtrusively at the brink of an enormous plot of land, had already drawn a curious figure.

Outside of number twenty-four Northvalley, a man quietly loitered by the sidewalk that hemmed the main road. He was swaddled in a dense overcoat that draped to his feet, his neck roped in a wool scarf. His features were obscured in the gloom. His stance was nonchalant, but his eyes were avidly watchful of his surroundings. He took into view a second man, who made his approach from the far end of the sidewalk.

As the second man came near, his murky silhouette acquired definition. He was bundled in a similar coat and scarf and was crowned with a wide-brimmed fedora. There was nothing peculiar about his appearance, aside from the fact that his burly frame towered at close to seven feet. His hands were plunged deep into his pockets, and his face was half-buried in his scarf as if he felt unusually chilled in the mild autumn weather.

The tall man slowed to a standstill by his partner. "Looks like the whole street is out," he remarked.

The shorter man nodded with a furtive glance across the empty road. "You did well."

"I toppled the entire pole. Did you hear the impact from this distance?"

"A dull thud. Hardly enough to wake anyone."

"Good." The tall man motioned toward the residence. "Let's get moving. We have only as long as it'll take them to restore the power."

Together, the men slipped through the opening in the wrought-iron fence that encircled the property. They surveyed the driveway ahead of them, which climbed a steep hill before broadening to meet the mansion's distant silhouette. As they began their ascent toward the house, they veered off the paved path, treading alongside the thickly hedged north border of the grounds. Upon coming halfway, they halted and expectantly cast their gazes skyward.

Even in the stifling darkness, it was clear to see that the clouds above number twenty-four Northvalley that night did not behave the way of ordinary clouds. Ordinary clouds do not churn and shift by their own accord, nor do they throb as if they were coursing with life. Ordinary clouds are not black like the heart of an abyss, nor do they glimmer with the sheer outlines of bones, claws, and skulls. However, these were not ordinary clouds.

The shorter man raised his hand, which was instantly touched with a lining of black sparks that leapt and crackled at his curled fingertips. In response, the rolling mass of clouds above the mansion jolted in its movement, like an idle puppet stirred by a tug of its strings. And as the man lowered his arm with an intricate wave of his hand, the clouds obeyed him.

Swiftly, the clouds began to descend, disbanding into seemingly sentient billows of smoke that weaved a veil to engulf the mansion's rooftops. They were like specters spawned from the darkness itself, and although they each moved as if by their own will, they acted as one force, murmuring to one another in venomous breaths that laced the air with poison.

But before the specters could enshroud the mansion completely, the two men were jarred by the rattle of an igniting engine. The instant they both turned their heads, they saw a pair of high-beam headlights flicker alive in the darkness. With the beastly roar of a motor and the howl of rubber on tarmac, a pickup truck suddenly careened down the mansion's driveway at a speed that was unsound, if not perilous, on such a steep incline.

The shorter man whipped back his hand and the specters' descent ceased instantly. The sparks about his fingertips blazed to kindle an orb of flame black as a cinder. He lunged, hurtling the fireball with devastating velocity toward the speeding pickup. But the truck thundered on without flinching in its course. In a blur, the vehicle had passed, and the projectile dissolved into the distance behind it.

The man shed the smoldering remnants off his hand and grimaced madly. As the car swerved onto the main road with a stammering screech, it sped away to leave only the drone of its engine clinging to the silence for several long seconds. "He got away." The man spun around to his partner in a fury that glared even through his shadowed expression.

"How could he have seen us?" replied the tall man in a harsh whisper.

"It was probably the shades that he saw. He must have been awake when I called them down."

"What do you reckon we do now?"

The second man turned back toward the mansion and resumed his ascent. "He isn't all we're after. We search the house regardless."

As the men advanced, the specters, too, gathered their pace and continued to envelop the house within their writhing funnel. For any who dared draw so near to the mansion as the two men now did, the specters' soot-black, smoky forms became far more defined: their visages were like those of skeletons—skulls with glaring, empty concaves for eyes, their fleshless jaws sealed in unbending grins. Arms and claws as gaunt as bone dangled at their sides like barbed chains, seeping from the amorphous robes that enswathed their emaciated frames. They hovered, gliding as if by the aimless currents of the wind, as they trickled further into the grounds about the residence.

The men hastened over the peak of the hillside until they both arrived at the mansion. Under the specters' ethereal pall, the house appeared as little more than a mirage. Its front entrance was carved into an ivied façade and preceded by a flight of stone steps. A bay window jutted out from the eastern section of the wall, not far from a half-opened garage from where the pickup truck had made its exit.

The men proceeded directly up the stairs and to the front entrance. A fleeting tug on the handle by the shorter man confirmed the door to be locked, though the fact did not appear to disturb him. As he brought an upturned palm to level with the door lock, a shadowy vapor stole over his hand.

Immediately, a plume of black mist and splinters erupted from the face of the door with a clamor of snapping steel. When the debris settled, the door lock had been mangled as if by an explosion, rent from its place in the wood, broken and scorched. The man delivered a crushing kick to the foot of the door and broke it ajar, the remnants of its lock clattering to the floor in warped fragments of metal.

"Wait," the tall man summoned his partner's attention. "What about the shades?"

"Leave them," the second man answered quickly, his boot already leaning over the doorstep. "No one can see them in this darkness anyhow. They will depart along with us."

The tall man returned a nod of approval, and the two entered into the mansion. The interior of the house was even darker than the grounds outside, and any fixture that could have illuminated it was rendered ineffective by the blackout. At once, both men swept their hands beneath the hems of their coats and each extracted a peculiar utensil—something akin to a flashlight, though far more unusual. It was a shaft with a leather-bound grip, on the head of which was mounted a closed steel funnel. Each of the men brought a hand around the lip of his flashlight's funnel and wrenched it, parting an interlocked disc of fine metal blades to bare a glass lens over the mouth of the funnel. And without as much as a flick of a switch or any other apparent method of activation, a flood of dazzling rays poured out through the lenses of both flashlights and penetrated the darkness.

Now dappled by the glow of their lamps, the men's features became at least partially visible. The shorter man had a sickly pale complexion and a face that was narrow and sharp, draped over with curtains of frail, wood-brown hair.

His jasper eyes were sunken in pools of shadows, fiercely accentuated by low-set, tapered eyebrows. His mouth appeared as if it had been carved by a knife, like an unpliable slit in a mask. The man's name was Noctell Knever, and his callous expression alone bespoke his character.

The tall man slackened the coil of his scarf, allowing it to sag around his neck. As he tipped up the brim of his hat, his face was unveiled. His eyes were deep garnet, burdened down by a thick and stony brow. His nose jutted like an ill-positioned hook that dangled over his thin lips, complementary to the shape of his face that was whittled to a dull point at his chin. His most prominent feature, however, was his skin—it was blood-red, blemished with patches of dry, hard scales. His fingers, wrought in the same scarlet hide, were tipped with honed, obsidian-black claws in place of his nails. His name was Raven Gaunt, and while he may have been a man, he was far from human.

Noctell and Raven both flitted their lights across the room, which appeared to be a foyer. Containing only a few wooden fixtures, a closet, and an opulent rug, the chamber was void of anything that could immediately capture the men's interest.

"What are we searching for?" Raven asked matter-of-factly.

"Nothing too specific..." Noctell drawled, his eyes trailing the ray of his flashlight. "Since the fool escaped before we could pry any answers out of him, we'll have to find answers in his possessions. Naturally, anything of use to us would bear the Winghearts' name—Brendan's or his son's."

Raven slung a bitter glance across the foyer. "The man is a book hoarder and this place is nothing short of a mansion. Finding anything of use here will take till sunrise."

"We're not returning empty-handed." Noctell twisted his head to direct a scowl past his partner. "Provided the power isn't restored sooner, we have four hours until dawn. Search quickly."

"We'll split up to cover more rooms," Raven added.

Noctell waved the beam of his lamp over the two door-ways in view, one each at the right and front walls of the chamber. "I'll go straight," he motioned ahead. "You take the other door. We'll meet up later on."

Raven listlessly obeyed his partner's command and sauntered out of the foyer. Noctell steadied his light to shine through the doorway directly in front of him as he advanced into the next part of the mansion—an expansive living room. Much of the furniture here was antique, Victorian in appearance. Twin settees were arranged at opposite sides of a luscious carpet, accompanied by a unique assortment of armchairs and a stout wooden table. A stone fireplace, stoked with cinders and half-charred logs, was constructed into the wall across from Noctell, its mantle cluttered with a variety of ceramic vessels and tarnished bronze ornaments. Bookshelves were abundant here also, scattered between glass display cases and vivid oil paintings that left no portion of the walls unadorned.

Noctell turned to the bookcase immediately at his left and skimmed its contents. Many of the tomes were impressively old, though few appeared to be organized in any particular manner. Shifting his fickle attention, he found the volumes on an adjacent shelving unit to be arranged just as chaotically. He began tearing out the books at random, casting to the floor anything he deemed futile, striving to uncover something of importance. But he found even the most intriguing volumes to be useless when he leafed them through.

He discarded what seemed like the last of nearly a hundred books and breathed an irritable sigh. Grudgingly, he conducted a final search of the room. His scrutiny wandered from a tidy stack of newspapers to four unopened envelopes and an erratically marked wall calendar. When none offered anything of relevance, he was drawn to a quaint red telephone on a cabinet by an armchair.

Noctell swept open the top drawer of the cabinet. From a mire of loose papers inside, he withdrew a tattered booklet in black faux leather—an address book. He scanned its entries with a sleuth's eye, but failed to see his target's name listed anywhere. Finding nothing else worthy of his attention, he ambled on through a second doorway.

This was the library and possibly the largest part of the mansion. Barely a sliver of the walls was visible here, for they were submerged behind an endless procession of bookcases that towered from the floor to the lofty ceiling. The chain of shelving was interrupted only by a vast window draped with tasseled red damask.

Noctell painted his new surroundings with his light. This place was nearly double the size of the living room and far more commodious. The largest fixture, a great round table with a threesome of matching seats, was positioned by the right side of the window. The other corners of the room, which stretched almost beyond the scope of Noctell's light, were speckled with various chairs and ornate lamps mounted on small cabinets.

Noctell strode to the opposite end of the room, his paces heavy and resonant on the hardwood. He faced the bookshelves nearest to the left of the window and scanned them downward from their unreachable peak. The books here appeared to bear more solid order, but their sheer multitude was devastating. If there were anything of value to be found amidst the myriad tomes, it would take well past dawn to find it.

He turned to a three-drawer table at the side of the bookcase, in front of the window. Its surface was bare, save for a potted ivy plant with flourishing vines that seeped over the table's edge. Noctell lurched open the widest, middle drawer to find a miscellany of household trinkets mixed in with scrawled-on stationery. He tore the drawer off its mount, its entire contents clattering to the floor at his feet. He kneeled, brushing aside a pair of scissors and a broken pocket knife to gather up the spilled pages, when the sound of approaching footsteps reached his ears. He rose and directed his beam ahead to see Raven emerge into the library through a distant second entrance.

Noctell waited until his partner had drawn close enough before hollering to him. "Anything?" he asked, his tone void of anticipation.

"Nothing," Raven replied snappishly. "The house is

monstrous. Either we waste an hour skimming the surface or spend a day hollowing out every bookcase and cabinet."

"We're not trying to find a cache of jewels," Noctell retorted. He stooped to recollect the papers, browsing them as he came upright. "Anything with a shadow of significance will suffice. Our chances are best if we limit our search to the library and rummage through any loose papers we see."

Raven allowed his eyes and his light to stray until they fell on an arrangement of furniture in the far-left corner of the room. There was an elaborate, multi-drawered writing desk—an escritoire—strewn with papers, adjoined by a high-backed armchair and an antiquated floor lamp. "Checked that desk yet?" Raven asked in barely a mutter.

Noctell responded with a shake of his head and followed the hulking shadow of his partner toward the escritoire. Raven batted a collection of ballpoint pens off the desk's surface and seized the remaining papers into his clawed grasp. These were letters, some unopened, others tucked inside torn envelopes. Noctell paused as if in thought, then cast aside the pages in his hand and tore open the left of the unit's two bottom drawers. He stole out a generous mound of tattered envelopes and riffled through them voraciously, only to come to a sudden halt at the sight of a familiar name.

Noctell grinned as if he had struck riches. "Let's go," he said in a brusque and startling command.

"What?" Raven turned to Noctell on impulse. Before another question could part his lips, his partner handed him an empty envelope.

"This letter appears to have been sent by Drake

Wingheart," Noctell beamed, discarding the rest of the envelopes in a fluttering rain of parchment. "His address is on it. We've found all we need."

Raven's brow twitched as his face came alight. "That'll do nicely." He greedily swiped the envelope and sheathed it into a pocket in his coat lining.

"Looks like we're finally closing in," Noctell added wryly. "It can't be much longer before Handel and Wingheart are both ours."

"It's taken long enough as it is," replied Raven. "I feel like I've spent half my life searching for a bloody address."

"No matter." Noctell padded away from the escritoire, his stare gripping the library window. "It's nearly over with now. Be thankful that all our efforts weren't in vain."

Raven drew beside his partner and gazed out the window from under the brim of his hat. "Where now? Do we hail another cab out of here and find Wingheart's street?"

"The address points to another city," Noctell replied. "And we haven't a clue how far away it is. We're not going to stage a break-in in broad daylight, and we have less than four hours until sunrise. It's unlikely we'll manage to find the house in that time. We'll transport back to MorningStar, then we can plan our next steps."

Raven nodded, and Noctell reached beneath his coat collar. He extracted an ominous-looking pendant—a small stone carved in the shape of a distinct form of skull and strung by a waxed black cord. The skull's scalp was round, like a flawless sphere, with a cork-sized, notched cylinder set below it as its teeth. The hollows of its eyes and nose were gaping and slanted upward, set in a contorted frown that seemed to convey too perturbing an expression for a simple stone neckpiece.

In the clasp of his fingertips, Noctell wrung the pendant's cylinder sharply, loosening it from its mount inside the skull before proceeding to unscrew it with forceful twists. As he delivered a final turn, prying out the cylinder entirely, a tempestuous flood of smoke-thin black ashes poured out from the cavity now exposed within the skull sphere.

The ash cloud took only seconds to swarm and enshroud the men. As if with a mind of its own, it wound about the bodies of Noctell and Raven, billowing to seal them within a cloak of cinders. The instant the cloud rose overtop Raven's fedora, it collapsed and dispersed into a lifeless mist while leaving nothing behind it. Devoured by the ashes, the men had vanished.

Cecil Handel lowered his binoculars. Far below him, Northvalley Crescent loomed like a canyon of shadows. His feet retained their tenacious grip on the crest of the thicketed hillside, though both his legs and arms coursed with tremors. The air, which carried scarcely a breeze, felt arctic against his sullen visage, while his every inhalation seemed to stoke the scalding fire that grew within the pit of his chest.

After narrowly escaping the assault on his home, Cecil had fled in his pickup truck to a secluded side street that grazed the summit of the valley's eastern wall. From here, he had managed to keep watch of his house by the glimmer of its intruders' flashlights behind its windows. But as the lights had suddenly disappeared, so had his ability to perceive anything in the blackout.

Cecil turned to survey the dead-end road behind him where he had parked his pickup, still not easing the double-handed clasp on his binoculars. Though the houses here were dark, the streetlights were operational. He hoped that, at such an early hour, he would not be seen as a dubious loiterer; but he knew that this was, by far, the least of his concerns.

He knew what were the creatures that had descended on his mansion. He was familiar with them—perhaps too much so. He knew from where they had come, and he had for over a decade been haunted by the dread of encountering them again. He knew the aims of the man who had sent them, and he feared gravely for the people who would be targeted next.

Cecil darted for his pickup, his shadow cleaving the still rays of the streetlights. *I feared this day would come*, his mind raced. He dove inside the car and slammed the door shut. *Sixteen years haven't made them give up.*

As the roar of his engine broke across the silent road, Cecil veered his pickup into a precipitous turn and sped off ahead into the night.

3

A Turn for the Worse

AGNUS KNEELED to collect the morning paper at the foot of the doorstep. Dawn's glow smarted his eye as he rose. The storefronts lining the opposite side of the street still lay partly in shadow, the sun's rays only beginning to seep over the contours of the eastern rooftops.

Magnus turned back to grip the chill-bitten handle of the apartment door, sunken behind the left end of the bookshop window. Proceeding through, he made his way up the steep flight of stairs that climbed to the second level of the building. Like much of the apartment and the shop below it, the staircase was timeworn but sturdy, barely mustering a creak under the weight of Magnus' step.

He entered the apartment. The living room was fairly large for a residence so discreetly nestled above a bookshop. Blanketed by the dull shine of a floor lamp, an oval glass table stood before a wide, beaten couch that was set against the wall, a pair of matching seats arranged nearby. Though the premises were well kept, they were piled with an abundance of dated newspapers and book-filled cardboard boxes that had found their way upstairs from the bookshop's confined storeroom.

Magnus proceeded to the table, where his gaze immediately took hold of the scintillant-lettered book that lay on the glass pane—*MorningStar,* by his father, Brendan Wingheart. Tucking the newspaper under his arm, he grasped the tome and brought it near to his face. It had been a little under a week since he'd first discovered the book. It was just the previous night that he'd finally turned its last page. His brother had promised him an answer to every one of his questions once he'd read the book entirely, and Magnus wouldn't waste a day to hear them.

Magnus turned and headed left, through the wood-trimmed doorway of the kitchen. Drake was there, standing by the counter as he withdrew a pair of porcelain plates from the overhead cabinet. He whipped around and hastily laid out the dishes on the dining table, outstretching a hand to the younger brother to accept the morning paper. "Thank you, Magnus."

But as Magnus approached, he discarded the rolled newspaper into a corner of the oblong table. He passed *MorningStar* into Drake's open hand, meeting his stare intently. "I've finished it," he declared. "Just last night. Now we can talk."

Drake gaped, as if caught off guard. He hardened his

grip on the tome and stammered at the first response he tried to muster, then laid the book aside and quickly diverted his attention back to the kitchen counter. "Later. Later this afternoon when the shop is closed. We can't spend time now discussing something so...complex."

"The shop doesn't open for a couple hours," Magnus protested. "Can't you at least tell me now why those books were hidden down there in the first place?"

"Please, Magnus, these aren't questions I can answer in five minutes!" Drake hastened to distribute cutlery over the table, dodging eye contact with his brother.

"You don't have to," Magnus countered. "We can talk over breakfast. I don't expect you to answer all my questions now; I just want to know why you'd hide our own father's past from me! I've waited a week to ask you!"

Drake picked up his head and attempted feebly to reply, but he was cut short by a clamant rapping on the apartment door. The brothers stiffened and turned on impulse in the direction of the noise. Seconds later, the knocking repeated. Drake glanced at his wristwatch as he hurried out of the kitchen. "Who in their right mind...?"

Magnus trailed his brother through the living room and down the entrance staircase, arriving at the apartment door. Drake strained to peer through the door viewer, then pulled away with widened eyes. He turned the lock and swept open the door. "Cecil!"

A middle-aged man stood in the entranceway. His wiry figure was of average height, his face framed with dark-gray hair that trickled down the length of his neck and brushed the collar of his olive-green trench coat. His sapphirine eyes gleamed brightly under shaggy eyebrows, but his smile was thin and faltering as he greeted the older Wingheart. "Good morning, Drake." He tipped his head, hands buried inside his pockets. "I-I apologize for disturbing you so dreadfully early."

"Oh, no disturbance at all! Come right in!" Drake showed Cecil Handel inside the tight vestibule, clearly startled by his former guardian's unexpected arrival. "But what on earth brings you here at this hour? Is everything alright?"

Cecil seemed more intent on sealing the door behind him than on answering Drake's question. He tossed his attention about with obvious anxiety, bringing it to rest on Magnus, whom he also greeted with a curt nod. "No, no, everything's..." he choked on his words as he turned to face Drake again. "Perhaps we'd best talk inside."

Drake read the dire urgency in Cecil's tone. He forced down his angst in a hard gulp, suddenly eager to divert from the subject. "Let me take your coat."

Cecil slipped off his coat and passed it to Drake as he followed the older brother up the staircase. Magnus lumbered behind, his paces made heavy by unease. He was disappointed at having been cut short in his questioning about the book, but his former guardian's solemnity told of far more pressing matters.

It was not a rare occasion that Cecil would travel to meet the brothers in their shop, despite the arduous length of the drive. Whether he would come to donate books from his immeasurable collection, or simply for an afternoon visit, he was a person who never seemed to abandon his joyous air—until today, when his usual cheeriness was replaced by a stagnant mask of dread.

The three headed into the kitchen, where Drake slung the coat over the back of a chair and nervously ushered Cecil into a seat at the dining table. "Have you...have you had breakfast yet?" he stammered.

"No." Cecil directed a boring stare through the older brother. "No I haven't. I'm afraid I left my house in a bit of a rush this morning."

Drake nodded weakly, clearly disturbed. He swiveled over to the counter, beginning to trifle with any utensils at his disposal, as if to stall while he devised a response. Magnus joined Cecil at the table and tried to speak also, but found that the troubling silence weighed his mouth shut.

As Drake passed a sideways glance over his shoulder, he saw that Cecil's stare had become affixed on the book *MorningStar* that Drake had laid on the table minutes earlier. The older brother turned to deliver a brusque explanation. "Magnus came across the book last week," he blurted out, then slowed his speech. "He just finished reading it yesterday night."

Cecil furled his brow in a display of inquisitive surprise. "I see." He took the tome into his hands, tilting his head in Magnus' way. "So?" he asked expectantly. "Did you enjoy your father's book, Magnus?"

Irritation hardened Magnus' expression. It was apparent that Cecil had known of the book just as Drake had. "An interesting read," he coldly remarked. "I didn't know that my father wrote fiction."

Cecil remained impassive. "Fiction?" He shook his head. "I assure you this is no work of fiction."

"None of the places mentioned in there ever existed," Magnus stubbornly objected, "and none of what it says ever happened...anywhere. But even if it did, it makes no sense. If this is my father's account of actual events, then why does it read like some surreal piece of fantasy?"

After a despairing pause, Cecil replied. "I wish I could tell you that every word of this book was purely fabricated," he said, "that this is no more than a tale of fantasy. But if that were so, I'm afraid I would not have come to alert you to the danger we face."

Magnus pulled a bewildered frown, looking to Drake from the corner of his eye. His older brother's face was marked by terror, more so than Magnus had ever seen. "What happened?" Drake exclaimed, buckling over to clutch the rim of the table.

"They found us, Drake." Cecil's tenor was dark and forlorn. "Last night, my house was attacked."

"Attacked!" Magnus nearly sprang upright. "Attacked by whom?"

Cecil was heedless of the boy's question. His attention remained fastened on Drake, who descended, trembling, into the third of the four chairs around the dining table. "By whom, Cecil?" Drake repeated Magnus' words with more sobriety.

Cecil reclined limply into his seat, sighing through

gritted teeth. "It was shortly after 2 a.m.," he began. "I was woken by an alarm, specifically one by my bedside that's triggered when my home security system is deactivated. The house was pitch-dark and none of the lights worked. By the looks of it, the area's power had gone out. I couldn't see much out of my window...until I looked up." He turned a disquieted grimace to the kitchen floor. "I'd recognize those ghastly clouds anywhere. An entire shade horde had gathered above the house."

"A *what?*" Magnus interjected, but was promptly silenced by his brother. "Please, Magnus," Drake barked, his voice quavering.

"I grabbed a flashlight, a change of clothes, and my coat, and made for the garage," Cecil continued. "I managed to get in my car just in time. As I sped out and down the driveway, someone assaulted me from the darkness, but I was moving too fast for them to land a hit.

"I escaped unscathed, thank heavens. I was forced to take a cumbersome detour because the road was blocked by a collapsed electrical pole—clearly the cause of the blackout and the doing of the people who attacked me. I headed for Meryle Drive, a cul-de-sac that overlooks Northvalley. From there, I was able to survey my house from afar with a pair of binoculars I store in my pickup. There were at least two people inside; their lantern lights were visible through the windows. But they vanished after barely an hour had passed. I can only assume that they found what they came for, else they wouldn't have fled so quickly.

"Whatever they found, of course, you'd be their obvious next targets. I stopped for supplies and made it here as fast as I could. I'm sorry to be the bearer of bad news, but...I suppose we knew this day would come."

"What is all this?" Magnus questioned his former guardian again in a more demanding volume. "Who attacked you? What were they after? None of what you're saying makes any sense until you explain!"

"I'll explain later, Magnus!" Drake pleaded, but his brother remained unconvinced.

"And why would they want us next?" Magnus persisted. "If we're all being hounded by a couple of book thieves, then we'll just call the police!"

"Book thieves! I wish!" Cecil scoffed grimly at Magnus' assumption. He pinned a scowl on the boy. "There is nothing the police can do. There is nothing we can do. We must flee from here by sundown or else risk being slaughtered in our own beds!"

"No!" Magnus snapped. "Not until one of you explains to me what any of this means! It's enough that I've had to wait a week just to ask why my own father's book was kept hidden from me; now we're blindly running away from something, and I don't even know what!"

Cecil took hold of Magnus' shoulder in a steadying grip. "Now is not the time, Magnus! I promise you, soon all will be explained, but for now we must leave! Leave! We are in danger, and that is all that matters!"

Magnus said nothing in reply. His eyes showed seething frustration for being left in such ignorance.

"I'm sorry, Magnus." Cecil breathed heavily, mellowing his anxiety. "We'll talk as soon as we're out of here and on the road."

"Where will we go?" Drake pulled a bleak frown.

"I believe the shelter outside Markwell would serve us best," Cecil answered the older brother, who appeared to understand fully. "It will, of course, take us most of the day to reach it. Assuming that Recett won't pull off another attack until dusk, we have plenty of time to pack and head out. Still, we'd be wise to leave soon and reach our destination before dark. Night will blind us by the time we reach the countryside if we leave here too late."

Drake propped his forehead in his palm. "Magnus..." he sighed without lifting an eye to his brother. "Go and pack any of your things you'll need for at least a week. We may be gone for quite a while."

"Pack a couple of sleeping bags also, if you have them," Cecil added. "In the place we're heading, I don't have much to offer in the way of a bed."

Magnus shook Cecil's clasp off his shoulder as he rose from his seat. With only a wordless parting scowl to each of his companions, he stole *MorningStar* off the table and briskly exited the kitchen. After a despondent pause, Drake turned again to his former guardian in an invitation to break the silence.

"Does he know...?" Cecil said in a voice barely above a whisper.

"Nothing more besides what he read," Drake answered.

"How did he discover the book to begin with?"

"He found it in the storeroom chamber. Somehow he stumbled upon the trapdoor while I was out."

Cecil's focus became suspended in a pensive trance over the chair where Magnus had sat. "Rather ironic, it is," he muttered, "how that book came to surface only a week before this whole mess started up again."

Drake nodded ponderously, bringing his head to rest in his hands. "I was naïve to think I could bury our entire past under the floorboards of a storeroom. It would have been better if he'd found that book long ago. Maybe then we could have done something to prevent this."

"That isn't something you can regret," said Cecil. "We could have done nothing. It seems no matter where we would have fled, we would only have been delaying the inevitable."

"Does this always have to be about fleeing?" Drake irritably replied. "Of course, nothing will ever change if all we do is run from one hiding place to another!"

"Can we do anything else?" Cecil answered, eyes tilting in a dismal expression. "Last night was a vivid reminder of the enemy we face. It is an enemy we are powerless against, and one that will stop at nothing to achieve its goals. We cannot fight it, and that is why we run from it."

Despair settled over Drake's face. He hauled himself up from his seat and plodded past the table, halting in the doorway of the kitchen. "You're right," he conceded. "We should start packing. We'll want to leave here by noon."

"We ought to take along any books that require safe-keeping," Cecil suggested, rising to draw beside the older

Wingheart. "Specifically those under the storeroom. I can load them on the back of my truck."

"Not many—only those of significant use or value." Drake turned suddenly to his former guardian. "And my father's satchel as well. The stone and the notebook should still be in it."

"Of course." Cecil gave a mindful nod. "We wouldn't want to leave behind the things we're being hunted for to begin with."

Magnus found himself growing less and less attentive of the situation at hand. As he abstractedly fed the contents of his dresser into the travel bag sprawled beside him, his thoughts were carried further off along tides of aggravation and confusion. Never in his life had he felt so lonesome—as if he hardly knew his own brother. The discovery of his father's book had already put into question much of what he'd been told about his past, but Cecil's bewildering warning seemed to suggest that far more had been kept from him.

Reviewing the lot of his belongings, Magnus shut the dresser vigorously and sealed the full bag. His gaze drifted to the ceiling as he fell back limply against the side of his bed. *"I wish I could tell you that every word of this book was purely fabricated,"* Cecil's voice throbbed in Magnus' mind, *"that this is no more than a tale of fantasy. But if that were so, I'm afraid I would not have come to alert you to the danger we face."*

Magnus turned around to retrieve *MorningStar* from where he had earlier left it on his bed. His hands embraced the vintage texture of the book's fabric binding. *Why should the reality of my father's stories be tied to Cecil's attack?* he mused to himself. He sought answers in the pages of the book, which he thumbed through vigilantly.

"...*Council of MorningStar*..." a fragmented medley of phrases flitted past Magnus' eyes, "...*mounted troops to the Serenian Border...swayed by councillor Larke's harangue*..." The words that had perplexed him over the course of last week were made no clearer after Cecil's arrival. This was a telling of a history that never existed, yet it was, according to his former guardian, no less than the truth.

"...*that Recett's forces had reached the outskirts of Nayr.*" Magnus was jarred by a single sentence that entered into his field of vision. Recett—it was as if the name were haunting him. The book was riddled with mentions of this supposedly powerful person, but strangest of all had been just earlier when Cecil himself uttered the name: "*Assuming that Recett won't pull off another attack until dusk*..." he had said.

Eras Recett, Magnus recalled the man's full name as he had read it in his father's book. *Who is he?* The book seemed to portray him as a councilman who became a cult leader and warlord—a general whose commanding might resided in his vast army of devotees and mercenaries. According to Brendan, Eras had seized one of the largest cities within a land known as Serenia, only to suffer a narrow defeat to the guard of the capital city of MorningStar.

But even the absurdity of that story paled in comparison to the book's offhand references to sword fighting, crossbows, and magical conjuring. Whatever sort of tale this was, it certainly wasn't factual. Cecil, however, had insisted otherwise. *Then what is it?* Magnus repeated a question that had plagued him from the moment he'd first picked up the book. The back cover offered nothing save for a silvery stamp that read "Elkridge Press." The first pages of the book contained what he assumed to be publishing details, but even these were maddeningly obscure.

"Have you finished packing, Magnus?" Drake's call from the living room jolted the boy from his ruminations.

Magnus hastily fitted the book into a side-pocket of his bag and slung the load crosswise over his shoulder. "Coming," he answered in a volume hardly loud enough for his brother to hear.

He exited his bedroom with a melancholy gait and proceeded down the short hall back into the living room. Drake stood there alone, saddled with a pair of swollen travel bags. He motioned to a third piece of luggage slumped at his feet. "Take your sleeping bag," he droned. "We're ready to go."

Magnus hauled the last bag over his free shoulder and straightened his overburdened frame. "Where's Cecil?"

"Outside, loading the pickup," Drake replied, his attention clinging to empty space. "We're taking along some of the books from...that room under the basement." He slanted an eye at the boy. "Did you take *MorningStar?*"

Magnus nodded, feeling for the bulk of the book along

the side of his bag. As the brothers retrieved their jackets off
the coat stand by the entranceway, Drake heaved a sigh and
trudged on down the staircase, Magnus following behind.

Each step of his descent, Magnus felt as if he were fading
ever further from his life of normality, and everything that
he had ever known to be true and sound. Even if he were
to soon return here, it did not seem likely that anything
would be the same as it had been before he discovered his
father's book. He struggled to assure himself otherwise,
but he remained unable to shake from his mind the sense
that things had only taken a turn for the worse.

Drake seized the handle of the apartment door
and swept it open, drawing the autumn wind inside
the vestibule. Cecil's pickup was parked across from
the bookshop, loaded trimly with a small collection of
cardboard boxes stowed with books. Enfolded in his trench
coat, Cecil himself stood by the driver's door of the vehicle.
His stance was solemn, his posture rigid, like the brothers'
dutiful chauffeur in wait to depart.

As Magnus shut the door behind him, following Drake
toward the pickup, he stole a savoring glance of the bookshop's homely storefront over his shoulder. It was hard not
to be gripped by the fear of uncertainty—whether or not he
would ever return here to see this place again. *You will*, a
wary inner voice promised him. *Once this is all over with,
you'll make it back here as if nothing ever happened.* But
still, the prospect seemed doubtful.

Magnus turned away mournfully, only to find himself
facing his brother. Drake's gaze was similarly fixed on the

shop. He did not appear to hold any more confidence than Magnus, nor any less fear that they would not set foot in their home's doorway again. His eyes shifted to lock with his brother's, but it seemed as if he could not look for longer than seconds before being assaulted by an unbearable sense of dread. He shuddered and whipped around impetuously, hastening for the vehicle that awaited them.

4

The Barren Road

DEATHLY SILENCE PREVAILED through the first ten minutes of the drive. It was as if neither of the brothers were bold enough to speak first. Cecil handled the wheel in an ironhard grasp, his attention riveted on the road ahead of him. Drake remained totally immersed in his worries, scarcely ever turning to his companions on either end of the truck's bench seat.

Magnus hadn't lifted his head once during the drive so far. His attention was dominated by his father's book in his hands—*MorningStar*, whose golden script caught the gleam of the sun flickering in through the pickup window. Though he sat unmoving, his mind was restless. The silence was growing difficult to endure, but it felt as if any words he formed on his lips were immediately stifled by the anxiety that was so thick in the air.

They drove on for another several minutes before turning onto the highway that led out of the city. At last, Magnus gathered the nerve to utter the first words anyone had spoken since their departure. "Where are we going?" he questioned, his eyes not shifting from the book in his lap.

"Far from here." Cecil's reply was surprisingly prompt. "To a remote hamlet named Markwell. A place deep in the countryside and virtually impossible to locate on a map."

"And your shelter is there?" asked Magnus, an ironic tilt in his voice.

"In a neighboring forest, yes," said Cecil. "The shelter isn't large, but comfortable. It was made for a situation such as this and should serve us well."

While Magnus dwelled in a pause, his brother suddenly joined in the dialogue. "How...did they find you?" said Drake, faltering in his speech. "I never got the chance to ask you in the apartment."

"I've been wondering about that myself." Cecil smiled dryly. "In retrospect, I suppose you could say it was a result of my own ignorance. About a month ago, I attended a national antique book fair with the hope of acquiring a few volumes I'd been searching for. While there, I made a couple of connections with some of the vendors...as well as one visitor who seemed to take an awful lot of interest in me and my collection.

"He was a well-dressed fellow, not much older than I. He struck up a conversation with me while I was browsing a book cart, offhandedly inquiring about what sorts of books I was looking for. We chatted a while. As it turned out, he lived just a couple of hours away from me. He was keen to see my collection for himself, so I gave him my phone number and invited him to call so that we could arrange a meeting. I never heard from him since. I'm inclined to believe that the only meeting that resulted from our encounter took place last night. And it wasn't a pleasant one, certainly."

The concern over Drake's face amplified. "You think he was the one who attacked you?"

"Not him, no," answered Cecil. "The man I spoke with must have only been a scout. Recett would have sent someone of greater caliber to carry out an attack."

"Attacker or not, that doesn't make much sense...what would one of Recett's scouts be doing at a book fair?"

"Looking for me, no doubt," Cecil snapped. "They know my trade. What better place to search for a book collector? They must have traced the phone number directly to my address. It's the only way they could have found me."

"But your number is unlisted."

"Makes little difference to them. Any number can be traced, especially for someone as persistent as Recett." Cecil irritably struck his palm against the wheel. "For over a decade, I've taken every measure possible to keep from view and prevent something like this from happening. Yet when one of Recett's own men walks up to me, I practically invite him to my home!"

Drake breathed a slow sigh. "You can't blame yourself. There was no way you could have known."

"After sixteen years of safety, one tends to let down their

guard," Cecil lamented. "The fault is mine. But there's no sense dwelling on it now."

Only seconds of silence passed before Magnus turned the subject back to his own questions. "That name," he said. "That name you keep mentioning. Recett...who is he?"

With no more than a glance in Magnus' way, Drake uneasily replied, "You...you read about him in our father's book, didn't you?"

"Eras Recett," Magnus recited the man's full name. "The book says he was a warlord."

Drake seemed to find difficulty in wording his response. "Eras...is the name he used to go by," he said with a mild stammer. "He's now known as *Daimos* Recett. He's...a powerful man who's been hunting us for many years."

"What?" Magnus exclaimed in disbelief. "Why didn't you ever tell me this? Hunting us for what?"

"For something he thinks we own." Drake's voice began to quaver. "Something of our father's."

"But what is it?" Magnus persisted, his tone more demanding. He flashed up the cover of the book that he held. "*MorningStar*?"

"No, no, it's..." Drake tried to answer, but suddenly fell mute, lost for words to explain.

"It's a collection of research done by your father," Cecil interjected. "Recett is after it because he sees it as a threat to his life."

"And why's that?" Magnus keenly inquired. "What's the research about?"

Cecil constricted his lips, anxiety returning to his

expression. "We'll have to discuss that later. The point of the matter is that we don't actually have the research. Recett only assumes so because of your being Brendan's sons."

Magnus frowned. "Then where is this research?"

"None of us knows. Most likely it's long destroyed. But Recett isn't willing to accept that."

Magnus pondered a moment, mesmerized by the light-play on the face of the book he was holding. "Why is it again that the police can't do anything about this? Regardless of what kind of criminal is chasing us, why are you so averse to getting the law involved?"

"Because we are not dealing with *criminals*," Cecil stressed. "We are not dealing with petty robbers who wield guns and knives. The law enforcers can't defend us from something they are powerless against."

"Then what in the world are we running away from?" Magnus barked, endlessly frustrated with the ambiguity of Cecil's answers.

Once again, Magnus' query was met with stagnant silence. It was as if neither Cecil nor Drake had even heard the boy. "Back in the apartment," Magnus said more slowly, "you said that...something had gathered above your house. What was it?"

Drake was clearly unwilling to respond. Cecil seemed pensive, answering only after a great deal of thought. "Imagine them as...living clouds," he said, "formed of some rather unusual beasts."

"What?" Magnus pulled a face of utter confusion. "Beasts? Like...birds?"

"Not quite," Cecil replied tentatively. "Perhaps beasts of more...ethereal quality."

"Why does every answer you give have to be a riddle?" Magnus retorted. "If you know what it was you saw, then tell it to me straight."

"In that case," Cecil drew a breath and began again in a more resolute tone of voice, "I will tell you that I was attacked by a horde of shades."

Magnus gave a dubious tilt of his brow. "And what exactly would that be?"

"Perhaps you've heard of them before," replied Cecil, "from mythology or elsewhere—a shade."

"Yeah..." the boy affirmed with hesitation. "A shade is a spirit of the dead, a ghost." He shook his head. "You don't seriously expect me to believe you were attacked by...spirits."

"No, Magnus, I don't," said Cecil, coming to an abrupt pause. "But it nevertheless remains the truth."

Magnus' mouth closed in shock. He glared at his brother, who did not even return the look. Neither of his companions showed the slightest sign of lying, but their sobriety did not sway Magnus from his skepticism. He riffled through the pages of *MorningStar* again in absent-minded frustration. "How could you even tell?" he asked, his sentence punctuated by the sound of his slamming shut the book. "What does a shade *look* like?"

"This certain kind is a unique one," said Cecil. "They are formed of black ash, and gather in colossal hordes. Individually, their appearance is something akin to a legless corpse dressed in rags."

Magnus winced at the perturbing description. "Are you sure you weren't...seeing things? How could you have known what that was?"

"How could I not? I'd recognize those ungodly creatures from a mile away."

"Recognize?" Magnus queried suspiciously. "Did you see them before?"

Cecil froze for a second, caught unawares by the question. "I did," he said. "We all did."

A sudden terror wrung Magnus' heart in icy claws, assaulting him with shivers. Cecil's stories were irrational and highly unbelievable—but Magnus could not seem to dodge the fear that they instilled in him. "I never..." he began, then cleared his throat. "That can't be. When? And where?"

Stillness returned as Cecil deliberated. "There's much to be explained," he finally replied. "There's much that needs to be told, but a highway isn't the place to tell it. The only thing you must bear in mind now is that I speak nothing but the truth, and that an answer to every one of your questions will be given in due time. Know that this is our fault and by no means yours. I'm sorry, Magnus."

Magnus found no words to answer his former guardian. He had heard enough to make him wary of asking further questions, fearing what horrors he would be told of next. He was possibly even more confused than he had been when he left the shop a half hour ago. But yet again, he would be forced to wait for clarity.

Magnus returned his attention to his father's book,

disregarding all around him. Stranded in unfamiliarity and doubtful of truth, he could do no more than void his mind and prepare for the long hours ahead.

They drove on through the day, stopping occasionally to eat and rest in the desolate villages through which the highway ran. Words were scarce, and conversation scarcer. Any dialogue that did not involve directions was spurred by Magnus' questioning about Cecil's attackers, and was promptly pushed aside with a vague response and another promise of future discussion.

Most of the way, Magnus gazed through the pickup window in a vacant trance. He had seen the sun soar at noon, and now watched as its blinding flames brushed the horizon on its slow descent. The day had drifted past like a faint reverie; Magnus was still unsure whether or not he was dreaming. How, in reality, could he have been so suddenly whisked from his home for the sake of such an elusive danger? It was all a simple nightmare, no doubt—a nightmare from which it seemed impossible to wake.

As dusk approached, their drive seemed to carry them into increasingly barren territory. Roadside barriers dwindled to be replaced by half-toppled wire fences, exposing acres of unkempt fields and distant forested hillsides. A handful of decrepit barns and farm houses went by, many of them long abandoned or razed by storms.

There were few others traveling this road, and the

absence of any signage suggested that it led nowhere in particular. They braked at the first intersection they met, veering left onto a similarly sterile stretch of road. "This is the way to Markwell?" Magnus asked in a sullen, empty tone.

"Indeed," answered Cecil. "It won't be much longer. We're getting near."

The road ahead, however, cleaved through miles of empty farmland with no foreseeable end or destination. They drove on for another fifteen minutes before arriving at a second crossroad, at which Cecil hung a sharp right. A dilapidated signpost caught Magnus' eye as they turned, but much of its text had been effaced with black paint. Only three names on the post had been spared—Evans Rd., Downey Rd., and Markwell.

They were taking Evans Road to Markwell. Magnus pried his attention away from the signpost as it diminished into the distance behind them. Not ten minutes had gone by before Cecil suddenly eased on the brake, making another right turn into a narrow avenue obscured by wild grass. After a downhill slope, a featureless, timeworn road sign jadedly greeted them: *Welcome to Markwell.*

The first buildings emerged into view almost immediately. With flourishing lawns and immaculate porches, the residences were old, though surprisingly well maintained. Among the houses, the glass frontages of a couple of storefronts caught the blaze of the setting sun, smarting Magnus' eye as they passed. There were few cars or open stores at this hour, though the occasional pedestrian was seen. Markwell was not the ghost town one would expect for a place so remote.

Cecil navigated the homely streets with a confident sense of direction. They turned twice, meandering into a quaint, shop-clustered plaza. While Magnus took in their surroundings with languid curiosity, Drake surveyed the darkened storefronts wistfully.

"Been a while, hasn't it?" Cecil remarked, rousing the older brother's attention.

"Hmm," Drake concurred in a mutter. "Too long."

"Perhaps too long..." Cecil nodded dismally. "...perhaps not long enough."

They headed down a side street that branched off from the plaza, where Cecil steered the pickup into a parking space along the side of the road. "Before we go any further, I ought to pay a visit to an old friend of mine," said Cecil, tugging the hand brake. "A herbalist. He owns the apothecary over there." He motioned toward a building across the street. "Markwell Apothecary" read the painted sign above the shop's display window.

"His help would be invaluable at a time like this." Cecil leaned past Drake and proceeded to rummage through the overfilled glove compartment, extracting a battered notepad and pen. "He travels to Serenia often as part of his work. He would know as much as anyone could about the province and its current state."

"Serenia," Magnus repeated inquisitively. "That was in my father's book as well. Where is it?"

Cecil pulled a dour frown. "Unfortunately no less

complex a question than anything else you've asked. Once again, all will be answered soon!" He unbuckled himself from his seat and exited the vehicle with haste. "If he isn't there, I'll leave him a letter. He'll be sure to see it when he comes in the next morning."

Slamming the car door behind him, Cecil hurried across the road against the boisterous current of the wind. He arrived at the apothecary entrance, scrutinizing its interior through the front window. A broad store counter speckled with medicinal wares extended across the left end of the shop; ceiling-high shelves teeming with bottles, flasks, and vials lined the walls behind and across from it. No lights were on inside. The shop was closed and its owner didn't appear to be in.

Cecil twice delivered a rapping to the door and waited, but received no response. He raised his notepad against the windowpane and attempted to write, only for his pen's ink to fade repeatedly. After a great deal of dry scrawling to restart the ink's flow, he spent minutes to cover both sides of the page in a constrained script—a terse letter outlining the assault on his home and offering a plea for help. He tore the page off the notepad and passed it under the crack of the door, tapping its edge to send it on through.

Cecil flitted back across the street and into his pickup. Drake turned to him as soon as the door was shut. "I remember him," he said. "Anubis, wasn't it?"

"Anubis Araiya, yes," Cecil affirmed, securing his seat belt. "You have a good memory. He once worked in MorningStar, if you recall."

"That's an odd name," Magnus remarked. "Anubis, I mean. It's the name of an Egyptian god, isn't it?"

"Ancient Egyptian," Cecil corrected. "And no, not a very common name around...here."

"Does he live in Markwell?" Drake asked before his brother could question Cecil any further.

"Yes, why?"

"You could see if he's home. The sooner we can get help, the better."

Cecil pulled the truck off the roadside and drove on down the street. "I'm not certain of his address exactly. The letter says that I'll be at the apothecary to meet him before noon tomorrow, so we're in good time for now."

Not long after they drew away from the plaza and the area around it, the storefronts dwindled back into scattered rows of houses. Mere minutes later, Magnus found that they had traveled back out into the same barren farmland from where they had entered. They didn't continue for long, however—Cecil steered into a side street that took them far off the main road and, gradually, under the flittering shadows of trees.

Magnus watched their environment darken as they slipped inside the grove. A bronzing canopy of leaves drowned out what little light of the day was left, upheld by great columns of oak that steadily encroached on the road. Only just as the thicket began to close in enough for its branches to graze the pickup, it parted, suddenly receding.

They emerged from the grove and into a derelict parking

lot surrounded by forest. There wasn't a single vehicle here, the only objects occupying the lot's twenty-some spaces being shattered tree limbs in puddles of dried leaves.

"This forest was once home to the Markwell Campgrounds," Cecil described, cruising past the empty lot, "which, as you can see, are long abandoned. The dirt roads are all that remain. They'll take us deep enough into the forest to reach the shelter by car."

"If there are any dirt roads left, they'll be buried in debris," Magnus noted. "That parking lot looks like it hasn't been driven on in ten years. We won't get far with a pickup truck in a place that's been abandoned for so long."

"Abandoned, perhaps, but not untrodden," replied Cecil. They drove through a second opening in the trees at the opposite end of the lot, reentering the umbrage of the forest.

"What do you mean by that?"

"Even if people don't camp here any longer, the forest is still used as a passageway for travelers."

Magnus cocked an eyebrow. "Travelers heading where?"

Cecil paused impassively. "You will know soon enough."

Magnus turned away, irate. Cecil's tone denoted that he would offer no more in the way of an explanation.

Before long, the asphalt road had faded to gravel and, eventually, to a compacted bed of twigs, leaves, and dirt. Trees of soaring stature hemmed the path like the walls of a canyon, their leaves eclipsing the roseate sunset sky. The way ahead was sharply illuminated by Cecil's high-beam headlights, but even still, every turn in the vague, meandrous road seemed to come without warning.

They advanced through the forest at a cautious pace, stopping often to ensure that they had not strayed from the path. They passed a campsite clearing along the way—a small field of bare earth where the carcass of a deserted motor home had been left to rust. It was peculiar how, despite the dilapidated surroundings, the path remained surprisingly unobstructed. However, after a wide turn at a crossroad, the terrain suddenly grew rugged. As the pickup slowed to a dead crawl, it became apparent to Magnus that they were no longer driving on any kind of road.

"We've gone off the path," Magnus alerted, peering out the edge of the car window.

"We have," Cecil confirmed rather nonchalantly. "The shelter isn't far from here, but we'll have to travel off the road to reach it."

"Then just park here and we'll walk the rest of the distance," Magnus suggested. The front end of the pickup took a harsh plunge as they drove over a furrow in the earth, jarring the vehicle's passengers.

Cecil readjusted himself in his seat after being rattled by the impact. "We can't leave the pickup out in the open or we risk giving away our location."

"We're already as close as we can get to being in the middle of nowhere. What are the odds that anyone would think us to be out here?"

"Heh..." Cecil laughed in a mutter. "You'd be surprised."

The forest was growing denser. Maneuvering was becoming a challenge, though Cecil seemed adept at finding just enough clearance between the trees to snake through.

At least twice did Magnus expect the pickup door to be stripped of its paint by passing too near to a tree, but his former guardian would each time prove him otherwise.

They came to a stop at the peak of a rippled hillside. Below, bowing trees speckled the slope, their exposed roots sprawled about them like earthy serpents. Cecil's sights were fixed on the partially obscured glade that lay at the bottom.

"Cecil, where—" Magnus could only begin his sentence before Cecil lurched the car off the hilltop and into the start of a precarious descent.

"Almost there. The shelter's straight below," Cecil assured, easing on the brake pedal to inch further down the slope. Like a thread through the eye of a needle, Cecil slalomed through the closely knit trees and coursed into the open glade, the car halting unscathed.

Magnus pulled himself upright in his seat and absorbed the eerily tranquil scene. This was a secluded area of the wood, enclosed by walls of forest mounted atop lofty hillocks. The color of the autumn leaves carpeting the ground was deadened to a muddy hue in the twilight.

Cecil drove a little further, into a shaded, overgrown corner of the glade. "Leave everything in the back for now and I'll show you inside," he said, shifting the vehicle into park.

"There's nothing here," Drake quietly observed.

"Not to unsuspecting eyes," replied Cecil. "Come." He made his way out of the pickup, Drake and Magnus following from the opposite door.

Cecil escorted the brothers toward the far end of the glade, to the foot of the steepest hillside. The slope's lower face was smothered in snarls of undergrowth, which Cecil began to press aside in a harsh snapping of twigs. Much of the debris was loose, as if it had been laid there deliberately. When the final branch was discarded, Cecil dusted off his hands on his clothes and stepped aside.

There was a door built into the slope. It was made of dense, fortified wood, free of rot and wear, fixed into a frame in a slant against the hillside. "Well concealed," Drake remarked with a nod.

"In a location as predictable as here, it needs to be." Cecil produced his keys from his pants pocket and selected one from the set. He unlocked the stout door and heaved it open by its handle, revealing a short flight of stairs descending into shadow. "Watch your step," he cautioned as he ducked inside.

Drake followed Cecil with wary pacing. Magnus stood a moment in admiration of the unlikely doorway before proceeding after his brother. Dusk's ghostly aura dwindled behind him, the stillness ruptured by the moan of the wooden stairs, a sound as shrill as the howl of a dying animal. As he entered the shelter, darkness came over his vision like a veil. He could only discern the contours of Cecil, who was walking ahead, and Drake standing nearby.

Cecil approached a table in the room's center and took up a peculiar bulk from its surface, something similar to a large tin can in shape. He separated the object in his hands, sounding a rattling of metal, and laid part of it aside on the table. Without much warning afterward, the room was suddenly and violently lit in an explosion of light.

Magnus flinched at the brightness, blinking to regain focus of his former guardian. Cecil appeared to hold a fist-sized hunk of crystal that emanated tremendous radiance, even more so than an ordinary light bulb. He set the crystal back inside from where he had taken it—a low pedestal on a thick steel base. From the table, he retrieved the second half of the object, a slatted metal-and-glass covering that resembled a miniature birdcage, and fitted it overtop the base to form a lantern of sorts. Taking hold of the lantern by a hefty ring chained to its cap, he swung it about to illuminate all corners of the chamber.

"And here we are." Cecil shrugged. "Welcome to my shelter."

The room they were in was moderately spacious, enclosed by wood-paneled walls, crammed bookshelves, and piles of unmarked boxes. The center table and its accompanying twin chairs were strikingly similar, if not identical, to some of the opulent furniture in Cecil's home. A somewhat ill-matching beige couch was placed at the table's right end, near an unadorned, bare stone fireplace.

Cecil ushered everyone's eyes across the three doors leading out of the room, two at the back wall and one on the left. "Our bedroom, bathroom, study," he listed, then swerved the rays of his lantern over to a final entranceway in the far left corner, "and the kitchen's through there. No windows, only a couple of vents to let in some outside air.

Not a very large abode, but it will keep us in safety and comfort for the time being."

"Incredible, Cecil!" Drake exclaimed, admiring the sturdy lodge. "Did you build all this yourself?"

"Heavens, no. I had the help of a few friends who did a great deal of the work."

Drake nodded, no less impressed. "I remember. You told me about this place when I was younger."

"Shame that it's only now you've gotten the opportunity to see it." Cecil wandered along the shelf rows, his lantern raised to the books' spines as he moved past. "Even this, unfortunately, is not a permanent solution. We should be able to stay here a few days, only until we've gathered our bearings and worked out what steps to take next."

Magnus roamed toward the kitchen, peering inquisitively inside the dark room. It was confined, with barely enough space to contain anything more than it did—an austere counter, cabinet, icebox, and an unfastened basin without any form of faucet.

"How will we get any water here?" Magnus queried. "This place doesn't have running water, does it?"

Cecil dismissed the boy's concern with an assuring wave of his hand. "We have other sources, not to worry. Why don't you go help your brother with the things in the pickup and I'll get us some water to drink and wash. After that, we'd best get some sleep. We have a lot of work ahead of us in the morning."

Magnus tried to protest retiring to bed so early, far too many questions still remaining. But he succumbed to his growing fatigue. He had heard enough for one day; he had heard enough to haunt him through many restless nights to come.

Cecil regarded the weary disappointment in Magnus' eyes with a sigh and a grimace. "Tomorrow," he said steadfastly. "Tomorrow, we will talk. I promise you, Magnus—you will soon know everything."

5

City of Ashes

 HE SUN NEVER SHONE here anymore. It was veiled by the thickest and darkest of clouds, the same ones that had first eclipsed it over a decade ago. The earth was barren, as arid as a desert, with trees as black and contorted as the withered roots beneath them. Nothing flourished here, nor grew at all. Serenia was a dead land, stricken by a plague of destruction, detriment, and ruin that had spread from its capital city.

Noctell Knever and Raven Gaunt ambled briskly down a sett-paved broadway, approaching the gatehouse of a heavily fortified citadel. The soot on the ground splashed in their tracks like smoke smoldering off their heels. The surrounding storefronts and residences, once lordly brick and half-timbered structures, now stood abandoned, stained with black ash and painted an infernal red by the flames of the roads' iron torches.

But the true horror of this place resided in the sky above it, in the impenetrable clouds that masked the sun. They were the shades, the scourge of Serenia, a sooty mass of tangled, groping limbs and skeletal visages that churned ceaselessly in the heavens. The clouds' spawn, the fiendish creatures themselves, soared over the rooftops with hollow gazes and slackened claws, like avian corpses carried by unseen strings.

This was the city of MorningStar—the former pride of Serenia, now a lightless, ashen hell.

The two men advanced through the grandiose archway of the open gatehouse and into the citadel. Buildings were more densely constructed here and possibly in even worse condition than those outside the fortress. There were other people as well, the idle guards of the city, ghost-pale men with languid postures and gaunt, bloodshot eyes that should have belonged to no one but the dead. They wore liveries of hard leather shadowed under jet-black cloaks; shortswords and miniature crossbows dangled from holsters at their belts.

Guards though they were, they had little to be vigilant of. The men who spent their days loitering in the derelict city could hardly be considered sentries of any kind. This place saw almost no passage from anyone other than the guards themselves, and any outsiders who dared enter risked a torturous death at the hand of the city's ruler.

As Noctell and Raven traveled through, they were regarded by the cloaked men with tentative nods of welcome. They were respected in MorningStar, not to mention feared, as elite members among the guards. Noctell, especially, surveyed the forlorn city with a contented disposition. Here, he was revered for his power. He was a necromancer, a puppeteer and conjurer of the undead, with skills that surpassed those of every other soldier in his master's forces. Spectral beasts such as the shades would bend to his will like mute, unquestioning servants, and those who worked beneath him were wise to do the same. He wielded his influence callously, satiating within himself a voracious thirst for dominance.

Raven was one of the exceptionally few nonhuman members of the city guard. He was a crimson-scaled giant with little in the way of a name to describe his species. Many knew him as a demon, a rare and accursed creature of uncertain provenance. Anyone foolish enough to press him for answers about his ghastly appearance was likely to face the demon's infernal temper.

The main road of the citadel ended far ahead at the loftiest, most direful edifice in sight—a small castle, comprised of a two-story base and a lone tower that spired into the void of the clouds. A podium of stone steps lay before its enormous double door, flanked by withered brambles rowed along ivied walls.

Noctell and Raven drifted into the open courtyard that encircled the castle. The torches' firelit stalks surrounded them, marking them each with scalding glares like those of red-eyed wolves. The eyes of another person, emerald-green and gleaming, fell upon them from the castle doorway. They belonged to a female figure, her lank silhouette painted by the smoldering, irascible glow of the torchlight.

Like Raven's, the figure's appearance was only mildly human. Her skin was light-gray, the color of stone, contrasting sharply with the veil of her jet-black hair and suit of dark, hard leather. On her belt were holstered an array of daggers and a slender shortsword. But what made her so vastly distinctive were the wings that branched off the back of her shoulders—featherless, like those of a bat, but as tall as her own stance, folded close against her frame. She was a harpie, a winged human of origins most certainly not in this plane.

"So our triumphant heroes return," the harpie greeted in a sardonic mutter.

"Indeed they do!" Noctell resounded, beaming. "But what manner of welcoming party is this, Medeva? Wouldn't you have gathered 'round all the men in celebration of our victory?"

"That depends on what manner of victory." Medeva walked off the steps to face the necromancer. Her inquisitive stare was fiercened by cutting scorn.

"We raided Handel's house and found this." Raven came forward, withdrawing the brown envelope from inside his coat pocket to pass to the harpie. "It's the address of Drake Wingheart, Brendan's son."

Medeva ignored the envelope, her glare unmoved. "And what of Handel himself?"

"He escaped," Noctell bluntly declared. "But it's no matter. Drake will be of even more use to us."

"For your own sakes, hope that Recett will think the same," the harpie replied. She stepped aside, motioning Noctell and the demon ahead of her. "Go on. He's expecting you."

Noctell ascended the podium, Raven following and Medeva trailing a short distance behind. The necromancer hauled back one of the double doors by its stout handle, and the three proceeded inside the tenebrous castle.

The door fell shut behind them with a roar like the sound of a crumbling monolith. The air here was laced with smoke and smothered in the scent of blood and putrid flesh. The entrance hall alone was one of the most terrifying parts of the castle. Beneath an ostentatious vaulted ceiling, the walls were rowed with thickset iron torches harshly ablaze, and arrayed with a macabre display—withered corpses, suspended by manacles and swathed in threadbare gowns of black cloth. Like the stuffed head of a buck flaunted by its hunter, these were the trophies of the castle's owner, the carcasses of long-forgotten enemies.

Noctell, Raven, and the harpie progressed through the sultry haze of the corridor. The corpses seemed to scrutinize them as they went by, looking down upon them with dead eyes shadowed in gaping concaves and parched lips sealed like notches in clay masks. The trio passed many doorways, but continued on until they reached a vast, circular chamber at the corridor's end.

This was the castle's heart, the throne room. Encircled by wall-mounted torches, a gruesome ebony throne loomed at the distant end of the chamber. An intricate lining of tendrils clasped its base, seeping upward into a spread of gargantuan, red-tipped talons that formed its backrest. Its feet were sculpted like a stallion's hooves, and from its armrests sprouted the heads of open-mawed dragons. The seat itself, however, was vacant.

Noctell and the others walked out into the chamber. Their soles clicked on a floor of chipped, discolored stone tiles—an ill-arranged mosaic sprawled from the mouth of the entrance hall to the foot of the throne. It bore the crude depiction of a skull: a set of sagging black ovals for its eyes and nose, enclosed by a bone-white circle with a barred rectangle of teeth extending from beneath it. The very same image could be recognized not only in Noctell's carved stone neckpiece, but also as the unmistakable emblem that branded every weapon and cloak of the city guards. It was a mark that was abhorred by many, and known by all as the insignia of MorningStar's feared usurper.

Footsteps resonated from beyond one of the room's many doorways. Noctell and Raven halted as they spotted the darkened figure of a man emerge from the leftmost corridor, hastening toward them in a half-crippled gait.

"Ah, sirs!" the guard eagerly addressed his superiors. "Pleased to see you've returned safely." He drew in front of the necromancer, scrawny hands clasped. He was an older man, his posture cambered and his ashen face marked heavily with creases.

Noctell flicked an upward nod in the direction of the throne. "Where is he?"

"In the dungeons, I believe," the guard said with a wry smile, "having a chat with his prisoners, another four herb-mongers we caught in the forest earlier tonight." He cleared his throat as if it were clogged with soot. "Anything else I can assist you with, sirs?"

"You may take our things up to our chambers." Noctell and Raven slung off their overcoats and passed them to the guard. Their garments underneath were well-fitting dark waistcoats layered over prim white shirts. Raven handed over his fedora as well, uncovering an oily slick of black hair matted to his scalp. Cradling the load, the guard dipped his head in esteem and departed through another doorway by the left of the throne.

Noctell and Raven immediately turned their attention over to a stone archway at the room's opposite end. They headed toward it, peering down the dimly lit spiral of stairs before them that plunged far beneath the castle. Bickering voices could be heard from below—one harsh, like the thrashing tongue of a viper, and the other fervid and snarling. The elite guards trampled down the steps, into the castle dungeons.

They drew to a standstill as they reached the bottom of the stairs. A yawning corridor awaited them, hemmed with metal bars fixed under a sunken, fractured ceiling. The asphyxiating stench of old gore wafted from the farthermost cells that were stained in blood and soot. Many of the enclosures here were the size of pillories, barely wide enough to contain two persons. Of the few that were comparably larger, one was occupied by a knot of four men. Outside the cell, a wiry figure shawled in a black cloak and hood drifted in idle paces.

"Oh, nothing? Nothing, you claim?" the figure continued the dispute. His voice was raucous, as if his throat were made of brass. "Trespassing! Thievery! Resisting arrest! What is your defense to that, knave?" It was difficult to tell whether it was ire or merely sarcasm that colored his tone.

"I wander about a dead forest outside my own city and you reckon me a trespasser? What kind of madman are you?" One of the four prisoners, a brazen-eyed, thin man with tousled hair, appeared to be at the head of the argument. He was clasping the bars of his cell with all his strength, fury seething through his locked jaws.

"*Your* city?" the figure scoffed, now clearly mocking the man. "Since when is this *your* city? MorningStar is my empire, the home of my army and all who serve me!"

"It is the land of corpses, ash, and ruin!" roared the man. "And you cursed it so! This will never be your empire, no matter how much blood you spill on it!"

The figure straightened its posture and confronted the prisoner, meeting his scowl with its own. "Your audacity tries your life, herbmonger. Perhaps I'd be more inclined to spare you if you'd be more reverent toward your jailer."

"I'd rather die twice," the man said through his teeth, "than hold any reverence to an undead beast-of-a-man who could only compare to the devil himself."

"Then I'm sorry to disappoint you..." A skeletal hand lunged out from the figure's shroud of cloth and seized the man's throat like a shackle. "...but I can only kill you once."

A dark aura suddenly stole over the figure's hand. The prisoner floundered, tearing at his jailer's grasp, but his struggle was in vain. As the figure drew back its claw, the aura clung to the man's throat in a fluid black helix of tendrils that remained tied to the figure's hand by a smoky cord. The other three prisoners recoiled against the back of the cell, wrenching away their eyes. They heard their companion's desperate shrieks diminish into guttural choking as the jailer's tendrils constricted tighter around their prey. After less than a minute, the man abruptly fell mute. A blunt thud on stone cut the silence.

The remaining prisoners loathly glanced back to see the man's body lying across the floor of the cell. Their faces were marked by a horror as dark as if their souls had been burned. They said nothing, nor did they look to their jailer, in fear of meeting the same fate.

The figure turned to face the elite guards who waited duteously by the dungeon entrance. As it approached them, it raised its knotted fingers and pulled back its hood, unveiling its formerly shadowed visage. It was a man, but one whose appearance was nothing short of cadaverous. He had no hair nor eyebrows and was almost entirely without flesh—only a mask of pallid skin over bone, with his nose and ears withered to cavitied stubs. The outline of his skull was distinct, his neck as thin as rope, and his sanguine eyes carved into gaunt sockets like blood-sodden pearls. His mouth was a gash with lips so thin that even the contours of his misshapen teeth were visible through them. He was the sheer image of the living dead—he was the indomitable warlord by whose rule MorningStar and all of Serenia had fallen.

"Lord Daimos." Noctell bowed his head, restraining an eager grin.

"You've returned quickly," Daimos remarked in a way that suggested disapproval. He stole a glance behind his men as if he expected to see them hauling the fruits of their victory. "I assume you've successfully apprehended Handel?"

Anxiety fractured Noctell's smile. "No," he answered. "I'm afraid he escaped in his vehicle as we were approaching the residence. He must have been awake; we cannot be sure why." Seeing his master's glower darken, he whisked the topic onto their notable accomplishment. "But we found all we need. Look."

Raven produced Cecil's envelope, which Daimos impetuously stole and scanned with a flicker of his eyes.

"The address of Drake Wingheart," Noctell proclaimed, arrogance evident in his temper. "It was on a desk in Handel's mansion. We returned here as soon as we'd found it."

"Did you?" Daimos replied with biting sarcasm. He set his glare back on his men. "And I assume you have taken into consideration the first place Handel will head to after your assault."

Noctell's pride was quelled by seeing no change in the warlord's surliness. "Yes, of course, but—"

"Brendan's son!" Daimos burst into a rage. "He and Handel will be halfway to God-knows-where by dawn! How could you not have seen that?"

"We considered it, milord, but it was only hours before sunrise," Raven interjected in a tone more steadfast than his partner's. "The address was in another city and likely distant. If we had started searching for Wingheart, we would have been forced to attack in broad daylight."

"Wingheart has been our sole target for the past sixteen years!" the warlord barked, his parched tongue afire. "You will attack at all costs! It makes no difference what the bloody time was!"

"Of course it does. We could have been seen!"

"Then seen you will be! In that world, you are more powerful than any force of law—than nearly every living soul! Yet you cower from them all and dodge between the shadows like fools!"

Raven abstained from argument, not wishing to anger his master further. In turn, Daimos directed his violent wrath back to the necromancer. "Go! Leave my sight!" he waved a twisted claw in Noctell's face as if stifling the urge to strangle him. "Find the address and bring me that man alive! If he and Handel are already gone, search the house and find anything that could tell us where they're heading." He sharpened every line of his face in the darkest of scowls. "Go!"

Scathed by their master's fury, Noctell and Raven nodded in accordance, retrieved the envelope, and hurried back for the entrance. They lurched as they nearly collided with Medeva, whom they were startled to find loitering behind them. The harpie stepped aside, allowing the men to pass her and ascend the dungeon stairs.

Medeva's impervious frown bored into Daimos. "They're right, you know," she said. "The consequences of drawing that much attention on Earth far outweigh your impatience."

"Consequences!" Daimos scorned the word. "No consequences outweigh sixteen years of fruitless irritation and our one chance at seizing our prize!"

"If Handel had escaped his house at the time of the attack, he would have reached Wingheart long before Noctell and Raven could have," the harpie noted. "It would have made little difference whether they had returned here to report or not."

"It's still their own ignorance that let Handel escape to begin with," Daimos countered. "And why should you care at all? You have no part in this."

"I will have a part in anything I please," Medeva retorted immediately. "You have spent over a decade and a half scouring both worlds for an elusive piece of research that may be useless altogether. You are wasting your own time, as well as mine."

"You're one to talk," snapped the warlord, extending a sickly finger. "It was you who told me of that parcel you saw Brendan give to Handel. Why should the research be any more elusive now than it was then?"

"Because if that research were of any significance," replied Medeva, "you would have been dead long ago. At the least, you would have seen an attempt on your life. So many years have passed in silence that it's as if Brendan himself never lived."

"Silence means nothing," Daimos delivered a stern rejoinder. "Simply because no actions have been taken, I should not disregard any imminent risks."

Medeva cocked her head. "So you plan to live the rest of your days weltering in the fear of death?"

"I fear nothing!" Daimos' rage was spurred again. "This concerns not only me, but you and the shade army as a whole! Your life is at stake just as is mine. You ought to be thankful for my vigilance."

"I believe you are mistaking vigilance for cowardice," quipped Medeva. "And for the latter, I have little to thank. Good night, Recett." She turned her wings to the warlord and sauntered out of the chamber, carrying not a shadow of emotion in her stride.

"You would be wise to watch your tongue, harpie!" Daimos bellowed to Medeva as she climbed the dungeon stairs, but unsurprisingly, he received no answer. Her footsteps fading, he returned to the cell that contained his dread-stricken prisoners.

"Well, then," Daimos hissed to an audience of gaping eyes and quivering lips. He coiled his hands around the bars of the cell with burning indignation kindled by the harpie's remarks. "Do either of you have anything else clever to say? Or shall I simply rush over to the part in which I slaughter the lot of you?"

"I-I'm..." A timorous stammer answered the warlord's threat. Daimos turned his attention to a prisoner cowering in the deepest gloom of the cell. "Yes? Speak, fool."

"I may be a-able to assist you," the man continued,

"with some information…regarding these p-people whom you seek."

"Oh?" Daimos turned his crushing shadow upon the man. "Then you will tell me all you know," he drawled, evocatively eyeing the corpse that lay within the cell, "if you value your life."

6

Myth and Magic

THE MORNING AFTER CECIL had brought the brothers to Markwell, Magnus awoke, wishing he were back in his brother's bookshop, safe and at peace. He wished to no end that the story of the shades and the shop's closing were nothing but a ghastly dream. But when he blinked open his eyes, he found himself lying under the cover of a sleeping bag, still beneath the wooden beams of Cecil's shelter. He poured out all his hopes in a sigh.

As Magnus passed through the door of his bedroom into the living room later that morning, he set eyes on Cecil, reclined in one of the opulent, timeworn chairs by the center table, browsing languidly through a slim, red notebook. The book *MorningStar* was laid on the table before him, next to a miniature satchel sewn of tattered leather. Magnus approached, baring a slight smile to Cecil in greeting.

Cecil lifted his gaze from the notebook to return the smile. "Good morning, Magnus."

"Morning, Cecil," answered Magnus, scanning the rest of the shelter in search of his brother. "Where's Drake?"

"He's walked down to Markwell to get us some breakfast," Cecil replied, motioning the boy to a seat on the second of the stately chairs. "Come. Sit down for a minute."

Magnus bobbed his head affably and sat by his former guardian as Cecil lowered the notebook onto the table. The place certainly appeared a lot brighter than yesterday. As Magnus swept his eyes across the ceiling, he noticed that the same peculiar lantern that Cecil had used when they first arrived was hung by a rusted hook above them, the crystal within it vibrantly aglow.

"Like it?" Cecil called the boy's attention away from the lantern.

"What is it?" Magnus asked in reply. "I mean, what kind of stone is that inside it?"

"A special kind." Cecil smiled thinly. "One I quite doubt you've ever seen before. I'll tell you about it later." He seemed to scrutinize Magnus' weary expression. "Did you sleep well last night?"

"Not really," Magnus answered tentatively. "When I woke up, for a minute I thought all this had just been a dream. Running away from the bookshop..." he lifted his dismal stare toward Cecil. "...the story of the shades..."

"Well, I suppose I still owe you a solid explanation for why we're here in the first place." Cecil returned the boy's look with empathy. "My frantic warnings were hardly enough to justify bringing you here on a whim."

"I suppose." A meager smile flickered over Magnus' lips. But Cecil rejoined too suddenly for the boy to even pose his first question.

"Then you must bear in mind that I have absolutely no reason to lie to you," Cecil said as if already anticipating Magnus' incredulity. "A lot of this may seem hard to believe, but you have to understand, I take no joy in messing with your mind."

Magnus concurred with a slow, wary nod. Cecil brought his hand to his mouth in deliberation. "Where do I start?" he muttered.

"The beginning," Magnus answered. "My past, my parents..." he trailed off, wavering over what to say next. "After everything I've just been told, I'm not even sure about where I was born."

"Fair enough," Cecil replied, nudging Brendan's book so that its cover was turned toward Magnus. "You were born in MorningStar."

Magnus stared blankly at the tome. "Then where is it? Where exactly is MorningStar?"

After a moment of directing his attention absently at the floor, Cecil rose from his seat to face the bookcases behind the table. From the topmost shelf, he withdrew a hefty, furled chart and brushed it free of a thick robe of dust. He opened it out on the table, flattening it over with his palms.

It was a map. It depicted a sea in which two islands were

nested; the first, to the east, was the largest, paired with a western island about three quarters of its size. At both the north and south borders of the map were the jutting crowns of two other land masses that faded off the edge of the chart. Though the map showed traces of its original colors, time had paled it to a lackluster sepia tone.

Cecil darted an intent glance across the surface of the chart until he placed a finger near the bottom of the eastern land mass. "Somewhere...here."

"On this island?" asked Magnus. "MorningStar is on this island?"

"Island?" Cecil gave an ironic smile. "These aren't islands, Magnus. These are far, far larger than islands."

Magnus peered closer at the antiquated chart through a dense frown. The map bore a great many names in a finely inked script, each one spanning a broad region of land. Depictions of planes, forests, lakes, and deserts alike suggested a vast array of climates.

"But they can't be that large," Magnus insisted, despite the seemingly gargantuan scale of the map. "I've never heard of MorningStar all my life. And I've..." He paused in an attempt to decipher some of the unusual names printed over the land masses. "I've never heard of any of these places, either. If this place is so huge, then show me, on a globe or atlas, where these...islands are."

"Well," Cecil replied, seeming to find difficulty in responding, "this is quite where they are. You could search every last globe on Earth, and I assure you that you won't find any of these places."

"So what are you trying to tell me?" Magnus asked with rising cynicism. "That this is another planet?"

"It's the exact same planet," Cecil answered, dragging his speech. "Just a different...version."

Magnus bounced a glance off the map and back over to Cecil, his frown now warped in total confusion. "Version? A different version? Where is this place?"

"Not *where*..." Cecil said in a near-whisper. He eased back into his seat. "*What*. This place is called Arkane."

"You're still not making any sense," barked Magnus. "I've never heard of any place called Arkane."

"No, I suppose you haven't." Cecil returned a grin to his face. For a second afterward, Cecil merely opened his mouth, as if he were angling for the right words to say. "You see," he said finally, "Arkane...is one of Earth's counterpart worlds."

Magnus didn't know if he had gotten the response he wanted or not. Cecil's answers were growing stranger with the boy's every question.

"Or, as many refer to them, *parallel dimensions*," added Cecil.

"That doesn't mean anything," Magnus persisted. "How could I've been born in another dimension?"

Cecil tilted his head to rest it in his hand. "I'm not explaining this very well, am I?" he sighed, kneading his brow. "Why don't I start from the top of things?"

He shifted himself in his seat until he faced Magnus directly. "Any universe, from a larger point of view also known as a dimension, can divide itself into a potentially infinite number of copies at the point of its creation," he said. "Each of these copies exists on its own plane in the dimensional spectrum, and as they evolve, they also diverge, growing increasingly farther apart from one another. Some evolve so drastically that they become separate dimensions altogether; others tend to stay relatively in alignment with each other to form what we know as parallel dimensions.

"Thus, a dimension parallel to ours is not far unlike our own dimension. Its cosmic structure is virtually identical to ours, meaning that there would exist in it a solar system with a planet Earth similar to the one on which we live. This particular version of planet Earth I now refer to is known not as Earth..." He fastened his palm on the open map. "... but rather, as Arkane."

"And this theory is...accepted by modern science?" Magnus asked with obvious sarcasm.

"Perhaps not *Earth's* modern science," replied Cecil. "Earth has its own theories, not to say that any of them are wrong. The origins of parallel dimensions have been forever disputed, even on Arkane, where science has a much better grasp on the subject. What I've just described to you is Arkane's most widely accepted theory—put in very simple terms, of course."

Cecil's talk of alternate universes did nothing but build on Magnus' frustration. The boy didn't believe much of any of this. But he bore in mind Cecil's candid insistence on having no reason to lie. "So I, Drake, our parents..." said Magnus, forcing away his skepticism, "we were all born in this parallel dimension?"

"Of course," answered Cecil. "I was also born in MorningStar, along with your father. Your mother was born in a nearby town in the same province, and I believe the same for your brother."

"Then how exactly would we have gotten here?"

"We have our ways," Cecil said firmly. "If I were to elaborate now, I fear I'd only be confusing you further and drawing away from the subject."

"And if we were all born in MorningStar," said Magnus, brow cocked quizzically, "why would we have left?"

Cecil's expression crumbled to dread. He folded his arms over his chest and heaved a dark sigh. "For the same reason I left my house, and for the same reason I sit here with you now."

Magnus bored his eyes into Cecil's. "Shades?"

Cecil nodded without a word in response.

Magnus was still not sure whether he believed the story of the shades. But just as with everything else he had been told, he hadn't much of a choice other than to trust his former guardian. "So then the shades came from Arkane?"

"Well, yes," said Cecil. "But no one knows exactly from where they originated. Some presume they escaped from another dimension, while others believe they were intentionally summoned."

"Summoned?" Magnus repeated, drumming his nails against the chair frame. "By whom?"

"Almost undoubtedly the same man who now controls them," Cecil solemnly replied. "Daimos Recett."

Magnus felt his heart lurch into the pit of his chest

upon hearing the name, though he knew hardly anything about their supposedly terrifying pursuer. "Drake told me about him yesterday," he recalled. "My father wrote about him in his book."

"You ought to know more about him than just that. I believe that this book may have been written before its final chapters could unfold," said Cecil, angling the luster of *MorningStar*'s gilded lettering into his eyes. "Decades ago, Daimos, or, more correctly, Eras Recett, was a councilman in the Serenian city of Anmer. He wasn't a person who attracted much attention...until he was linked to an uprising of the notorious New Order cult within the city. In the months that followed, Anmer suffered a violent revolt that led to the collapse of the city council. Eras assumed control of Anmer as a warlord.

"While the rest of the province scrambled to take action, Eras launched a second attack on Serenia's capital city of MorningStar. Thankfully, his army, which consisted mostly of mercenaries and New Order followers, was small and poorly constructed. He was struck down by the MorningStar Guard and fled into hiding. Your father, who was part of MorningStar's council, made an enormous contribution during the battle and the restoration of the city. It was because of his immense support that, months later, he was elected as head of the city's council."

"I already read most of that in my father's book," Magnus interrupted. "What did you mean about its final chapters?"

"I didn't say this was the end of the story," Cecil replied.

"It was about three years later that something strange began to occur. Every night, a small band of shades would soar down from the skies and attack the city's guards. They were nothing like anyone had ever seen before. As a rule, such spectral creatures tend to remain in a single location, guarding their place of death or something of importance to them. These particular shades attacked the city's guards with a vengeance. They were no more than small assemblies at first and were easily driven away...but the threat grew worse. The shades' numbers would multiply, night after night, until two weeks had passed and the guards could barely maintain their defense."

"On the fifteenth day, the worst yet of the dangers they had faced arrived at the gates of MorningStar." Cecil dwelled in a wistful pause, laying *MorningStar* back onto the table. Though his vision was affixed on the book, his mind's eye was mired in the images of MorningStar's battles that were so deeply carved into his memories. "I remember it distinctly," he began. "The city was awoken in the dead of the night to an approaching army of few men but thousands of shades. Leading them was a man who appeared more like a walking corpse than a powerful general or summoner. He had no flesh, only bones under a mask of gray skin.

"When he arrived at the city gates, he ordered that MorningStar surrender, else be attacked. Most incredible of all was his claim that he was, in fact, Eras Recett—and many of his old allies were gathered around him to prove it. He declared that he had been bestowed with a new, immortal form, and that his name was now Daimos, a word meaning 'terror' in an old Arkane language.

"When MorningStar refused to surrender, Recett unleashed his shade army on the city. The battle raged on for hours, during which a great many guardsmen and civilians were killed. Attacking in hordes, the shades were close to unstoppable. Recett's men were formidable, but at least they were mortal—Recett himself was left unscathed by all manner of attacks. Aside from being tremendously powerful, he even took the shot of a crossbow bolt to his heart and barely flinched. It became apparent that he was, indeed, the undead corpse he appeared to be."

"Undead?" asked Magnus. "As in...reanimated from the dead?"

"Well, yes, but the exact definition can vary," said Cecil. "One who is undead is not always reanimated. Your father believed Recett to be possessed by some form of dark spirit, possibly something alike the shades themselves. A powerful possessor can leech away the life of its vessel, replacing it with its own ethereal life and rendering the body useless. This would explain why any form of physical assault was futile against Recett."

Magnus had long abandoned his cynicism for the sake of the conversation and now found himself rapt in the tale. "So then how did you defeat him?"

Cecil's expression again turned dreary. "We didn't. The MorningStar Guard, aided by the Serenian army, managed to fend off the shades for long enough that Recett and his men retreated. But it didn't end. The nightly shade attacks continued relentlessly. Brendan and the rest of the MorningStar council knew that if Recett were to strike a second time, the city wouldn't have the strength left to defend. They needed something powerful enough to fight back.

"The council concurred that the shades' summoner, Recett, would have to die if the shades were to be stopped. Since Recett was impervious to death by any normal means, it seemed that he would need to be exorcised of his possessor beforehand. Now, an exorcism is ordinarily quite possible if the spirit's vessel is unwilling of the bond, or if the spirit is particularly weak. The spirit in question was neither weak nor did it have an unwilling vessel, considering what Recett had become. He would have to be exorcised by force, and with a possessor powerful enough to immortalize him, that was no simple feat.

"Brendan recognized that any spirit of such strength has an elemental affinity—usually of either light or darkness. Since Recett, in his new form, appeared to detest light almost as much as his shades did, it was obviously the latter. Something of tremendous radiance would be needed to drive out the spirit within him.

"Brendan spent many days compiling research in pursuit of something capable of eradicating Recett's immortality. From what I remember, he happened upon a centuries-old record of some bandits living in the Galem mountains. Allegedly, they had discovered a prodigious boulder of crystal in a crater, probably the relic of a meteorite. The boulder was described as being bright as the sun, and it was said that a man had been permanently blinded by a light burst that was released when he tried to break off a piece. Along with the name that the boulder was given by the bandits, Luminous Rock, this is practically the only record that remains of it."

"That sounds like that stone in your lantern," Magnus remarked, eyeing the encasement of the illuminated crystal hung above him.

"I guess you could say that." Cecil brushed a glance over the lantern. "The mineral inside is a common gemstone on Arkane known as *lucidus*. It's a type of crystal that captures and exudes light, often used in lamps and lanterns such as mine. The Luminous Rock is simply one of the most, if not *the* most, concentrated forms of lucidus ever found.

"Brendan hoped that the light released from even a single shard from the Rock would deliver a strong-enough blow to weaken Daimos' shade army, and most of all, rid Daimos of possession. Later that week, Brendan set out for Galem to find the Rock and confirm its existence. Astoundingly, he returned some days later to say that he had found it, and he had a shard of the Rock to prove it!"

"Without having been blinded?"

"Oh, it was a simple matter of protecting the eyes. The bandit was only blinded because he wasn't aware of what would happen. A couple of days after obtaining the shard, Brendan concluded his research and made plans to return to the Rock to gather more crystal."

"Then how come Daimos isn't dead yet?" Magnus asked immediately after Cecil had ended his sentence.

Cecil was weighted deeper into his seat by dejection. "It did not go unannounced that Brendan had found a way to conquer the city's greatest enemy. It's not surprising that news of his plan reached Recett. Not long after Brendan finished his research, Recett returned to rampage the city with the full force of his army. It was clear this time that he had aims other than just the capture of MorningStar—he wanted to find whatever it was that was such a threat to his life. As could only be expected after the unrelenting attacks of the shades, the MorningStar Guard, wounded and weary, didn't stand a chance in the fight. The city was evacuated, sending thousands of people scurrying to this world, while others were captured or killed."

"What about my parents?" Magnus asked in a fretful murmur. He didn't know what to believe about his parents' fate. He had hardly believed the story of their drowning, and he wasn't sure if he believed much of Cecil's story, either.

"During the attack," said Cecil, "I gathered my friends—three ex-captains of the guard and a former councilman—and ran to your father's house. He asked me and the others to take you, Drake, and your mother, and get the three of you someplace safe. We tried to convince your father to come as well, but he insisted on staying. He told me that he had to help defend the city. He said that no matter how many others would die, he'd be the last to give up. It was, sadly, because of his determination that he met his ultimate demise. I later heard it confirmed by other survivors that they saw Brendan swarmed and killed by Recett's men in the MorningStar citadel."

Magnus sealed his eyes and drowned his face in the darkness of his palms. "And my mother?"

"As we made it out of the city," Cecil thinned his voice to a whisper, "something was following us. It soared in the air, soundlessly, like a bat, watching us. But after we thought it was gone, I saw it, skulking in the shadows. Before I had a chance to stop it, it fired an arrow at your mother, killing her instantly. My friends rushed to fight the creature; they managed to chase it away, but not before one of them suffered the same fate as your mother. After that, we escaped to this world, where we have remained to this day."

A stifling silence followed Cecil's words. Magnus almost wished he hadn't heard any of this, whether or not it was true. "I don't know what to believe anymore," Magnus said in a voice bent by the restraint of his tears. "If everything that you and Drake ever told me about my past was a lie, then why should this be any more real? And if all this *is* real, then why would you lie?"

"The reasons are not all black and white, Magnus." Cecil placed a tender grip on the boy's lap. He reached across the table and swept up the leather satchel that lay beside *MorningStar*, then prodded forward the notebook he had been reading before the start of their conversation. "When your father asked me to take you and your brother someplace safe, he gave me this satchel, and told me that it held this notebook containing all the research he had ever done about the Luminous Rock and Daimos."

Cecil produced from the satchel a fist-sized fragment of rock, which he set down onto the face of the open map.

"Along with the notebook, your father oddly included this stone in the satchel. None of us really knows why, or what it has to do with anything."

Magnus picked up the stone and studied it closely. It was quite unremarkable—a coarse shard of rock, such as one might find lodged in the dirt. "Could this have anything to do with the Luminous Rock?" he asked. "Didn't you say he managed to break off a piece?"

"Yes," Cecil answered with hesitation. "But that piece was unfortunately stored in a holster on his belt when he was killed. I'd offered to take the shard in the satchel, but he said he'd keep it with him should he have a chance to face Recett himself. He never did, and the shard was almost certainly found and destroyed."

Putting aside the stone, Magnus reached for the notebook and breezed through its discoloring pages. The book contained a gamut of incomprehensibly scrawled formulas that appeared meaningless to the boy.

"Through my years of studying that notebook, alas, I've found it to hold no reference whatsoever to Daimos or the Luminous Rock," Cecil lamented. "Thankfully, I can almost guarantee you that Daimos never actually found the Luminous Rock, else we wouldn't be in the situation we're in now."

Cecil accepted the notebook back from Magnus. "It was for your own safety that we didn't tell you about any of this. Recett must have feared the shard at first sight; that's why he's been searching for us. He thinks we're the only ones who know what Brendan was researching."

"Are we?" Magnus inserted a doubt.

"Just about," said Cecil. "There were others in the council who were partly aware of his plans, but not to the extent of knowing where the shard had come from. There were six others who journeyed with him to Galem, but they were sworn to secrecy, and Recett has no way of tracking them down. Even I don't know their identities, let alone if they're still alive. The three of us are the perfect targets, since we're probably believed to be harboring the original research containing everything about the Rock, from its exact location to how Brendan planned to use it." Despair burned deeper into his frown. "Of course, the notebook we received from Brendan contains nothing of the sort. Neither Drake nor I know where the actual research is. For all we know, your father could have given us the wrong book. Drake never spoke a word of this to you because he didn't want anyone else to have to bear the burden we do."

"That wouldn't have stopped us from being hunted," retorted Magnus.

Cecil nodded regretfully. "Alas. We kept the irrational hope that Recett's legion would eventually be quashed by some other province. Years later, that has yet to happen."

Magnus lowered his head in somber reflection. A final question entered his mind as he looked back upon the map: "If MorningStar was evacuated, then why did its people come here? Why didn't they just move to another part of Arkane?"

"Some did, if they were able," replied Cecil, "but many did not, believing that Recett's ruin would follow them.

Relocating to another continent was unthinkable, seeing that Arkane's eastern continent is the only one solidly inhabited by humans. Making way to a separate continent would have meant starting a new civilization. Earth seemed like a perfect refuge to most, given the options."

Even after Cecil's response dwindled to a close, Magnus scarcely moved his eyes from the open chart; these tangled lines on parchment were all that sculpted the land in which his past supposedly resided. "All that you told me..." he said, "...sounded a lot like you were reading me a story straight out of a fantasy novel."

"True that it does, though it's nonetheless fact," replied Cecil. A smile lightened his expression. "I hope you can still believe me."

"Well, I..." Magnus stammered, finding no more to say.

"Tell you what," Cecil said brightly. "After breakfast, meet me outside in the clearing. And I'll show you just how real 'fantasy' can be."

Fire, Wind, and Water

MAGNUS EMERGED FROM the shelter doorway and stepped out into the forest clearing, his steps lingering at the foot of the hillside. Nothing here had changed since yesterday. The pickup stood idle in its spot on the earthy plane, glazed in the rays of the freshly risen sun that trickled through the overhanging mesh of branches.

Drake was seated limply on the ground at the clearing's edge. His head was tilted down toward his hands while he inattentively toyed with a withered twig. He seemed immersed in his thoughts and greatly distressed. Magnus' approaching footsteps called him to his senses. He looked up at his brother, struggling to shed a smile.

Magnus found a seat next to Drake between the serpentine roots of a broad oak and bared a narrow grin in sympathy. "You've been quiet all morning," he said.

"I..." Drake pulled a hard grimace and rubbed his tired eyes. "I just didn't sleep well last night. I couldn't take my mind off what happened yesterday." He released his grip on the twig, sighing bleakly. "I hope you're not still mad at me. I'm sorry I never told you any of this...I just—"

"Please, Drake," Magnus cut short his brother's apology. "I'm the one who should be sorry. After what Cecil told me this morning, I understand now...why you kept all this from me."

Drake remained silent. The past week had stirred in his mind the memories that he had taken over a decade to put behind him. After yesterday, he feared that history was about to repeat itself. "It's one thing to witness so many innocent people die," he said, "but it's another to watch your mother be murdered right before your eyes."

Magnus' breath was stolen by grief; his body grew cold as if his veins had turned to ice. "You saw it," he replied grimly. "You saw our mother die."

Drake said nothing in direct response. "We were almost out of the city," he began to recall. "I was running alongside Cecil, who was carrying you, only an infant. Our mother was falling behind. Cecil said that we were being followed and urged us to pick up pace, but our mother wasn't fast enough. As we turned a corner, she was shot in the back by an arrow. I heard her scream—I saw her fall dead. That was it."

Magnus couldn't bear to hear any more. He lifted his gaze to the oak's thinning canopy, as if to escape his own thoughts. He would have preferred to believe that their parents had merely drowned, as Drake had used to tell him. He would have preferred to believe anything to avoid the terrible truth.

"I never want anyone else to feel the way I felt that night," Drake continued. "I never wanted anyone else to see a person they love die in that wretched place. That's why I hid this from you."

"But if I hadn't found our father's book," said Magnus, "would you ever have told me about MorningStar?"

Drake was cautious in responding. "I can't count how many times I had the opportunity to," he said. "But I couldn't. I could never work up the nerve to admit I'd lied to you and to tell of a real past that would make me sound like I'd gone insane. When you were younger, Cecil and I both convinced ourselves that it would be best to wait until you grew up before you could handle the truth. As you got older, we feared how you'd react if you were told the truth. It was for the best that you discovered that book when you did." His last words were stolen away by a frail gust of wind that died into silence.

"What about other family?" Magnus asked. "You and Cecil always told me that we had none..."

"A few, I think." Drake shrugged. "Distant relatives. None that Cecil or I remember well. Perhaps we'd have had a chance of finding them if I hadn't stayed so secretive."

"You did all you could," Magnus commiserated. "You were only trying to protect me. It seems like this was bound to happen one way or another."

Drake laid a hand on his brother's shoulder, offering a fickle smile. "Put your mind off things for now," he said with an indicative tilt of his head toward the right end of the clearing. "Cecil is waiting for you. He has something he wants to show you that might help lift your spirits."

Magnus exchanged goodbyes with his brother on a lighter note and made way to the clearing's edge. Here, a tapered dirt slope coursed down into a much smaller, deeper glade curtained by the trees around it. Cecil could barely be spotted at the base of the slope, seated on a fallen tree. He turned and raised a hand in greeting as he caught sight of the boy standing high above him.

Magnus returned the gesture and began his descent down the slope with wary footsteps. Drawing aside the brittle net of tree branches that obstructed his path, he skidded into the depths of the glade. It was considerably darker here than in the shelter clearing. The forest domed around this place so densely that light was scarce to filter through. But in patches where trees had already cast off their leaves or where their branches parted in windows to the sky, the sun's rays cascaded into the glade in resplendent, heavenly shafts.

"Hello, Magnus," Cecil welcomed cheerily, his back half-turned to the boy. "Glad you could join me." He was toiling at a stocky branch rested in his lap, whittling its end to a spear-sharp tip with the blade of a small pocketknife.

"What are you doing there?" Magnus pried, coming around the fallen tree to face his former guardian.

"Just setting ourselves up." Cecil snapped shut the pocketknife and sheathed it in his pocket. With the sharpened spar in hand, he trod into the center of the glade, where an identical branch had already been impaled upright in the earth. He speared the second branch into the ground a few feet away from the first, then returned to the fallen tree.

"To begin with," said Cecil, crouching to retrieve what appeared to be some form of staff deposited at the rotting base of the tree trunk, "why don't you tell me what you think this is?"

Magnus accepted the staff as it was handed to him. It was near five feet in height, carved of a profusely knotted wooden stalk and embellished with an impressive array of fine gems. On the head of the stalk, an entwinement of branches sprouted from the wood and crept over the immaculate surface of a stunning, flame-red hunk of crystal, gripping the stone fast in place.

"Honestly," Magnus dragged his speech, reluctant to admit the undeniably fantastical appearance of the staff, "it looks a lot like something a sorcerer would use."

Little emotion touched Cecil's face, but his smile broadened. "What if I told you that your guess wasn't far from the truth?"

"I probably wouldn't believe you," Magnus said candidly, "but after yesterday, I don't seem to have a very accurate grasp on what I should or shouldn't believe in."

"That's quite understandable." Cecil gave a sharp nod. "You'll find that much of what you may have once considered fiction no longer seems so implausible. You must simply open your mind..." As his sentence drew to a pause, he reacquired the staff from Magnus and portentously extended its crystal headpiece. "...or allow me to open it."

When the crystal suddenly gleamed, it could have been perceived as no more than the light of a sunray caught in its lucent prism. But then, to Magnus' astonishment, a flame flickered to life on the surface of the gem and devoured the headpiece. Cecil lanced the burning crystal outward like an iron spear still lit by the fires of its forge, and an astounding ribbon of flames leapt from the staff, attacking the first of the branches impaled in the center of the glade. Torched, the branch shuddered and collapsed into the dirt. The blaze evaporated as abruptly as it had materialized, leaving not even the slightest smoulder in its wake.

Magnus was rattled and silenced by complete disbelief. He couldn't even begin to fathom how Cecil could have propelled flames out of a crystal. "What—" he stammered, lifting a doubting hand toward Cecil's staff. "What exactly was that?"

"Would you believe me if I told you?" asked Cecil staunchly.

Magnus tried to respond, but choked on his words in hesitation. He renewed his breath and spoke again: "I've seen and heard enough to know that I can't stay a skeptic. Tell me anything."

"In that case," Cecil replied, resuming his seat on the fallen tree, "what you have just seen is what one might refer to...as a spell."

Magnus bit his lip with painful reluctance, but quickly shrugged off the feeling. "Fine." He gestured to the crystal headpiece bound atop the staff. "Then how? How did that thing catch fire?"

"That's a simple question with a less-than-simple answer," Cecil began, admiring the crystal against the flittering sunrays. "Magic, spellcasting, call it what you wish. It's an ancient art that has existed on Arkane for millennia, and even once found users in this dimension. Through the ages, countless people, nations, tribes, and races have attempted to harness the unseen forces of nature and bend them to their will. One of the few that succeeded, as a world, was Arkane, where magic was practiced even by common folk with the use of enchanted gemstones—the basis of almost all Arkane spellcasting."

"What do you mean, 'enchanted'?" Magnus asked in an ironically slanted tone of voice. He lowered himself to a seat beside his former guardian. "How are they enchanted?"

"That, even I cannot say." Cecil smiled and shrugged. "The enchantment of gems is a whole different science altogether. From the little I know, it involves the use of a runic language that predates Arkane civilization. Now, the enchantment process specifies what elements of nature a gemstone can conjure. However, each variety of gem tends to have an elemental affinity that makes it apt for conjuring a specific element over another. For instance..." He rapped the blood-red crystal headpiece. "This is a ruby. It is enchanted to conjure fire, which is its natural affinity."

"This," Magnus exclaimed with widening eyes affixed on the fist-sized jewel, "is a ruby? Cecil, that staff must be worth thousands!"

"On Earth, yes, perhaps," Cecil answered under a placid

laugh. "But not on Arkane. The gems we consider rare in this world are far more abundant on Arkane."

"And these..." Magnus scrutinized the variety of smaller gems that adorned the staff's trunk. Some were a brilliant blue; others were colorless and translucent, stirred with a rainbow spectrum as light shone through.

"Sapphires and quartz crystals," Cecil confirmed. "Water and air, respectively. The fourth and last of the basic elements, earth, is best conducted by emeralds."

"Why only those four kinds of gems? What's so unique about them?"

"Oh, other gemstones can be enchanted just as easily," said Cecil. "But they're often considerably less effective in conducting the elements as opposed to the four I just mentioned."

Magnus was caught off guard when his former guardian turned to pass him the staff. "That's enough of my talk," Cecil declared, beaming. "Now it's time for you to try it."

"Try...?" Magnus blankly took hold of the staff.

"Of course," Cecil affirmed. "Did you think spellcasting was an art reserved for only the well-trained and power-ful? Get up, stand ahead of that branch, and hold the staff close to yourself."

Dazed by Cecil's abrupt instructions, Magnus staggered to his feet. He faced the remaining one of the two branches skewered upright in the dirt and took a two-handed grip on the staff, his nerves tinged with both angst and enthusiasm.

"Start with something simple," said Cecil. "A gust of wind. Anything strong enough to knock back the branch."

Magnus wavered a second before loosening his clutch on the staff. He realized that he was clueless as to how he could work the so-called enchanted gems in any way. "How?" was all he could think to ask.

"You must feel what you aim to conjure," Cecil directed. "Begin by closing your eyes. Notice the most subtle breeze even when it seems there is none."

Magnus gave a nod and shut his eyes. Without vision, he allowed the forest's full splendor to reveal itself through his other senses. The fickle serenade of birdsong was joined in a chorus of rustles muttered by the leaves; the wind, previously imperceptible, now fell over the glade like nature's own whispered breaths.

"Clear your mind of disbelief," Cecil continued his instructions. "Pay no attention to what you are actually trying to do, but rather, concentrate on what I tell you to do. Seek out the wind. Grasp it. Concentrate until you feel that it is in your very control."

Magnus did as he was told. At the moment that the finest sinew of wind licked his flesh, he seized it, arresting it to his staff like the taut string of a marionette. It was a peculiar sensation—how every movement of the staff seemed to draw the wind along with it. Evidently, there was far more to the gems than had first met Magnus' eye.

"When the wind is within your grasp," said Cecil, "expel it. Open your eyes and lunge with all your strength!"

Magnus constricted his fists, savoring the power that he clutched inside them. He advanced a single step, blinked open his eyes, and thrust out his staff with a heated focus pinned on the upstanding branch. The wind was spurred into an instant rage, shattering against Magnus' back as it tore the branch out from the dirt and cast it flat over the earth.

The gale subsided quickly. Magnus retracted the staff as if he were, all of a sudden, wielding a dangerous instrument. He found it difficult to believe that he had actually manipulated the wind, but it could hardly have been coincidence.

"Well done," Cecil ended the uncertain silence. His lip twitched to a smile at Magnus' childlike amazement.

"This..." Magnus muttered, incredulous, "...is unreal. How is this even possible? How can any of this...work?"

"Such things cannot always be explained through Earth's feeble spectacles of science," Cecil cryptically remarked. "The gems are enchanted. That may sound hopelessly absurd to anyone in this world, but what is often considered fictitious on Earth is the norm on Arkane."

"But why?" Magnus persisted. "How can it be that all the mythology we ever dreamt up in *this* world exists as reality someplace else?"

Cecil's smile widened as if in amusement. "That is because much of the mythology in this world isn't exactly dreamt up. A multitude of parallel dimensions once co-existed, trading their secrets and sharing the tales of their lands. There was once a time when spellcasting was accepted on Earth, but there also came a time when the practice was abused by those who harnessed its power for darker means. Shortly after the Middle Ages, magic was forbidden and shunned as an evil practice. As the worlds slowly diverged, their inhabitants drifted apart with them, and the reality of one world was left as the mythology of another."

"Then why did it stay that way? I mean, why doesn't anyone on Earth know about magic?"

"Because of the chaos that would result if they did." Cecil's tone saddened. "It's inconceivable, Magnus. Can you imagine what would happen if spellcasting were revealed to Earth in this day and age? Science would collapse, weapons would become obsolete, anarchy would erupt if an ordinary man were suddenly capable of wielding untold power. It became clear long ago that this world could not handle Arkane's technology—why, it can barely handle its own. Arkane has fought for centuries to protect Earth from magic and the consequences that would follow. We are lucky that they have succeeded so far."

His attention having strayed onto the toppled branch in a reverie, Magnus was brought to his wits only when he felt Cecil place a palm to his back. He turned to find that his former guardian had drawn beside him. "Now I want you to try an element you can see, not just feel," said Cecil, indicating the staff's bulbous ruby. He walked over to the branch that had been felled by Magnus' wind spell and restored it to its original upright position. "The element of fire. Scorch the branch to a cinder!"

Magnus flinched at Cecil's abrupt command. "What am I supposed to do this time?"

"Seek the element you wish to conjure," answered Cecil, stepping back from the branch. "Embrace it, empower it, and expel it. Such is the method for all elemental spellcasting."

"But there isn't any fire around here," Magnus argued. "Or heat, for that matter."

"Then find it," Cecil replied. "The elements are ever around us. Heat can be found in the deepest cold, even if it is from within your own clenched fists. Feel the singe of flame on your palms, and the staff will guide you through the rest."

With a nod of acknowledgment, Magnus shut his eyes a second time. He sifted through the autumn air to locate the element he desired—the scorching heat of a fire as vivid as the midday sun. A gradual warmth seemed to swell over his fists; before long, he believed he could feel the same heat emanating from the head of the staff. Opening his eyes to the sight of the ruby headpiece caught aflame, he thrust away the staff on impulse to avoid being burned by the gem's now-searing temperature. The fires bickered at his jostling and scattered wisps of flame, nearly dying, but endured long enough for Magnus to regain his focus and salvage the spell. As he braced his stance again, he cast out the head of the staff and shed a staggered flicker of flames toward the branch.

Unlike Cecil's earlier demonstration of the same spell, Magnus' frail blaze skimmed the peak of the branch and instantly set fire to the wood. It took the boy a second after the magic had dissipated to realize that he was gaping at a steadily burning wooden stake—which, of all places, stood in the center of a glade enveloped by forest.

"Quickly now," spurred Cecil. "Put it out before it spreads. What douses fire?"

"Water, but..." Magnus' speech faltered in uncertainty.

"All elements are conjured in the same manner," Cecil reminded. "The mere water vapor in the air is enough to summon a flood, if you are skilled."

Closing his eyes and renewing his mind, Magnus filled his lungs with the barely discernible scent of morning dew that still laded the air of the glade. An invigorating chill washed through his veins as he exhaled. His palms around the staff grew clammy, as if the sapphires adorning the wooden trunk had begun to leach a damp trickle of moisture. Once his grip on the element was fastened, he opened his eyes to lunge out and discharge an icy surge of water onto the flames that crowned the branch. With the fire extinguished, the charred branch wearily slumped aside.

Magnus let down the staff in a bout of stunned silence. Cecil broke the quiet with a leisurely applause. "Impressive." He smiled again. "Especially for a skeptic like you."

Magnus returned a grin of candor. "Even though I know everything you've showed me is real," he said, "it's still no easier to believe it."

"Indeed," his former guardian concurred. "Your perception of reality has been inverted in a matter of hours, but you've shown yourself to be willing. Accepting the very notion of magic is no easy task."

Cecil plunged a hand into his pocket and delicately retrieved a miniscule, gleaming artifact. Gesturing the boy to reach out, he deposited the object in Magnus' open palm. It was a golden ring, inlaid with a flawlessly cut jewel as clear as glass. "I want you to have this," said Cecil. "It is an enchanted diamond ring. While the gems I've just showed you can only conduct a single element, a diamond is one of the few precious stones whose unique properties allow it to conduct all four basic elements: fire, air, water, and earth."

Magnus was awestruck at the ring's sheer beauty. Every tilt of the fine jewel refracted the sun's rays in a dazzling coruscation of light. "Cecil, I don't know what to say but... thank you!"

"Though a diamond's power, by far, does not equate to that of, say, a ruby or emerald," said Cecil, "it's nevertheless an excellent tool for a beginner in the practice, or for one who simply wishes to use magic for everyday tasks, rather than for combat."

"Combat?" Magnus questioned the word. "You mean, you use magic to fight with?"

"Surely you didn't think that magic's only purpose is to ignite wooden pickets," Cecil replied with a motion toward the two charred branches. "Spellcasting is an art that knows no bounds, nor limit of power. Taking magic as what you've seen today is as if you were to judge the sharpness of a longsword by the pommel of its hilt. Some of the art's most powerful and magnificent capabilities lie in combat, a practice you might well need to learn soon." He sighed. "Where our situation stands, you never know when your skills may be called upon against the dangers that we face."

8

An Old Friend

IN LOCATIONS LACKING *sufficient elemental vapor, the desired power of a spell must sometimes be attained through a succession of multiple, weaker conjurings.* Magnus scanned the yellowed pages of the book in his lap. *Chain conjuring, as the technique is known, thus lades the air with vapor through the initial conjurings, allowing the use of substantially more powerful spells in turn.*

Magnus eased the tome shut, his eyes and mind both weary. Cecil had given him the book, a compendium on elemental spellcasting, earlier that morning after first introducing him to the art. Not surprisingly, the book's convoluted subject matter seemed hopeless to grasp.

Magnus was seated on the ground of the clearing outside the shelter, a tree for his backrest. As he reclined his head, the glare of the noon sun fell against his shut eyes in white-hot rays dampened by chill breaths of wind. He reflected on all that Cecil had told and shown him that morning. In mere hours, his sense of reality had been turned on its axis until there was virtually nothing left he could consider fiction. After being taught how to materialize water and fire from thin air, he felt like a fool for at first holding any skepticism against Cecil's tales of alternate dimensions.

Magnus blinked open his eyes as he sat upright. Cecil had left for Markwell at mid-morning to meet with the herbalist Anubis Araiya, acting on the note he had slipped under the apothecary door the previous day. He would be back by noon, he had said, but there was no sign of him yet.

Dim footsteps ruffled the silence. Magnus shifted his attention to see Drake clamber out of the shelter's skewed doorway. The brothers exchanged frail smiles of greeting as Drake approached to find a seat in the dried foliage near Magnus. "An interesting read?" Drake inquired, slanting his eyes toward the book in Magnus' hands.

Magnus chuckled, playing his fingers along the tome's spine. "Quite. Did you ever...do any of this yourself? Spellcasting, I mean."

Drake shrugged placidly. "Well, yes, but not very much, nor very well. I was only nine when we escaped Arkane. And I wasn't able to practice such skills openly here, especially as you got older."

"Right..." Magnus said in a mutter. He was called from his wistful trance when the sound of voices touched his ears from a distance. He picked up his head to look in the direction of the hillside opposite the shelter, where he spotted

Cecil alongside another man, looking down into the glade from the peak of the hill.

Cecil raised his hand high in an eager welcome. He had a sizable travel bag slung crosswise over him, as did the other man. With skillful footing, Cecil shuffled down the incline until he reeled to a halt on the ground of the clearing. The second man hastened after him. He was slightly taller than Cecil and rather lank, his limbs supple and thin like a willow's leaves. His long, lackluster dark hair, parted in the middle, fell along the sides of his face in flaccid, ill-cut curtains and onto the collar of his navy leather vest. He smiled meekly, with gleaming eyes that lent him an appearance as innocent as that of a child.

"Sorry for my lateness," said Cecil to the brothers. He ushered the man forward. "This is my friend Anubis Araiya."

"Magnus, I believe," Anubis amiably greeted, shaking the boy's hand. He addressed Drake in the same manner. "And Drake! I remember you—it's been far too long since we last met."

"Since MorningStar," Drake said with a plaintive smile. "Wonderful to see you again...though unfortunate that it should be under such circumstances."

The herbalist puckered his face. "Yes," he slurred. "Yes, indeed."

"Magnus and I can take your bags," Cecil promptly offered, extending a hand to receive Anubis' load. "Drake, why don't you show our guest inside?"

Anubis handed over his luggage with a gracious

thank-you and followed Drake through the shelter door, down the lopsided stairs beyond it. Magnus shouldered one of the two bags—a sleeping bag—as Cecil gave it to him. He was about to proceed after his brother when a rustle stole his attention away from the shelter. He was certain he had spotted something dart past his feet.

Ineptly, Magnus swiveled around to peer behind himself. To his astonishment, his eyes locked with another pair that was beady, emerald green, and brilliantly lustrous. He was looking upon a reptilian creature, a crimson lizard with four spindly paws and a long, lithe tail. It snarled, flaunting a maw of needlelike teeth before it scuttled after Anubis through the door of the shelter.

"Ah," Cecil noted. "That would be Anubis' pet salamander, Ember. Marvelous creature and, as you'll find, remarkably intelligent."

"Huh," Magnus gathered his brow, intrigued. "I've never really seen any kind like it."

"No..." Cecil said with a curled upper lip as the boy ducked inside the shelter. "...I don't believe you would have."

Magnus watched the sunrays ebb behind him and the shelter's mellow lamplight rise to replace them. He entered the main room, looking back as Cecil descended the stairs after him. "Where should I lay out Anubis' sleeping bag?"

"Oh, just leave it by the doorway, thank you," Anubis cut in. "I'll be sleeping out in the clearing."

"The clearing?" Magnus whisked his glance in the herbalist's direction, then back to Cecil in an astonished gesture. "Why?"

"We've practically been arguing on the subject all the way here." Cecil gave a crooked smile. "Anubis says he doesn't want to take up any of our space, and he insists that he'll sleep outside, no matter what I say."

Magnus turned again to Anubis, who merely waved aside the subject with his hand. "Please don't concern yourself, Magnus. It's already settled."

Magnus shrugged and deposited the sleeping bag by the foot of the stairs. He gathered with Cecil and his brother by the center table while Anubis surveyed the homely shelter.

"Exquisite construction, Cecil," Anubis praised, approaching the nearest of the bookcases. He brushed a fingertip along a row of well-worn spines. "And as marvelous a collection as always. You never cease to amaze me with some of the volumes you've managed to acquire."

Cecil grinned rather modestly. "These would include many of the rarer variety of my collection." He lifted the second of Anubis' bags off his shoulder and laid it on the floor by the table. "Most being from Arkane, I reckoned that they'd be safest stored here."

"Of course," Anubis muttered, selecting a book to thumb through its pages.

"Safest, relatively speaking, of course," Cecil added with a melancholy sigh. "At a time like this, safety doesn't appear to be very certain, regardless of the location."

A strange silence followed Cecil's statement. Anubis gawked at the open pages of the book in his hands with barely blinking eyes, as if he'd never heard Cecil speak.

"You alright, Anubis?" Cecil prodded the herbalist out of his reverie.

"Hm? Oh, yes—yes, sorry," Anubis tore his focus off the book as he closed it, fitting it back inside its slot on the shelf. He immediately plunged his hands inside his pockets, arms pulled tight against his sides.

"Are you cold?" Magnus asked.

"Just a little," Anubis answered with hesitation and cringed in a mild shiver. "I'm alright, thank you."

"It's chilly, isn't it?" Cecil concurred, eyeing the bare, sooty hearth of the fireplace. "There's a chimney vent at the top of the hillside. It'll likely have to be cleared of debris before we can stoke the fireplace again." He motioned to the older brother. "Drake, would you like to come along? We ought to check the vent and gather some wood."

"Sure," Drake readily agreed and headed for the stairs with Cecil behind him.

"Magnus, stay here in case Anubis needs anything." Cecil looked back to the boy before leaving. "We'll be outside if you want us."

Waving them off, Magnus watched Cecil and his brother drift out of sight beyond the shelter doorway. He slipped into a chair by the center table. "Can I get you anything?" he asked Anubis.

"Oh, I'm fine, thank you." Anubis glanced a smile in Magnus' way and found a seat at the end of the adjacent couch, sighing contentedly to himself.

"So you live in Mark—" Magnus tried to begin speaking,

but his sentence was throttled by the sight of the herbalist's pet salamander. It scurried past him a second time with the sound of claws snapping on the hardwood. "That lizard again...Ember, is it?"

"Correct!" Anubis exclaimed. "Cecil told you?"

"Yeah. I saw it outside a few minutes ago." Magnus twisted his head to look past the high backrest of his chair. There behind him, the reptile stood still. He could see it with more definition now—its head was extraordinary, like that of a dragon, snouted and adorned with short, sloping spines that sprouted from its crown and trickled down the length of its back to its tail. Its scaled hide was stippled with veins of ochre and scarlet, interwoven like a tapestry. It was enough to know that no ordinary salamander possessed claws as this one did, but this creature was unlike any Magnus had ever known to exist.

"What...kind of salamander is it?" Magnus wondered aloud.

"He's a Zephyrian salamander," Anubis answered. "From the Arkane province of Zephyr. A notably rare breed. They're best known for their exceptional intelligence."

Magnus couldn't help but give an ironic smile. "Everyone I know or meet lately seems to be from Arkane," he jested, eyes trailing the salamander as it darted around to the opposite end of the table.

"Would you care to meet more?" Anubis quipped and returned a grin. "You may be surprised at how many people from Arkane live in Markwell."

"Why? What's so unique about this place?" Magnus'

attention strayed back to Ember as the salamander latched onto the table's edge in a deft leap and trod out onto its surface.

"Its location, chiefly," answered Anubis. "Did you know that Markwell itself was founded because of its proximity to the MorningStar rift?"

"MorningStar rift?" Magnus raised an eyebrow. He saw Ember nestle into a graceful pose in front of him, draconic eyes affixed on him in a way that suggested he was listening.

"Ah, Cecil mentioned that you were new to this sort of thing." Anubis acquired a pensive frown. "Where to start? Has Cecil told you much yet about the science of parallel dimensions?" he asked, and received a nod from the boy. "Good. Well, then a rift is that which bridges one dimension to another. Overlaps, if you will, between the worlds."

Magnus hesitated. "What purpose do they serve? Are they some kind of...portals?"

"Portals, yes, if you choose that kind of terminology," said Anubis. "By definition, they are natural tears in the fabric of space and time through which it is possible to traverse the dimensions—parallel dimensions, usually. The more closely related one world is to another, the greater the number of rifts connecting them. But they can lead to much stranger places as well."

"What would one...look like? Unless I don't really grasp the concept."

"They're difficult to describe. You could consider them invisible, but a discerning eye can spot them. They appear like translucent veils where things seem to shift and sway as if they weren't entirely there. Walking into one instantly transports you to the other side in the world that it leads to."

Magnus pulled a face of stunned incredulity. "That sounds unbelievable. How can something like that not be known to Earth?"

"Oh, Earth knew about them at some time or another," said Anubis. "But rifts are fickle things. They materialize over millennia, yet can collapse in seconds if not kept stable. Dimensions like that of Earth didn't have the kind of knowledge necessary to study or properly understand such things, so as many of these rifts faded over time, the concept was ignored and forgotten." A quiet laugh cracked his sobriety. "It's ironic, really. Nowadays, if any ancient records are discovered that cite mystical gateways and alternate worlds, we indisputably regard them all as fiction."

"What do you mean by Earth not having the knowledge?"

"Insight, understanding..." Anubis listed vaguely. "Remember that Arkane's people are a civilization that was born with a remarkable grasp on the unseen forces of nature. Rifts, just like spellcasting, are one of these forces. Why Earth should have evolved any differently, it's impossible to say. Arkane has had knowledge about rifts and spellcasting for so long that trying to trace them to their origins would be like...trying to single out the identity of the person who discovered fire."

"Then where *are* these rifts?" Magnus asked somewhat dubiously, even while trusting the herbalist in his explanations.

"All over the place, really." Anubis' response was disappointing at first, but he elaborated after a moment's consideration: "In locations where the environment allows it. Rifts tend to materialize in places where the ties between dimensions are strongest—typically isolated places surrounded by the elements, say, a thick forest or a mountain's peaks, or even the depths of an ocean. Naturally, this rule applies to both sides of the rift.

"Rifts exist in this fashion because they thrive off the elemental energies around them. The moment these energies are disturbed, as is the case when civilization encroaches, the rifts weaken and, ultimately, collapse. The people of Earth have destroyed countless rifts this way without even being aware of it. This leaves only the rifts that exist in places so remote that almost no one ever discovers them by accident.

"Arkane, on the other hand, has learned to study and maintain these rifts so that they may utilize them. A perfect example would be Markwell—a rift to the forest west of MorningStar can be found in the deepest parts of these woods. You could say Markwell was founded as a sort of camp for those whose work or professions required them to travel often between the worlds. With civilization being established just near enough that the forest is left undisturbed, the rift remains active and strong."

"Then why would this place have been designated a campsite?"

"Because the campgrounds preceded the hamlet. They served the same purpose, of course, but without being very versatile or suitable for longer stays. And they were prone to receive too many visits by ordinary folk believing this place was nothing but an ordinary grove to pitch a tent in. As the hamlet developed over many years, the campgrounds fell out of use, until they were abandoned entirely. No one comes here anymore, besides those who know about the rift."

Anubis' answers were incredible to Magnus; nevertheless, the boy accepted them. After a morning of witnessing things that shattered the bounds of imagination, it would be irrational to respond any other way. "Hasn't anyone ever entered a rift by accident?" he asked. "And what happened when they did? It seems amazing that anything as big as another dimension could stay a secret to everyone in this world."

"Yet bigger secrets have been kept." Anubis beamed at the irony. "People *have* unknowingly wandered into rifts before. Imagine, though, if the other side of the rift were not much different than the side you entered from, would you even notice the rift at all? By the time you did, you'd be far from it. To the people of Earth, you'd have vanished without a trace, but your real fate depends on what sort of world you'd stumbled into."

"Suppose that world were Arkane?"

"Then you're likely to encounter civilization immediately. Every Arkane rift is stationed with people who vigilantly monitor its traffic, incoming and outgoing. Border guards, you might call them. Anyone exiting Arkane must state their reasons for doing so; anyone entering must explain whence they came. Generally, cross-dimensional traveling has complex restrictions and isn't allowed unless absolutely necessary. If a person should have entered from Earth by a fluke, steps are taken to ensure that word of Arkane does not escape to Earth. The same applies to those visiting Earth from Arkane."

"So in other words...you kill them?" Magnus smirked, his response clearly in humor.

"Oh no, no, certainly not," Anubis answered under an amused bout of laughter. "But the authority that oversees the rifts is a powerful one, and those who know this are not inclined to upset it." His lips halted a moment as his smile faded. "MorningStar's rift, of course, remains the only one not currently under guard. The reasons for this are...evident." He blinked forcefully, as if suddenly jostled out of a trance. "But there hasn't, to date, been any trouble with people straying in. Too remote. The forest, I mean. No one comes here anymore, as I said."

"Cecil said you've been to Arkane recently," Magnus shifted the subject. "What's it like there? ...after what happened with Daimos."

The herbalist cleared his throat and lingered in responding. "Oh...well, I only return to MorningStar every now and then to gather some of the herbs I need for the more specialized stock of my apothecary. Dried herbs, of course. I know quite a few of my colleagues who do this also. I haven't been to the other regions of Arkane in a long time, but I believe they've remained mostly untouched."

"Then what about MorningStar?" Magnus added. "What's it like?"

"Not...a very pleasant city, as it is," Anubis slurred through a sigh. "It's abandoned now, save for Daimos and his men. With the ash clouds blotting out the sun, the whole of Serenia is a wasteland. But the damage is, at least, limited to the province."

"Ash clouds?" Magnus' eyes gaped.

"Yes...yes, the shades are formed of ashes, you see," said Anubis. "They gather into clouds so thick that even the sun cannot penetrate them. Shades are normally scattered by light, but...when they're gathered densely enough, virtually nothing can affect them." He turned his head sharply in Ember's direction as the salamander scampered off the table.

"So you've seen them before?"

"I...have, yes." Unease touched Anubis' roving gaze. "Their clouds are quite hard to miss, almost anywhere in Serenia."

"What about...up close?" Magnus asked, lowering his voice.

Anubis could only respond with a dry stammer before he was interrupted. The whine of footsteps on hardwood signaled Cecil and Drake's descent down the entrance stairs from outside. "The vent's in perfect condition," Cecil announced. His arms were full with brushwood, as were Drake's. "Everything should be clear to start the fire."

"Ah, let me help you with that," Anubis avidly exclaimed and leapt to Cecil's aid.

"Thank you." Cecil rolled the assortment of spindly branches into the herbalist's arms. "I should note that it would be wise to limit the use of the fireplace, especially during the daytime," he said. "Smoke is discreet, but still visible from a distance. We wouldn't want to give Recett's men another way to spot us."

Anubis crouched by the edge of the hearth to deposit the brushwood, when Magnus strode up behind him. "What about Daimos?" the boy continued on the subject as another question sparked to mind. "Have you ever seen—"

"T-that reminds me, Cecil, I ought to be preparing my things outside in the clearing." Anubis abruptly staggered upright to face Cecil, as if he had completely failed to hear Magnus behind him.

"Oh...yes, yes, of course." Cecil nodded, chilled by the sudden angst in the air. Anubis hurried off, hands fastened inside his pockets, casting back a feeble attempt at a smile. He swept up his bag in a trembling fist and flitted up the steps, out of the shelter.

"What was that about Daimos?" Cecil asked warily.

Magnus turned between Cecil and his brother, partly stunned. Drake was in the midst of clustering the leftover brushwood at the edge of the fireplace when he lifted his head to listen as well.

"I just asked if he'd ever seen Daimos," Magnus replied. "We were talking about MorningStar...and what it's like there now."

Cecil skewed his lips, grimacing. "It may be best to keep from the subject with him," he said. "He acted similarly when I spoke about it on the way here. Considering that part of his trade involves gathering Serenian flora, I'm afraid to ask at all about what kinds of horrors he's encountered being so near to MorningStar."

Distress flared over Magnus' expression. "What do you mean?"

"The shades, for one thing," said Cecil. "In large-enough swarms, they are easily deadly. And Recett's men are always scouting about for those they consider trespassers. Countless innocent people have been arrested and killed for as much as setting foot in the province."

Magnus' concern turned to horror. "That's just...what could anyone have to gain by slaughtering travelers?"

"Absolutely nothing," Cecil answered bitterly. "It seems Recett kills without reason other than to satisfy his blood-lust. Ruling over a barren empire in this way for more than a decade...he's long lost his sanity, if he even had any to begin with."

Noctell suspired, but his apprehension did not leave him. He eyed Raven beside him, the demon displaying no less anxiety. With a leaden grip, Noctell hauled open the MorningStar castle doors.

Torrid, ash-sodden air gusted into his face. The entrance corridor gaped ahead, its darkness ready to devour him. Although Noctell and the demon almost always lugged a choking sense of dread when they returned to their master, few times compared to today. Empty-handed from their raid on Wingheart's bookshop some hours ago, they were prepared to suffer Daimos' searing wrath for their failure. Whether they were even to blame for their targets' escape, their master was not one to be rational when disappointed.

Noctell was first to head in, followed by Raven. They cringed at the thunderous echo of the door falling closed behind them, like the gate of a cell shutting to trap them in confinement. The paced past the corpses' wilted frames until entering the throne room. Here, their master awaited them.

The contempt that was carved into Daimos' face showed even at a distance. He was leaned out of his ebony throne in an agitated posture, his glare set upon Noctell and Raven from the moment they'd set foot in the castle. "Nothing, I presume?" he droned. "Nothing at all?"

Noctell halted at the center tiles of the skull mosaic; Raven boldly advanced a few feet further. "We searched all corners of the apartment and the bookshop below it," said the demon, his stare lifting no higher than the ungulate feet of his master's throne. "It appeared that at least two people had been living there, all of them now clearly having fled. A hidden cellar of Arkane books was discovered...but it seemed that Wingheart had already taken anything of value."

"What the devil *else* do you think he'd do?" Daimos' acrid snarl echoed. He rose from his throne. "*Clearly having fled,* you say? How observant of you! Did you expect to tie the lot of them up in their sleep? Did you expect to find anything at all at that damnable address after Handel escaped?"

Raven's submissive air became mingled with irritation. He was long tired of Daimos' sophistic scolding, though he knew that defiance would do him no good. Noctell held his ground in silence, remaining oblivious to the argument that inevitably concerned him.

"Here we return to the start!" Daimos stormed toward the men, cloak rippling in the firelight. "Just as things were a decade and a half ago! Searching without a lead for this man who continually eludes us!" He confronted Raven at a distance that did not allow him to be stunted by the demon's height. "No, not us, in fact...but you two! He who has eluded you long enough to make fools of you!"

"Milord, this is no fault of ours," Raven countered. "We did exactly as we were told. The plan simply didn't foresee Handel's escape."

"Then whom are you trying to blame?" Daimos lunged out, igniting a blaze of dark energy ignited in the air before him. "*Me?*" Like a nine-tailed whip, the blaze clutched the demon by his stout chest and constricted, buckling him over. Raven let out a shivering scream at the pain, a sensation as though his bones were being wrenched out of place.

As Daimos dispelled the blaze, he affixed his wrath on the mute necromancer. "And don't think you'll be spared for the sake of your silence!" With a flash of black cloth, his claw was wrapped around Noctell's throat. Noctell gasped, struggling, while still too terrified to move. Tendons of dark energy joined his master's clutch and pulled taut, choking him suddenly. He staggered back, coughing, when Daimos finally relieved his hold.

"However..." Daimos sobered his tone. He exchanged glances with Noctell and Raven, who had both withdrawn to a cautious distance. "...you may consider yourselves lucky. Later the same night that you returned from Handel's residence, an unlikely prisoner offered his services to me as a scout and spy. Apparently he knows a great deal more about our targets than we do. Provided he doesn't fail us, we may locate Wingheart soon enough."

Shock and ire formed on Noctell's expression. "Then what was all that about returning to the start?" he snapped.

"The scout is but a last resort," the warlord answered acutely. "Your tasks are your own matter, and you are to treat them as if our entire mission relied on them. No one should ever trust the aid of an outsider." He glowered. "Nevertheless, we have discovered through this outsider that Wingheart is residing with Handel somewhere in the Markwell forest. You are to set up camp there and await further instructions. I will contact you at the scout's next report."

Noctell and Raven dipped their heads in a blend of timidity and anger, scarred by their master's brutal rebuke. Without another word, they turned and hastened out of the chamber.

9

Faithful by Fear

AVEN BORED HIS PONDEROUS stare into the campfire before him. As the flames heaved and rippled, their warmth lapped the demon's half-hooded face. No wind was present, though the air was touched with a coldness. Over the lip of the fire's red haze, he observed Noctell slumped against a buckled tree across from him.

Noctell and Raven had headed for the Markwell forest in immediate response to their master's orders. With few instructions other than to keep watch for their targets, their mission seemed more like punishment in the form of tedium. The evening had trickled by listlessly, leaving night to descend on the forest like a stagnant black fog.

Raven's eyes trailed the sparks of the campfire as they were spat from the flames to leap into the cloudless heavens. He turned up his head, bringing it to rest against the tree at his back. He was mesmerized by the night sky—an unbounded void tinged with cosmic shades and blanketed with stars that seemed to increase in multitude the longer one looked. It was a spectacle that could not be seen from beneath MorningStar's ashen shroud. Raven heaved a sigh.

"Clear night, isn't it?" the demon remarked.

"Hmm," Noctell replied with only an indifferent drone, absorbed in his own reflections.

"The skies above MorningStar have grown so clouded by ash," Raven continued in a wistful mutter, "that it's almost impossible to think they once looked like this."

Noctell gave no response. The almost-mute crackle of the fire prevailed over the silence for a minute before Raven spoke again: "Ever wonder what would happen if we just never went back?"

This time, Noctell picked up his head. "To where?"

"MorningStar..." Raven answered into the sky, "...our master. Suppose, for once, we didn't return."

Noctell uttered what might have been a quiet laugh. "We'd be hounded within an inch of our lives, of course." He paused, speaking again in an almost sarcastic melody: "What gave you such an absurd idea?"

"Oh," Raven mimicked the necromancer's tone, "nothing at all."

Silence returned as the men brooded. Conversing only through their facial expressions, they could tell that they were of like minds. Noctell rubbed his neck indicatively; Daimos' clutch still burned him. "I've lost count of how many times he's done this to us," he said. "Thrashing us like dead animals..."

"If I listen to any more of his tirades, they may actually start to sound reasonable," Raven added. "Unless I just fail to understand his logic."

"He has none," Noctell replied. "Rage is his logic. We're the highest-ranking men of his guard, yet he treats us no better than his prisoners. No gratitude for our loyalty."

"Just what is loyalty?" said Raven. "Loyalty is voluntary and steadfast allegiance, not servitude out of fear." He looked pointedly at Noctell. "Which do you think best describes our *loyalty* to Daimos?"

Noctell hunched lower against the face of the tree. The answer was clear, but he was loath to speak it. "And?" He shrugged irritably. "Is that such a bad thing?"

"Ask yourself that very question the next time you're floundering in Daimos' grasp," Raven countered.

The necromancer fell silent without words to respond. "Loyal or not," he said finally, "we can't do much about it, can we? Standing up to him in any way will only worsen our punishments."

"Sadly true." Raven pulled a dismal grimace. "Best not to dwell on it right now. With that new scout on his side, this hunt might be over sooner rather than later. Then he should have less reason to scold us."

"Unlikely," Noctell scoffed. "But at least our search will be done with."

Noctell's reply died off into uneasy silence. The men's eyes did not meet, but instead clung to the perpetually swaying flames before them. "Better get some sleep, I suppose," Raven muttered, as if to sever his own train of thought.

"I'll take the first watchman shift," Noctell volunteered.

Raven took up one of the two sleeping bags bundled with the rest of their supplies by the edge of the camp. Unfurling the tattered bed, he clambered in and collapsed on the side of his burly frame, his back to the necromancer.

Noctell returned his languorous gaze to the fire. Though his eyelids were leaden, his mind was restless. He had been through this before. Tonight wasn't the first time he had questioned his loyalty toward his master, and he was certain it wouldn't be his last.

"*Loyalty is voluntary and steadfast allegiance,*" Raven's barbed insights echoed, "*not servitude out of fear.*"

Noctell was by no means loyal to Daimos—he feared him. He sought to please him, dreading the punishment he would receive if he did not. His throat tightened at the mere memory of the countless stranglings he had endured at his master's hand. Suddenly short of breath, he withdrew from the pulsating heat of the flames, trying to shed the sensation. But instead, his doubt returned twofold.

How long has it been? he asked himself.

Eighteen years, he responded. *Eighteen years since I joined Daimos' ranks. I hardly remember how things were before then.*

I was free, he answered again.

You were weak, a second voice entered his thoughts. But he disregarded it.

I could be free again, he continued. *It's not as hard as it seems. There's nothing holding me back from leaving Daimos. I could stay in this world and never be fearful again.*

You will be hunted.

I will be. But who am I to be concerned? Between Raven and me, none of Daimos' forces will be able to stop us.

What has gotten into you, Noctell? The second voice established a clear identity in his mind. It was alluring, placid, and laced with ill intent. *Why do you doubt your loyalty?*

Because it is false loyalty, Noctell replied. *I obey Daimos out of fear over his rage and threats. How long can I keep fooling myself into believing this is loyalty?*

Pay no heed to what Raven has told you, for he is blinded by the frustration of his failure, said the voice. *You will think on your own. Can you not see all the benefit that your master has given you?*

I try to, but I fail to see any at all.

Then compare who you are now to who you once were. The voice grew in sharpness, searing the walls of Noctell's skull. He began to drowse, his eyes blinking slower and heavier each second. *You were a weakling,* continued the voice, *a coward with little strength of your own. A forlorn orphan child burned by anguish. But you are powerful now, a mighty captain of the greatest guard on Arkane. You are wealthy, brave, and fearless, as well as feared.*

Noctell struggled to oppose the voice's beguiling tenor. *I am a servant*, he said, *chained to my master's will.*

You are not chained, but merely fixed on the path that is right for you. One grows errant without a friend and master to guide them.

If you consider anyone in that festering wasteland to be my friend, Noctell snapped, *you are sorely mistaken.*

Is Daimos not your friend?

The fire's blaze seemed to languish, its tongues drawling, coming still. *Perhaps once*, Noctell answered, *but no longer.*

Am I not your friend?

Noctell coiled his hands into ashen fists, his head throbbing fiercer until the pulsations resonated in his mind like the sound of a hammer striking iron. He felt strangely cold within, as if his blood were waning. The sight of fire dominated his vision; all around, it fell dark as the night sky. *Perhaps once...* he repeated. His own voice now resonated vividly. *...but no longer.*

I was once the only friend in the world to you, the voice thundered in return, *yet now you disown me?*

Leave my mind, Noctell demanded, seething. *It was you who confined me to Recett to begin with. No good has ever come from listening to you, and none ever will.*

When you first came to me, young, foolish, and feeble, hissed the voice, *you thought otherwise.*

The voice seemed to fade into the direction of the fire, from where a thick black smoke began to seep up. At Noctell's eye level, the smoke lingered and curled, its threads weaving to form a sculpture of smog—Daimos' unmistakable skull icon.

Noctell was overcome by fury at the sight of the icon. He lunged over the flames and thrashed at the smoke, tearing apart the image into a sinewy mist. Immediately, the fire was extinguished as if it were a flame as frail as a candle's. Sheer blackness flooded his surroundings.

Noctell dared not raise his head. On his knees, he shivered, his stare clinging to the stark earth. The dark was so oppressive that he believed he could feel its weight on his back. His mind was silent, but he knew he had not heard the last of the voice. Gathering his nerve, he looked up.

He was no longer in Markwell. He was in a forest clearing, but the trees that loomed upon him were ancient, gnarled, and dead, and the abyssal sky above him held no stars, clouds, nor moon. As he looked around, he saw no one and nothing but a sparse assembly of rotting wooden grave markers and shattered, nameless headstones. He had been here before—it was the place of his nightmares, and one that he had wished he would not need to lay eyes on again.

Unsteadily, Noctell came to his feet. He scouted his surroundings, eyes wide with fear and nearly unblinking. He embraced himself for warmth, but felt no heat; his skin was pale as bone and cold to the touch. A slow rustle from the gloom of the trees seized his attention.

A man emerged into the cemetery clearing. His hair was long and chalk-white, shawling a narrow face of bloodless complexion. As he approached, the shadows wafted off his figure. His body was leather-clad, draped over with a black cloak woven with tenuous red veins. He directed his scarlet eyes toward Noctell, his thin lips unbending.

"Hello, Knever," the man greeted the necromancer by his last name. It was this man's voice that Noctell had heard in his mind.

"Go," Noctell replied bitterly, still shivering. "Leave me. I don't want to see you any more than I want to listen to you."

"It's been a while now, hasn't it?" A smile glimmered over the man's lithe features. "I was beginning to believe your loyalty had finally solidified."

"I was beginning to believe I was finally rid of you," Noctell retorted.

"Why would you wish to be rid of me?" The man appeared amused at Noctell's remarks. "In your anger, you cast aside even the one who gave you hope and new strength at a time when you had none? Your lack of fidelity is lamentable, I am sorry to say."

"What you gave me was a curse in the guise of a blessing," the necromancer growled. "I don't care what you say; I have no freedom. The instant I even try to question my loyalties, you torment me until it feels as if I have no mind of my own! Why should you even care about my service to Daimos?"

"Because you aided me, Knever," said the man, his voice innocently enticing, "and I wish to aid you in return, simply by fixing you on the path that is best for you." His expression fell solemn. "It would grieve me to see you revert back into the weakling you once were."

"I was never a weakling," Noctell spat, channeling a violent black glow into his skeletal pendant, "and never will be!" But as he outstretched his arm toward the man, his attempt at a magical assault gave off no more than a dying flicker of energy at his fingertips. He snarled, lunging in his rage, only for his legs to be stricken with a sudden infirmity. He lurched and fell gracelessly at the feet of the man.

Noctell pried up his head; his scowl was met by the man with a saddened, pitiful frown. "Your memory fails you," said the man. "Had you not been a weakling, you would not have come to me as you once did. Remember the agony of helpless solitude, and you will remember the worth of my gift."

Noctell staggered upright, his stare jaded and heavy with anger. His jaws quivered, but no words emerged.

"I am not your enemy, Knever," the man continued. "I am no less your friend than I was eighteen years ago. I commiserate with your frustration, but you must learn to endure your pains for your own profit. Upon my return, things will be different."

Noctell's expression had turned lifeless. He no longer even appeared to be thinking. "When will that be?" he asked, his voice just as vacant.

"That will depend on the devotion of my followers," the man answered. "Should you remain staunch in your service to Daimos, you will see the Order's rise before the first frost of winter." He widened his eyes, which scintillated like glass prisms. "I told you once before that you were fortunate enough to live in the age in which you would witness my ascent to power. That time is now nigh, and more so than ever."

Noctell heaved a breath, his shuddering subsiding. Still, he said nothing.

"Do you vow to serve Daimos as your master?" The man's tone was mellow, but demanded a straight answer; with great reluctance, Noctell delivered one.

"I—" the necromancer stammered. His lips were loath to move. "I do." He shut his eyes in a grimace, as if he had swallowed poison.

"You are wise." The man beamed. "And thus you will begin to see the fruits of your labor sooner than you would expect."

"Then please let me leave this place..." Noctell lowered his head timidly. "...and don't haunt me any longer."

"You will leave soon enough," said the man, "but you must first affirm your vow." He paced further away, his cloak lingering in his wake like a veil. Turning to face Noctell again, his robes settled to reveal an enormous headstone that had manifested behind him. Noctell felt every tendon in his body turn frigid and brittle at the sight.

The headstone's foundation was a colossal plinth from which rose a pair of emaciated arms and hands. Within the clasp of the hands, raised as if in an offering to the gaping black heavens, was a giant skull of stone—an immaculate sphere with a broad, notched cylinder of teeth fitted beneath it, and a set of drooping hollows for its eyes and nose. The sculpture's detail was remarkable, unscathed by the wear that had claimed every other headstone around it.

But most mysterious of all was perhaps the lone hilt of a dagger that protruded from the crown of the skull; it appeared as if its blade had been caused to melt into the very stone, leaving not even the slightest fracture in its place.

"No doubt you remember this," said the man. "Grip your dagger, and our bond will strengthen, so that I may better guide you through times of confusion."

"I don't need your guidance," Noctell replied in an irate mutter. "I'll do as I'm told."

"Apparently not," the man rejoined, "else I would not have brought you here. You are fickle and require a rigid hold. Should you stray again, you will only lead yourself further toward ruin."

With a sigh of submission, Noctell confronted the headstone. The skull's cavernous gaze seared him like black embers; atop the sculpture, just above eye level, the dagger hilt gleamed. Acting on an impulse of determination, Noctell reached out and clutched the hilt, which, even to his pale flesh, was colder than ice. He felt the man's gauntleted hand come upon his shoulder in an instant.

A writhing numbness struck the arm in which Noctell gripped the knife. The sensation permeated his skull, deadening his mind and slashing apart his vision to a throbbing, sanguine haze. Total blackness descended on him again. When his senses returned, he found his shoulder still fiercely gripped—but not by the man.

"Wake up." A baritone voice and a firm jostling spurred Noctell to open his eyes. He was facing Raven, back in their forest campsite.

"You fell asleep," Raven droned, letting off his grasp on Noctell's shoulder.

"S-sorry..." Noctell palmed his face, kneading his eyes. "I..." His mouth was parched and barely capable of forming words.

"Forget about it." The demon pulled himself to his feet and shambled back to his post at the opposite end of the camp. "I'll take over. You get some rest."

"Thank—" Noctell drowned his reply under a cough. "Thank you."

Stroked by the familiar warmth of the campfire, Noctell was calmed. He seemed unable to think or hold open his eyes wider than a slit, but he took pleasure in the stillness of his mind and body. He folded his arms close against his chest and lifted his gaze to the night sky's vividly speckled canvas. Only in the profound silence did his own thoughts still whisper:

Forgive me, master... Noctell shut his eyes to the forest around him. *...for doubting you.*

10

Potion Crafter

THOUGH HE WAS by no means a chemist, Magnus was certain that the formulaic text of his father's notebook was anything but ordinary. As he breezed through the pages, his eyes were assailed by messily scripted symbols, words, and numerical strains— interwoven, ill-aligned, and seemingly without order. Much of it was barely legible.

This was the book that Cecil had received from Brendan on the night of Daimos' final assault on MorningStar. Passed along with the stone and the satchel in which it had been given, it encompassed, according to Brendan, all the research he had ever done on the portentous Luminous Rock. However, it was apparent to anyone who scrutinized it that this was untrue.

Magnus was seated at a small writing desk in the room he and his brother shared in the shelter. The notebook, the sole item on the desk, was open before him. A diffuse, radial glow was the only light, shed from a lucidus-stone lantern suspended above.

Magnus heaved his eyes off the inky bedlam that smothered the pages, blinking hard. He rested his gaze by allowing it to wander the confined room, which, aside from the desk, contained only a pair of mattresses laid over with sleeping bags. Even after having spent all morning absorbed in the notebook, he was unable to make any more sense out of his father's enigmatic scrawl than when he had first seen it. It was even more disheartening to think that Cecil had studied the writings for years without avail. Magnus was forced to consider the bitter prospect that the book may be useless altogether.

It was all too likely that, in the heat of the battle, Brendan had simply included the wrong notebook in the satchel. A petty error had sealed the fate of MorningStar, shattering all hopes for Daimos' defeat. Cecil and the brothers were now being hounded for an object they didn't possess, unable to retaliate and doomed to flee until their inevitable capture.

But Magnus refused to accept such a pessimistic outlook. He realized that if Brendan had left the research behind, Daimos would almost certainly have found it; yet the warlord's continuous pursuit suggested this was not the case.

Then where is it? Magnus pondered. His fingers crept mindlessly back into the pages. *Wherever...it definitely isn't here.*

The groan of the door summoned Magnus' attention. He swiveled around to see Cecil lean into the room.

"If you need anything, I'll be outside with Drake for a while." Cecil motioned to the shelter entrance. "We agreed he ought to brush up on his spellcasting as well. You could say he's gotten just about as much practice as you have in the past few years."

"Sure." Magnus smiled wearily. "Have fun."

As his former guardian departed, Magnus saw Anubis standing by the table in the main room to wave Cecil off. The herbalist turned in Magnus' direction and beamed with sleepless eyes. He slouched to the bedroom doorway, propping his shoulder against the frame. "What's that you're reading?" he inquired.

"It's my father's notebook," Magnus replied, a discernible gloom in his voice. "Has Cecil told you about it yet?"

Anubis hauled himself into the room on his spindly legs and set a crooked stare on the open pages. "Yes, I believe so..." He took the notebook into his hands. "Haven't had the chance to look over it yet myself."

Magnus watched Anubis glance over the next three pages with fierce interest. "What do you think it all is?" asked the boy.

"Some sort of herbology notebook, by the looks of it," answered Anubis. "Very hastily written. I can barely make out the script..."

"Herbology?"

"Potion crafting, more precisely. These are all formulas, recipes, for potions."

"Medicinal formulas? Or what exactly?" Magnus gave a quizzical frown. "What *is* a potion?"

"Just another word for a herbal concoction, really. Occasionally, it involves the use of magic, but often, potions are simple medicinal remedies not much different than those used on Earth."

"Then my father was skilled in...potion crafting?"

Anubis pursed his brow, leafing the pages more slowly. "I'd be just as surprised as you'd be. I didn't think your father would have known so much about herbology."

Magnus was lent a flicker of hope by Anubis' remark. "Then do you suppose the book isn't even his? Maybe someone else swapped it with the research."

Anubis shook his head in a display of doubt. "I don't know. Cecil said he was pretty certain it was Brendan's handwriting." Turning another page, he shook his head harder. "Extremely odd. It's like all this was copied out of a book...not jotted down as experimental potions or herbology notes."

"Well, what kind of potions are they?" Magnus asked, unsure if it was a foolish question.

"Nothing out of the ordinary," replied Anubis. "There's the odd formula that seems a bit complex, but most of it isn't anything you wouldn't find in a textbook."

Magnus turned away as his thoughts deviated. "You don't suppose I could learn a bit?" he asked after a pause.

Anubis' eyes shifted to lock with the boy's. "Learn?"

"Learn herbology. At least a little...to help me understand that book. Maybe things wouldn't seem so hopeless then."

"I don't see why not," said Anubis. "By all means, you should have a grasp of what your father passed on to you." He tipped his head askance, in the way of the door. "Let's go into the study. I believe Cecil has some books on the subject you might find useful."

Magnus followed the herbalist out of the room and through another doorway in the adjacent wall of the shelter, entering the cluttered confines of the study. Bathed in pale light, indistinguishable mounds of items—mostly books—teemed from boxes heaped around a table with a wheeled wooden stool and a sturdy chair. There were only a couple of bookcases, whose shelves bowed under the weight of the ponderous tomes that lined them.

"Pardon me a moment..." Laying the notebook on the table, Anubis went to work on prospecting the miscellany around him. Magnus' gaze sauntered over the heaps while he waited.

Every one of the books piled about here held great intrigue. Magnus selected one at random—*Galem: The Rise and Fall of Arkane's Most Powerful Nation*, by R. Deglaugh. Bound in a similar hardcover as *MorningStar*, the book was dense, though not unusually large. He thumbed its pages, whose edges were painted a dull red. A black-and-white flurry of fine text filled his vision until he came to a stop. "*Headed by Darius and Vadier, a party of twenty men was hastily dispatched in search of Ignis' body...*" read the opening of one paragraph.

Magnus shut the volume and placed it aside. He leaned toward a much larger and heftier tome plainly titled *Atlas of the World*. Without lifting it from its perch on the top of a stack, he peeled back its cover and glanced over the first three pages to arrive at a colored chart. It was identical to the parchment map that Cecil had shown him yesterday, depicting Arkane's two continents and the jagged rims of its poles. The following page was a stunning geographical rendition of the eastern continent; the next page focused in on the continent's lower half, divided into a trio of provinces.

Magnus glided his fingertips over the landmass. The chart's details were so vivid he believed he could feel the terrain's cragged mountaintops and sprawling forests as he grazed them. His touch lingered over the name of the westmost province, seven letters arched across a lush plane: SERENIA. A bright-red marker denoted the location of its capital city, MorningStar.

He looked north, to the utmost province on the page: NEMUS. This land was deluged in greenery and interwoven with rivers, though copiously speckled with markers of cities. From here, his eyes drifted southeast, over a prodigious mountain range that marked the borders of both Serenia and Nemus, and onto a similarly large province occupying another corner of the continent. GALEM, spelled the letters printed over it. This was the place where his father had journeyed in the days before his death, where the Luminous Rock resided. Would Magnus ever see the province for himself? The idea was so foreign that it seemed unlikely.

"You may find these interesting…" Anubis called the

boy's attention away from the atlas, laying a small heap of books onto the table. "Take a seat."

Magnus lurched into the chair, sidestepping Anubis' travel bag, which he found to be propped against a table leg. Anubis dropped himself onto the wheeled stool and swiveled to face the books in front of him. He lifted a hefty volume off the pile and nudged it before Magnus. *The 3786 Eldred Herbology Encyclopaedia*, its cover read.

"Thirty-seven-eighty-six," Anubis repeated the number aloud. "It's a year, see. Arkane's calendar is far older than Earth's."

Magnus raised an eyebrow with fascination. "So what year is it there now?"

"Thirty-eight-o-eight," answered the herbalist. "The calendar has an offset of exactly 1,816 years from Earth's. That would mean you were born in thirty-seven-ninety-two...of course, the year of the evacuation." He paused a moment, suddenly solemn, then threw open the tome. "Anyhow..."

Magnus winced as the scent of stale paper gusted into his face. He balked at the sight of the towering columns of text that climbed across the open pages.

"Take a look through," Anubis urged. "You may find it interesting to explore a bit of Arkane botany. It's much different from Earth's."

While Magnus leafed the encyclopedia's cumbersomely thick pages, Anubis returned to browsing the notebook. "These are what you use in potions?" Magnus asked.

"They're most of the basic ingredients, yes," Anubis

replied without turning away from the book in his hands. "The art of potion crafting is constantly expanding and has few known limits. Some more unique brews even call for the use of foliage from other dimensions."

Magnus arrived at what appeared to be another section of the encyclopedia. Here was a simple entry, a page titled "Acer Tarensis." Enclosed densely by text, there was a set of three meticulous color sketches—a sinewy tree, a shred of bark with white-stroked furrows, and a leaf that branched to three points.

"Ah," Anubis tapped the encyclopedia's sketches observantly. "The taren tree; it's a relatively common species on Arkane. Its bark has highly medicinal properties." He displayed the open pages of the notebook. "Common potion ingredient, too. Here."

The herbalist indicated a scrawny paragraph at the top of a page from the notebook. Magnus was only able to discern a few words—*taren* among them. "Some simple potions involve no more than a single item," Anubis detailed. He traced the handwritten text with a finger as he went on to describe it. "This calls for a base of plain water...cold...into which is mixed the taren bark, crushed as finely as possible. This concoction alone serves as a potent anti-poison."

"Hmm," Magnus muttered. "What could a more complex potion do, then?"

"Though most potion crafting is medicinal...probably a lot more than you would expect." Anubis resumed leafing the notebook's pages, now with more speed. "See this." Again he turned the open book in Magnus' way. Here was a tremendously verbose formula that covered at least two pages, complete with glyphs and symbols that seemed bizarre enough to be considered another language altogether.

"Advanced potion crafting such as this straddles the line of an even more intricate practice," said Anubis, "namely alchemy."

"Turning lead into gold?" Magnus playfully remarked.

Anubis pulled a smile. "Possible, in fact, but realistically too much work to turn a profit. No—alchemy is the art of altering, enhancing, and enchanting natural materials. How else do you suppose a ruby is made to conjure fire with a mere thought? Alchemy, you could say, is the source of all magic."

"And how is that done? What *is* the source of all magic?"

Anubis pulled his shoulders with candor. "Alchemy is far beyond me, I'm afraid. It's arguably the most complex and delicate science to master. From what I understand, it relies on the use of the runic languages that predate known civilization. I wish I could tell you more..." He waved the open notebook. "...but I'll have to admit that this is as far as my knowledge goes."

"Then how far is that?" Magnus narrowed his eyes at the notebook's scrawl. "Would you know what this is?"

"Certainly," Anubis replied with little hesitation and turned the book back to himself. "This appears to be a formula for a potion that is used as a method of tele-transportation," he said, "better known as teleportation."

Magnus gaped in response. "Teleporting with potions?"

"About, yes," Anubis affirmed nonchalantly. "Not in any psychokinetic manner. In this world, I believe the term was made popular by writers of science fiction. On Arkane, quite ironically, the practice itself has existed for much longer."

"How does it work? I can hardly imagine a...potion being anything more than medicinal."

"Well, it isn't simply a concoction of herbs, in this case," Anubis answered, readjusting himself on the swivel stool. "Enchantment plays a considerable role. The potion works to transport any object it comes in contact with to the place of its origin. Not the location where it came from, exactly, but from where it ultimately originated."

"So it only works on items, then?"

"No, no...see, the process also transports anything in immediate contact. Suppose you applied the potion to a tree branch, which you are holding. Along with the branch, you would be transported to the tree from which the branch had grown—its place of origin. Nearby objects tend to be extracted as well, though the selection is altogether quite random."

"Could you...make the potion yourself?" Magnus asked with discernible anticipation.

"With some help, yes." Anubis nodded diffidently. "The few times I've brewed the stuff, I've had an alchemist friend carry out the more complex half of the recipe. I may have a bottle with me, in fact..." He dove into his travel bag that rested against the table. "I brought along some basic potions and ingredients, should they be needed," he said under a rattle of glass as he searched the bag. He emerged from under the table with a five-inch bulbous flask in his fingertips. "Though this would be anything but basic. Just something practical to have on hand."

Anubis set the flask before himself. It was enmeshed in wire, its glass opaque black. A screw-on cap sealed it, reinforced by a metal clamp with a miniature latch. "A teleportation potion," he proclaimed. "Powerful substance; dangerous, too. It'll be safe as long as it's kept shut."

Magnus took up the flask, his hands shivering on contact with the strangely frigid glass. He recoiled in surprise as a bolt of static leapt beneath the surface of the vessel, though nothing else could be seen through the glass itself.

"The flask requires its own enchantment to resist the effects of the potion," Anubis added. "As a result, the concoction is in constant reaction with its vessel."

"Is that why it's sparking?" Magnus withdrew a hand to see another sinuous static bolt explode behind the wired glass.

"Yes, though it's completely harmless." Anubis paused, his eyes momentarily wandering to the ceiling and back. "Just ensure that the potion never actually makes contact with a living being, including yourself. The results would be disastrous, and likely fatal."

Magnus entertained the thought of the potion's nature, but it soon began to unsettle him. Upon realizing what manner of artifact he was handling, he placed the flask back in front of the herbalist.

"It's well sealed, of course. Else I wouldn't be carrying such a thing around with me." Anubis stole up the flask with a speed that seemed irresponsible after his warnings. "Still a highly controversial item. Illegal to trade, actually, across all six Arkane provinces. The only lawful way to get a hold of one is to brew it yourself."

"Is it that dangerous?" Magnus asked, eyeing the potion with even greater concern. His heart lurched on impulse as Anubis lowered the flask back onto the table.

"Oh yes. But only to the reckless. Teleportation through potions is not a practice to be taken lightly or used freely. Should you ever acquire a flask of the potion, it's to be used only in an utmost emergency. Emerging in a different place is probably the least of your concerns...compared to the risk of mutilation, severe burns, or instant death, all of which are reported cases."

Magnus' expression twisted with horror. "Why?" seemed to be the longest response he could muster.

"Because of the potion's volatility. A single flaw in its preparation could be enough to kill the user—and even if the potion were flawless, such methods of transport are always hazardous, some just more so than others." Anubis curled his lip to a grim half-smile. "The defiance of space-time is not without consequence."

Magnus heaved his shoulders in blank disbelief. "Incredible," he remarked as if lost for other words.

"Isn't it?" Anubis beamed. He returned the flask to his bag before reaching out to sift through the remaining books on the table. "You'd enjoy a look through this,

I reckon." He proffered a navy-blue tome: *The Modern Compendium of SCIENCE, MAGIC, and TECHNOLOGY,* it was titled.

"Herbology is mostly medicinal, as I said," Anubis continued, passing the book to Magnus, "but Arkane technology is a truly fascinating study that combines a gamut of different sciences."

Magnus leafed the volume, slowing as he became rapt by its contents. His fingers idled on a page that was too intriguing to pass: "Luminal Pattern Containment and Projection," the chapter was named. The ink sketch of an intricate prism and a spread of clear slates rested at the foot of the page.

Anubis peered sidewise at the opening lines of the chapter. "Ah, lucidus...photosphorite," he pronounced a peculiar mineral name. "Another product of alchemy; photosensitive crystal, essentially."

Magnus scanned the text, gleaning words at random. "What's it for?"

"It's a composite of lucidus and photosphorite, both Arkane minerals. It has many uses," answered Anubis, "photography being one of the most common." He outstretched a finger to the illustration of the slates. "Those there would be photographic slides. Quite similar to those used on Earth, only much more sensitive."

"You mean you use cameras on Arkane?"

"Certainly. They're called *occulas*—simple spring-loaded mechanisms, just capable of exposing a slide to light for a fraction of a second. But the images are of stunning quality, some say almost three-dimensional." Anubis momentarily held back his speech in thought. "Perhaps you've seen one... unknowingly. Have Cecil or Drake ever showed you photos of your parents?"

Magnus returned a solemn shake of his head. "No. I didn't know any existed. Are there any?"

"Oh yes. Your father was head of city council, after all."

"Yeah..." Magnus clasped his lip in his teeth. "Cecil and my brother always told me that whatever few photos were in existence had been either lost or destroyed. I never really took that. Now things make more sense."

Stark silence arose from each person's hesitation to continue speaking. Magnus placed his focus back onto the pages in search of a change of subject. "And this?" He pointed to the illustration of the prism beside the slates.

"Oh...that would be a cloaking prism," Anubis replied in a sudden slur, as if rattled from his thoughts. "Made of a similar mineral composite, but less sensitive and more potent. Think of it as being able to capture a panoramic photograph."

"And it's called a...cloaking prism? Why?"

"Because of a very subtle difference in its design," said the herbalist. "A photographic slide is made to capture a light pattern—an image—and display it. A prism does the same, but rather than containing the image, it imposes the light pattern onto the area around it."

"Then it's a projector?"

"Only much more so. With a few hours of exposure, a prism can capture an extremely vivid impression of its surroundings. This light pattern cannot be viewed in the prism itself, but it is refracted as light passes through it from an external source. The refracted image is often so lifelike that it's an illusion undetectable as such to the naked eye. Depending on the prism's shape, the illusion can be focused on a single area—a wall, perhaps. A door, an entranceway, any sort of object could be concealed entirely. This deceptive process is what we know as *cloaking*."

"That's amazing," Magnus said in a near-whisper. He traced a finger along the outline of the prism, winding himself deeper in his reflections. "...all of this is." Page by page, he continued to explore the vast compendium. A barrage of text glided by, interspersed with ink illustrations that varied from simple shapes to confounding diagrams. After some minutes, he lifted his eyes to Anubis, who was still immersed in Brendan's notebook.

It seemed that the herbalist had stopped leafing to scrutinize a single page. Magnus pulled himself closer with a weary moan of the desk chair—the page was one he distinctly recognized. Contrary to the rest of the notebook's content, the recipe here was penned clearly and diligently. It was neither lengthy nor complex—more like a simple list of components.

"Wait," Magnus alerted, placing a hand on the edge of the page. "What potion is this?"

"Nothing I can clearly make out," Anubis muttered. "I don't recognize any of these ingredients in use together. No description, either."

"It's just the way it's written...it's so—"

"Neat?" Anubis surmised. "I know. Not scrawled like the rest of the book. I can't imagine why... It doesn't seem any different than anything else in here."

"But you said you'd never seen anything like it."

"Exactly. Half of these formulas are incomplete or irrational, so this is just about the same. The only difference is its chirography." He held a finger to a set of words that had been effaced in a scribble of ink. "There are corrections, too. This was something Brendan must have worked on, not just copied."

"It's the only one in the book like that," Magnus added. "I saw it earlier when I was looking through. Don't you think that means something?"

"It's strange, yes, but I'm afraid its purpose is still completely undefined." Anubis smiled dryly. "Why don't you make it yourself? That's bound to be the only way you'd ever know."

Magnus' eyes gleamed with enthusiasm. "Could I?"

"Oh...well, I suppose, if you wanted to." Anubis reacted as if his previous comment had been in humor. "It's a straightforward concoction and it looks harmless enough to try, but...I personally wouldn't waste my time with such a thing. If you're interested, I mean, I'd be more than happy to familiarize you a bit further with the subject—introduce you to some of the more common foliage and such."

"I'd love that, thank you." Magnus nodded amiably. "Even if my father wasn't a herbalist..." He withdrew the open notebook. "...this was my father's. Whether it has any purpose at all is another matter."

"Yes, unfortunately..." Anubis replied, already having returned under the table to rummage through his bag. "Give me a moment here and I'll gather my supplies. Get out that encyclopedia again when you're ready."

Sifting away the clutter, Magnus extracted the herbology encyclopedia and laid it open in front of him as before. His hold lingered on his father's notebook; he stole a second to inattentively thumb its pages again before forcing it aside and out of his mind. *I won't drive myself mad over a set of irrelevant notes*, he ruminated. *But that book is anything but irrelevant. Whatever my father's reason for giving it to us, we'll know yet.*

11

Bird in a Cage

N TIME, MAGNUS FOUND himself able to distinguish the unmarked road that led away from the shelter. As he walked, he navigated by the distinctly meandering pattern of the path and the notable sights around him. A crooked slope, an arch of wilting cedars, a fallen tree with monstrous roots—Magnus recognized many of these landmarks from the drive to the shelter two nights ago.

Cecil and Anubis had left for Markwell earlier that day for supplies—enough to last them, hopefully, the remainder of their days at the shelter before they would seek more permanent lodgings. Magnus had tagged along with them as far as the campgrounds' crossroad, from where the path to Markwell was clearly marked by trodden dirt. He had walked back to the shelter for the afternoon, but had arranged to meet up with Cecil and the herbalist by the crossroad at dusk, when they were to return.

It was close to dusk now. The sun had fallen to a place on the horizon from where its light caused the trees to appear as if they were burning, gilding them with fire, casting shadows like endless spires. Magnus cupped a hand to his eye to shield from the flickering rays. He turned east, from where the darkness was already encroaching. He had brought Ember along with him; the salamander was weaving in and out of the trees along the edge of the path, always near, though never fully in sight. Often the reptile would halt far ahead, only to withdraw back into the umbrage at the boy's approach.

Magnus could tell he was nearing the crossroad. He was surprised at the ease he felt in walking the forest alone. Though he had only explored this route twice, he had observed it well enough to traverse it without any fear of losing direction. Should the night arrive too soon, he had a flashlight in hand to guide him the rest of the way. It was ever tranquil here; the richness of the air alone seemed to lure his mind away from all concerns.

He staggered down a short incline into a stretch of clearing. Ember scampered in front, but this time came suddenly still. Magnus ambled on at first, but also halted when he discovered that the salamander was no longer following him.

"Ember?" Magnus called over his shoulder. Almost before he could completely pronounce the creature's name, Ember lashed his head around and hissed fiercely into the void of the forest. Magnus glanced about, seeing nothing, turning back at the chitter of the salamander's claws on tree bark.

Ember scuttled up the side of an elm and slipped between the sprawl of half-leafless branches. As Magnus hastened underneath, the salamander snapped open his draconic maw and hissed down at the boy even harsher.

"Ember, what is it?" Magnus cried up the tree, but the salamander paid no heed.

A rustle behind him gave only a second's warning. In the moment Magnus turned to look, a stone-hard blow came against the back of his head.

Magnus tried to open his eyes, but his lids remained heavy. His face was resting on the earth. Had he fallen asleep? He was unable to move. It was only after some time that he realized he was hearing the mutter of voices.

"If he is, he can lead us to the others," said a man. Magnus wasn't certain, but it may have been the voice of Anubis or Cecil. He remembered stumbling to the ground. Perhaps the others had found him.

"Don't keep your hopes up," said another man. "He's too young to be Drake, and I can't imagine what he'd have to do with either of the men we're after."

It became apparent to Magnus that he was not among friends. Also, he was not immobile out of weariness—it felt as if he was bound at his feet and hands. When he could at last pry open his eyes, he saw a blur of seated figures in dark garb. A coldness rushed over his body as his heart gathered pace. He shut his eyes to continue eavesdropping on his captors.

"Anyone in this forest is suspect," replied the first man. "Especially someone like him. If nothing else, we know he's from Arkane by that ring he was wearing."

Ring? Magnus wondered. He promptly remembered the enchanted diamond ring that Cecil had given him some days ago. But when he now wiggled the fingers of his bound hands, he found the ring to be missing, likely stolen by the men.

"I saw him move." The baritone voice of the second man jarred Magnus like a dagger to his gut. There was a steady rustle of footsteps. He suddenly received a belligerent kick to his shoulder that rolled him onto his back. He opened his eyes to the sight of a monstrous, red-skinned man looming over him.

"Well, hello," Raven drawled, his tongue slithering with derision.

Magnus stifled his fear under a scowl. "Who are you, and what do you want from me?"

"We're conducting some interviews among the local residents." Noctell strode up beside the demon. His tone of voice was equally caustic. "We are hoping you could spare us a moment to answer a few questions."

"I don't have much of a choice, do I?" Magnus retorted, struggling against his bonds.

"No, you don't, actually." Noctell gestured to his partner with a cock of his head and moseyed away.

Raven came forward to clutch the boy by his shoulders and heave him off the ground. Only as Magnus was lifted up did he see what giant of a man was handling him—if he could be called a man at all. The boy was forced into a seat against the base of a knotted tree, legs folded upright. He could see that his ankles were tied in a band of coarse rope, and he could assume the same for his wrists that were fastened behind his back.

Magnus seized the opportunity to assess his circumstances. He tested the strength of his bonds, finding them as tight as chains. His odds of escape were slim. He was in a clearing he did not recognize, in what appeared to be the campsite of his captors. The sun had dropped from sight, though its roseate aura still lingered. It was seemingly minutes away from nightfall.

Noctell returned from the edge of the camp carrying a threadbare coil of rope. He unraveled it, kneeling as he began to wind it around the boy's body. Magnus flinched at the touch of the slivery cord, which pricked him as if it were wreathed of barbed wire. "I already can't move. You don't have to be so paranoid and tie me up twice," Magnus quipped irately.

"I'm not concerned about you escaping, boy." Noctell finished binding his hostage and secured the rope entwinement with a strangely loose slipknot. But as the necromancer rose and drew back, Magnus felt the cord come taut around him like a python constricting its prey. These ropes were not ordinary, nor inanimate.

"Cooperation is painless," Noctell remarked.

"I don't plan on being stubborn," replied Magnus.

"What is your full name?" The necromancer asked as if it were a threat.

Cooperation aside, Magnus could not afford to be truthful with the people who were obviously in search of his brother. His eyes flickered skyward in thought. A shimmer of movement in the leaves stole his interest. *Ember!* Magnus spotted the salamander nestled vigilantly in the branches above him. He faced Noctell so as to divert attention from his animal companion. "Emburn," he lied on impulse. "Mark Emburn."

The instant the name left his lips, the threadbare ropes viciously contracted. Magnus shuddered and screamed at the pain, a sensation as if his chest had been clamped in irons. It was several seconds too many to bear before the cord finally slackened.

"The ropes can sense a lie from truth," Noctell said impassively. "Don't displease them again, or you will endure worse."

Bruised and shivering, cold in his blood, Magnus dropped his head and yielded to his interrogator. "Magnus Wingheart."

Noctell and the demon gaped, disbelieving. But the ropes did not twitch. The boy was being truthful. "What..." Noctell stammered. *"Magnus?"* He exchanged glances with Raven, who was similarly speechless. Vehement, he turned back to his hostage. "Are you the brother of Drake Wingheart?"

Magnus barely nodded.

The grin that eased across Noctell's face was like a flame set to a mask of ice. Raven scoffed and beamed profusely. "Lucky catch," the demon crowed. "Nearly forgot about you, didn't we?"

"We focused our search on Drake because he was the elder." Noctell half-turned to his partner. "The fact that Brendan had a second son was irrelevant. We didn't even know if he'd survived the assault on the city."

"Wasn't it Medeva who said she saw Cecil escape with an infant?" Raven noted. "We knew he survived. He was just never enough in the foreground to concern us."

"Yet here he is now, right in front of us!" Noctell clasped his palms together and laughed in a whisper, nearly euphoric. "Tell us, boy—where are the others?"

Magnus gathered his wits, breathing hard. If he revealed no physical symptom of a lie, he could not see a way for the ropes to tell; with enough concentration, he was sure he could deceive them. "In the town. They're—" But his response was cut short by his own agonized cry as the ropes constricted again. Just as it felt like his rib cage were on the verge of shattering, the torture subsided.

"What are you trying to do?" Noctell jeered. "Are you a martyr, boy? Speak the truth and save yourself the torment!"

Magnus did not answer, nor look at the men. The ropes could not harm him if he stayed silent.

"Speak!" Noctell whipped out his hand as if he were drawing a pistol. Magnus saw nothing but a glint of black light before he was struck by a surge of excruciating pain. He gave a writhing scream and withdrew into his original position, unresponsive to his captor.

"You realize we will torture you through the night if necessary," the necromancer threatened. "If that fails, you will be turned over to Daimos, who may not be as courteous. As long as your lips are still able to move, every bone in your body can be broken on a whim."

Daimos... The name struck a harsh chord in Magnus' mind. The enemy that Magnus had until now only heard of suddenly became a vivid and terrible reality.

Noctell's frown softened, though it was unclear if he was merely feigning empathy. "For your own sake, Wingheart, comply. No more harm will come to you or your companions if you do. Your knowledge is all that we want."

Magnus weighed his options, which he realized were few. If he allowed himself to be mutilated by his captors, what would he achieve? The discovery of his companions was inevitable if they stayed near Markwell much longer, whether he revealed their location or not. "They're in the forest," he finally answered. The ropes remained inert.

"I could figure that much, fool," Noctell spat. "Where in the forest?"

"How do you expect me to answer that? You want an address?" Magnus picked up his head and snarled.

Noctell pulled a dour grimace. "You will lead us to them."

"How?" the boy replied in near-mockery. "I can't lead you anywhere if I don't even know where I am."

"We'll take you to the crossroad. Would you be able to find your way from there?"

Magnus scanned the enclosing forest walls. Night had just about descended. "It's too dark," he said. "I wouldn't be able to navigate."

"We'll have plenty of light."

"That won't matter. I'd need to see as much of my surroundings as possible."

Noctell narrowed his eyes to piercing slits. "Have you ever traveled this forest after dark?"

Magnus' response was resolute: "No." Again, his bonds did not twitch.

Noctell beckoned Raven aside, withdrawing deeper into the campsite. "The ropes can only detect a definite lie, not an opinion," Noctell said quietly. "He may still be able to lead us in the dark, even if he says he can't."

"Then we take him to the crossroad regardless," Raven presumed.

"That's one option. Alternatively, we take him straight to Daimos."

"Wouldn't that be nice?" The demon bared a full-faced grin. "Imagine our master's delight at such an unexpected offering."

"Ah, but it could be even better," Noctell added zealously. "Suppose we brought the lot of them—Handel and the other Wingheart. They're not far out of reach with the boy to aid us."

Magnus strove to listen in on his captors' discussion, but heard nothing above a toneless whisper. He turned his attention to matters of escape, seeing the men at least partially distracted. Should he agree to lead them, his ankle bonds would have to be removed; it wasn't a plan by any means, but it would grant him the ability to maneuver.

Then a familiar scuttling sound grazed Magnus' ear. He swiveled left, where he glimpsed Ember for an instant before the salamander slipped beneath his arched legs. As Magnus felt a vicious tugging at his ankle bonds, it became apparent what Ember was attempting. After a few short seconds, the bonds fell limp—Ember had clawed them loose.

"So we have him lead us," said Raven, half in question.

"Perhaps..." Noctell replied irresolutely, "...but that would risk the boy failing us. Better, we let the others come for him. A few hours is all it will take."

"They might not find us."

"We'll rekindle the fire and light all the lanterns to draw them. If they don't show, the boy will take us to them at dawn."

"They'll put up a fight, no doubt. We ought to know what we're up against."

"I wouldn't worry," Noctell replied superciliously. "Handel would be adept, but not dangerous. Drake isn't much of a concern."

"What if there are others?"

Noctell answered by turning back to his hostage. "Wingheart," he barked to seize the boy's attention.

Magnus stiffened as his captors' eyes fell on him again. He feared that Ember might be spotted, but the salamander remained concealed behind his legs, staunchly unmoving.

"Is there anyone else traveling with you besides Cecil and your brother?" Noctell inquired.

"Yes," Magnus replied flatly.

"Who?"

Magnus restrained himself from answering at first, but soon saw no point in withholding the name. "Anubis," he said.

"Can't you speak more than one word at a time?" Noctell snapped. "Anubis who?"

"Anubis..." the boy muttered, then paused to think. "...Araiya."

Noctell and the demon exchanged blank looks of question. "Never heard of him." Raven shrugged dismissively.

"Neither have I." Noctell returned his voice to a subtler volume. "I'd take my chances with whoever he is; certainly won't be anyone more powerful than us."

Ember leapt out of hiding the moment the men turned on Magnus. He slithered into the crevice between the boy's back and the tree, and grappled onto Magnus' wrist bonds with both teeth and claws. After a fervent struggle by the salamander, the rope shattered into fibrils at its weakened point and collapsed into the dust-smothered roots. Only the threadbare ropes remained around Magnus now, but they secured him to nothing. Given the right opportunity, he was free to make his escape.

Magnus could sense that his captors' conversation was

drawing to a close. He prodded the salamander off, and it reluctantly abandoned him to retreat behind and up the tree. Not three seconds after Ember had escaped from sight, Noctell and Raven trudged back toward their hostage.

Magnus locked his legs together tightly, so as not to reveal the looseness of his severed ankle bonds. He made a discreet brush of his hand to ensure that the cord once fastening his wrists was tucked out of view behind his back. Noctell knelt dangerously close to undo the threadbare ropes that clasped the boy's body, but moved away without noticing Ember's subtle deed.

"No need for these anymore," Noctell declared, bundling the frayed cable. "Looks like you'll be staying the night." After discarding the ropes by the camp's edge, he moved past his partner and into the shadows. "You keep watch while I gather the firewood," he called out. "Make sure there's plenty of light on."

Magnus saw a clear beam, like that of a flashlight, flicker to life in front of the man before he was engulfed by the forest. Then another glow was ignited in the clearing, this time from a swaying lucidus lantern clutched by his remaining captor. Raven set the lantern by the ashen remnants of the campfire; he proceeded to light a second, identical lantern, which he carried back to his hostage. Situating the lantern beside himself, he folded to a seat against a tree opposite from the boy.

Magnus' bonds may have been cut, but escape was still no simple task. Should he attempt anything brash, his captor would be upon him in an instant. He eyed the lattice of branches above him, where Ember lurked. The salamander was poised intently, as if prepared to strike Magnus' gargantuan captor—but the man was too far out of reach for Ember to leap. Nonetheless, Magnus spied an opportunity.

If the man were to come near enough, Ember would easily be able to attack. Magnus was averse to putting the salamander in any more danger than it already was, but he trusted that Ember would be swift enough to flee without getting harmed. A second's diversion was all Magnus needed to escape. He had only to draw his captor toward him.

Raven folded his burly arms, assuming a leisurely posture. His gaze clung to the boy like a lead weight. After some time, his fingers wandered into his vest pocket to extract what appeared to be Magnus' diamond ring. He toyed with the band in his claws, admiring the scintillating crystal while remaining noticeably vigilant of his hostage.

"Is that my ring?" Magnus asked with urgency.

A scathing smirk crossed Raven's lips. "Yes, perhaps it was."

"Can I have it back?" Magnus bluntly requested.

The demon raised a jet-black eyebrow. "Do you take me for a bloody fool?"

"What could you want with it?" Magnus replied, feigning total ignorance. "It's only a ring. And your fingers are too fat for you to wear it."

Raven's flame-tinged eyes came alight with irritation. He sheathed the ring in a massive fist. "You have some nerve, don't you? You can get out of this unharmed. Don't make matters worse for yourself."

As Raven took the ring back into the pincer-grip of his claws, Magnus stifled his fear and continued to speak. "Just be careful not to scratch it," he said. "It must be hard to hold anything with nails like that."

"I can close your mouth for you if you're having trouble doing it yourself." Raven flashed the most forbidding of scowls. He slipped the ring inside his pocket and settled back in place. His eyes were now riveted on the boy, with no sign of languor. Mustering audacity, Magnus spoke again: "You're not a human, are you?"

Raven gave no response this time. His expression, too, was strict and silent.

"What are you, then?" Magnus persisted.

"A magical woodland fairy," Raven answered with mordant inflection. "Are you quite done commenting on my appearance?"

"You don't look like a fairy," Magnus vacantly replied. "Are you...a Minotaur?"

Raven played deaf to the boy's question, but his fury was beginning to show.

"No, you couldn't be...your skin is completely red," Magnus observed, making a show of scrutinizing his captor in the lantern light. "Or do you only turn that color when you're angry?"

"Have you lost your mind, boy?" Raven bellowed, his rage overtaking him. He impaled a clawed hand into the dust as he kneeled forward. "If you have nothing useful to say, then don't speak a word!"

"Or what?" Magnus retaliated. "I'm too valuable for you to kill me."

"I can wound you," Raven menaced. "And I will do so until you are silenced."

"No, you wouldn't." Magnus shook his head, his speech losing clarity in his nervousness. "You wouldn't risk my death at all."

The demon's face warped into a snarl. "I needn't risk your death to cause you pain."

"Go ahead, then," Magnus retorted. "Claw off my arm instead of barking threats like a coward."

Raven rose to his full, devastating stature. "With pleasure!" But he managed to take only two steps toward his captive.

Like a scarlet dart, Ember catapulted himself out of the treetops. Raven received no warning before a reptilian figure latched onto his face, inflicting a gruesome pain as if his flesh were being punctured. With a shrill roar, the demon reeled aside and plunged to the ground like a toppled colossus.

Raven clawed blindly at his attacker, but the creature was gone as swiftly as it had appeared. He clutched his facial wounds to smother the raw pain as he struggled to his feet. Thoroughly disoriented, he was almost certain that his eyes were deceiving him when he saw his hostage bolt into the shadows of the trees. But a double glance revealed only a pool of mangled ropes in Magnus' place. The boy had escaped.

"Noctell!" Raven thundered to his absent partner.

Alerted by the clamor, Noctell sprinted into the camp within seconds. He hurled aside the stack of brushwood in his arms and raced to Raven's side.

"The boy's escaped! I don't know how the devil he did!" Raven cast out a hand southward. "We split up and chase, now!"

Magnus staggered over root-woven terrain in a desperate attempt to flee. Grazed relentlessly by tree limbs, he tore through the darkness without aim or sense of direction. He had no way of telling how closely his captors were pursuing him, unable to hear over the rustling of his own breathless pacing.

Then a holler reached his ears from a distance. Magnus tried to accelerate, but his legs could carry him only so fast through the undergrowth. He glanced behind, then turned back in front. When he saw the gully, it was already too late.

His heel skimmed the lip of the eroded precipice and he hurtled forward. Black earth churned around him until he struck solid wood. With that, his world shattered like glass.

12

Echoes

ITH NO KNOWLEDGE of where he had been before, Magnus found himself surrounded by darkened buildings. He was not familiar with this place, but he did not question it. Instead, he walked on down the bare road that lay ahead of him.

An intangible haze coasted over the near horizon. Shadows seemed to cling to every plane. It may have been night, but Magnus never looked skyward to be sure. He panned his eyes across the desolate cityscape. These buildings appeared centuries old in their design. Most were grand, multi-leveled edifices; some were modest-sized shops and homes. Magnus could have presumed the entire town to be vacant were it not for the lackluster glow that emanated from every window of every structure. Yet even then, that glow was an eerie, dead light—as if all existence stood frozen in time.

Magnus felt no fear at first. He walked until the road seemed to drift like a single, undying wave that coursed through an unmoving sea. But Magnus was not roaming without direction. He knew with certainty where he was heading. Now the buildings around him were beginning to fade from clarity; only their incandescent windows remained sharply in sight, suspended in a shapeless void.

In time, a castle emerged. Soon Magnus found himself treading a court that encircled the walls of the castle itself. He did not feel the need to look up and admire the full height of the structure. Rather, his vision was consumed by the walls' monolithic slabs. He extended a hand to graze the face of the wall as he moved past it. The stone was warm to the touch. It felt safe, and intensely familiar. *They will come*, a strain of unspoken words wafted through Magnus' mind, *but here we will stand strong against them.*

Magnus turned from the wall. He was no longer alone. The court was occupied by hundreds of uniformed men. Suited in crimson cloaks and military jackets, they wore metal close helms with glass-like visors. Many were armed with small crossbows; others wielded imposing blades and shields. But not one of them was moving, nor did their eyes stray from the distance. Because there was no wind, even their cloaks hung still like petrified silk.

Magnus paced down the rows of solemn soldiers. Dread surrounded the men so thickly that Magnus could feel it on his skin, a sensation like cobwebs enswathing him. His feet were becoming leaden. When he halted, it was as if his position amongst the soldiers had been sealed, and he had become one with a greater entity. A visor covered his eyes now. His hand grew heavy with a sword in his grip. He turned in the direction in which every other soldier was facing.

The castle was no longer in view. The soldiers were standing before a lofty stone wall with a gatehouse that was drawn shut. If Magnus looked hard enough, he could see something moving far beyond the iron gate—like a storm of shadows, a mile-wide cloud of devastating mass that thundered through the darkness and toward the wall. The sound of a myriad shrieks was surging out of the silence; the dread in the air was worsening. When the storm reached the gate, the scene erupted into bedlam.

Soot-black clouds rushed through the gates and deluged the court, and the soldiers charged onward against them. A furor of battle cries and clashing steel ensued, but it was drowned in the loudening shrieks. Magnus knew he was to aid the soldiers, but his legs were heavy as stone. When he tried to take a step, he staggered. Gravity wrenched the sword from his hand, which was suddenly too weak to maintain a grip. Amidst billows of smoke, glaring flashes, and a torrent of projectiles, the melee raged around him.

Magnus' senses were beginning to fade. While he stood rooted, helpless, the sight of the fray dissolved into obscurity. The noise receded until he felt nearly deaf. A sense of desperation overcame him, and he lunged into the haze, screaming. He fell, but never struck the ground.

Magnus was stolen off his feet by an irresistible force. He began rapidly drifting backward, though he himself was not moving a muscle. He was being carried away. As sound returned to his ears, his vision snapped back into focus. He was back on the road he had first walked before reaching the court. Only now things were not as tranquil.

Buildings were aflame. Soldiers' bodies littered the floor, their garb torn as if by the claws of some beast. The air flowed with unearthly wails, while dark-cloaked men astride vicious mares stampeded past. *"The citadel has fallen!"* a horror-fraught cry sounded. A chorus of warning horns sundered the noise. *"The citadel has fallen! Retreat to the forest! Retreat to the forest!"*

Still drifting, Magnus could not move nor speak. Through unblinking eyes, he watched the dark-cloaked men rise in numbers until they dominated the road completely. Aiding them was a stranger breed of creature—savage airborne entities like plumes of black sand that mingled with the smoke of the burning buildings. Magnus watched one soar down with terrifying velocity and assault the back of a fleeing soldier, slaying him in a deft flash of claws.

Magnus was able to shut his eyes now. But the clamor continued, perhaps even louder. Incessant shrieks, thundering hooves, cries of assault, pain, and death—the echoes of war surrounded him, unrelenting. Then there was a scream; it pierced all other sounds, shattering them. It was that of a woman. A pain struck Magnus' chest like an arrow through his heart. After that, there was silence.

Magnus had stopped moving. Fearfully, he opened his eyes. Though he was still on the road, he was alone again. The fire and smoke had withered away. No one, dead or alive, remained. Buildings were marred with soot; many were damaged beyond repair. The ground was smothered in black ash, like the wasteland surrounding a volcano, yet the air was cold as an arctic desert.

Magnus enfolded himself in his arms, but it gave him no warmth. He felt afraid without knowing why. He felt as if he had lost something dear to him, without knowing what. His heart still smoldered with pain. *The citadel has fallen,* he found himself declaring in his mind, *the ashes rise in its place.*

A shiver grazed Magnus' spine. He became aware that someone was behind him. He turned suddenly, locking eyes with a smoky black skeletal visage. A scream burst from his lungs and he spurred away as fast as he was able. He could sense that the creature was gaining on him, but he did not waste a second to glimpse it. *"Flee..."* a whisper as dark as death touched the nape of his neck. *"Flee all you want. It will lead you nowhere better."*

As Magnus ran, his surroundings dimmed and dissolved. The ground no longer felt as solid. A pair of frigid claws lunged against his back, causing him to shudder uncontrollably. There was a shriek. He staggered and went blind again, the terrain plunging to an incline. His head struck the ground when he toppled forward and cascaded down the slope. He came to rest at what felt like a tree trunk, and opened his eyes.

He was in a forest now. Nothing was ill-boding about this place—in fact, it was a haven. Shadows caressed the spiring, leafy pillars; starlight gilded the branches. The darkness rippled like a silken veil, not as if blown by the wind, but as if moved by a sentient force. Magnus knew he was safe here. He rose to his feet.

Many voices spoke to him, in whispers, as he walked. They spoke of times past, of things that the trees had witnessed. But Magnus did not regard them. Ahead of him, he saw a silhouette shift in a way that broke the current of the shadows. He slowed his pace to a standstill as he watched the silhouette, that of a man, emerge to face him.

Though his features were eclipsed in the gloom, the man was acutely familiar to Magnus. He proffered a hand, which shone bright and pale in contrast to the rest of his body. Knowing the man as an ally, Magnus came forward to meet him. But the man turned up his palm at Magnus' approach. He stepped aside, ushering the boy past him with a sweep of his arms.

Magnus abided by the man's instruction and strode on into a murky grove. He heard the man speak to him from close behind: *"The bloodshed you have just witnessed,"* he said, *"has roots that run deep."* His voice was like a stream through a vast, empty cavern. *"What I show you now is truth. May this knowledge serve you well."*

There was an ominous shift in the air. Before Magnus realized it, the man was gone. His sense of safety was overcome by disturbance. The shadows that had earlier woven amidst the trees were dispersed by the stagnant, pallid shine of the moon. He was in a clearing, but more distinctly, a ruined cemetery. Rubble piles and rotted grave markers were scattered around him. Only a single headstone stood tall and prominent in his vision. Its foundation was a colossal plinth from which rose a pair of emaciated arms and hands. Within the clasp of the hands, raised as if in an offering to the gaping black heavens, was a giant skull of stone—an immaculate sphere with a broad, notched cylinder of teeth fitted beneath it, and a set of drooping hollows for its eyes and nose. The sculpture's detail was remarkable, unscathed by the wear that had claimed every other headstone around it. It was horrifying beyond its mere appearance, emanating vice and dread. Magnus recoiled from the sculpture in terror-struck awe.

A slow rustle sounded from afar. Someone was approaching, but Magnus held his stance at the clearing's edge without any fear of being seen. He watched a person lurch into the cemetery from a trodden forest path. It was an indefinable figure, swathed thickly in a hood and robe in an obvious attempt to hide its identity. Dragging its left leg in a limp, it walked on the support of a gnarled wooden staff that was crowned with a gem-inlaid metal ornament.

The figure staggered before the great headstone and cast aside its staff. Lifelessly, it dropped to its knees and collapsed forward, its face in the dirt. In the silence, Magnus could hear it weeping. It was a man's voice.

"For..." the man muttered into the earth, his voice broken by sobs. "For...give...m-me..." He clenched his hands into shivering fists. "Forgive me...master..."

The man's lamentations persisted for a minute before he came quiet. Now everything was still. Rather than approaching, Magnus stood in wait. He felt a wicked breeze surround him like a helix of serpents. When the wind subsided, there was a second figure in sight. It was a vaporous specter, blurred as if not completely set in reality. It had long white hair that flowed well past its shoulders. As it drifted by the headstone, mist smoldered off its back. The specter halted before the weeping man.

"Eras..." a voice called out. Startled, the man tore his upper body off the ground to lock eyes with the figure that loomed over him. He shrieked and leapt away in utter horror. He was still trembling when he struggled upright several feet away. The specter raised a consoling hand, but the man would not be calmed.

"What..." the man barked and stammered. "You—! You can't..." He retreated slowly, faltering on his weak leg. "Mad! I've gone mad! I can't bear this anymore!"

"Eras!" the name was called again, this time as loud as thunder. The man crumpled to his knees, shuddering, mute. The specter lowered its hand. "You are not mad, Eras," it said, now speaking in a tranquil melody. "I am not an illusion. I am who I appear to be."

Eras picked up his head meekly. With hesitation, he drew back his hood. A short black beard over his chin and upper lip was all the detail that could be seen of his face from a distance. He gaped at the specter for a long while before he staggered forth, wilting to a lowly bow. "Forgive me, master!" he howled. "Forgive—"

"Calm yourself, Eras," the specter interrupted firmly, then eased its voice to a whisper. "I do not understand your distress. Why do you beg forgiveness?"

"My army..." Eras whimpered, not daring to lift his head an inch above the ground. "My army has fallen...fallen. Serenia has crushed us. Those who are not dead have deserted me. I have nothing...n-nothing left with which to serve you, my lord."

The specter was silent at first. "I see," it returned two curt words. Its displeasure was clear. "But do not believe that you have been rendered futile." It turned its back on the man and took a couple of paces away. From Magnus' viewpoint, the specter's face was still veiled by its hair.

"Master, why?" Eras' voice withered even further, still quavering. "Why do you show yourself to me? I have failed the Order. I do not deserve your presence!"

"I will decide who deserves my presence." The specter turned to Eras again. "You are one of my most devout and prominent followers. I have every reason to choose you as the first to whom I appear."

"The first..." Eras choked on his reply, suddenly speechless. He raised his folded hands high to the specter. "Master, the honor! The honor! You have gathered your strength at last?"

"Scarcely," said the specter. "I have gathered strength enough to project myself into the physical realm. But doing so drains me further. I will not make such an appearance without purpose."

"Of course, my lord," Eras answered zealously. "What is it you desire? I will aid you in any way."

The specter tilted up its head, exposing the contour of a pale narrow face. "It has been a thousand years since my death in this world. Time has repaired my soul, but only to an extent. I require the very essence of life to regain my full power." There was a painful silence. "I require a part of you, Eras," it continued. "In return, I will bestow upon you a part of me."

"Say it and it is yours!" Eras exclaimed. Then he spoke in a grating whisper: "I would lend my soul to you, dear master."

"That won't be necessary," replied the specter, pausing again. "A mere fragment of your soul is all that is needed."

Eras seemed to lurch with shock, but he was not swayed from his fidelity. "Anything, master," he hissed, "for you."

"But you will not go unrewarded," the specter added enticingly. "Imbued with my spirit, you will be changed. Power will flow raw in your veins; you will be impervious to all physical ills. You will be ageless, and above all, immortal."

Eras was left truly speechless. What words he could finally muster were of almost hysterical gratitude. "Thank you—thank you, master!" he gasped. "I could not ask for anything more!"

"I am the one to be thankful, Eras," said the specter. "Know that you will be strengthening me greatly."

"But how? How will it be done?"

"Remember that a lich is capable of such things." The specter flaunted a sickly thin hand. "I must simply be allowed to touch you—though in my weakened state, any direct interaction with the living would be impossible." It palmed the surface of the great stone skull. "This grave is my gateway. It is where my body resides, and thus it is where our realms intersect. Forge a bond with my headstone, and my power will be allowed to flow into you."

Eras set a yearning stare on the sculpture. "How may I forge this bond, master?"

"An object solely of this realm must become one with the headstone," said the specter. "A blade—yes, a blade will do."

Eras plunged a hand into his cloak and avidly unsheathed a short dagger from his belt. He proffered the weapon to the specter. "Will this dagger serve your purpose, my lord?"

"Yes," the specter answered immediately. Fervor was growing in its voice. It flicked its palm off the surface of the sculpture while keeping an arm outstretched to the skull's mournful visage. "Plant your blade in the crown of the headstone, and the bond will be made."

"What—?" Eras faltered at the specter's instruction. He clutched the blade by its hilt, withdrawing it. "I could never defile your sacred headstone! Is there no other way?"

"Do no consider it sacrilege as long as the act is under my will," the specter insisted. "Impale the dagger in my headstone; that is my desire, and my command."

With an unwilling nod, Eras steadied the weapon in his grip and rose to his feet. He hoisted the blade above the headstone as if preparing to slaughter an animal for sacrifice. After several seconds, he was still rigid with hesitation.

"Brute force is not necessary," said the specter. "Bring down the blade, and I will do the rest."

Eras grimaced and sealed his eyes. Taking the hilt in both his hands, he stabbed the blade downward. There was a sound like a knife slicing flesh. Eras' eyes leapt open wide with terror. The blade had dissolved into the skull, leaving not the smallest crack to scar the surface of the stone. He tugged the hilt, but the dagger was solid in its place.

The specter wasted no time to react. It lunged out ravenously, clamping Eras' shoulders in gaunt claws. Though Eras recoiled on impulse, he seemed unable to pry his hands off the dagger hilt. An inhuman whisper set the air aflame. The specter bounded forward, its hair lashing about its face as its legs shattered to mist. It broke through Eras' body in a wreathing storm of vapor and light, and the man emitted a scream that echoed a soul-rending agony. Eras was knocked backward as if by the shot of a cannon, striking the ground limp.

Now scarcely a shadow in the haze, the specter hovered over the lifeless Eras. "Thank you," it breathed, "my loyal servant." Along with its words, the specter faded. The stillness that followed seemed to last for an eternity.

Magnus guardedly approached the headstone and the man sprawled before it. The closer he came, the more likely it appeared that Eras was, in fact, dead. Magnus regarded the dagger in the crest of the headstone, keeping his eyes from meeting the skull's abyssal gaze. He turned to face Eras, who was clearly not breathing—the specter had murdered him.

But then Eras blinked opened his eyes.

Magnus reeled back at the shock. Vertigo overwhelmed

him, and his world spiraled upward. When he regained stability, he was lying flat on his back. He knew at once that something was horribly amiss.

He struggled onto all fours, still faint. His hands were not his own—they were withered, fleshless, misshapen, and knotted. His fingernails were like charred splinters of bone. He gritted his teeth, which crumbled to dust in his mouth. His throat was as hard and dry as iron. He tried to scream, but coughed black ash, which dispersed into the air like smoke.

His legs were deathly numb. Unable to stand, he hauled himself toward the headstone on his broken claws. Every movement he made caused his bones to dislodge, as if he lacked any ligaments to bind them. He lurched and grappled onto the headstone as his only support. He could no longer move. His stare was fixed on the sculpture's plinth. Two words were carved here, in a coarse, jagged script. Like hellish embers, they smoldered in the stone: SAXUM DIABOLI.

Knives and needles flooded Magnus' arms as fire scalded his eyes. When all faded to black, the words still throbbed alight in his vision. Gradually, they dwindled as well, along with the pain. He was left in a familiar state of profound silence and total blindness. But just as when he had first entered the forest, a sense of serenity filled him.

His surroundings became bathed in a diffuse glow. The light was emanating from behind him. He turned, discovering the figure of a man standing some distance away from him. The man carried a memorable aura—he was the silhouetted stranger whom Magnus had met in the forest. Like before, the man was masked in shadow. A crystalline pendant was strung around his neck. It radiated a vibrant white shine, but the light did no more than graze the outline of its bearer.

As Magnus approached, the pendant's rays became searingly bright. He stopped only inches away from the man's face, though the pall over the stranger did not fade. In response, the man raised his necklace by its cord and dangled the pendant before Magnus' eyes. It was a translucent jewel, cleaner cut than any Magnus had ever seen. Embraced by ten golden talons, it scintillated as if it housed a thousand mirrors. Magnus had only seconds to admire the neckpiece before it was withdrawn by the man.

Magnus returned his attention to the void of the stranger's face. He saw the man nod, and that was all. Blindness came over him again; only this time, he opened his eyes.

Magnus was still in pitch darkness, but his surroundings were considerably more vivid. He tried to pull himself upright, clawing a handful of dirt-sodden roots. He remembered—he was at the bottom of the gully he had stumbled into after escaping his captors. His head was glaringly sore. It seemed he had been knocked unconscious upon falling. His mind was rampant with gruesome memories of places he knew he'd never seen and things he knew he'd never witnessed. All of it, from the vacant town to the bloody onslaught, the specter, and the ruined cemetery, had been nothing more than a nightmare.

Magnus groped for support until he found a sufficiently sturdy root. Seizing it, he hauled himself up and clambered over the peak of the gully, out onto the forest floor. Even in the open, he had almost no range of vision. He was still very likely being hunted by the men from whom he'd escaped, and he risked recapture every minute he lingered here.

He considered returning to the gully for refuge. He would be safe as long as he remained unseen. But if Cecil and Drake came searching for him, their lives would be put at equal risk. *Ember!* Magnus remembered in turn. The salamander was no longer at his side, and possibly just as lost as he. Reality was beginning to feel not much different than the dream from which he had woken.

Magnus boldly crept into the murk. His eyes were adjusting to the dark now. He was quite certain he had emerged from the opposite side of the gully, which meant he was traveling away from his captors' camp. Wherever his blind navigation would take him, he needed to keep moving if he wanted to find Cecil and his brother.

He became paralyzed when his ears caught the sound of movement that was not his own. Someone was rapidly approaching. He sprinted aside in a panic, only to hear the intruder flit past him. He turned, but saw nothing. Looking down at his feet, he found what he had suspected—the salamander had returned to him.

Magnus respired, dispelling his angst. Ember's appearance alone was more than he could have asked for.

"We have to find our way back," Magnus said in a whisper, "before those men come..." But Ember darted in front with almost no heed paid to the boy. Stunned, Magnus bolted around and took after him. The salamander didn't appear to be fleeing, silently weaving a path through the dark. Magnus was finding it hard to keep up. Just when Ember's form was growing faint in the distance, a light gleamed up ahead.

Magnus stiffened as the light approached. He would have run for cover had Ember not streaked dauntlessly onward. The beam of a flashlight glanced his face. Then came a desperate shout: "Magnus!" It was the voice of his brother. Magnus charged into the light, nearly colliding with Drake.

"Keep your voice down," Magnus cautioned before another word could be uttered.

Drake gaped, momentarily speechless. "Are you alright?" A second flashlight beam was cast in Magnus' way. Cecil hastened into view from behind the older brother.

"Use as little light as possible and keep your voices down," Magnus repeated as Cecil rushed to his side. "Daimos' men are in the forest."

"What?" Cecil exclaimed and snapped off his flashlight.

"I was captured by two of Daimos' men," Magnus explained, short of breath. "I escaped, but they're bound to be searching for me. We have to get back to the shelter."

"Heavens, Magnus, you're lucky to be alive." Cecil ushered the brothers along with speed, Ember trailing them. "Are you sure they're not following you?"

"Pretty sure." Magnus clutched the side of his still-throbbing head. "I fell into a ditch when I was running away and got knocked unconscious. If they were following, they could have recaptured me there."

"My..." Cecil sighed, wordless with dismay. He gathered pace. "We have a lot to discuss, but only once we get to safety. We may be forced to leave this place sooner than we'd planned."

13

Saxum Diaboli

EVEN WITH ITS LANTERNS vividly alight, the shelter seemed darker than ever before. Magnus and Drake were seated on the couch close by the center table, Anubis and their former guardian across from them. After hearing of Magnus' ordeal, the herbalist had maintained a state of mute, wide-eyed anxiety. Cecil balanced on the edge of his chair, rapt and solemnly thoughtful.

"How much did they find out?" Cecil queried the boy.

"Not much," replied Magnus. "They know my identity, and that we're sheltering somewhere in the forest. I escaped before they could force me to lead them here."

"That must have been quite some feat."

"Ember clawed off my bonds when they weren't looking." Magnus eyed the salamander nestled by the hearth. "But the tall one came back to keep watch while his partner left to gather firewood. I lured him close enough so that Ember could attack him; then I was able to make my escape."

"You're *very* lucky to be alive," Cecil said gravely. "Is that when you fell?"

Magnus nodded. Cecil slumped back into his seat. "It seems we'll have to rush our plans. Now they'll be scouring this forest more than ever."

"Do you think there are other scouts here?" Drake speculated.

"Probably. If there aren't, there soon will be."

"Then what are we doing next?"

"That's what we have to decide," said Cecil. "I've been thinking for a while now, where we'd head from here. Simply put, our first choice is between Earth and Arkane."

"Arkane?" Magnus balked at the suggestion. "Isn't that where we want to avoid going?"

"Serenia, maybe. But any of the remaining five provinces would be an asylum for us."

"I doubt that," Drake differed. "Recett has far more eyes on Arkane than he does here. He'll track us down faster there than he ever could on Earth."

"What alternatives are we left with?" Cecil shrugged. "Do we duck into another burrow and pray Recett doesn't find us for ten more years? You know we won't be any better off if we keep scurrying from one hiding place to the next."

"At least we'll be safe!"

"We will never be safe," Cecil sternly retorted, "unless something is done to end this. Recett will hunt us down no matter where we are. On Arkane, we have friends; we have protection. Here, we have no one. We are alone."

Drake sobered his expression. "Why didn't we go before?"

"Because we were never threatened," replied Cecil. "Our safety was in optimistic ignorance. We hoped Recett would be slain by some miracle. After being rudely awakened from that fantasy, we have no better option." He looked to the younger brother. "And there was Magnus. As long as he knew nothing about this, he was our self-made excuse for not taking action all these years. But now things are different. If we have to flee again, then we flee to Arkane."

Magnus dwelled on Cecil's proposal. "And then what?"

"Rally support, gather our allies...there are many who would be eager to aid us. With the right people, we might even be able to find some answers about Brendan's research." Cecil glanced at Anubis, who was still resolutely silent.

"The nearest rift leads to the MorningStar forest," Drake replied, "and we don't want to go anywhere near there. We'd have to enter Arkane from somewhere else."

"There's a rift map in the study," said Cecil. "We'll look it over and plan our best route."

"Where to? Zephyr? Nemus?"

"We have allies in both provinces. Considering Nemus' proximity to Serenia, Zephyr is the safer bet. We could take the Evanderal rift."

"Where is it?"

"Oise, France. We'd have to catch a flight."

There was a sullen, uncertain pause. "Then that's it?" asked Magnus. "We're leaving?"

"As soon as we can, yes," Cecil sighed. "The longer we stay here, the greater the danger gets. If all goes well, we might be able to leave by the morning after tomorrow."

"Why the wait?" Drake asked fretfully. "Shouldn't we be leaving by sunrise?"

"That would be ideal, of course," Cecil replied, "but that would also mean running blindly. We need time. We need not only decide where we're heading, but what we plan to do when we get there. We need rest, and, most importantly, I need to teach you and your brother enough spellcasting so that you can at least defend yourselves. As long as we stay low, the shelter is still a haven."

"Are you sure the Evanderal rift is our best choice?" Anubis suddenly interjected.

"Well, if we decide on anything better..." Cecil trailed off. "Why not Evanderal?"

"Any rift that's guarded by the Magistrate, really," Anubis answered in an impetuous slur. "The moment we reveal our identities to them, all of Arkane, including Recett, will know that Brendan's sons have returned."

"But all the rifts are guarded by the Magistrate," Cecil countered. "And they mean us no harm. We'll have to reveal our identities either way."

"There's one rift..." Anubis averted his eyes.

Cecil gathered his brow, unsettled. "We can't take the MorningStar rift. That's foolhardy."

"It's the only one that isn't guarded," Anubis argued. "We don't have to come near MorningStar at all. We can cut through the forest and travel straight north to Nemus."

"Then we'll be forced to reveal our identity in Nemus. What difference does it make if it's there or at the rift? We can't stay anonymous if we want help from our allies."

"It's...the time that's an issue." Anubis faltered again. "Recett surely has spies in the Magistrate, and he'll find us sooner if we pass through a guarded rift. We may not have a chance to establish any sort of protection before he comes for us."

"That still doesn't outweigh the risk we take by traveling weeks across Serenia on foot," Cecil disputed. "As much as I see your point, it's just too dangerous. There are so many more obstacles we face in taking the MorningStar rift."

Anubis nodded, withdrawing into submissive silence. Cecil kneaded his weary eyes. "We'll review the rift map," he concluded. "Then we can decide for certain."

"I'd need to close my shop," Anubis brusquely added. "The apothecary. I'd have to close it...at least until further notice. There's no telling how long we'll be gone for."

"Oh, yes, I suppose," Cecil hummed. "I really appreciate your coming with us, although I certainly don't want to put you through any more trouble than we already have."

"You've put me through no trouble, and I want to aid you as much as I'm able. I could leave tonight, close the shop, get some rest, and be back here by tomorrow noon."

"Well, thank you, Anubis," Cecil said, then frowned

in concern. "But I'd think twice about traveling the forest this late. Especially knowing that Recett's men lurk here."

"Oh no, not to worry. I can navigate with very little light. I want to be back here as soon as I can to help you prepare for the trip."

"You'd still have enough time if you left in the morning."

"Sunrise comes late in the forest. If I left after dawn, I wouldn't be back until well into the evening. I insist, Cecil, you needn't worry about me."

Cecil was disconcerted, but reluctantly agreed: "Alright. Get out of the forest as quickly as you can. If someone comes at you, attack and flee. It's quite unlikely that anyone you encounter here will be on our side."

Anubis nodded. There was quiet again. "Well," Cecil declared, as if for the sake of ending the silence, "I suppose I'll get the map." He was partway out of his chair when he was halted by the younger brother.

"Wait," Magnus exclaimed. He said nothing more at first, as if his words were caught in his throat. Then he continued: "There's something else I want to tell you. Before the memory fades."

"Certainly." Cecil reclined back into his seat. He tried to face the boy, but Magnus refused to shift his gaze away from the floor.

"When I fell unconscious in the ditch," Magnus dropped his voice to a mutter, "I had a dream. It might be meaningless, and I don't want to fear something just of my imagination...but imagination or not, it might be important."

Magnus had scarcely finished reciting the details of his dream when Cecil leapt to rummage the bookcases behind them. Drake didn't appear to have any better a grasp on the subject than his brother did; Anubis remained silent and unreadable. Cecil was suddenly more occupied with scanning the spines of his volumes.

"After he pulled the necklace back..." Magnus recalled, trailing away. "That's all I remember. Then I woke up."

Cecil wrested out a book from the tightly packed shelves. Glancing at its cover, he forced it back into its slot and resumed his search. "You do realize that *Eras* was Daimos' former name," he said, his back still to Magnus, "before he turned into the skeletal abomination he is now."

"I know," Magnus replied. "But if that man was Daimos, then who was the ghost? The one who the grave belonged to?"

"I have an idea," Cecil answered into the shelves. He extracted another book for examination, immediately slamming it back into place. "It must be in the study..." he surmised, and took for the doorway to the right of the bookcases.

Anubis and the brothers waited in eager silence. Some minutes later, they saw Cecil emerge with a tome in hand. Cecil deposited the dark-cerise package onto the table as he dropped back into his seat. Magnus recognized the book immediately—*Galem: The Rise and Fall of Arkane's*

Most Powerful Nation. He had come across it in the study just yesterday.

"Saxum Diaboli," Cecil began, delving into the book's pages, "I believe, is Latin for 'Stone of the Devil.' And if I'm correct, it isn't a name you simply dreamt up." He breezed through to the index, then leafed vigorously until coming to a stop near the end of the book.

"What is it, then?" Magnus asked with some impatience.

Cecil was already engrossed in his reading. "A name..." He tapped a finger to the open page. "...given to a grandiose, unmarked headstone discovered in the Venieres Forest. Yes, I remember now!"

"What?" Magnus gaped, his brother reacting likewise. "Then the grave is real?"

"Yes, yes it's real!" Cecil vehemently asserted. "I quote: *'Void of an inscription, the headstone was lent the ungodly name Saxum Diaboli for the sake of its infernal appearance—that of a frowning skull hoisted on a pair of cadaverous hands.'*"

"That's it!" Magnus cried out barely before Cecil could end his sentence. The headstone's image resonated through his mind with a vividness too great for a mere memory of a dream. "Then...whose grave is it?"

"Unknown, but..." Cecil paused to scan another paragraph. "...the ancient cemetery in which the stone is found is populated with many other, less significant graves. Many of them bear infamous names, alluding to the owner of the Saxum Diaboli having an equally infamous identity."

"Who?"

Cecil shut the book and spun its cover over to Magnus. "See this title?" He laid it down. *"Galem: The Rise and Fall of Arkane's Most Powerful Nation.* Over a millennium ago, Galem was the mightiest province—or, as it was at the time, kingdom—on Arkane. With its sheer size, military strength, economy, and technology, it rose above all others...but do you know how it fell?" He paused, sharpening the air with suspense. "It fell to the most powerful warlord who ever lived," he concluded, "Sennair Drakathel. It's believed that the Saxum Diaboli is his headstone."

"Sennair..." Magnus recited to himself. "...Drakathel. I don't remember hearing that name in my dream. Is there some description of him?"

Cecil tilted his head in thought. "A number of portraits exist, as with any historical figure. You could say he had quite a noble appearance—much in contrast to the callous madman he was."

"Did he have long white hair?"

"Yes...yes, he did. Chalk-white. Probably his most striking feature."

"Then that was him. He was the ghost."

"What was he doing with Eras?" Drake wondered aloud.

"Performing some kind of ethereal exchange, perhaps?" Cecil proposed.

"No, I mean, why would Eras even come to Sennair Drakathel's grave?"

"That doesn't surprise me." Cecil laced his tone with

dark irony. "After all, Daimos is a devout follower of Sennair's cult."

"Is he?" Magnus took on a startled expression, as did his brother. Anubis maintained his petrified stare.

"Certainly. Eras himself has made that known," said Cecil. "All the destruction he wreaks is in the name of his dead master's cult, and the same is true for all his own followers. The fact was always irrelevant, of course...the Order is a sect of mindless fanatics and its beliefs are delusional. But it's massive, nonetheless, and its disciples are notoriously powerful."

"The Order?" Magnus repeated in question.

"Yes, the New Order is a cult that was founded by Sennair Drakathel close to a millennium ago. It's the one that Recett spurred into an uprising in Anmer, when he was still a councilman. The cult advocates what you could call an extreme form of anarchism—the abolition of all of Arkane's monarchies, governments, and controlling powers, with the goal to rebuild the world as a single nation. Paradoxically, they worshipped Sennair as their living god and ageless king. And to this day, they still do! As far as they're concerned, their master isn't even dead."

"Really," Magnus hummed. "Even with the grave and all?"

"They believe that Sennair's death is only temporary." Cecil skewed his lip wryly. "In fact, they claim that Sennair's ghost swore his physical resurrection. How else could such a cult still thrive? The Order's disciples have such unswerving faith in their master's promise that they would go on five thousand more years without doubting it."

Magnus wavered between disturbance and skepticism. "Is that at all possible? Resurrection?"

Cecil sobered immediately. "Under most circumstances...no. The souls of those who have passed on cannot be recalled into their original mortal vessel. However, that applies only to *most* circumstances." Again, he immersed his attention in the Galem history book. "Sennair Drakathel was not considered much more than a war general when the Order was first founded," Cecil described, thumbing the pages. "His greatest feat was the brutal usurpation of the Galem throne sometime around, I believe, 2790. It wasn't much later that the Order's followers began to view Sennair as more of a deity than a commander."

Taking up the tome, Cecil read: *"They believed he had become the impossible, the immortal. Those nearest to him claimed he had taken the form of a lich, the greatest of ethereal beings, fueling him with life everlasting."*

He looked to the brothers expectantly. "A *lich*, by definition, is essentially a being that is just as much a spirit as it is a mortal. Liches are rare, not to mention supremely powerful."

"How would you become something like that?" Magnus asked dubiously. "And what does that have to do with resurrection?"

"Because an unnatural life makes for an equally unnatural death," replied Cecil. "A mortal body can be destroyed easily enough, yes, but a spirit? A spirit is immortal. A being that is both mortal and spirit becomes nearly impossible to kill. Despite that, Sennair was mysteriously proclaimed dead at the end of the twenty-eighth century. You have the choice to believe one of two sides—history, which logically dismisses the legend that Sennair was ever anything more than a mortal, or the Order's followers, who claim that their master did not die entirely, and that his soul lives on in some sort of ethereal prison."

Magnus hardened his expression. "What do you believe?"

"It seems logical to side with history," Cecil answered promptly, "seeing that, a thousand years later, the immortal Sennair Drakathel still lies under six feet of earth. However, your dream, Magnus, lends further strength to the Order's beliefs."

"The similarities between Sennair and Daimos are uncanny. Each immortal, each a warlord with the same cause, each..." His voice declined. "...the leader of a deathless army. Sennair, you see, was most feared not for his alleged immortality, but for the inhuman legion he commanded." Cecil returned to leafing the book, then halted to read:

> *"But perhaps most appalling of all were the chimerical monstrosities that now joined him in battle. From the cockatrice and wraithlike specters that eclipsed the sky in myriad hordes, to the phantasmal quadrupeds that broke and cast aside the bodies of the mightiest soldiers, it was certain that Sennair Drakathel had acquired an army of the most fearsome beasts ever to exist on Arkane."*

Cecil raised a sinister eye back to Magnus. "Quadrupeds and cockatrice perhaps not," he said. "But 'wraithlike specters'? Sound at all familiar to you?"

"Shades," Magnus replied, almost automatically. "You mean Drakathel controlled the same shades that Daimos does?"

"Impossible to prove for certain," said Cecil, "but as evidence suggests, very likely. Many of the Order's followers believe so. They say that Sennair's army was much greater, but that Recett has been the only person in a thousand years to be capable of reawakening the shades."

"So..." Magnus drifted into a moment's silence. "What do you make of it?"

"If we suppose that your dream is a recollection of actual events," answered Cecil, "it seems logical to think that the entity possessing Recett is Sennair Drakathel's ghost."

There was an exchange of troubled glances between the four. Drake spoke next: "Then Eras was turned into the living dead by Sennair...who possessed him through a dagger in his headstone? Does that make any sense at all?"

Cecil dropped his head in a pensive gesture. "It may." He rose, wandering back over to the shelves.

"Then Sennair isn't trapped," Drake added. "Or is he? If he was able to interact with Eras, how could he be?"

Giving no response, Cecil stole up a small object from the end of a shelf. He ambled back to his seat, presenting his company with a capsular wooden case, a tool akin to a pocket knife. With a twitch of his finger, a miniature magnifying glass snapped out from the side of the case like a switchblade. "There is the mortal realm, in which we live," he said. From a separate slat, he unsheathed a second magnifying glass. "And there is the spirit realm, in which the soul lives on after mortal death." He prodded the second lens just behind the first, overlapping their edges to form another, double-lensed space between them. "But there is a third realm—the ethereal realm, the intersection between the worlds of the living and the dead. It is known as the nether realm, the realm of the mind, or the dream realm." He indicated each division of the overlapped circles, calling them out as he did. "Body, mind, and soul. We know this as the *Treus Aetherae,* the 'three realms.'"

Cecil shut the lenses back inside their case. "For any spirit to interact with the realm of the living, it must either exist in, or channel itself through, the nether realm. Accepting the myth that Sennair's soul is trapped, we can assume he resides in the nether realm. What was it again, Magnus, that you heard Sennair call his grave? A gateway?"

"In my dream?" Magnus paused to dissect his memories. "Yeah...his gateway to the mortal realm."

"Precisely." Cecil flicked his thumb over the wooden implement again, this time unfolding a slim knife. "A powerful spirit can forge gateways through locations that are closely related to it. Thus, naturally, a spirit holds great power over the place of their burial." He swiveled the blade downward, suddenly spearing its tip into the scarred wooden surface of the table. "When Eras impaled Sennair's headstone, he fused a mortal object with one over which Sennair held power, establishing a direct bridge from the ethereal to the mortal realm. It was through this bridge that Sennair stole away a part of Eras' soul, replacing it with a part of his own. Imbued with ethereal life, Eras was warped into the inhuman, immortal creature he is now."

The brothers were left thoroughly bewildered. Drake leaned his chin against his fist as he brooded. "Even if Sennair possessed him, why would he want to? What does he have to gain?"

"I don't know." Cecil gave a puzzled shrug. "Daimos doesn't seem to be doing anything in Sennair's favor besides having annihilated Serenia. He may not even be conscious that Sennair possesses him."

"Sennair said he would be 'strengthened greatly,'" Magnus mentioned.

"Clearly not enough to be resurrected," said Cecil. "That cemetery meeting must have taken place almost twenty years ago." Then he amended, as if in reminder, "If it ever did."

Magnus nodded faintly, jaded by his thoughts. "I don't understand how I could dream about something I've never known of. And with so much detail! Dialogue, faces, scenery...everything was so clear, like I was there when it all happened. Yet I wasn't."

"Or were you?" Cecil added a peculiar doubt. "At least for the first part of your dream. The onslaught you witnessed sounds glaringly identical to the one that evacuated MorningStar sixteen years ago."

"But I..." Magnus tried to contradict Cecil, but stopped himself. "...I was there," he realized.

"As an infant," Cecil confirmed. "I carried you as we fled. Even if unknowingly, you saw it all. You saw the shades, the bloodshed. You heard your mother scream."

Magnus flinched and shuddered. His brother cringed, drawing his arms closer around himself.

"In our deepest states of unconsciousness," Cecil continued, "sometimes we remember things we were never aware of knowing. The blow you took upon falling may have incited some of your earliest, most disturbing memories."

"And the Saxum Diaboli?" asked Magnus. "I've never heard of it, or Sennair Drakathel, in my life."

"One does not always have to know of something before dreaming of it," said Cecil matter-of-factly. "You gain the knowledge of something by witnessing it, experiencing it. But who's to say that can't be done through a dream?"

"Because dreams are constructs of the mind," Magnus answered. "It's impossible to dream of a reality that you never experienced."

"Yet what did you just do?" Cecil rejoined. "You cannot view such things from the shallow perspective of Earth science; it knows nothing of dreams. Half our dreams are mental constructs, yes, but the rest are observations."

"Observations of what?"

"There is a reason why the nether realm is known as the dream realm." Cecil took on an enigmatic melody of voice. "Some say that a fragment of our consciousness exists there at all times. Hence, through our dreams, we observe a small part of the nether realm as if it were reality. How would a vision of reality find its way into the nether realm?"

He anticipated Magnus' next question. "Because that is the nature of the realm. It is a cache of memories, and etched within it is every event that has ever taken place—down to the spoken word—in the worlds of the physical realm. Like an echo, the past lingers there."

"Then I just dreamed of Sennair Drakathel by fluke? Between centuries worth of memories?"

"That would be unlikely. There are those few who have learned to selectively draw upon the knowledge of the nether realm, but for anyone else, an aid is needed." He pondered briefly. "That man in your dream. The one whose face you never saw. You don't have any idea who that could be?"

Magnus shook his head with assurance. "His necklace was all I saw of him."

"Then the necklace—what did it look like?"

"It had a really clear crystal, like I said...and it was glowing bright."

"Anything else?"

"It had these golden claws around it." Magnus cupped his hands to mimic the talons gripping the jewel. "That's all."

Cecil suddenly pried out the blade from the table and sheathed it back inside its container. "Come to the study." He leaned out of his seat, urging the others to follow him.

"It is said that the spirits of the deceased have the most direct access to the nether realm," Cecil continued as he rounded a corner and entered the study, Anubis and the brothers at his back. With the room too confined to allow the four of them in, Magnus headed after his former guardian, while the others remained by the doorway. Cecil turned to search the most cluttered of the bookcases. "Occasionally, those spirits use the nether realm as a channel to convey a message to the living—the message, in this instance, being an ethereal memory."

Cecil withdrew an ominous package from beside a bookend, patting it free of as much dust as he could. It was a flattish object, neatly swathed in brown cloth. "Through the nether realm, the historical knowledge that the dead possess is infinite," he said. "It's not irrational to think that a spirit may have passed that memory on to you, believing you would find it of use."

Cecil unfolded the cloth package and bared the object inside it for the younger brother to see. Magnus became light-headed at the sight—it was a crystalline pendant necklace identical to the one he had seen in his dream.

"This is an enchanted diamond pendant." Cecil clutched the jewelry piece by its scintillating chain. "Only three of these exist. They were made at the request of your father. One belonged to him, one to your mother, and one to me."

"Then..." Magnus tried to reply, but lost his words immediately.

"I believe that the man in your dream was your father," Cecil concluded. He proffered the pendant. "There's no other explanation. He showed you the necklace as the only way to confirm his identity."

Magnus speechlessly accepted the pendant. Its cord trickled off the edge of his palm like a wisp of gold silk. The gem's luster was just as he had dreamed. "Why my father and...and why now? And why me?"

"Why not your father?" answered Cecil. "Who else, of all the deceased, would want you to know such a thing? Why you and why now? There could be many reasons. Age is a factor; the minds of the young are said to be most receptive to visions of the nether realm. And you certainly wouldn't have been capable of dreaming such a thing if you were in any less deep a state of unconsciousness."

"So it should just happen that..." Magnus trembled as he spoke. "...that I pick up some message by my dead father two days after I find out everything I never knew about him?"

"That could have something to do with it," replied Cecil, bundling the cloth. "The subconscious has a way of mangling dreams that may come across as surreal or incoherent. Had you not opened your mind to these supernatural matters, as the past few days have forced you to do, you may not have remembered such a dream at all." He went to place back the cloth shawl in the bookcase. Magnus extended the necklace to return it, but Cecil waved aside the offer. "No, no. That is yours to keep."

Magnus' startled eyes flitted between Cecil and the dazzling gem. "Cecil, I couldn't. This was my father's gift to you..."

"And he would want you to have it." Cecil folded the boy's fingertips over the pendant. "May this be a replacement for the ring that you lost to those men." He beamed. "And may it serve you so that no such danger will ever again come near."

Magnus breathed a sigh of gratitude. "Thank you, Cecil." He savored the feel of the jewel in his palm. It sustained a familiar warmth—like the radiance it shed when worn by the man in his dream. He knew who that man was. The sight of his father's shadow-masked face would never leave him. He drew the pendant's cord over his head and around his neck. "Does this change anything?" he asked abruptly. "Even if my father wanted us to know Daimos' history, does that knowledge change anything at all?"

Cecil turned somber in reflection. "Not that I can see," he said. "Recett still must be slain, and the only ways of doing so remain the same. Our knowledge of Sennair Drakathel's involvement has given us no advantage. If nothing else, perhaps your father only wanted to reveal to us... our true enemy."

14

Fool's Gold

NO DARKNESS COULD COMPARE with that of MorningStar after nightfall. With the moon under the ashes' eclipse, the city's only light was that shed in searing plumes from the torches that lined the citadel roads like ritual obelisks.

From among the many guards here who loitered in careless, leaning stances against the walls of shadowed alleys, or who chatted with one another as they drifted by, there emerged one man who was unlike any of them. He was tall and lank, shawled in an ill-fitting black hood and cloak that concealed most of his features. He advanced down the desolate road that led to the mouth of MorningStar's castle, the towering, malefic edifice that seemed to cast its shadow miles off into the city. The guards skimmed glares of disdain over the man as he passed, but he did no more in response than pull his head between hunched shoulders and duck into the shroud of his robe.

With hurried yet reluctant steps, the man entered the castle courtyard in the heart of the citadel. His field of view was steadily devoured by the castle's vast double doors, where the harpie Medeva stood sentinel, reclined against the building's ivied façade. In a slackened grip, she held the misshapen ebony trunk of a halberd crowned with a deathly sharp spearhead. The weapon's blade was wide and slender, arching down in a broad half-moon disc before lifting at its tip, its edge accented menacingly in the torchlight.

The harpie had her emerald eyes on the man long before he reached her. "It's about time," Medeva barked. "You had two days to report. What could've taken you so long?"

"I-I was delayed." The man swallowed hard. "I didn't get a chance until tonight."

The harpie grudgingly abandoned her post and drew nearer. "You're lucky that Recett is in a fair mood today," she said. "If you have what he needs, he might just forgive your delay and let you live."

Staying mute, the man wrung his hands into fists and ascended the steps to the castle entrance. He hauled back the right of the double doors and peered into the torchlit void that awaited him within. With ponderous steps, he advanced, the harpie trailing him.

The man fixed his vision on a staunch path ahead, keeping his eyes from wandering onto the nightmarishly disheveled corpses whose manacled limbs bowed over him on his way past. Before long, the entrance hall broadened into the capacious room where Daimos was laggardly sprawled in his throne. The warlord rapped his scabrous fingernails against his seat's armrests in rhythm to the approaching footsteps of the man and the harpie.

"You've finally returned, I see," said Daimos, creasing his lipless mouth into a smirk.

"G-good evening, milord," the man stammered as he came to a halt before the throne. "I have a report for you."

"Go on..." Daimos lifted his brow in zealous anticipation. "Where are Drake and Cecil hiding?"

The man gaped and shivered before trepidly responding. "They're hiding in a shelter...in the Markwell forest," he said. "It's concealed underground, in a hillside, in a clearing a-about one and a half miles southeast of the crossroad. One mile...south from the end of the east road."

Daimos eased back into his seat, appeased. "Excellent work."

"Then I trust...no harm will come to the pursued? As promised?"

Daimos gave a condescending smile, as if in agreement to some childish request. "Yes, yes, as promised. Now how about your reward?"

"Reward?" the man blurted, then appeared to arrive at a realization. "Ah...my reward. Y-yes, of course."

Daimos rose and hooked up an arm in a gesture to follow. "Come with me," he beckoned, guiding the man toward a doorway at the far right of the throne room. The man followed his master out of the chamber, Medeva close at his back.

Beyond the doorway, under the shine of two distant torches, gleamed a tightly winding spiral of iron steps that climbed up into the impenetrable gloom of the castle tower. Near where the tower steps met the floor, the ground opened into a vast coil of stairs that half-circled the chamber before descending to a lower level of the castle.

Led by the warlord and tailed by the harpie, the man was ushered down the basement stairwell. The glow of the torches waned as the passage deepened, shaded over by the ceiling that encroached on the opening through which they had entered. As the three arrived at the end of the stairs, the darkness was interrupted by a fluttering carpet of light that streamed from beneath a cross-barred wooden door. Daimos swept aside the metal crossbar without effort and flicked up his hand against the door, knocking it ajar to reveal a stark, torchlit corridor.

The warlord hastened into the passage, followed by the man and Medeva. The man found an immediate difficulty with breathing in the sultry confinement of the corridor, and what air did reach his lungs was musty and doused in the scent of blood. Curiosity lured his eyes to the left wall of the passage, where a vivid, almost hospitable light flooded in through an expansive doorway. But as keenly as he turned in the direction of the illuminated entrance, he wrenched his sights away in revulsion—within the bright room, beneath a canopy of dangling shackles, lay a torture rack morbidly reddened by the blood of its victims.

The midpoint of the passage was marked by another door, this one reinforced by bolted steel plating and a stout iron padlock. Daimos swept open his cloak and withdrew a hefty key ring from the belt that clasped his gaunt waist. Strumming a knotted finger across the assortment of metal instruments on the ring, he selected a thick-toothed key and stabbed it inside the padlock. With a jolt of his wrist, the warlord slipped the unlatched padlock into the shadows of his robes and swung open the door to allow through the man and the harpie.

The small room that they entered appeared to be a treasury of some sort. A tarnished lantern gave the only light here, stationed on a desk against the right wall. A threesome of fortified chests lined the back end of the room, near a table heaped with pouches of gold coins at the base of an ancient balance scale.

Daimos lashed out a skeletal arm and stole an impressively swollen pouch into his wiry fingers. He whipped around, casting the pouch to the man's feet. "Your reward," he drawled, "as promised."

The man's intrigue was sparked by the sight of the bulging purse. He kneeled, quivering, to gather his prize, but his fingertips prickled when he found the pouch to be considerably lighter than he had anticipated. He opened the pouch by a tug of its drawstring and tilted it into the cup of his hand, only to have his palm fill with worthless, biting-cold ashes.

Daimos' withered mouth parted in a snide laugh. The man was now trembling beyond control as he tilted up his head to the warlord. His timidly questioning gape was met with bloodshot eyes narrowed in scornful amusement.

He glanced sidelong to the harpie, whose stare gripped Daimos with unreadable, bitter emotion, before he turned back to the sneering rack of bones that he dreadingly called his master. The pouch dropped from his tremulous hold, striking the floor in an eruption of smoke-thin cinders.

"Are you truly that driven by greed?" mocked the warlord. "You should be thankful that I chose to free you, rather than kill you. Your true reward is your life."

The man delivered an obedient, shivering nod at Daimos' reminder. Only a few days ago, he had been captured by Daimos' men and imprisoned in the citadel dungeon, along with three of his colleagues. Daimos had already brought a swift and brutal death to one of the prisoners, but the man who now stood before the warlord had lent his aid as a scout and spy in return for his and his remaining companions' release.

"You may soon have your gold..." Daimos' claw hovered back over the table to cull a second burlap purse. This time, he turned the pouch over in his hands while he opened it, releasing into his palm a shower of glistening gold coins. "...but not yet, for your work here is needed still." He tipped down his hand, spilling the gold into the ashes at the man's feet in a tantalizing gesture. But the man passed no more than a fleeting look over the coins.

A whip of Daimos' black veil was all the warning the man received before a hand lunged out to clasp his neck. The man writhed and sputtered as he was lifted onto his toes, brought to level with the warlord's inhuman grin.

"Of course," continued Daimos with the lisp of a viper,

"there is always the alternative." His bony fingers constricted around the throat of the man who flailed breathlessly in his hold. A mantle of dark energy stole over Daimos' wrist, engulfing the hand in which he fettered his prey, draping the man in ethereal, serpentine black tendons. "Now listen to me, herbmonger," said the warlord, "for I must request of you another task."

15

Once Human

 HE SKY ABOVE the Markwell campgrounds darkened with each passing hour as it surrendered to the clouds of an arriving storm. Before long, the forest was stripped of its last light and descended into total shadow.

Raven Gaunt trod among the legion of trees, his gargantuan figure stunted in comparison to the towering oaks around him. He thrashed his claws at each branch that jutted into his path, prying his way through the densest, most inhospitable regions of the abandoned campgrounds. For all he knew, he was miles away from Noctell and their camp. But he cared not—he wasn't going back until he found the child who had humiliated him, escaping right before his eyes.

After sixteen years of searching in vain, at last, they had found one of the Winghearts. If Noctell and Raven had delivered him back to the citadel, they would finally have proven their competence to Daimos. For once, they would have received praise rather than endure the pain that their master would often wreak upon them in his fury. But instead, the boy had escaped. Now, yet again, they would wind up returning to their master empty-handed.

Raven's thoughts were halted when his boot became snagged under an exposed root. He staggered, nearly falling, only managing to support himself by latching his claws onto the face of a tree. He stabbed his knuckles at the trunk with an indignant growl, shattering the bark.

After Magnus' escape, Noctell and Raven had separated to scour the forest for their fugitive hostage. They could not even inform Daimos that they had found and captured the boy Wingheart, for along with their tale of triumph would come the inevitable truth that they had allowed him to escape. But Noctell was not to blame—it was under Raven's watch that Magnus had slipped away. It was the demon who was at fault, and no one else.

Then from the clouds above began to trickle a slight rain, which swiftly escalated to a downpour. Raven drew up his hood to buffer the frigid sting of rain on his scalp, but it did not keep him from being drenched by the torrent. Within minutes, the forest floor had been rendered a swampland, and the demon had been soaked completely. It had become hard enough for Raven to see in the dark without the rainstorm, but now he was close to being blind.

Raven could not bear any more of this. He planted his

boots in the mud, lashed back his head, and flooded the overcast skies with a furious roar. He had long lost direction, and all that surrounded him was blurred by the flickering veil of the rain. He lunged out at a nearby tree with no aim other than to vent his insatiable rage, thrashing the bark with a ceaseless assault of swipes, cursing himself under his every breath.

Finally, Raven reeled away from the tree and slumped his hulking frame against the trunk of an oak behind him. His arms and legs were equally worn; his mind surged in an infernal tempest of wrath, hatred, and dread. As he crippled to a seat at the foot of the oak, he folded his head into quivering hands.

It was Raven's own rage that had allowed the boy to escape. It was because of his own fury that he now sat, drenched by an unforgiving storm, alone in the depths of a tenebrous forest.

"Do you only turn that color when you're angry?" Magnus' taunts rang strong against the walls of the demon's mind. Raven lifted away his palms to gaze down at his crimson-scaled flesh. The boy had been clever enough to see Raven's bane—the demon despised his own appearance more than anything else.

Leaving his hands to rest in his lap, he threw his grim, lifeless stare onto the ground before him. A shallow puddle of water had gathered at his feet. Pelted by ripples but still strangely clear, it beamed the reflection of his own demonic visage back into his garnet eyes. His face was still degradingly marred with the claw marks of the creature that had aided the boy in his escape. He formed a trembling fist and clawed at the puddle, slashing the mirror image into a hundred watery wisps of red hue. But as the rainwater settled, it once again mockingly flashed up his likeness. *"It must be hard to hold anything with nails like that,"* Magnus' voice resonated in his memory.

The demon could not stand to look at himself without being maddened by the sight. His chimerical appearance was like that of a cross between a snake and a man. But most maddening of all was the reminder that he hadn't always been as he was now.

Raven had once been human. Once, he had lived a life of normality. Now, he boasted scales, claws, and played servant to a merciless master whom he was beginning to loathe. He knew that nearly two decades ago, he had made a dire mistake, fueled by his pride, jealously, and thirst for recognition of his strength, that had warped him into his current monstrosity.

What have you done to yourself? Raven pondered wretchedly over the face that stared up at him through the watery portal. *You're a ruin—you've destroyed your life and there's no way to undo it.*

A crack of lightning cleaved the night sky, retorted by a deafening blast of thunder.

Why would you want to undo it? A suaver, calmer voice entered into Raven's mind. *You consider your life destroyed? Even after all you've received?*

What have I received? Raven growled in return. *I've been wrought into a beast and I live in a blood-stained hell! I didn't receive this—I was cursed with it!*

You should consider yourself gifted, the alluring voice suggested. *What you may now think of as a place of destruction is merely the rubble of an old dominion that will soon be born anew, rich and flourishing. And your demonic form has bestowed you with great strength.*

Strength doesn't replace what I've lost, Raven countered immediately.

The voice assumed an almost laughing tone, abandoning its charisma. *What have you lost? Your life in that worthless town and that fool brother of yours?*

Fool or not, Raven cut short the voice with rising anger, *he was smart enough not to sell himself to your godforsaken cult.*

Oh... sneered the voice, *...and you were not?*

Raven dropped back his head to cast his yearning eyes into the void above. The cold rain gnawed at his skin. *No,* he answered. *I wasn't. I was the fool to begin with. I followed you only because I was too blind to see how much you had ruined me.*

I gave you such power, the voice replied, *yet you say I ruined you? Do not be troubled by your appearance, Raven. You have extraordinary potential. Use it to serve your master, Daimos, and soon, very soon, you will gain your reward.*

I've had it with Daimos just as much as I've had it with

you, Raven barked. *He treats me like a slave, and I have no reason to be loyal to him. Why should I serve a man who's done nothing for me?*

Daimos has done much for you, answered the voice. *You just fail to see it.*

Raven irately dug his claws into the soggy earth. *And why should I be listening to you? You're the one who cursed me to begin with!*

It was your own decision, the voice said resolutely. *Need I remind you? You were the one who came to me, in need of my aid. I gave you what you desired, for the small price of your human form.*

Why don't you just get out of my head? Raven finally retorted.

The voice loudened under a derisive chuckle. *Why should I?*

The demon's reflection in the rainwater pool began to blur, losing color and definition. Raven cupped his hand to his forehead as his world swayed and darkened, his field of vision diminishing until all that seemed to remain was his view of the puddle directly before him. Steadily, his reflection reformed to display the face of another man—his long, fluid hair ghost-white, and his skin deathly pale. The man's eyes gleamed a devilish hue of red brighter than flame, and his thin mouth was curled into a malevolent grin that heightened the sharpness of his face.

Raven cried out and assaulted the puddle with a fury-filled swipe of his claws. But as his fingertips grazed the surface of the water, a sprawling cloud of soot was swept into his face. Raven retracted his arm, petrified to discover that a pool of ashes lay in the hollow where the water had once accumulated. Along with it, the rainfall had ceased. Warily, he rose to his feet.

He was no longer in Markwell. He was in a forest clearing, but the trees that loomed upon him were ancient, gnarled, and dead, and the abyssal sky above him held no stars, clouds, nor moon. As he looked around, he saw no one and nothing but a sparse assembly of rotting wooden grave markers and shattered, nameless headstones. He had been here before—it was the place of his nightmares, and one that he had wished he would not need to lay eyes on again.

"Hello, Raven." The same voice that had infiltrated the demon's mind now sounded from behind him. Raven lashed around to see an ominous specter approach. It was the white-haired man whose face he had seen in the water. His body was clad in plates of hard leather and arrayed in a black cloak woven with tendrils of blood-red. His sinister smile remained set on his face as he paced toward the demon.

Raven gritted his teeth in an acrimonious scowl. The man was one he knew well, and one he took no more joy in calling his master than he did Daimos. His name was Sennair Drakathel. "No..." Raven muttered aversely. "No! I don't want any part of this! Get me out of this place and leave me!"

"I only wish to speak with you," said Drakathel in a calming, benevolent tenor. "Why do you say you have no reason to be loyal to Daimos?"

"Because he's a madman who gives no respect to the people who serve him," Raven delivered a swift retort. "Give me any reason why I should be loyal to him."

"Wealth, power, influence..." answered Sennair. "Is that not want you want?"

"Of course it's what I want," the demon said more somberly. "But not at the price I'm paying. What do I care if I have wealth and power if I have nothing else?"

Drakathel uttered a throaty, pitiful laugh. "You had nothing to begin with, Raven," he replied. "Without Daimos, you would be poor and feeble, and still have nothing else."

"You consider the freedom I once had as nothing?"

"Freedom is an irrelevant luxury," said Sennair. "Look at where you stand now. After faithfully serving Daimos and me, you are wealthy, powerful, and a soldier of the greatest guard Arkane has ever seen." He paused, turning his back to the demon. "Now, look at your brother. After refusing to serve the Order, he has gone to dwell with the robbers and castaways in the mountains. While you grew powerful, he became but a petty thief."

"My brother is not a petty thief!" Raven snarled through his teeth, his rage spurring him into an onward charge. But before the demon's claws could impale the specter, Drakathel whirled around and unsheathed a longsword from the shroud of his robes. Raven's assault was met with a sweeping arc of the lich's blade and a thunderous flare of dark energy that effortlessly propelled the demon backward to the ground.

Raven's shuddering breaths broke against the forest

floor as he lay buckled over sideways in agony. This was a
dream, a nightmarish phantasm, and nothing more, but it
did not stop him from experiencing the pain of Drakathel's
blade as if it were a material weapon.

Raven turned up a spiteful glare that was quickly
sundered by the lich's intimidating stance. The longsword
that Drakathel wielded so dominantly was a far-from-
ordinary weapon, its blade forged of a metal blacker than
the deepest abyss. It was a weapon whose sight alone was
enough to remind Raven that Sennair Drakathel was not
to be defied.

"And if none of my words have convinced you so
far, then bear this in mind," said Drakathel, sheathing
his sword. "If you cease your work for Daimos, you will
remain exactly as you are, a demon, for the rest of your
life. If you continue to serve Daimos as his loyal follower,
you have my solemn vow that when I return, I will restore
to you your human form."

Raven pulled himself to his feet and acknowledged
Drakathel's oath with a hesitant scowl. Gradually, he
dropped his head into a silent nod of agreement. He could
not, at any cost, abandon his sole chance of regaining his
humanity—even if it meant remaining a pawn to his master
Daimos.

Sennair beamed from under an expressionless mask.
"Very well," he hissed. "Then I must ask of you one final
task." He stepped aside to reveal a towering headstone
behind the place where he had stood. It was a horrid
sculpture, though marvelously carved, and like Sennair

and the ancient forest cemetery, it was a sight that caused Raven's heart to writhe with dread.

The headstone's foundation was a colossal plinth from which rose a pair of emaciated arms and hands. Within the clasp of the hands, raised as if in an offering to the gaping black heavens, was a giant skull of stone—an immaculate sphere with a broad, notched cylinder of teeth fitted beneath it, and a set of drooping hollows for its eyes and nose. The sculpture's detail was remarkable, unscathed by the wear that had claimed every other headstone around it. But most mysterious of all was perhaps the lone hilt of a dagger that protruded from the crown of the skull; it appeared as if its blade had melted into the very stone, leaving not even the slightest fracture in its place.

"Grip your dagger," said Drakathel, "and our bond will strengthen, so that, upon my return, I will be able to return to you your original form."

Raven trudged up to the headstone. He locked his sights on the dagger hilt that shimmered viciously even in the darkness of the forest. *I will continue to serve Daimos,* he told himself, *only for the sake of my demonic curse. Then I will leave, and I will be free.* Without allowing his words of assurance to fade from his mind, he swept out his hand and grasped the burning-cold hilt. The instant that Raven's fingertips met the steel grip, Drakathel laid his own gauntleted hand upon the demon's shoulder.

An immediate numbness swelled over Raven's arms. His surroundings collapsed into a speckled haze of light and shadow, as if he were losing consciousness. His senses continued to dwindle until he could have considered himself no less than dead, before his blindness suddenly dissipated, and his vision cleared.

To his relief, he found himself still sprawled against an oak in the middle of the Markwell forest. Though his head throbbed unremittingly, the rain had ceased and the clouds had receded, giving way to the light of the moon that now shimmered off the bark and earth still damp from the rainfall. Upon clambering upright, Raven could only imagine for how long he had been gone from his camp, and how far he had strayed.

Haphazardly estimating which direction to take, Raven sprinted off into the trees. He paid no heed to the roots that tugged at his feet or the branches that grazed his face as his route drew him out from the forest's asphyxiating density and into more open, trodden paths. As the skies had cleared overhead, so had Raven's perception. Before another hour had gone by, he came across a familiar stretch of dirt road that steered him on toward his camp.

A warm, smoldering glow soon stole over the shadows of the distance. Raven hastened until he arrived at the source of the blaze—a lambent campfire in the center of a small clearing. Noctell's lank figure was arched over the flames, lapped by the sparks of the fire. The necromancer turned at Raven's approach, baring an austere glare in greeting. As Raven set foot in the firelit glade, he was halted by the singe of cold steel at the nape of his neck and a caustic murmur from behind him.

"What a surprise to see you here." The harpie Medeva

paced up to Raven's side, her halberd blade fixed at his throat. "What made you decide to stop by?"

"I was in the area," Raven returned a cynical quip. He tried to continue walking, but was barred again by the trunk of the harpie's polearm.

"Why the delay?" Medeva's lips crept apart in a livid snarl.

Raven flitted his eyes between Noctell and Medeva, skimming their expressions. Fortunately, it did not seem as though Noctell had told the harpie of Magnus' capture and escape. "We split up to search for Wingheart," replied Raven. "I got lost on my way back. And what brings you here?"

"Recett just received word from his new scout," Medeva began, retiring her halberd's threatening position, "who reported that Drake was hiding out with Cecil Handel in an underground shelter in the forest. Recett was anticipating to attack tonight, but thanks to your lateness, we'll be forced to put off his plan until tomorrow."

"What?" Raven puckered his brow. "Why?"

"Do you have any idea what time it is?" Medeva lashed her tongue at the demon. "Dawn is an hour away. With the shades alongside us, we need to ensure that the sun doesn't rise before we've located the shelter and carried out the attack."

"We don't need your shades," said Raven in a half-enunciated mutter. "Noctell and I can handle the both of them ourselves."

"I'm beginning to doubt that, considering you already

let Handel slip away once," retorted the harpie. "Recett does not wish them dead, but he certainly doesn't want for them to escape again. The shades will be there to overwhelm and enforce, not to destroy. If your master had ordered a swift kill, he could have sent me alone." A passing haughtiness curled off Medeva's tone and fashioned her mouth into a wry grin. "I'd best be off," she said as she withdrew to the clearing's edge. "I enjoy the sunlight no more than the shades do."

Unfurling her great bat-like wings, she marked Noctell and Raven each with a parting scowl. "I'll be back at sunset," she warned. "Be ready." Not a second after she had finished speaking, she propelled herself into the forest's canopy with a powerful stroke of her wings. Then, leaping off the trunk of a lofty cedar, she took to the night skies and vanished from sight.

Raven sealed his eyes and suspired. "Once Daimos hears that we had to put off the attack...he'll be furious."

Noctell smiled thinly. "Be grateful that we aren't the messengers to bear him the bad news. He can't wring our throats as long as we're out here."

The demon fell to a seat on the ground by Noctell and propped his head in his hand. "All is my fault," he lamented. "Daimos can't even know that we found that boy after I let him escape. Now his entire plan was delayed because of me."

"Well, we can't do much about it now, can we?" Noctell droned, his stare lost to the blaze of the campfire. "Let Daimos wait. With any luck, his rage will have calmed by the time we get back to MorningStar."

Raven picked up his head to set his sights back on the wavering flames before him. Although voices of doubt, confusion, rage, and hesitation did not cease to bicker in his mind, a lone, whispering strain still prevailed above the fray: *I will continue to serve Daimos only for the sake of my demonic curse,* he repeated to himself. *Then I will leave, and I will be free.*

16

Earth, Ice, and Lightning

GAIN NOW, WITH YOUR eyes open," Cecil directed. "Fire, water, air."

Magnus swept out his hand, his pendant aglow. A wisp of flame sparked to life over a patch of leaves. As the boy whisked his hand in the opposite direction, the blaze was doused in a splash of water. Extending the same hand, he cast out a jet of wind to disperse the remnants of the smoke.

"Good," Cecil praised. "Never slacken your concentration or speed." He crouched to retrieve a wooden staff he had laid near a fallen tree. He tossed it to Magnus, who deftly snatched it. "Ready to learn something new?"

Magnus studied the enchanted weapon. It was not unlike the first staff Cecil had shown him two days ago. A sizable emerald crowned it, enmeshed in branches that seeped from the head of the trunk; a double band of sapphire studs was set into the wood inches below it.

"Earth is the last of the basic elements," said Cecil. "Unlike fire, water, and air, earth is not a simple and invariant element. How do you define earth? It's not only the soil on which we walk. It is the trees, the plants, the mountains, and so much more. You cannot conjure such things. They can only be manipulated, utilized to our advantage by our magic."

Cecil withdrew the staff and hoisted its gem to catch the sparse sunrays of the glade. "Like any element, you must feel what you intend to manipulate—whether the trees..." He glided the staff through the air. The branches reaching over him fluttered as the emerald headpiece passed beneath them, like a hand across the strings of a harp. A warm rustle flooded the glade. "...the ground..." He brought down the staff to tap the damp soil. An unseen force flashed across the earth in a sprawling crack, casting up tendrils of mud. "...or flora itself." He upturned the staff so that its emerald hovered over a snarl of bronzing ivy at the base of a tree. With a gleam of the gem, a fickle green tinge swelled over the drying leaves, partially rejuvenating them.

"This is the magic of earth," said Cecil. "Not very impressive at first, but potent in the hands of someone more experienced. A powerful terramancer might be capable of anything from spurring an earthquake to uprooting a full-grown elm in the blink of an eye." He tossed the staff back to the boy. "You try now. Lay your hand against the trunk of a tree and grip the element with all your concentration."

Magnus eyed his pendant necklace. "A diamond can cast all elements, can't it? I can use the pendant."

"True, but you'll find greater difficulty in doing so. An element's purest conductor is always most effective to use."

Magnus gave a nod and strode up to a stout tree nearby. Hardening his grasp on the staff, he shut his eyes and locked his other palm against the tree trunk. He filled his mind with only the sensation of the bark at his fingertips, which began to feel as coarse as the surface beneath them.

His arm was numbing. A profound weight was growing upon him, as if he were upholding the tree by its roots. He opened his eyes as he looked skyward. His vision was blanketed by a high canopy of branches woven with shimmering threads of sunlight. As he pulled aside the staff, those branches swayed in unison as if by the work of puppet strings. He swept the staff in the opposite direction, and the branches followed. He stood mesmerized a moment, until his focus grew weary and collapsed. The branches came still. He blinked violently and readjusted his stance.

"That should be a good exercise to start with," Cecil advised. "When you can grip the tree without touching it, move on to anything else you can. Shift the earth, enliven the plants...there is no right or wrong way, nor any specific method to be taught. Once an element is in your grasp, you may bend it however your power permits." He received another tired nod from Magnus. Cecil's own expression turned melancholy. "So much to learn and virtually no time to practice it. I'm sorry to be rushing you through all this."

"At least I can try," Magnus replied. "That's the best I can do." He planted the staff at his feet, playing its gem in the sunlight. "What else is there? Are those all the elements there are?"

"Oh, no. The base elements are all you've seen. There is a vast array of secondary elements—combined elements—and there are the ethereal elements, light and darkness."

Magnus' eyes sharpened with intrigue. "And how would that work?"

"Well, the ethereal elements are certainly the most challenging to manipulate," said Cecil, "but also the most potent. You'd best learn some light magic before we head for Arkane tomorrow. Secondary elements are rather straight-forward." He took the staff back from Magnus, twirling it to exhibit its full array of jewels. "Emerald and sapphire, for instance," he said. "The base elements they conjure, earth and water, form the secondary element of mud."

In a movement too swift for Magnus to follow, Cecil impaled the staff in the earth until it was buried nearly half its length deep in soil. At second glance, Magnus saw that the ground under the staff had become totally sodden, almost liquefied. As Cecil let go of the knotted wood rod, the ground solidified instantly, taking fierce hold of the staff. Not a trace of moisture remained.

"Now...pry out the staff," Cecil instructed. "Your magic, of course, being a necessary aid."

Magnus clasped the staff with some hesitation. His concentration wavered as he debated how to act.

"Using water or earth alone would make the task far

too difficult," said Cecil. "Conjure them in tandem. It's not as hard as it sounds."

Obeying, Magnus evoked a shroud of moisture to the staff. He turned the rest of his attention to the ground, which he absorbed into his focus with the staff as his conductor. He felt the two elements mingle in his clammy hands. When the earth began to loosen, he honed his focus further so that his magic resonated through the entire length of the rod. He finally wrested out the staff from the muddy shaft, staggering back.

"Good!" Cecil exclaimed and accepted the staff back from Magnus. In a flicker of sapphirine light, the staff was doused in water to rinse it of dirt, and the mud hole withered to a dry dent in the earth. "Now another." He returned the staff to the boy. "Use your pendant as well this time. Try...ice."

"Water and..." Magnus stalled in consideration. "...cold? How?"

"Air is easiest manipulated for temperature. Seek out the cold and wield it as its own element."

Magnus stepped ahead and recollected his focus. As moisture came over the staff again, he worked to garner the subtle chill of the branches' thin shadows. His hands grew cold to the point of being numb. When the dankness became biting and unbearable, he flinched, dispersing his magic in a trickle of frigid water.

"Never dwell on your conjurings," Cecil advised. "Expel them!"

Magnus seized the tail end of the wet cold before it

faded, and empowered it a second time. The clear aura of his pendant seeped into the glow of the sapphires. Assuming a firm stance, he cast out the staff in a cleaving arc, as if it were a sword. A whip of water lashed forth and solidified to ice on contact with the air. With treacherous velocity, the icy saber hurtled into the trees and shattered to glass-thin splinters.

"Well done again," Cecil said with more emphasis. He drifted to Magnus' side. "Though often a concentrated assault is more effective than one that's outspread. Always shape your attack to combat your opponent's unique defense."

Magnus met Cecil's suggestion with visible surprise. "You mean, in battle?"

"Naturally," Cecil replied, but seemed lost for further words.

"Then how? You can't do all that much damage, can you?"

Cecil gave a somewhat ironic expression before he cupped Magnus' pendant into one hand and took hold of the staff in the other. In the following instant, there were two flashes—the first from the diamond neckpiece, and the second from a bolt of lightning that leapt from the head of the staff to meet the ground directly in front of them. A clap of thunder sent Magnus reeling away in shock. Quivering flames clung to charred leaves in the spot where the lightning had struck.

Cecil dispelled the frail fire with a stroke of water mist. "Arkane magic can be deadlier than any weapon ever crafted on Earth," he said. "Its power is limited only by your ability. A lightning bolt is hardly the most destructive thing one can conjure."

Magnus' eyes followed Cecil as he wandered back into the center of the glade. "Then what is?"

"How destructive are the elements?" Cecil asked rhetorically. "How destructive is a hurricane? A tidal wave? An inferno? Of course, I exaggerate...but such things aren't totally farfetched for the mightiest spellcasters."

Cecil found a seat on the fallen tree while he half-mindedly inspected the staff's jewels. "By its very nature, the most destructive form of magic would be calimancy—the manipulation of dark energy. So destructive, in fact, that all of Arkane forbids its use outside the guard and military. Even where it is legal, its morality and safety are strongly questioned."

"How can..." Magnus faltered. "What *is* dark energy?"

"Are you familiar with the concept of antimatter?"

Magnus hesitated at the peculiar question. "I've heard about it. Don't know anything about it, though."

"Antimatter is the counterpart to matter," Cecil described. "It is extremely volatile and tends to annihilate all matter particles it comes in contact with. On Earth, to date, there has been very little success in generating it. However, on Arkane, a stabilized form of antimatter, known there as dark energy, has been employed as a weapon for millennia. It is conjured through enchanted abylite crystal, a rare and highly prized Arkane mineral recognized as being blacker than pitch. Still, due to its inherent volatility, quite a few unwise folk have died through the improper handling of dark energy. Only to a well-versed calimancer, the element becomes an amorphous weapon with the capability to devour all matter it touches."

Magnus cringed and grimaced. "But it's illegal," he repeated for clarification, as if in a way to assure himself.

"For most people, yes. Though that doesn't stop Recett and his men. Many of the Order's followers are powerful calimancers, and no law will inhibit them. Regretfully, this is the enemy that we face."

Magnus deadened his expression. "How do we fight it?"

"Fire is fought with water," said Cecil, "and dark is fought with light. Even then, though its magic is unmatched in defending, light is incapable of directly inflicting harm. A luminomancer must rely on physical weaponry in close combat." He stood up, artfully twirling the staff to catch it in a combative grip. "A staff is an effective blunt weapon, for instance. It takes a lot of skill..." He tapped the trunk to the nape of his neck. "...but it's possible to render someone unconscious with a well-aimed blow."

"What about guns? Explosives?" Magnus lifted a wry eyebrow. "Doesn't that seem more effective?"

"Than a jeweled branch? Of course!" Cecil barked in jest. "But can a gun conjure the elements?"

"What if you put a gem on it?"

"Arkane weapon smiths have tried and failed," Cecil replied. "Using an explosive device as a magical conductor yields nothing but unintended detonations. The mix is simply too volatile. The odd enthusiast might own a revolver or something of the sort, but most people on Arkane favor other, more effective weapons when it comes to combat."

"Such as?" asked Magnus keenly.

Cecil tipped the staff's head in the way of the shelter door. "Care for me to show you?"

The first item that Cecil set on the study table was a worn hard-leather scabbard at least four feet long. A stout hilt protruded from its end, branded with an intricate, rhombic insignia. In its pommel was embedded a cleanly carved rock of gold-tinged crystal.

"This is a lucidus longsword." Cecil unsheathed the full length of the blade and laid the weapon before Magnus. Age had not significantly tarnished the metal. It coruscated in the lantern light. "Not that the blade is made of lucidus—it's the stone on its hilt."

Magnus leaned from his seat to stroke the faintly gleaming gem. "Why lucidus?"

"Enchanted lucidus is the conductor for light magic." Cecil tipped his head to the ceiling lantern. "Just like that one. But enchantments vary. A fragment of lucidus used in a lantern will never be as effective as one prepared specially for magical weaponry."

Magnus' fingers strayed onto the surface of the blade. He became mesmerized by the sight of his eyes' reflection in the thin steel mirror. "Did you used to wield this?"

"Certainly." Cecil took up the sword, gauging its weight

in an outstretched hand. "I served in the MorningStar Guard some thirty years ago. The same for your father, in fact. That was how I first got to know him. Remarkable fighter, he was. When the war came, he..." He trailed off in seeing the inevitable grim end of his reminiscing. He swiveled the blade to bring its edge against his thumb. "A little dull," he muttered, as if to return to the subject of the weapon.

"So people fight with swords?" asked Magnus after some silence.

"Among many other things," said Cecil. "Dirks, war hammers, bladed staffs...depends on your preference. But the most widely used piece of Arkane weaponry is not one for close combat." He laid down the sword to search the same corner of the study from where he had taken the scabbard. From an open crate of ill-stacked books, he lifted out a mahogany case that was not much larger than the tomes beneath it. Placing it in front of the sword, he unfastened the latches that sealed it and bared its contents for Magnus to see.

Set inside a felt-lined cast was a handheld mechanism that resembled, quite ironically, a clockwork revolver. It was comprised of a metal shaft attached to a barrel chamber, complete with a grip, trigger, and a cylinder, seemingly for housing ammunition.

"It's a gun," Magnus bluntly observed.

"Actually not." Cecil took the weapon by its grip, regarding it from all sides. He clutched a second, flat trigger that protruded from the back of the handle, causing a pair of convex metal limbs to snap open from the sides of the shaft. The weapon now clearly resembled something of a miniature crossbow.

"It's known as a handbow," said Cecil. "Think of it as a highly advanced model of the medieval crossbow." He denoted each component of the device: "Nine-shot cylinder, foldable limbs, and automatic reload powered by dual pistons in the shaft chamber. The bowstring, alas, I removed after it broke almost twenty years ago. Though its mechanics are still operational."

Cecil squeezed the trigger. There was a powerful, rapid hiss of air, but the weapon was otherwise unaffected. "The bow is normally fastened to the nib..." Cecil indicated a small stopper situated where the shaft met the cylinder. "...which is released by the pull of the trigger, propelled forward by the bow, and instantly retracted by the pistons."

"What do you fire?"

"The ammunition? Bolts. Small ones, about two-thirds the size of your hand. Don't have any with me at the moment...bound to be somewhere in this mess. They're light, barbed, and deathly sharp. With the extreme high-density bow cord used to propel them, they can easily approach the speed of a bullet."

Magnus took hold of the weapon as Cecil passed it to him. Despite the handbow being virtually ineffective without its string, he handled the device as if it were a death trap on the verge of release. "A bullet-less pistol..." he thought aloud.

"Better than that!" Cecil amended. "The handbow

becomes a weapon of limitless power when combined with magic." He swept the contraption back out of Magnus' hands to exhibit the quartz prism embedded in the right side of its grip. "Air magic is especially effective. In manipulating the wind, one could totally alter the direction of one's shot in flight or accelerate it to incredible speeds and distances, not to mention what's possible with other elements. One could set a projectile ablaze, empower it with light, imbue it with deadly electricity...to name just a few possibilities."

Magnus bound his sullen stare to the weapon. "What about dark energy?"

"Of course." Cecil gave a bleak shrug. "A bolt charged with dark energy could tear clean through its target. That would require some skill, mind you. Not to say that many of Recett's men don't have skill..." He took a seat on the study's desk stool and wheeled himself closer to the table, laying down the handbow. "We only hope they're more intent on capturing us than on killing us. There exists armor designed to protect against such weapons, but I own none."

"Like what those soldiers were wearing in my dream?"

"Yes, to some extent. That would be full fighter's armor," said Cecil. "Body armor, to be exact, is made of an alchemically crafted fabric so dense that it causes bullets and bolts alike to ricochet. Surprisingly lightweight, too. But it won't make you invincible by any means. Should you be assaulted by dark energy or otherwise, armor alone can only soften the blow. Magic must remain your chief defense."

As Cecil ended his sentence, a second conversation could be heard taking place in the adjacent room. He swiveled his stool aside and rose to glance out through the doorway. "Anubis is here." He turned to Magnus before leaving. "Rest a while. We'll continue practice in the afternoon."

Cecil strolled outside the study to find Anubis speaking with Drake. The herbalist was saddled with a fresh piece of luggage over one shoulder. He shed a smile in welcome, but it faltered as Cecil approached.

"Closed shop?" asked Cecil.

"Yes. Yes, the apothecary's closed. For now," Anubis replied in staggered phrases. His eyes never completely met Cecil's.

Cecil warmed his expression as he clasped Anubis' shoulder. "How are you?"

"Fine, fine, thank you, fine," Anubis jittered. "Just didn't get much sleep." He heaved a breath and beamed contentedly.

"Let me get that for you." Cecil motioned an offer to unburden the herbalist. Anubis gratefully handed over his bag.

"Thank you. Just a few extra things I picked up from home. Tools and such. Didn't have any weapons, I'm afraid. Sorry."

"I didn't expect you to bring anything at all, so you certainly have no reason to apologize," Cecil laughed lightly. He shouldered the bag, turning back toward the study. "Shall I leave it with the rest?"

"Yes, but—one thing, just..." Anubis stammered to call

back Cecil's attention. "I was just talking with Drake and... ah, we plan to leave tonight, yes?"

"No, actually, tomorrow morning," answered Cecil. "I still need to teach Magnus some light magic, and Drake wanted to practice a bit himself. I'd prefer if we were all at least relatively equipped to defend ourselves before we enter Arkane."

"Ah." Anubis gave a shivering nod. "So Magnus still needs to learn?"

"Light magic, yes. I don't expect him to combat Recett's men, but at least..."

"I could teach him," said Anubis in a voice suddenly resolute. "I have experience with the shades. I've dealt with them often enough in my expeditions to the MorningStar forest."

Cecil tipped his head amiably. "Yes...yes that wouldn't be a bad idea. I'd appreciate that greatly. Then I could spend more time training Drake."

"Certainly," Anubis exclaimed. "So this evening, then? I'll take Magnus out for practice."

"Wouldn't it be wiser to practice during the day?" asked Cecil. "You're more liable to be spotted by Recett's men after dusk, using that kind of magic. And light is far harder to conjure in the dark."

"Exactly as it is in Serenia," replied Anubis. "Perpetual darkness is the condition we face all across the province. If Magnus doesn't learn how to fight in that condition, he'll be just as powerless against the shades as he is now."

"But we'll be heading to Zephyr. There's plenty of light

there," Cecil rejoined. "He'll have time to hone his skills before we ever face the shades."

A forced smile flickered over Anubis' lips, but died to a distraught frown. "Hopefully."

"Hopefully," Cecil affirmed with optimism. "Don't fret. Things will be different once we reach Evanderal."

Anubis gaped in an attempt to reply, but his breath was locked in his throat. His eyes sank to the floor. "Provided... we..." he muttered, barely audibly, only to find that Cecil had already turned and departed.

17

A Weapon to Wield

MAGNUS WATCHED the black scrawl of the branches steal over the sky. Light was dwindling further with every step through the undergrowth. Anubis had led him far from the glade where Magnus usually practiced his spellcasting, down an untrodden, inhospitable path. They eventually stopped in an area that was terribly overgrown. Though it was early afternoon, here it was dim as dusk. "Right, then." Anubis turned to face the boy.

"Why out here?" Magnus asked, freeing his sleeve from a snarl of twigs.

"Light is more challenging to conjure in the dark," Anubis replied. "Since shades can only function in the dark, an encounter with one could only take place in the dark. As such, it is in the dark that you must practice. With enough luck, we won't have to face the shades immediately when we arrive on Arkane. Nevertheless, we need to be prepared for the worst."

Magnus grimaced, nodding. He wandered a few steps until he found a suitably uncluttered channel between the trees.

"To start," said Anubis, "you should know what manner of creature it is we're dealing with. Recett's shades are ethereal creatures, therefore they cannot be affected by physical means. In their dormant state, they are black ash—inanimate and harmless, but can blind you easily enough in a squall. Once awoken, those ashes vaguely take the form of an airborne skeleton. As far as anyone knows, a shade is also impossible to kill. It can only be driven back by light."

Anubis displayed a broad golden band on his right ring finger. It was fashioned in the likeness of a coiled cobra, the crest of its head serving as a pedestal for a small yellow gem. "Light magic is channeled most efficiently through enchanted lucidus, such as the stone on this ring, though other precious gems can be used." He pointed to Magnus' neckpiece. "Diamond is a favored alternative. Versatile and potent if enchanted for use as a weapon."

"Is mine?" Magnus inquired, swiveling the jewel in his fingers. Anubis came forward to take it in his grasp. The diamond flared suddenly bright in his fist, then dimmed as he released it. "Seems so," he replied. "Such an enchantment allows for faster conjuring. It's an indispensable feature in combat."

Anubis withdrew to a distance. "There are three

fundamental uses for light magic: as a torch..." He swept out his hand, which became swaddled in silken rays of light emanating from his ring. "...as a shield..." He cleaved the air with his palm, and a trail of radiance smoldered in its path, like ripples in molten glass. "...and as an offense." Anubis turned to a side-facing stance, raised his hand, and lunged. The light swelled and exploded against a wiry tree, which quivered at the impact.

"First is the matter of conjuring light," said Anubis. "It's not an action that can be straightforwardly taught. Light is an element you see, not feel, and you cannot conjure something out of visualization alone. But light energy is something different—an ethereal force. That is what we conjure. Close your eyes now, just to try it," he directed, and Magnus followed.

"Summon all your vigor inside yourself," Anubis continued. "Dwell on it, empower it. Feel strength itself. But at the same time, know that strength as light. See the noon sun glaring down on you even in the deepest darkness, and take hold of it."

Magnus steered his mind through Anubis' instructions, but to little avail. Trying to invoke the brilliance of the sun in such gloom was like an attempt to kindle damp wood. He managed only a withering glow to his pendant.

"When there is no light to see with the naked eye," Anubis added, "use your mind's eye. It can see anything at all, whether visible to you or not."

Without opening his eyes, Magnus silently acknowledged Anubis' advice and renewed his concentration. It took him at least a minute before he was able to completely dismiss the blackness of his vision. Then, from some immeasurable distance, he saw a sun spark into existence. He had forgotten that he was standing in the darkest furrows of a forest and that the horizon he surveyed was an image fashioned by his mind. The sun flared large and fierce in the void. As its rays reached their climax, they dissolved the shadows.

Now the light was in Magnus' hold. He opened his eyes to see that his pendant had caught a tremendous glow. The light faltered when he lost focus, but he salvaged the spell before it could die out.

"Good, don't lose it now," Anubis cautioned. "Try to expel it. Gather strength and cast it out."

Magnus tried, but failed repeatedly. Each time he would extend a hand to release his burgeoning magic, the light refused to leave him. Like flames clinging to a rag, the glow of his pendant swayed without dispersing. The light was exhausted more with every attempt until it guttered out.

"You're doing fine. Don't stop trying," Anubis urged on.

Magnus returned light to his pendant and empowered it even more than before. When the brightness became so great that Magnus could no longer sustain it, he forced out the light with as much mental strength as he could muster. A flash erupted, and the light expired instantly.

"That will do, for now," said Anubis. Though his expression was unreadable in the murk, his voice carried concern. "Practice as much as you're able. If nothing else, a flash like that will do to scatter a small shade swarm. That's the least you need to be capable of."

"Cecil said you can use light magic to fight..." Magnus mentioned. "...as a defense against dark energy. How?"

Anubis propped his jagged shoulder against a tree, fidgeting in his stance. "Light alone, of course, can do very little as an offense besides momentarily blinding someone. The physical aspect of light energy is the raw force it becomes in its purest form. Using that force, a burst of light could deliver a blow as strong as a hurricane wind. All comes with practice."

"And defending?"

"Same process. Once you can grasp the element, it's just a matter of bending its force." Waving his palm, he renewed his magic and painted a sheer veil of light in front of him. It diffused like a fast-dying ember. "Shields are actually quite challenging to conjure. They can't be sustained for very long, either. You might raise one to repel a single strike... though that would make up about a fraction of a second in battle." His arm shivered and drooped to his side. "A spell fight can be even faster paced than a sword fight. A luminomancer, a conjurer of light energy, will always have the upper hand in speed...but a calimancer, a conjurer of dark energy, is more apt to inflict harm. Considerable harm."

Magnus watched Anubis stand lost in his dismal brooding. "But you can defend yourself well enough, can't you?" the boy asked, hoping to put Anubis at ease.

"I..." Anubis lurched out a sound. "No, I can't. Against the shades, maybe, but not against Recett's men."

He sighed to recover his composure. "I'm a herbalist, not a fighter. Recett's men are fighters. And years of dwelling in a wasteland have hardened them." But then he turned back to Magnus, suddenly bolder. "Again," he said. "Another light burst."

Anubis padded across the trees' broken shadows while he watched the boy gather focus and conjure a flash that ruptured the darkness. "If you can, wait for a shade to get as near as possible before attacking it," said Anubis. "The less the distance, the greater the effect of the light. A stunned shade will seek refuge in the ash clouds until it recovers from the shock. Now again," he instructed, and Magnus repeated the practice with a light of even greater strength.

"It's also important to note that a shade does not wound its victims," Anubis described. "It kills, and will do no less. Its claws can slice through leather, and will instantly stop the heart of whosever skin they penetrate." He drew behind Magnus. "Once more."

A fourth time, Magnus charged his amulet and expelled its light. As the flash died from his eyes, he felt his energy beginning to drain from him. His stance slackened.

"Spellcasting exhausts the conjurer," said Anubis, "especially something as straining as the use of light magic. Take a rest."

Magnus dropped his weight against a tree, grappling onto the jutting stub of a broken branch above him. "Shades..." he mused aloud, "...what are they exactly? Ghosts? Animals? Any description I've gotten has been so vague that I don't know what image to hold of them."

Anubis didn't respond for some time. He turned and wandered in short paces. "That is because shades are vague beings," he said. "They surely aren't animals, and calling them ghosts would imply that they were the spirits of the dead."

"And they aren't?"

"Thousands of unaccountably tainted souls? If not Hades itself, I can't imagine what kind of world they would have been summoned from. They were introduced to us as shades by Recett and his men, though that term isn't quite accurate. Scientifically speaking, a shade is a visible ghost confined to this world by an attachment of some kind. That description doesn't seem to match the creatures we're dealing with."

"Then what are they? They can't be human."

"Some refer to them as elementals of ash." Anubis shuffled to a halt. "Elementals being any natural element given life, like an animated golem made of mud or rock. That would assume that these seemingly undead creatures are some kind of soulless, animated dust."

Magnus pulled a frown. "How is that possible?"

"It is. It's possible for there to exist an entity driven solely by energy—without spirit or a functioning body. Dead elementals, as they're known. Nothing exists of them but an indefinable force; nothing is capable of destroying them. How thousands of such creatures could have come into existence is beyond me. With what we know, we can't do more than repel them."

Magnus gave his silent acknowledgment, attention

half-stolen by his own observations. He found it hard to believe that the person who now lectured him so extensively about the shades was the same person who, only two days ago, could not even bear to hear mention of the subject. Anubis' usual smog of apprehension was still present, but different.

A smirk rose, then vanished, on Magnus' lips. "That just leaves Daimos' men. Like the ones that captured me last night."

"Yes," Anubis answered brusquely. "As I said, Recett's fighters are a separate danger altogether. If you encounter one again..." He stopped, shaking his head in agitation. "No. You will do all you can to ensure that you don't. Crossing paths with one of Recett's men is as good as turning ourselves in."

"No, it isn't. I escaped them," Magnus reminded. "They're not out to kill us, are they? All they want is that lost research of my father's."

"Does that make the thought any more comforting?" Anubis retorted in a whimper. "We don't have what they want, and they'll torture us to the brink of death before they realize that."

"Then that still means we have a better chance," Magnus persisted. "It's easier to shoot an animal than it is to capture it. Any chance we have to flee or fight is better than none."

Anubis' stiff bearing crumpled away. He lowered his hands into his trouser pockets as if the cold silence disturbed him. "You're braver than I am, Magnus," he professed, and said nothing more.

Magnus shrugged diffidently. "Maybe I'd think otherwise if I had to face the same things you did."

"That's why someone like you is needed to give a more rational perspective." Anubis shed a rare smile, but the expression lasted only a moment. "Ready to give it another go?"

Magnus plodded back to his original position. "So, suppose I were to meet another of Daimos' men..." he revisited the unsavory subject.

"Attack and run," said Anubis. "A direct burst of light is enough to blind someone for a second or two. The trees will lend cover as you escape."

Magnus winced as the memory of his kidnapping was stirred in him. "Provided there are trees at all. I like to think that we've seen the last of those men in this forest."

Anubis withdrew into the shawl of his hair. "Nevertheless, we've got to be wary of the things we never even want to imagine." His voice was suddenly quieter. "Remember that we're not in safety yet."

"Is everything clear?" Medeva drawled to her company.

Noctell reclined his head against the tree where he sat. His expression was set with languor and fashioned with malevolent intention. "Clear," he droned. Across the undulating flames of the campfire, he watched Raven tinker with a metal armband nearly large enough to clinch a human neck. The demon snapped open the band by a latch and clamped it onto his mammoth left wrist, matching one he wore on his right. Between ruby studs, its surface was carved in a wicked ravel of symbols that bristled with flame as Raven stroked them.

"Then the plan is set." Medeva rose from her crouched posture. "The forest is being swarmed by soldiers as we speak."

"Is that necessary?" Noctell scoffed. "It's already ridiculous enough that the shades have involvement in this."

"Any more ridiculous than the number of years it took for you and Recett to get to this point?" Medeva replied. "We leave no room for error, and no exit unguarded. Within three hours, no one will be able to escape the forest."

Raven clawed at the fire, spurring it into a rage with a gleam of his jeweled armbands. The tall flames became wreathed into a vine, which Raven snatched at its peak and spun into a lambent orb in his palms. As he extended his hands, fingers splayed, the orb ruptured in a cyclone of flames that stole the campfire into its tongues, devouring it as the blaze expired to smoke. The demon came to his feet with the poise of a living monolith. "Ready."

Silent, Medeva turned past her winged shoulder to lock gazes with the darkness. There was a distant sound, vague enough to be considered the wind were it not for its shrill and discordant melody. Then it repeated—a scream like one uttered in a tortured, dying breath—and multiplied until the air shivered with pain. A black plume glided past, followed by a second, then a third. Ash whirled thick in the shadows, weaving a frayed tapestry of bone. Noctell picked up his head to see the waning moon give in to the billows of the gathering horde.

The screams subsided, and the shades came still. Medeva turned to face the others. Her subtly scintillating eyes seemed to lend the only light. She spoke as if no words had the authority to follow her own: "Let's go."

18

Fight or Flight

ECIL TRACED HIS PEN along the inky ridges of the Mediterranean coast. His stare hovered over the map a moment, then shifted onto the opposite page of the rift atlas, where he compared his observations to a chart of Arkane's eastern continent. Multicolored pinheads denoted the locations of the rifts. *Athens-Silvryn, R054012,* one was tagged in fine print. Cecil riffled deeper into the volume.

"Our choices are between the Evanderal and Silvryn rifts," Cecil declared to Anubis, who was seated at the opposite side of the center table.

The interruption of the silence seemed to jar the herbalist as if he'd never expected to hear another word. "Whichever you think is best," he replied through a cough.

"The airline will make the final decision for us,"

said Cecil. "France or Greece. We'll take the fastest and most direct flight."

"Which airport?"

"That small one about three hours south of here." Cecil wavered between two sections of the book before settling on a map of the province of Zephyr. "Evanderal is my preference. Farther from Serenia, and the Zephyrian Archives should be of good use to us." His posture wilted in exhaustion. "Have you packed yet?"

Anubis seemed like he was about to answer, but then simply nodded instead.

"I'd much prefer if you'd sleep inside tonight," Cecil added. "Despite your insistence on not cluttering my space, it would give me a better night's rest to know you're safely sheltered."

"I...understand, Cecil." Anubis nodded again. "Thank you."

Cecil suddenly frowned and tipped his head aslant. "Did you hear that?"

"Hear what?"

"It sounded like...an explosion. From somewhere out in the forest." Cecil slunk out of his seat and stole toward the door, leaving Anubis arrested by angst. He eased up the stairs and leaned on the wood with a vigilant ear.

A blast erupted against the door from outside. Cecil reeled away, shaken to the bone. His quick footing barely saved him from being knocked off the steps. Not a moment later, Magnus and Drake bolted out from their room at the noise. Ember scurried into sight to stand by Anubis, who was already trembling profusely. No one dared move or speak.

"You know who we are," a voice bellowed from behind the door, stifled by the wood. "We've found your rabbit hole. Come out now. No harm will come to those who comply."

Sixteen years of hope were unraveled in a single breath. Cecil and Drake's eyes gaped, empty, as if the soul beyond them had withered. Magnus felt his blood flare with anger throttled by numbing fear. In the brutally unnerving quiet, Anubis uttered a whimper.

"No...no! No!" Anubis bound himself in his arms as if to restrain his helpless quivering.

Drake turned to his former guardian at a total loss. Cecil was no less disconcerted, but offered what encouragement he could. "We haven't given ourselves up yet," he said. "They can't kill any of us without risking a loss of valuable information. They'll have to catch us, and we'll make sure that they don't."

"Did you hear me, Wingheart?" the voice behind the door hollered again. "You have two minutes to exit peacefully, else we break in."

Cecil spent no longer than a couple of seconds deliberating. He beckoned everyone near. "Depending on how many people we're facing, we'll try to escape the forest," he whispered. "That may involve a bit of a scuffle." He motioned to the boy. "Magnus, give your necklace to Drake. Come with me to the study and I'll get you my ruby staff. Anubis, you have your ring."

Drake accepted the pendant necklace from his brother,

but stalled in hesitation. "Cecil, you take it; I'll use your other staff."

"I have my own weapon," Cecil waved aside Drake's offer and hastened away with Magnus. He swerved inside the study and seized the ruby-crowned shaft leaned at the doorway. "Can you make do with this?" he asked, handing the staff to Magnus beside him.

"Yes. And what about you?" In the harsh lantern light, Magnus barely recognized the object that Cecil had stolen off the table—it was the scabbard his former guardian had shown him earlier that day.

Cecil clipped the leather holster to his belt and drew its blade with the skill of a swordsman. "I've never forgotten how to wield this." He played the weapon in his wrist like a feather-light baton. "Now to sharpen..."

Leaving the sword on the table, Cecil delved into the clutter around him. From a crate containing an assortment of unusual implements, he removed a fist-sized stone slab secured within a metal grip. A pale emerald was entrenched atop it. He returned to the table with the slab in hand and nailed his opposite palm against the hilt of the sword.

Greenish light swelled over the jeweled device. As Cecil glided the stone across the edge of the blade, sparks of the same color gushed into the air and dissipated. He turned the weapon over and repeated the stroke. The sword gleamed like cut crystal.

"Combined with magic, an emerald grindstone can

sharpen any blade in an instant," Cecil noted, sheathing the weapon. "We're ready."

Cecil and Magnus took for the shelter door, where the others awaited them. Anubis was on his feet now, but had by no means calmed.

"We head out together," Cecil strategized. "Drake, stay with me. Magnus, stay by Anubis. After we've stalled long enough, I'll make the first move."

"Are we planning on fighting them?" Drake gave a troubled eye.

Cecil returned the look with regret. "Only for long enough to distract. Then we flee at the opportune moment."

"Which will be...?"

"When I call out your name. That will be our signal to break away. Given the chance, I'll try to create a diversion. Now, Anubis..." Cecil turned to the herbalist, who cringed as if he were being threatened at knifepoint. "Take Brendan's satchel on the table. Fill it with any herbs you have and wear it when we head out. If they find the notebook inside, they won't think anything of it."

Anubis' answer was a twitch of his terrified frown. He complied with Cecil's instructions, sweeping the satchel off the center table on his way into the study.

"It's been long enough." The voice outside loudened with impatience. "Show yourselves!"

The group's hearts lurched with every dwindling second. Anubis was swift to return, carrying the now-swollen purse on his shoulder.

"When we flee," said Cecil, "Magnus and I will head one way; Anubis, you and Drake go the opposite direction. We'll leave the forest and regroup in Markwell, by the pawnshop at Kingsley. All clear?"

The brothers nodded faintly. Cecil filled his lungs as if he were about to plunge into a river from whose waters he would never emerge. "Let's go."

Cecil wrenched the knob and shouldered open the door, weapon drawn. A smog of light surrounded him, diffusing from a pair of lucidus torches set on the ground and aimed precisely at the shelter entrance. Beyond the scope of the light, the darkness was made denser in contrast.

"Have we been summoned by invisible men? Or cowards?" Cecil called into the gloom. Anubis and the brothers came to stand beside him.

An ominous rustle of footsteps through dry leaves sounded in return. Two figures approached the verge of the light, where they stood, unflinching, at either end of the clearing. One had the stature of a giant. Magnus had no doubt that he recognized these men as his captors from the previous night.

"Good evening Handel, Wingheart," Noctell scrutinized each of the shelter's occupants, flinching bitterly at the sight of Magnus. "Of course, our young fugitive." He eyed the herbalist last. "And you...Anubis Araiya, isn't it?"

"Glad to see you know us all so well," Cecil quipped derisively. "May we have the pleasure of your own introductions?"

"Certainly," Noctell crowed. Every word that curled off

his tongue was doused in nonchalant arrogance. "My name is Noctell Knever. This is my associate, Raven Gaunt. We are elite soldiers of the new MorningStar guard."

"Splendid," replied Cecil. "Now that we're all familiar with each other, I suppose you two ought to be going."

Noctell hummed, unamused. "You will come back with us to MorningStar. Your cooperation will ensure you a safe return."

Cecil crept two paces forward. "What are our other options?"

Noctell motioned to the darkness surrounding them. The shadows were murmuring; when Cecil gazed into them, he was certain that they were moving. "Shades surround the clearing," said the necromancer. "The forest and the town are swarmed with our men. You have no other options besides that we drag you all out of here on the trails of your own blood."

"I don't think the dead are very good at answering questions."

"Did I say anything about killing you? Suffer a few broken limbs and you'll still be perfectly capable of moving your lips."

Cecil's impassive stare did not twitch. "What is it you want from us, exactly?"

Noctell mocked a gesture of surprise. "Are you that ignorant?"

"How would you expect us to know? I assumed Recett was just out to murder us."

"Does the name Brendan Wingheart sound at all

familiar?" Noctell droned with a cynical slant. "He's the one we're after. But a corpse can't speak, you see. The fool fought himself to death before he could be arrested. Surely the man's closest family and friends could—"

Noctell suddenly assumed a defensive stance at seeing Cecil's weapon flare alight. A radiant explosion collided with a swell of dark energy. Noctell hurled the dark billow at the ground before Cecil, where it shattered to sparks. Without a warning, the battle had begun.

Raven's menacing bulk loomed toward Anubis and the brothers. Drake summoned a light to his pendant and expelled its force in an unbroken beam, like a lance, but Raven had already fashioned a barrier of flame in defense. The light dispersed on contact with the shield, whose fire was kindled tenfold. A lash of the demon's claw wove the flames into a knot of ravenous tongues that rippled over the leaves on the ground, igniting them.

Noctell leapt closer and thwarted a second light burst from Cecil. Two more blocked assaults, and the pair was now battling at close range. Cecil spun a labyrinth of swipes with his blade, but was consistently opposed by the necromancer. Light-charged blows shattered against plumes of dark energy with unremitting tempo. Noctell was given no chance to attack, but he maintained his defense as if it would never falter.

The fires roped about Drake's feet, encircling him. Raven beckoned the blaze to rise, and the flames spired up like the bars of a cage. Drake strove to douse the fire, but the water he called forth was meager. Standing barely three feet away, Anubis couldn't press past his anxiety enough to make a move. Magnus was desperately occupied in his attempts to generate any magic at all. Moisture glimmered over the jewels of his staff, only to fade faster than it was conjured. He almost failed to notice that the demon's shadow was now directly upon him.

Raven played the flames like a curtain that bowed and bulged with each sweep of his arm. The fire straggled out in cords, which he steered to entrap both Anubis and the boy. Magnus lunged, narrowly dodging the flames, and heaved his staff to bludgeon the demon's lofty head. But he saw a gargantuan limb swoop down on him before he'd made it far. His shoulder was struck with the weight of a rockslide, and he toppled to the ground.

Then Raven uttered a raucous howl, as if in pain. Magnus, buckled sideways in the dirt, just managed to glimpse the creature latched onto the demon's thigh by its claws and teeth—Ember. The salamander must have escaped through the open door of the shelter. With Raven's concentration broken, the inferno trembled and subsided to a puddle of flames.

Raven scarcely spared a look at the reptile before sweeping its lithe body into a fist. "You!" He recognized Ember as the creature that had assaulted him the night before, prior to Magnus' getaway. He cried out again as the salamander flailed its bladed paws, slashing him. "Sickly rodent!" With merciless strength, Raven hurled Ember against the nearest tree trunk. A pained shriek knifed Magnus' ears, and the salamander crumpled limply to the ground.

Cecil maneuvered his back to the clearing's edge without a stammer in his onslaught. At the precise moment, he would make the call to flee. But the single backward step he took was enough to allow a rebuke from his opponent. Noctell outspread his arms and whisked from the air two smoky veins, which he brought to collide in a shockwave that caused the surrounding light to quiver. Cecil shielded himself, though the blow was still strong enough to rattle his fighting stance. Now Noctell was on the offense. A storm of dark energy bled and burned from the necromancer's arms, converging in his palms to form dual blades black as the fabric of an abyss.

Cecil swept up his lambent sword to meet Noctell's blades. Sparks erupted with the fury of a lightning strike. Each time Cecil would prepare to retaliate, his weapon was struck aside with such force that he was driven backward. Clearly, Noctell's aim was to disarm rather than kill, and he was close to succeeding.

Anubis was robbed of his breath by devastation. He careened over the flames, singeing himself as he scrambled to Ember's aid. The salamander still showed life, though he was immobile and evidently wounded.

Raven irritably dissolved the last of the fire and approached the herbalist from behind. Anubis suddenly stood upright, shuddering with stifled anger. His valiance was met with a provocative smirk from the demon, but he was too enraged to be daunted. He found the courage to kindle power within his lucidus ring. Faster, Raven veiled himself in a burning red miasma. When Anubis released his assault, the light was immediately diffused in the demon's shield.

Raven stirred the mist with his claws, which became gilded with flames like obsidian torches. Anubis recoiled, his bravery withering. He had been impetuous in confronting the demon. He returned a feeble light to his ring, trepidly prepared to defend.

Magnus streaked to rescue Ember from the fray. With the injured salamander cradled in his arms, he retreated to the umbrage. His brother waded through the tatters of burnt leaves and cinders as he readied his pendant with light. Drake couldn't attack the demon with Anubis standing between them, so he flitted ahead for another approach. From his eyes' periphery, he glimpsed a shadow pass him in the opposite direction at nearly twice his speed.

Drake gripped the dirt with his soles and whirled around. The yawning darkness glared back at him. He expelled a light burst, which, in the second before it faded, gave shape to a humanlike figure poised on the hillside above the shelter. Then a glint of metal cleaved the void. Drake felt a brutal sting pierce his left shoulder, and he crumpled with a scream.

All heads turned at the cry. Cecil flinched, yielding his opponent an undefended strike. A bolt of dark energy hammered his side and knocked him onto his back. He raised his sword to defend again, but Noctell had withdrawn far from his reach. As he returned to his feet, he saw the darkness begin to churn. The malevolent seething of the wind told that the shades were encroaching.

A familiar host of shrieks thundered down the length of the valley. Sooty cadavers deluged the clearing in seconds. Magnus doubled over the salamander to protect it, shutting his eyes to the gruesome display. Bones enfolded him with a touch colder than death; claws raked his back, beckoning him, only to leave his heart impaled with a festering barb of despair. When the shades' presence subsided, he dared to look again.

Noctell and Raven were gone from sight. The melee had ceased, and the clearing was stagnant. In the stark glower of the torchlight, Drake writhed on a bed of leaves that was glazed with blood.

19

Blood and Ink

ANUBIS EASED DRAKE upright while Magnus looked on with dismay. Drake's left sleeve was doused in splashes of red; strands of blood wove a trail to the weapon that had landed the blow—a sleek throwing knife.

"Don't move. We'll carry you inside." Anubis threaded a shoulder under Drake's uninjured arm.

Drake wrung his face with deep agony as he was raised onto his feet. "It's okay..." he gasped, steadying himself. "I can walk."

Cecil skimmed the clearing's edge with the glow of his sword. Their attackers had vanished inexplicably, along with the shades. The faintly reflective hull of Cecil's pickup truck caught the light. The vehicle had not gone unnoticed by the men—it was leaned drunkenly on four slashed tires, one of which had been clobbered inward. Its open hood exposed a mangled engine.

Magnus followed Anubis and his brother into the shelter, Ember slung in his arms. Cecil hovered a short distance behind. He stopped and turned dauntlessly, as if daring the darkness to oppose him. He waited for that sudden assault, for the men to return and seize them unawares. But his unspoken challenge was met with moribund silence. If nothing else, he was certain their attackers had not fled without reason.

Cecil stooped to gather Magnus' discarded staff off the ground. Just before departing, his eye was caught by the bloodied throwing knife. He sheathed his own sword and stole up the weapon, a finely weighted blade wrought from a single sliver of steel. He trailed Magnus and the others inside.

Drake plodded down the stairs with Anubis as his crutch. A step away from the floor, he went limp in a shiver and buckled against Anubis' side. He recovered, but proceeded with more difficulty than before.

"Are you alright?" Anubis exclaimed in a panic.

Drake shed the pain through an ivory-white fist and nodded off any concern. "Just...weak. I'll lie down." However, his shivering had not subsided.

Cecil closed the door behind him and hurried to catch up. He made a fleeting attempt to inspect the knife in the lamplight. Mingled with a crimson smear, a slick of some murky substance smothered the blade like oil. Cecil's breath grew short; he gathered pace.

"Anubis." Cecil flashed the knife. "You'd better look at this." He rushed beside Drake and the herbalist, who halted at the stern suggestion. "There's a coating on the blade."

Anubis took the weapon into fingers aquiver. Distress consumed him at once. He returned the knife to Cecil and raised a hand to Drake's forehead. "Help me carry him, quick," he urged. "The blade may have been poisoned. He's already running a fever."

Cecil hastened to lift the older brother from his wounded side. Drake was paling, shivering more violently. His legs raked the floor as he was hauled inside the bedroom. Magnus fervently pursued them. "How can we help him?"

"I have taren bark anti-poison," Anubis hollered back. "Leave Ember on your bed and bring my bag from the study."

Drake was laid on his mattress, his body feeble as a reed. He winced at the beam of the lantern that smarted his blood-rimmed eyes; needles swelled in his chest when he tried to breathe. His hands, too weak to hold a fist, were turning numb. Magnus put Ember to rest on his own bed before heading to the study. He promptly returned with Anubis' clattering sack of vials and herbal reserves.

Anubis tore open the bag and fished out a four-inch bottle filled with a chlorochrous fluid. Its label was marked with a fading pen scrawl reading "Taren."

"Extract of taren bark," Anubis denoted, opening the cap on a hinge. "Very potent. Enough to counteract most simple poisons." He placed the bottle to Drake's lips. Swigging a mouthful of the antidote, Drake heaved a cough at the acrid fire it stirred in his throat. He slumped flat on his back as the burn abated.

"The symptoms should subside within an hour." Anubis returned the sealed bottle to his bag. "With two to three hours of rest, he should be in better condition."

"Thank you, Anubis." Cecil dipped his head graciously. "You've proved an indispensable aide in the past few days."

Anubis immersed himself in the clutter of his bag again; only he didn't appear to be rummaging as much as he was trembling in another spell of nervousness. He tried to pass a smile through a cleft in his hair, but the expression was wrenched by an already present frown. Gathering some cloth and a spool of bandage, he hustled his eyes back to Drake and his wound.

"I thought they didn't want us dead." Magnus folded to a seat on his mattress, beside the injured salamander.

"I thought the same," Cecil bitterly concurred. He sank into the chair by the desk. "Perhaps the poison wasn't lethal."

"Then what would've been the point of wounding him?"

"What was the point of the whole assault?" Cecil snapped. "They just fled! For no conceivable reason!"

Magnus gingerly scooped Ember into his lap. The salamander had its left hind leg taut, as if it were sprained; it appeared otherwise unhurt. Its lids unfurled, exposing eyes like emerald-capped pearls, which flitted to lock stares with the boy. "Those were the two men who captured me last night," said Magnus. "Maybe we put up too much of a fight for them." But not even he seemed convinced.

Cecil shook his head. "I'd like to think that. But that calimancer still managed to knock me back in the end. If he wanted, he could have captured me then and there."

"You're not hurt?"

"No, I'm not, thankfully. Dark energy can be shaped to something either totally harmless or mortally dangerous. Seeing that he chose the former, he wasn't even intent on wounding me." Cecil tousled his hair in fretful contemplation. "But he was powerful, no doubt. And with the ease he showed in defending himself, I can't imagine I was much of a challenge for him." His scabbard knocked the desk leg as he sat upright. He glanced at the weapon as if he'd forgotten it and unlatched it from his belt. "What about the other one? Raven, was it?"

"I think," replied Magnus. "He seemed pretty powerful. I'm not even sure what kind of monster he was. I've never seen any man that huge. And his skin was *red*—blood-red." He looked questioningly to his former guardian, but Cecil didn't seem to have any better insight.

"There are stranger beasts on Arkane than on Earth," said Cecil with a lopsided shrug. "There's the common race of the elves, who are typically taller than humans...but not to the extent of Raven. Not to mention that an elf's skin is actually pallid in comparison to a human's."

"When I was captive at their camp," Magnus added, "Raven was angered by my taunts about his appearance more than anything else. I asked him what he was, but he wouldn't tell me."

"He looked like something of a demon," said Cecil, sounding quite incredulous of his own reply. "Only, a true demon is an ethereal creature. This one looked more like the product of a botched alchemical experiment." He unsheathed the first few inches of his sword and pensively swiveled its edge in the light. He tore himself from his own thoughts as he rammed the blade back into the scabbard. "He was the one who threw the knife, wasn't he?"

"No." Drake strained to speak. "There was a third person. Someone who never came into sight."

Cecil's eyes flickered a little wider. "But you saw him?"

"Only..." Drake winced as Anubis dressed his wound in a strip of damp bandage. "...only briefly. It was too dark. She was hiding..."

"She?" exclaimed Cecil, fiercely intrigued.

"I couldn't tell...for sure," Drake muttered. "It looked like."

"What did she look like?"

"She was fast," replied Drake, "and quiet. I heard nothing. I only saw her a second before she attacked me." His lips stiffened as he shuddered. "I couldn't be sure but...it looked almost as if she had...wings."

"That sounds too familiar." Cecil's expression turned dark and hard as ebony. "I suspect this isn't first we've seen of her. And the last time, her quarry wasn't so lucky."

Drake breathed a wordless lament. In the silence, Magnus grasped Cecil's morbid implication. "The one who killed our mother," said the boy.

"Either that, or some other creature almost identical to her," Cecil confirmed. "I've only ever seen one winged human in my life; she shot Myra on the night we escaped MorningStar. She would be recognized by mythology as a harpie, a beast that's only known to exist in the dimensions outside of Arkane. I can't imagine how or why she would be a follower of Recett."

Anubis fastened Drake's swathe with a knot and packed away the rest of his items. "I salved the wound. It should be mostly healed by tomorrow," he said. "I'll take care of Ember in the study, where I have a little more room to work. Call me if Drake starts to feel any worse." Shouldering the bag, he took the salamander from Magnus' arms and into his own. He scuttled out of the room at once.

Magnus' eyes drifted away from the vacant doorway and back to Cecil, posing a tacit, dismal question. Cecil deepened his frown. "Plans have changed," he declared. "The pickup truck is obliterated; someone slashed the tires and destroyed the engine." He glanced out across the main room as if he were still witnessing the battle in its heat. "Before the attack...that must have been the explosion I heard from outside."

"Then we walk," Magnus proposed. "It will be easier to escape the forest on foot anyhow."

"The nearest airport is a three-hour drive away from this outpost," Cecil replied. "We'll be captured before we make it out of Markwell. After that bizarre escape stunt they pulled, I'm wary to even step outside the door."

Magnus palmed his brother's hand, which seemed warmer than before. "We can't confine ourselves in here," he said. "We'll have to leave the shelter either way. The only question is where we plan to head."

Cecil angled for an answer, but found none. "We don't know that yet," he replied. "The longer we travel, the likelier our arrest. The MorningStar rift could be our best choice, seeing how things stand."

Magnus shed a look of dark misgiving. "Isn't that where the men are coming from?"

"Alas, yes." Cecil held back a shiver. "But at the moment, it's no more dangerous than Markwell. We'll be risking our lives regardless of our route; the shortest one will be the safest." He paused, as if having run out of words. "We depart as soon as Drake is well."

Magnus slumped, his arms on his knees. His eyes floated onto Brendan's satchel deposited at Drake's bedside. A leafy bulge obscured the outline of the notebook inside.

"You may as well start packing if you're ready," Cecil suggested bleakly.

"I will, soon." Magnus reached for the flaccid strap of the satchel. "I have something to ask Anubis first."

"How's Drake?" Anubis inquired the moment the boy entered.

"He's alright. Cecil is with him." Magnus paced inside

the study. He dropped the satchel between the slovenly piles of books on the table. "How's Ember?"

"Doing better, thanks," Anubis replied. He was in the process of bandaging a sliver of wood to the salamander's leg as a makeshift splint. "A bad sprain, but thankfully nothing more."

Magnus stared in silence for a moment, then pulled out the contents of the satchel—a sheaf of herbs, followed by Brendan's notebook and the inexplicable stone that had been given along with it. "When you're done...I wanted to talk to you about my father's things."

Anubis fastened the bandage and left Ember to rest. He faced Magnus with fear-wide eyes and a scarcely perceptible smile.

"Cecil thinks we should leave as soon as Drake heals," said Magnus. "The pickup truck was destroyed by the men, so we'll have to travel on foot. We'll be packing light, and this book might be the only one in the shelter that we'll be able to salvage."

Anubis' expression took on a dismal contortion. He crumpled back into his seat and abandoned his gaze in space.

"I know that Cecil spent years looking over this without finding anything of use," Magnus continued, clutching the booklet as if it were strung to his soul. "But whether these notes are totally useless or whether they have even a shred of value to offer, we risk losing everything from the moment we set foot in the forest. This might be the last chance we ever get to find something that can help us, out of the things in my father's satchel."

"Of course, Magnus," Anubis lifted his posture an inch. "But besides exploring what's already been explored, I don't know what else we can do."

"Neither do I. I just..." Magnus thumbed through the notebook as if he were trying to locate the rest of his sentence. He swiped the stone off the table and proffered it determinedly. "What about this? It was in the satchel as well; it should be just as important as the notebook."

Anubis halfheartedly swiveled the stone in his fingers as though any hope of discovery had long left him. "It's doubtful that it got added in by accident, so it must be of some significance. But with that said..." His optimism fleeted as he set down the item. "...a rock alone cannot tell us its purpose."

"It can tell us something," Magnus persevered. "Could it have anything to do with what my father was researching?"

"The Luminous Rock?" Anubis tilted the stone in the light. "I can't see how. It looks like a coarse chunk of basalt. The Luminous Rock was supposed to be formed of lucidus."

"Does the notebook say anything about it?" Magnus flashed his father's scrawl.

"I'm quite certain it doesn't. I reviewed much of it, and the closest any of those concoctions come to geology is a gemstone polish."

Riffling keenly, Magnus sought out a distinct and familiar page from the book. "What about this one?"

Anubis leaned in to inspect Magnus' proposal. It was perhaps the sole oddity of the notebook—the recipe whose orderly script told that it had received an unusual amount of attention from its author. "We looked at this one the other day, didn't we?" asked Anubis in a half-mutter.

"Yes. You even said it was strange," Magnus noted. He gave Anubis a moment to reexamine the text before continuing to query him. "You said you didn't know what it was for, but...is there any way we could find out?"

Anubis shrugged candidly. "A more experienced opinion, maybe? I've been in the field for twenty-some years, but spent only a quarter of that time on Arkane. Experience aside, of course, I can assure you that this doesn't look much like a potion recipe." He stroked the finely woven ropes of cursive text. "This is a set of lists; repetitious ones at that."

"There's more than one?"

"It seems like there are four, though they aren't much different from one another," said Anubis. "Ah, one of them is, slightly," he amended. "Here, have a look."

Magnus dropped onto the desk stool and wheeled up to the herbalist's side. His eyes were steered to the top left of the page, onto a scribbled blotch of ink that capped a list of eight items. The scribble was adjoined by the ambiguous title "Sample 1."

"Here's the first one," Anubis identified, then denoted a neighboring column of text about half the size, "and the second." His finger traced a wide black bracket that encompassed both lists. "This seems to indicate that the two are related." The bottom left column extended under a similar ink blot that was aptly labeled "Sample 2."

The final column beside it was punctuated with text edits and was ill-aligned in comparison to the others. "And the third and fourth, respectively," Anubis motioned a circle around the lower two columns. "Their connection isn't expressed, though they share many of the same ingredients."

"Then which is the one you said was different?"

"The third column, sample two. It's quite unlike the first two, but similar to the fourth. And the fourth..." Anubis studied the columns more intently. "...also shares many of the same ingredients as the first two. Not knowing any better, I'd say the fourth column is a combination of samples one and two. The edits would indicate this isn't something that was copied."

Magnus angled the book toward him. "And you have no idea what the samples could be?"

Anubis shook his head in a reverie. "The ingredients are a muddle of herbal extracts and common chemicals. Since all four blends contain either curranthium or imrynic acid, they're poisonous, and clearly not meant to be ingested. The combinations would have no drastic effect on their own, and the notes don't specify any use for them otherwise."

"So you don't suppose this is at least...a part of my father's research," Magnus warily surmised.

"Maybe." Anubis shrugged a shoulder. "But that doesn't account for the part that we lack."

"We make do with what we have," said Magnus. "A part of the research is better than none." He scanned the perplexing array of paragraphs. The majority of the substance names eluded him. "Do you have any of these ingredients with you?"

"I may have all of them." Anubis lifted his eyes off the page to look sidelong at the boy. "You plan on mixing these concoctions?"

Magnus returned an affirmative glance. "We have a couple of hours. Is that enough time?"

"More than." Anubis hoisted his canvas bag onto his lap to rummage through it. "I don't want to discourage you, but I'm not sure what results you expect from this."

"I don't expect anything," Magnus replied. "I just want to have done all I can before we risk losing everything. Potions will be less suspicious than papers, anyhow. If they confiscate the notebook, at least we'll have something left of it."

"The notebook isn't what's of most value to them." Anubis' lip flickered with grim irony. "They much prefer a person who can answer a spoken question..." He culled a couple of vials from his bag and set them aside. "...and bleed if they do not."

Magnus picked up each vial that Anubis produced, comparing its minuscule label with the recipes—*ardentine* was a vermillion powder; *junet* was a near-black water whose fickle green veins shone at only the most precise tilt in the light. Anubis had already brought out an additional five vials by the time Magnus had scrutinized the first two.

"What say we start with the one in the fourth column?" Anubis assembled the vials to unclutter the space in front of him. The last object he withdrew before placing the bag at his feet was an empty vial a little larger than the rest.

"The one with the corrections," affirmed Magnus. "Do we have everything we need?"

"Oh yes." Anubis whisked open the tallest of the vials. "Straightforward concoction. Shouldn't take longer than a minute." A thread of silvery, limpid water pooled behind the glass as he tipped the vial into the empty container. He then added a roseate liquid, followed by the junet, which eclipsed the clear mixture with straggling black tendrils. A trickle from three of the remaining vials was poured next, inciting no more than a placid hiss. The ardentine was last; it dispersed on contact with the surface of the water, where it settled like a film of ochre dust.

Anubis capped the vial containing the mix and stirred it heedfully. The result was an inky fluid that left a sopping black stain in each place it lapped the walls of its vessel. "Well, then," Anubis tepidly exclaimed. He reopened the vial and set it before him. "The mystery potion unveiled. At least one of them, anyway."

Magnus scraped the vial closer, peering within. "Could we try using it on the rock?"

Without much in the way of a response, Anubis returned to his bag to extract an immaculate handkerchief. Thoroughly dousing its tip in the potion, he used the cloth to daub the basalt fragment. The black water seeped over the rock like paint too thin to leave a mark; Magnus' anticipation dissolved along with it.

Anubis pulled a face of commiseration. "Next one, then?"

Magnus lifted away the sodden handkerchief as the

herbalist delved back into his supplies. His inattentiveness, however, led him to trickle more than a few stray drops of the mixture onto the notebook's open pages. Irritably, he wadded the cloth and gripped his sleeve to mop up the spill. Horror wrung his gut when he saw the ink swim away with the droplets.

Magnus smacked the table's edge in a fury. A distraught frown was all he could offer when Anubis leaned near in concern. At least a dozen letters had been effaced, with not even a smear, but only a bare ripple in their place. Anubis, conversely, appeared more intrigued than disturbed.

"Peculiar..." Anubis gathered the last of the droplets with a dry corner of the cloth. "The potion causes the ink to evaporate on contact, but..." He indicated the first two paragraphs, which, though wet, remained intact. "...not all of it."

Magnus' dismay turned to unblinking curiosity. "Sample one," he muttered the header aloud.

"An ink," Anubis announced suddenly, as if in a revelation. "Sample one and sample two are different kinds of ink." He riffled a few pages on, to one of the many unremarkable entries in the notebook. With utmost precision, he used the handkerchief to moisten the tip of a paragraph. As the parchment drank in the solution, the scrawl did not just vanish as before—it changed.

Magnus and Anubis both gaped. On a quivering impulse, Anubis soused the whole paragraph with the cloth, and promptly after, the entire page. The ink that wafted away in the watery stains yielded to another swarm of letters, as if some unseen force were molding the potion's black pigment. As the moisture subsided, a flood of new words were born:

With the knowledge of a hundred antiquated maps and history books to pave the untrodden route I've chosen, I hope to leave for Galem tomorrow. For the sake of Serenia, may this expedition not be in vain.

20

Well-Hidden Words

NBELIEVABLE." CECIL LEAFED the notebook with hypnotic fixation. Penned on still-damp pages was an entirely different volume—one that had lingered in disguise since its author's untimely death. Herbal recipes had dissolved from existence, replaced by a valiant chronicle of Brendan's search for a weapon to destroy the warlord Daimos and the immortal army he commanded.

Cecil rested a thumb on the page containing the remnants of the original four-paragraph recipe. "This is the potion that caused...this?"

"Yes," Anubis confirmed, adding a nod to Magnus seated by his brother. "If it weren't for Magnus' perseverance, it would have gone unnoticed along with the rest of the book. The recipe was so vague that I never paid any attention to it myself."

Cecil looked up from the book for the first time since he had been shown its new text. "What is it exactly? I can't imagine Brendan would have been so skilled in herbology to concoct something even you wouldn't recognize."

"I believe I never recognized it because it was not the form of herbology I'm familiar with," replied Anubis. "There is general and medicinal herbology, which are the fields that I've studied. I do have some basic knowledge of alchemical herbology, but not much about chemical herbology. The latter is the category under which that recipe would fall."

"What defines chemical herbology?" Magnus interposed.

"Any concoction whose product is a chemical, or that causes a chemical reaction, as opposed to a more practical potion. A chemical recipe has little to distinguish itself, other than that it doesn't usually appear very coherent."

"Then my father knew...chemistry?"

"No," Cecil answered, but with a positive inflection. "Myra did. She was a nurse by profession, but she took an interest in this sort of thing—chemistry, that is. I think it's still safe to say that the other herbal formulas were copied out of a book as a guise."

"But you believe that Myra was responsible for concealing the text?" Anubis asked, to which Cecil responded with a cautious shrug.

"Someone must have," said Cecil. "And I can't think of anyone Brendan trusted more than Myra. It's his handwriting, no doubt, but it wouldn't be farfetched to call Myra its creator. Would you say the recipe is very complex?"

"Hard for me to judge, really." Anubis stood by Cecil's chair and slanted a look at the open pages. "After seeing the product, I at least have a clearer picture as to what all this is. I imagine that sample one is the ink he used to write the original text; sample two is the ink used to write the potion notes as a façade.

"The first potion under sample one contains imrynic acid, a mild solvent." Anubis pointed to the upper-left cluster of ingredients. "That suggests its purpose was to dissolve the original text. The subsequent column lists no acid, but junet, a potent herbal dye, which I assume would be responsible for restoring the same text. The third potion, the one under sample two, also shares the use of acid... so I would think that its purpose was in dissolving the false text. It appears that Brendan and Myra's goal was to combine the second and third potions, creating one that could dissolve the false text while repairing the original. The fourth potion would be the result of that endeavor, since it was the one that altered the writing."

Cecil stared at the scrawl in solemn disbelief. He turned a couple of pages, then flipped them back, as if he feared the text would slip away as suddenly as it had appeared. "I spent a decade with this book before passing it on to Drake," he recounted. "Six years later, on the night we face our pursuers...that's when everything we've ever searched for reveals itself."

"Why didn't my father tell you the real text was hidden?" Magnus wondered aloud, zealous for an answer.

Cecil flinched at the unnerving memories that rushed

back to him on an impulse. "Brendan had every intention of meeting up with us again once the battle was over. Myra was with us; surely she'd have been able to tell us, should anything have happened to her husband. There was no need for Brendan to explain anything at the time. But by some wickedly bad luck...we lost them both on the same night."

"Then why did he hide the text to begin with?"

"For its own sake." Cecil lowered his head to the book as he closed it. "Brendan had enough foresight. He knew that Recett would return to seize whatever it was that had been declared his bane. Concealing the text behind the potion notes was probably the wisest thing to do. Only I don't think it was his wish that it stay concealed for so long."

"He never expected to die," Drake muttered from his recumbent posture, his voice a little more substantial than earlier.

"He evacuated the people for the sake of their safety," Cecil added. "But he never thought MorningStar would fall the way it did."

Anubis brushed Drake's forehead with the back of his hand. "How are you feeling?"

"Surprisingly well." Drake pulled himself to a reclining position. "How long has it been?"

"Barely three quarters of an hour..." Anubis' sentence dwindled to a perplexed pause. "Even your fever is down considerably. With the symptoms you showed earlier, I expected you'd take at least twice that time to heal. For any poison to be cured that fast..." he entertained his unspoken suggestion with arrested breath, "...it must have been nothing more than a shock poison."

"Shock poison?"

"A nonlethal poison that throws the body into a transitory state of trauma," Anubis described. "The symptoms are like those of the deadliest poisons, except that they scarcely last thirty minutes."

"Then it was a ploy," Cecil inferred. "But to what aim?"

"To slow us down?" Drake proposed.

"That only shows they had quite a more intricate plan than we ever imagined." Cecil gave a flustered shrug. "If we don't first go mad by paranoia, I dread to think what awaits us outside."

"Whatever they've planned is beside the point," Magnus replied audaciously. "My father learned how to fight these people, and he recorded it all in that book. If that knowledge can't help us, I don't know what else can."

Cecil sighed away his anxiety. "Alright," he said, seeming neither to agree nor disagree. He delved back into the notebook. "The first pages are dedicated to the research of mineral amalgamation," he reviewed, "an alchemical process in which multiple gemstones of the same kind are fused into a larger piece. It seems that Brendan considered using amalgamated lucidus as a weapon against Recett and the shades, but then concluded, I quote:

'Amalgamated lucidus for military use proved too
costly and labor-intensive. An individual piece of
amalgamated lucidus lacks the density to perform

an exorcism. According to Mhersol, even an arti-
ficial density increase through alchemy could not
yield a luminosity higher than 400 percent. Higher
densities of lucidus are only possible in nature.'"

Cecil looked back to his company. "In summary, Brendan deduced that a light source great enough to force Recett's exorcism could not be crafted artificially, but could only be found in nature. The person he refers to, I believe, is Edmund Mhersol, an alchemist who worked for him." He leafed a few pages on as he continued. "He proceeds to reference a slew of books and archival records, listing the highest-concentrated lucidus deposits known at the time. Most of them are stroked out, as if they were ultimately insufficient."

"What's considered sufficient?" asked Magnus.

"Brighter than anything that's humanly possible to conjure," Cecil replied. "The spirit possessing Daimos Recett is powerful enough to render its vessel immortal; something of equal power is required to exorcise it. Nothing with such luminosity was recorded to exist."

"What about that thing he was after..." Magnus recalled. "...the Luminous Rock?"

"Yes, this was probably how he first heard of it," said Cecil. "Almost nothing about it would have been documented. In his catalog of lucidus deposits, he makes note of a few locations in the Galem mountains." He turned a page, then another. "His studies swerved to a very specific direction after that."

Cecil scanned the next paragraphs voraciously. "Much of this is familiar to me now. Brendan based his subsequent research on the 600-year-old account of a mountain bandit. As he describes it:

'The man happened upon the crater of a meteorite somewhere in the central-west region of the mountains. In the crater was a cavern, within which he discovered a boulder of golden, luminous crystal. The man tried to obtain a fragment of the boulder by chiseling off a piece with a knife. When the boulder was fractured, an explosion of light was released, which instantly and permanently blinded him. He was rescued by his clan mates, who were the ones to christen the boulder with the name by which it is now vaguely known: the Luminous Rock. Should this account be accurate and truthful, I can infer that the Rock is a super-concentrated lucidus deposit with a luminosity of at least 850 percent.'"

Cecil turned the book out to exhibit a sprawling equation. "He'd done the math, it appears. He was able to estimate the power of the Rock by determining how concentrated a deposit of lucidus would need to be to cause a blinding explosion. A luminosity of 850 percent is unheard of besides the Rock. If Daimos is disturbed by light magic, a blast like the one that blinded the bandit is sure to exorcise his possessor.

"So, as we know, Brendan set out for Galem to locate the Rock for himself," Cecil continued after a pause and a turn of the page. "He goes into some detail about his route; we must review this later. Upon reaching his destination, he writes:

> *'We've found a pit of rubble that may be the described crater. After a thorough excavation, we've uncovered a cavern...I assume something that was carved by the meteorite on impact. Exactly as I'd read, the Rock is within. What an awesome sight it is! Clearly this is some remnant of the meteorite, perhaps its core. To think that this marvel fell from the stars! Blindfolded for safety, I chiseled off a shard of the boulder. The explosion was beyond astounding, even with my eyes protected. Should my troop be followed by Recett, I've veiled the cavern entrance with a cloaking prism. We leave for MorningStar at dawn.'"*

Cecil skipped over another four pages, gleaning sentences at random. "Of course, he returned to MorningStar..." His hands suddenly came still. "And then it ends." He hovered over the margin where the writing gave in to blank sheets like an interrupted song. "He returned to MorningStar to complete his research, and made plans to harvest more lucidus from the Rock," Cecil continued, no longer reading from the book. "Just a few days later, Recett launched a second assault on MorningStar and bludgeoned away what was left of our defenses. When Brendan stayed behind to fight, with the shard of the Rock carried in his dagger holster, he was overwhelmed and slain."

"Not to sound cynical," said Drake, "but there isn't much in those notes that we didn't already know."

"That is true, regrettably." Cecil turned back the pages with a leaden touch.

"But now we know where the Rock is," Magnus reminded. "Didn't you say he wrote all that detail about his route?"

"That might come in useful when we have a course set for Galem, and a lot more people to aid us," answered Cecil. "Right now our course is set for refuge."

"A course through Serenia?" Magnus asked incisively.

"Our best chance to avoid capture lies beyond the MorningStar rift, I am sorry to say." Cecil lifted his head and turned to the others. "Would everyone agree?"

"I trust your judgment," Drake replied. "As much as the thought of that city vexes me, it's the last direction they'd expect us to flee."

Magnus signaled his agreement with a firm nod. The threesome's attention descended on Anubis, who stammered in accord, "I-I concur. We're left with no wiser alternative."

Cecil clasped the notebook and waved it pointedly. "Then know that we now carry something more valuable than all our knowledge combined. Should we find ourselves in imminent danger, this book must be burned immediately! But even then, we will do all we can to ensure that not a word of Brendan's work is wasted. Now...we set course for the rift."

"We can steal across the outskirts of MorningStar," said Anubis, motioning a circuitous path through the air in demonstration, "if we travel far enough northwest before exiting the forest."

"And we can still approach Route 20 directly?" Cecil inquired, and was assured by Anubis.

Magnus' eyes pendulated between the open atlas and the familiar scene of his brother, Cecil, and Anubis crowded around the center table. Drake's wounded arm had been fastened in a sling. Ember sentiently observed the discussion from his roost in Anubis' arms, immobilized by the splint that held his leg.

"Route 20 will take us north to the region of Yewcrest at the Nemus border." Cecil defined the said location on the map, then used his hand to measure the distance from MorningStar, about the breadth of three fingers. "Approximately a two-week hike," he added. "The road passes through a number of towns, but I wouldn't try my luck with any place in Recett's empire, inhabited or not."

"We have no choice but to go on foot?" asked Magnus.

"Recett's wasteland doesn't make for easy travel," said Cecil. "Horseback is a convenient method of transport on

Arkane, but I can't imagine that Serenia has any living horses to speak of. Am I right, Anubis?"

"I would believe the same, yes," said the herbalist. "No animal could survive in a barren land for long. Recett's own men live off food smuggled from outside of Serenia."

"What about velocipedes?" Drake proposed, arousing his brother's curiosity.

"A much more modern and conventional method of transport," Cecil remarked to address Magnus' imminent question. "On Earth, the velocipede is known as the predecessor of the bicycle. The velocipede on Arkane is essentially a mechanical motorbike. Even if we found one..."

"They were destroyed," Anubis interjected. "At least, from what I heard..."

Cecil grimaced, bewildered. "Intentionally?"

"Yes, Recett's doing. Maybe for the same reason all the trains are derailed, and the lampposts are toppled and replaced by torches. He seems to have an ire for anything of modern construction."

"He's a raving madman," Cecil murmured in half a growl, half a sigh. "As if we weren't aware of that already."

"What do we do once we reach Yewcrest?" Drake returned to the subject of their journey.

"We travel on to the capital city of Silvryn," said Cecil. "But the worst of our trip should be over by then. Nemus was a close ally of the old Serenia, and I doubt that its loyalties have swayed to Recett. With its council's support, we'll arrange an expedition to Galem to find the Luminous Rock." His proclamation was echoed by his own silent amazement. "I never thought I'd hear myself say that," he sighed.

"And when we find the Rock," said Magnus, "How do we use it?"

Cecil pensively retrieved Brendan's journal from the table. "That's thinking far ahead." He leafed his way through the book again. "Brendan said something about using..." His fingers slowed and stopped on a page. "He believed that an explosion identical to the one that was released when he broke off the shard...could be simulated by fracturing the shard itself."

"Just breaking it?"

"Either that, or, as he also suggests, overcharging its container. Quote:

'It has been proven that lucidus' volatility increases with its luminosity, becoming more prone to rupture upon overcharge. Lucidus with a luminosity as low as 350 percent, occasionally, has been known to shatter with the use of powerful luminomancy. With this in view, I note that a), the Rock's lucidus is too volatile to be used as a spellcasting aid, and b), shattering it through overcharge is more effective than using physical force.'

"In summary, super-concentrated lucidus can be fractured simply by overcharging it. For something as massively concentrated as the Rock, an overcharge wouldn't require much more than conjuring a weak burst of light."

"Which would shatter it," Magnus recounted, "releasing an explosion bright enough to kill Daimos Recett?"

"Only to render him mortal," Cecil corrected, his expression falling melancholy. "And only supposedly. Even with the depth of Brendan's research, using the Rock to force an exorcism remains an untested theory."

"I don't think my father would have gone to such lengths to study this if he didn't believe it was effective," Magnus adamantly replied.

"No, he wouldn't have," Cecil concurred in a monotone. He shook off his frown. "You're right. I would never doubt Brendan."

The discussion faded, as if there were no words left to offer. Exchanging a mute affirmation with his companions, Cecil heightened his posture to assume a suddenly dauntless air. "So it's set," he declared. "To Serenia."

21

Fleeing Toward the Enemy

ECIL UNSHEATHED HIS SWORD from under his coat and crossed it against the dead air. His shadow knifed the beams of the lucidus torches on the floor of the clearing as he stepped forth. He was followed by Magnus, then Drake, who wielded Cecil's ruby staff as a crutch, and finally Anubis, who sealed the shelter entrance behind them. The click of the door lock signaled their departure from safety.

Cecil stood against the wall of the darkness as if he were facing an armada. To the breathless throb of his heart, his eyes pried into every crevice of the trees in search of their elusive opponents. But the silent abyss did not stir.

"Take the torches and shut them," Cecil instructed in a whisper. "Keep them on you in case we need them later, and don't conjure any light unless absolutely necessary."

Anubis hastily gathered the torches. He twisted each

one by the rim of its opening, inciting a mechanism that masked the torch's lens with a circlet of interlocking metal blades. After the second device was shut, the clearing plummeted into stark gloom.

"Anubis, take the lead." Cecil beckoned his companion ahead. "We'll follow the best-hidden route you know."

Anubis deposited the torches in his shouldered canvas bag, from where Ember peered out afloat a pool of vials and cloth packets. Padding past the slaughtered pickup truck, Anubis ushered the party down the knotted slope that threaded into the glade below the clearing. Reaching the edge of the glade, they plunged into the forest's inscrutable depths.

Magnus secured the straps of his backpack and put his hands before him to paw any obstacles in his path. His eyes gradually adjusted to the night, though he could still see very little. He stumbled often, never seeming to find level ground, as if he were walking on broken cobblestones. When the terrain undulated, he thought he would fall if he didn't grapple the trees for support.

A hushed warning from Cecil jarred the line to a halt; a tense but empty silence arose. "Must have been an animal," Cecil dismissed his alarm and urged Anubis to proceed.

"How far to the rift?" Magnus inquired.

"Four miles, give or take," Anubis replied. "If we plan to stay off the trodden road for most of the way, it's bound to take a couple of hours."

The ground eventually leveled out like a wave extinguished by the shore. As the path broadened, so did the pillars of bark that walled it. The wind was intangible, scarcely with a temperature, yet Magnus felt a chill that seemed to reverberate inside him. He buried his chin in the collar of his jacket and glanced off into the silhouetted treetops. The moonlight that speckled the leaves was guttering with the arrival of a cloud cover. Within another half hour, the skies were overcast and the party's range of sight was diminished to nothing.

Anubis retrieved one of the torches and parted the shield over its lens to a crack. Shedding a meager glint of light on their surroundings, he closed the device and trudged on blindly with Cecil and the brothers. "We should be fine as long as we maintain our direction," he said.

"How will we know when we've reached the rift?" Magnus asked. The shadows seemed thick enough to smother his voice.

"We'll first reach the side road that forks off from the eastern crossroad," answered Anubis. "We'll follow that directly to the clearing where the rift is located."

Magnus acknowledged Anubis' direction with a barely audible drone. His vision rendered ineffective, the darkness seemed to become an inky mirror in which his mind's eye was reflected. An apparition of Raven's red face wafted past him—red like the cover of his father's notebook, red like the ruby that crowned Cecil's staff, red like the blood that had poured from his brother's wound. He wondered what Daimos Recett might look like; he dared to sculpt the warlord's image in his thoughts, out of what macabre descriptions he had been given by Cecil.

From the phantasmal murk emerged a skull warped by a miasma of death. Its gaze seared him in a way that was painfully familiar. He had seen these eyes before, in his nightmare, on the visage of the Saxum Diaboli. He thought he heard the echo of a scream, the one he had heard when he witnessed the spirit of the headstone attack Eras. But then he rattled himself out of his reverie, profoundly disturbed.

He wondered if Serenia was as dark as this. He wondered again, even if foolishly, whether Serenia was real or simply another realm of the endless dream in which he'd found himself trapped for the past four days. Perhaps, if he entered the rift, he would finally awaken.

The group's trek was interrupted several more times, either by their halting to confirm direction or by an ominous rustle that was more likely to be a passing critter than an enemy. Now the ground had become noticeably flatter. Anubis skimmed the forest floor with his light again, illuminating a well-trodden dirt path. "We've reached the side road," he announced.

It was brighter here, too. When Magnus looked skyward, he saw why: trees were sparser in this region, but, more curiously, every one them was leafless. His attention was abruptly summoned back to the path when he was forced to hurdle a fallen trunk with the aid of Anubis' light. He helped his brother across, using his brief moment of sight to inspect the area. "The trees here all look dead," he observed, a second before Anubis snuffed his torch.

"That would be caused by dimensional overlap," Cecil

whispered in return. "The vicinity of a rift tends to develop according to the environment on the opposite side of the rift. What you see here is a glimpse into the withered MorningStar forest."

Magnus stroked the body of each tree he passed, his senses heightened in the soundless umbrage. Bark as cold as ancient bone burned his fingertips. These trees spoke of a plague more wicked than death and mirrored a world untouched by light for over a decade. He would soon be venturing into that world—a place more distant than the farthest planets, yet as close as a forest barely a day's journey from Drake's bookshop, and a place that, according to his brother and his former guardian, was his true home.

The final minutes of the hike blurred into a few erratic seconds, as if time had become irrelevant. Magnus could no longer feel the trees' stony columns alongside him. He slowed until Anubis revived his light. They had entered a bare clearing domed by straggling, emaciated branches. The earth here was far too black to be ordinary; when Magnus stepped forward, soot swirled at his heels.

"Here we are," Anubis declared. "The rift is ahead. You three proceed first, I'll go last."

"Drake, you go after me," Cecil directed. "Magnus, after Drake." He moved in front, with Anubis' torchlight at his back.

Magnus flinched when Cecil suddenly slipped from sight like a candle doused by a gust. In the emptiness left behind, he watched the light become snared and muddied by an unseen haze. Squinting, he saw the air scintillate with waiflike gray static and sway with the quality of liquid glass. Here before him was a rift, a cleft in the fabric of reality and a gateway to Arkane.

"Just walk straight through," Drake told his brother. "You'll emerge instantly. I'll meet you on the other side." With that, he followed Cecil through the aery curtain and vanished as well.

Magnus stared across the deserted arena and readied himself. He had no qualms about proceeding; there was only one way forward, and it could lead him to no worse a situation than the one he and his company were in now. He strode forth, into the rift.

The atmosphere shifted abruptly. For a moment too brief to be measured, Magnus was permeated with a sense of immateriality unlike anything he had ever experienced. Anubis' light had vanished, but it shortly reappeared to sweep the clearing. Drake and Cecil were again standing near him.

"Welcome to Arkane," Cecil sighed with indignant grief. "Welcome home."

The blackness resealed its veil as Anubis shut his torch. "Alright," the herbalist quavered. "I'll take us somewhere secluded where we can camp for the rest of the night." He returned to the lead and began to chisel a path through the void for his companions to follow.

Magnus staggered along at the same pace as before. Here, the darkness was absolute. Neither the sky nor the trees nor the ground gave the vaguest glimmer that would allow one to be distinguished from another. He felt an impulse to embrace himself, as if to ensure that he still existed. There was an ever-present reek of scorched ruin, though he knew that the ash here was not spawned from any fire.

This was Serenia—the land whose name had loomed over his mind for days like some ivory tower. He was nowhere on the face of the Earth, but in a twin reality known as Arkane.

Anubis stopped again and reopened his torch. They were standing at the mouth of a high metal fence that rambled into the dark on either side. The gate was ajar, fixed with an impressive padlock that was rusted fast in place. A little ahead, the dirt path transitioned into a road paved with ash-marred setts and dotted with extinguished lampposts. Cutting the light, Anubis led the others down the east branch of the forest road.

"Are rifts normally locked in?" Magnus queried, brushing the icy gate on his way past.

"Yes," Cecil replied, "and well guarded. Although those who prove their travels to be with fair intentions are allowed entry. Rifts are some of the most secured places on Arkane...save for this one, of course."

Cecil's voice gave in to the hypnotic patter of their feet on the pavement. Magnus spoke again, in a voice almost as quiet as a thought: "You came through here when you escaped?"

"We did," Cecil answered at an equal volume. "And I remember hoping to no end that things wouldn't be like this when we returned."

Magnus shuddered under the suddenly crushing weight of the darkness. After Anubis paused a couple of more times to measure their progress down the road, he steered Cecil and the brothers off the paved path and up a hillside ridden with toppled dead wood. With black ash to slick the soil, every step of their ascent was arduous. The hill rose to a precipitous crown before falling about half as steeply, then rippled on for another mile. The hike ended with a treacherous scramble down the wall of a valley, where Anubis drifted to a standstill.

"I hope this place can offer...sufficient protection." Anubis painted the unsightly canyon with his light. The floor was a mire of ash and wilted underbrush. Exposed roots clawed out from the hillside like the withered hands of half-buried cadavers.

"Thank you. We're as safe out here as we can get." Cecil walked ahead and unshouldered his backpack at the foot of a bowing tree. "Lay out your sleeping bags and try to get a bit of rest. I'll stay up and keep watch."

"I'll take the first shift," Anubis offered. "We should have about four hours; we'll switch in two."

"Thanks again." Cecil nodded and sheathed his sword. "Shut your torch once we get settled. If any of Recett's men approach, we'll see their light before they see us."

Working with haste, Cecil and the brothers unpacked and unfurled their sleeping bags on the brambly soil. Once done, Cecil removed his remaining bag—Brendan's satchel—from under his coat and tucked it between their backpacks gathered in the center of their camp.

Magnus saw the light go out moments after he clambered inside his sleeping bag, which did little to dampen the coarseness of the forest floor. He was surprisingly untired; any fatigue in him was throttled by an incessantly pounding heart. Calming himself was futile. His surroundings were the same, whether his eyes were open or shut. If he drifted asleep, he doubted he would feel any different.

22

End of the Road

AGNUS THOUGHT HE FELT something collide with him, perhaps in the midst of a dream. His eyes lurched open when he realized he was being violently jostled.

"Get up, quickly!" A harsh whisper hammered at his ear.

Magnus scrambled out of his sleeping bag. Anubis rose beside him, his lucidus ring aglow. "Shades are approaching," he grievously announced.

A second light emerged ahead, conjured by Cecil with his sword. Drake stood by his former guardian with his ruby staff fast in hand. The four gathered close, guarded and primed to fight.

It became clear that what Magnus had first believed to be the howl of the wind was the voice of something more sentient. Cecil fired off a piercing shaft of light, which was retorted with a familiar shriek. A trio of frayed shadows suddenly wreathed around them. Cecil expanded his light again to repel the creatures, a moment before a fourth shade narrowly hurtled past his shoulder. Raising his sword, he invoked a luminous explosion that lit the gully with the intensity of a lightning strike. The shades scattered like dust in a squall.

"Grab your bags and keep close," Cecil instructed, stealing up his backpack from the pile. "We've got to leave, preferably for open ground."

They retrieved the last of their luggage, along with Ember nested in Anubis' canvas bag, and sprinted for the hillside. Scarcely five feet on, a slender projectile cut across their path. Cecil dug in his heels and returned a flash from his sword in the opposite direction, but their assailant had already fled.

"That certainly wasn't a shade," Cecil muttered. The tail of his sentence was mangled by another shriek. He expelled a blast to fend off the returning shades. In sequence, a second projectile flitted past Anubis' back.

"I thought Recett didn't want us dead," Drake snapped.

"We thought the same before that harpie slashed your arm," Cecil replied, spurring the others to gather pace. A third projectile soared so precisely over his head that it seemed more of a taunt than a miss. Irate, he lashed out at the dark with a vicious arc of light. He perceived the fringe of a darting figure before his illumination faded.

"Cecil," Anubis timorously called for his partner's attention. "We won't make it out of the forest. I...know a place nearby where we can hide."

A curt rustle whisked everyone's eyes aside. "Lead the way," Cecil approved, and Anubis steered the party back into the gully with his lit ring as a beacon. The shades' voices crescendoed again, then ebbed with the return of their assailant's rapid footfall. Cecil half turned in motion to set his tracks ablaze with light, but the path behind them was empty.

The four streaked across the length of the gully until it thinned back into denser forest. As Cecil pulled his bag tighter over his shoulder, he suddenly gaped and stalled. "The satchel!" he exclaimed. "Where is it?"

"I put it in the backpack, don't worry," Anubis assured, barely slowing.

Cecil nodded and resumed his retreat, when his light was clipped by a shadow that seemed to vault into the tree-tops. He stabbed his radiant sword skyward and seized a glimpse of a lithe, winged silhouette as it flickered against the raveled canopy. "It's the harpie," he warned, dread clenching his throat. "She won't be easy to lose."

Drake shivered at the memory of the harpie's gruesome blow that had disabled his arm. If this was indeed the same beast that had murdered his mother, they had every reason to fear it. But while Cecil and the brothers fought to pick up speed, Anubis began groping voraciously through his bag. He extracted a miniscule bottle of fluid and locked his stance.

"Drake, your staff," Anubis requested, taking the older brother's weapon. He urged his company on and employed the staff's ruby headpiece to ignite the cork-like seal of the bottle. Turning a shoulder, he lobbed the burning bottle into the murk and scuttled after Cecil.

The paltry flame glimmered alive for no longer than two seconds before it ate through the seal and licked the fluid inside. A small but violent explosion tore the glass vessel to shards, unleashing an opaque white smog that billowed to fill aisles of forest around it. When it settled, it hung stagnant as if everything within it had been effaced from existence.

Anubis had just escaped the tail of the smog when he caught up with the others and retook the lead. "The cloud will temporarily blind and suffocate anyone in range," he said breathlessly, returning the staff to Drake. Cecil canceled the glow of his sword, leaving Anubis' light alone to guide them. They ran on a little farther, then stopped at a receding strip of trees along the peak of a short slope.

Anubis withdrew one of the lucidus torches from his bag and poured its beam into a clearing just beyond them. "Across that glade," he described, "there's a grotto...where we can hide. But the glade curves, and the grotto isn't visible from here. I'm going out to make sure it's safe." He passed his bag to Magnus and his torch to Drake, who ineptly wielded the device in the hand of his injured arm. "Take Ember and my light. If the way is clear, I'll signal each of you to come; not all at once."

"First I'll go, then Magnus, then Drake," Cecil advised. Anubis gave a distracted nod and hurried out to take position in the center of the glade. His lucent ring opened a porthole in the shadows through which his upper body was only just visible. Scattering furtive glances around himself, he beckoned Cecil to proceed.

Cecil stole out from the scraggly row of trees and across the empty glade. A step past the bend, and he was gone from the brothers' sight. Anubis motioned the next person forward after a few seconds' delay. But when Magnus moved ahead of his brother, the herbalist dismissed him with a fervent wave of his hand and pointed to Drake.

Magnus twitched back beside his brother, securing Anubis' bag on his shoulder. "I think he wants you to go first."

"Why?" Drake crooked an eyebrow. But he knew that their situation allowed for no complaint. Abandoning hesitation, he followed Cecil and swerved behind the wall of the glade.

Now only Magnus and Anubis remained. He slanted a look at Ember inside the bag, then back at Anubis in anticipation. Even when nearly a minute had passed, he received no signal. He gestured a request to advance, but the herbalist firmly shook his head.

Anubis' stare was distant, as though he had stopped thinking. Their plan must have gone awry. Magnus peered deeper into the glade, troubled for his companions. He wondered what could cause Anubis to appear so anxious while not conveying any indication of imminent danger. Then Anubis inched backward, lowering his light.

Magnus attempted a step into the glade; Anubis lurched with a hand outstretched in fierce yet timid opposition. *No,* the herbalist mouthed. Terror welled behind his eyes.

Go...go back, his lips and arms thrashed to pronounce a voiceless scream. Magnus withdrew, caught between fright and disarray. Anubis' expression guttered to what looked like a desperate plea for help, but only for a moment before he turned and bolted deeper into the glade.

Meanwhile, Drake skimmed his lucidus torchlight over the mouth of the grotto. The entrance was no taller than three feet, framed by lopsided sheets of rock embedded in a low hillside. Crouching, he tucked his staff under his free arm and threaded himself through the gravelly aperture. He dropped to a stand a fair height below. The first thing he saw upon raising his torch was the torso of a man who was definitely not Cecil.

A pair of limbs lunged from behind Drake to clasp his chest and mouth, tearing him backward. When he inhaled to scream, an asphyxiating chemical stench billowed into his lungs. His strength, then consciousness, abandoned him.

Drake heaved open his eyes. Smears of black and orange reeled around him like grimy water. He rolled on his side, hoisting himself off the cold stone and onto a crooked kneel. As the blizzard of dark speckles shriveled off his vision, his environment solidified.

A crowd of at least a dozen armored men encircled him. He was in a stark firelit cavern with twin corridors yawning off in either direction. Cecil was standing beside him; his brother was nowhere in sight. His shoulder sling had been torn off, inciting the pain of his wound to flare as if his arm were skewered with nails. Any possessions he and Cecil had earlier carried—weapons and bags included—were now in the hands of the soldiers that surrounded them.

"And so it ends," said one of the men, who wore a magisterial black watchcoat. It was Noctell Knever. His usual unfaltering aura of pride was magnified by sardonic satisfaction. "Wonderful to see you both again."

"Spare us your fond greetings," Cecil bitterly replied. He shifted his attention off Noctell as an agitated stream of footfall wafted into the cavern, followed by a diffident glow that opened the darkness of the tunnel ahead.

Anubis emerged to stand at the mouth of the chamber. His eyes met neither those of Noctell nor Cecil nor Drake. He was visibly trembling, as he often was, though he didn't seem in any way surprised at the soldiers' presence. Likewise, the men paid him little regard.

"Ah, Anubis...Araiya, is it?" Noctell greeted the herbalist nonchalantly. "My apologies—I've only just been informed." He patted a gloved hand against Anubis' back, his lips unfurling to a grin. "Thank you...for your generous services."

Drake and Cecil gaped in unison. They were engulfed by confusion, followed by thunderstruck disbelief. "No..." Cecil breathed a single word in hope that Noctell's statement would be met with some objection. But Anubis' treachery was affirmed in his silence.

Rage twisted Drake's expression with the weight of hot iron. "Godforsaken double-crosser!" he roared, arms quivering in a restraint of his urge to lunge at the traitor. "What have you done with my brother?"

A spark of realization leapt across Noctell's face. "Excellent question." He swiveled back to Anubis. "Where's the youngest one?"

Anubis angled his eyes even further away from the necromancer. "He...he escaped before I could bring him through the glade."

Noctell gave a look of skepticism mixed with bored irritation. The guard nearest to him keenly offered his help: "I'll head out with a search party."

"Thank you." Noctell tipped his head to the guard, who beckoned the four men at his left to follow him out of the chamber.

"How could you?" Cecil snarled at Anubis through the slit of his teeth. "You knowingly led us into a trap."

"He deserves credit for a lot more than just that," Noctell interjected a wry compliment. "We may never have found you in Markwell without the help of your good friend."

"Then why the devil didn't you just arrest us there, instead of fleeing and chasing us from one burrow to the next?"

"Because you're all brazen idiots and you would have fought yourselves to the death like Brendan if we hadn't pulled away," Noctell replied with an acrid tongue. "You owe us thanks for doing all we could to ensure you reached your destination unscathed."

"You call this unscathed?" Drake indignantly pointed to his bandaged arm.

"Oh, come on now, that was barely a scratch." A sneer enwrapped Noctell's gaunt features. "Just a minor addition to the plan to keep you from running off too soon, courtesy of Medeva."

"Medeva," Cecil recited the name with distaste. "Is that what you call that oversized bat?"

"Sometimes," Noctell answered in a savagely sarcastic tenor. "I more often use the name *oversized bat*."

A cautious chuckle droned from the soldiers. Drake cast a scowl to the sickly-faced figures. "She was the one who chased us here," he added, "right after your men nearly shot us dead."

"The only person I sent after you was the oversized bat." Noctell stifled a laugh. "And take my word, she could have driven an arrow through your skull from half a mile away if she wished you dead."

Drake and Cecil glowered without another response. Noctell shrugged at the silence. "Well, now that everything's cleared up..." He returned his supercilious grin to the herbalist. "Lord Daimos will already have been informed of the prisoners' arrival by the time you reach him; he awaits you with your reward. As you may know, the tunnel will lead you directly into the castle dungeons."

Anubis wrested out the courage to lock eyes with the necromancer. "No harm will come to them?" he requested, though his quavering voice was hardly resolute.

"Why should you care?" Noctell sighed in smiling mockery. "...you godforsaken double-crosser."

Anubis recoiled as if in pain and ducked behind the

cape of his hair. Staggering on his first step, he careened past the crowd and hastened deeper through the tunnel.

"Enjoy this hell as it is!" Drake bellowed into the shadows that steadily immersed Anubis. "You've destroyed all hope for it!"

"Lock them up in cell six," Noctell instructed his men with an offhand wave. "I'll join the search for the youngest one."

The soldiers gathered behind Drake and Cecil to prod them on in the herbalist's tracks. Swiping a lucidus torch from his belt, Noctell headed in the opposite direction with his remaining three men. The last soldier to depart the chamber raised a glove to the light of the torchflames behind him, which were snuffed at the close of his hand.

Anxiety bound Magnus to his spot with the weight of granite shackles. Though it was too dark to see through the glade ahead, he was loath to conjure a light for fear that an enemy would spot him. If his companions were not in danger, they were in hiding—but the stillness told him nothing that could explain either.

He blindly reached for the herbalist's bag to ensure Ember was still safe with him and felt the spined creature flinch under his touch. It was then that, out of the corner of his eye, he saw a diffuse light intrude on the darkness. An instinctive terror filled him, tailed by the hope that his companions had returned. He stole three steps into the glade to peer beyond the curve. Alas, his fears were realized.

A throng of black-clad guardsmen lingered at the mouth of the grotto. After scouring their immediate surroundings with their lucidus torches, they rapidly dispersed. Magnus leapt from sight, his heart and mind spurred to a pace faster than he'd ever thought possible. He bolted for deeper forest, though it seemed as if his fate had already been sealed.

23

Vagabond

NUBIS DRAGGED HIMSELF down the dungeon corridor. He clasped his chest in arms trembling to the point of feeling numb. He was too preoccupied to even notice how long he had trekked through the tunnel to reach here. The throbs of his breath and footfall struck his ears like a gently rapping mallet that, after its thousandth blow, had become agonizing. But he would rather hear anything than silence, for in silence, he would hear his thoughts.

Anubis fought to suppress the memory of the betrayal he had inflicted on his friends. As long as his mind did not stir, there was no guilt. But his concentration faltered repeatedly, allowing the voices of his former companions to echo back to him. He doubted that Drake's condemning shouts would ever leave him.

A far-off clamor jarred Anubis back into awareness. He

inadvertently glimpsed what may have been the mutilated remains of an inmate, and he tore his sight away, dissolving the image in a blur of torchflame. For the remaining stretch of the corridor, he made sure not to lift his eyes any higher than the sparsely blood-mottled floor. He dared not even steal a glance of his old cell, fearing he'd find the corpse of his murdered acquaintance still sprawled inside.

He had been here four days ago—Anubis, along with three of his colleagues, had been arrested by Daimos' soldiers as herbmongers trespassing in the MorningStar forest. For no purpose other than alleviating the warlord's boredom, they were confined and harassed, one of them killed. The surviving three may never have seen freedom had Anubis not offered his aid to Daimos as an informant.

It began as an impulsive excuse to bargain for release. Anubis had never believed he would be pulled into such depravity. A few names, perhaps an address, were the most he had expected to give. But Daimos saw too great a potential in the herbalist to liberate him so quickly. Enlisted as a spy, Anubis had been assured by Daimos that, should he fail on his mission, he would be hunted down and duly punished. His fate became sealed when Daimos' guards escorted him back to Markwell and discovered Cecil's note. Caught between the plea of an old friend and the threats of the most terrifying man conceivable, Anubis could do little but witness himself betray his companions into the same dungeons where his ordeal had begun.

Anubis reached the stairwell at the end of the corridor and left the gory cell rows behind. Scaling the pitch-black shaft on a helix of steps, he plodded through the top door-way and entered the throne room. Daimos, predictably, was sunken in his seat of power. He was in the midst of a heated discussion with Medeva. At Anubis' approach, the warlord stopped and twisted his head on the misshapen stalk of his neck. "Araiya!" he hollered amiably, beckoning the herbalist with an exaggerated gesture. "Come right in!"

Medeva stepped aside, and Anubis shuffled to the center of the floor mosaic, a cautious distance from the throne. "E-evening, milord," he returned the greeting, his head locked in a bow to avert eye contact.

"I've just been informed of your success." Daimos grinned, molding his face to match the vivid outline of his skull. "Splendid. Our gratitude is immense."

There was a pause before Anubis realized he was expected to respond. He gave a faint nod. "Yes...yes, thank you. With everything in order, I trust that...no harm will come to the prisoners, as agreed?"

"That depends," Daimos cut in with a sudden sternness, like the pound of a gavel.

Anubis waited for an explanation, but the warlord said nothing more. "On...what?"

"On whether you finish your work," Daimos answered matter-of-factly.

"What do you...I thought I—"

"Handel and the eldest Wingheart are safely stowed away, yes, but I believe we're still missing a third member." Daimos rose off his throne. His threadbare cloak rippled about him like an aura of smoke. "After the assault in

Markwell, Noctell brought to my attention the existence of Brendan's younger son, whom you entirely failed to mention in your report. Where is he?"

Anubis gawked as if he'd been asked some impossible riddle. "He...he fled before I could lead him into the tunnel. He could be anywhere by now."

"How unfortunate," Daimos commented starkly. He came to stand in front of Anubis, who would have seemed petrified if not for his trembling. "Any member of Brendan's family is valuable, and so that boy must be captured. Bring him to me and you may have your reward and your freedom."

"But I don't know where he is!" Anubis exclaimed, slurring his sentence into the length of a single word. "Noctell sent the guards to search for him. There...there isn't anything else I can do."

"Does the boy know about your betrayal of the others?" Daimos inquired.

Anubis stalled in search of an appropriate answer. "I don't know," he replied.

"Clearly he knows enough to have fled in the first place," Daimos pointed out. "What was it that he saw?"

"I don't know," Anubis repeated, growing more anxious still. "He could've seen anything. He just...ran."

"Perhaps he heard something." Daimos' tone turned scathingly insinuative. "Perhaps he heard a warning. Perhaps some confused fool told him every detail of the plot in a desperate attempt to thwart the inevitable."

When Anubis failed to answer with anything but a

speechless stammer, Daimos seized the timid man by his throat. Anubis strove to hold his ground, tautening every muscle in his body against his shuddering.

"I know you're lying," Daimos condemned with a glower hard enough to shatter steel. He constricted his grasp, wresting a guttural cough from his victim. "Are you going to make it up to me? Or is your last use to me as another trophy to mount in my hall?"

Anubis shook his head with mindless conviction. He was scarcely listening to Daimos. Eyes shut, he flailed and clawed at the warlord's bony shackle like a feral animal. Daimos was unperturbed, but growing irritated. He abruptly cast Anubis to the floor. "You're worthless," he spat, waving dismissively. "Get out of my sight."

Anubis gaped up at the black-shawled skeleton. He couldn't believe what he'd heard. But Daimos snarled and reaffirmed his demand: "Go!"

Anubis was barely on his feet before he began to run. He waited for the warlord to deceive him and murder him at the turn of his back, but the assault never came. He shrank into the distance until he hurtled himself against the entrance doors, ramming them open to a crack just wide enough to slip through. When the doors growled shut, Anubis was gone.

Daimos immediately turned to Medeva standing nearby. "Follow him," he ordered. "There's a fair chance he'll lead us to the one we're after, the younger Wingheart."

Medeva regarded the instruction with an insipid twitch of her brow. "I suppose you want them alive?"

"The boy, specifically. Araiya's fate is irrelevant."

Medeva gave no further response and exited the chamber in measured paces. Her vision not shifting an inch from the doors ahead of her, she followed the entrance corridor out of the castle.

The courtyard lay in its usual sepulchral slumber. The torchlight only reached as far as the battered buildings at the periphery of the court, but Medeva had perfect sight of Anubis scurrying down the main road. Her vision was unlike that of any human—she saw clearest in absolute darkness. Beneath the shades' ever-present umbrage, her stealth and perception were unparalleled.

On a mighty flap of her wings, Medeva vaulted into the air. With no effort, she climbed to the skies. The citadel stretched below her as a grid of cinereous stone interspersed with flames, drowned in a miasma of ash. She observed Anubis scuttling through like an insect on a desperate run for its life. The loitering guards would seize him at every corner, harassing him with questions about his haste for no purpose but their own amusement, only to release him in their boredom.

After some time, Medeva saw Anubis reel through the citadel gates and slacken his speed in exhaustion. The harpie glided to rest on the roof of the gatehouse, from where she watched her target trudge into the city streets with a conjured light to illumine his way. When Anubis reached the brink of her vision, she soundlessly dove off her roost and followed.

The buildings beyond the citadel were mostly intact,

but derelict nonetheless. MorningStar was a city swept not by destruction, but by death—like the long-forgotten grave of a king whose glory still coruscated behind each soot-stained window. Even so, it remained an insoluble abyss that darkened with every step away from Daimos' fiery keep.

Medeva soon overtook Anubis and dropped to a perch on a fourth-storey balcony littered with broken shingles. Beneath her lay Galliard Square, once the bustling heart of the city. A dry fountain jutted out amidst an arena of bleached flagstone, which wound off in an arabesque pattern of walkways. There were none of the citadel's crude stone torches here, and the ornate lucidus lampposts scattered about were either toppled or non-operational. Striking frontages of all sizes—those of canopied artisanal shops and decorous public buildings—gazed out across the court with an unperturbed air of eminence. One could take the scene for a glint of brilliance frozen in time; to a more rational eye, it was like a crowd of ghosts unaware that they were no longer amongst the living.

In due time, Anubis hurried into the square and lingered by a lamppost to catch his breath. Medeva looked on dutifully, unblinking, unflinching. Her hair always half-curtained her face without ever seeming to obstruct her vision. Her profoundly indifferent expression showed a level of reserve unmatched among most human beings.

Medeva no more than touched on the thought of pity for the man scampering below her. Anubis had his life so helplessly laid in the harpie's palm without even knowing it.

She was invisible to him; at any given moment, she could hurl a knife and strike him dead. In letting him live, she was simply postponing a worse fate that had been clear to her from the moment Daimos unhanded the man.

Anubis exited the square, westbound. Medeva hurdled the balcony railing and slipped back into the skies on the black sail of her wings. For miles she trailed him, every so often descending to skulk across the highest rooftops. Anubis' stamina was impressive for someone of his scrawny build, though his fatigue showed. He staggered on with crazed determination all the way to the outskirts of the city. Ascending a broad hill, he met a crossroad marked with a tarnished signpost: Court St.; Markwell Rd.; Elm Rd.; MorningStar-Markwell Rift 2.5 miles. The MorningStar forest rolled out across the base of the hill like a prison of charcoal swords. Anubis followed Markwell Road off the bank, directly into the forest.

Even in the confines of the woods, Medeva was undetectable. She lurked in the scraggly weavings of the treetops, crawling as though on wire mesh, never gripping a branch too thin to hold her. Her abilities were decidedly inhuman—apt for a creature inhuman as her.

She maintained sight of Anubis whatever his pace or direction. He seemed even more frantic here, with very little sense of where he was heading. It became apparent that he was looking for something, or someone. The truth came in his desperate shrieks to the darkness: "Magnus!" His voice was only a strained whisper at first, but it loudened when his search wore on without result.

Anubis eventually found his way down into the gully where the harpie had attacked him and his companions earlier that night. "Magnus!" His calls were relentless. He cast his light over every foot of parched earth to no avail. When he stopped shouting, he began to pace around aimlessly as if he were wrestling with an array of unsavory options. He finally bolted south, down the winding channel that led out of the gully.

Medeva knew Anubis' destination with such certainty that she was tempted to simply proceed ahead of him. She only remained in his tracks for a chance of spotting the fugitive Wingheart. As she had anticipated, she followed Anubis directly into the glade surrounding the entrance to the citadel dungeon tunnel. For one last time, Anubis glanced about, then turned with a cringe and a shudder and clambered inside the grotto.

Medeva withdrew to the overarching peak of the cedar on which she was resting. Anubis was hurrying to rescue his companions, no doubt, after having failed to track down the boy. He would be captured in the castle with pitiful ease.

Just then, another, frailer light glinted far below the harpie. It emanated from a figure that began to tail Anubis with ponderous hesitation. Medeva stole to the lowest branches of the tree for a clearer view. It was the younger Wingheart. As he padded through the glade, the boy didn't seem to be stalking Anubis as much as he was simply unsure whom he was following. Medeva prepared to lunge, but decided against it when she watched the boy slink inside the grotto after Anubis. There was no use in causing any commotion here; all loose ends would be tied once the runaways reached the dungeons.

Medeva soared over the forest again. Acres of straggling black spears cascaded under her vision while she surveyed the ground beyond. She spotted the occasional one of Daimos' soldiers, who lingered about with evidently little interest in the manhunt they were meant to be conducting. The lot of them looked as if they'd given up by now. Among the few still actively searching was the man who proclaimed his authority with his imperial watchcoat. Medeva swooped down behind him.

Noctell whirled around with his lucidus torch extended to the harpie. Medeva grimaced at the light and indignantly batted the lamp aside. "The boy you're looking for followed Araiya into the tunnel," she reported.

"What?" A scowl flared over Noctell's face. "That can't be. We've been searching the forest for hours."

"Am I to blame for your incompetence?"

"You're to blame for your own incompetence! Why didn't you seize the boy when you saw him?"

"Because there's no use in trying to seize an animal already bound for a trap," replied Medeva. "I'm heading back to inform Recett. Get a move on to the tunnel, and we'll corner both the boy and Araiya in the dungeons."

"If that's how you decided to scheme things..." Noctell gave a deprecating shrug and bustled past the harpie. A sudden squall lashed his back. When he glanced behind, Medeva had already leapt out of sight.

Anubis walked every step through the tunnel with the fear of seeing an enemy's face emerge from the dark. The light cast by his ring extended hardly three feet in front of him. Walls of coarse limestone, occasionally patched with bricks, flowed alongside him to no end. His legs shivered from weakness, but he was too determined to care. No matter Daimos' threats that had forced him into the role of traitor, Anubis knew he alone was responsible for his companions' capture, and he alone was responsible for freeing them.

He hovered his light over the half-empty bottle in his hand, something he had found near the tunnel entrance. An enwrapping label explicitly denoted the substance as *athamine*, an inhalation anesthetic most often used as a knockout drug. The rest of the label teemed with safety precautions. From his left vest pocket, he pulled out a wadded cloth rag he had found with the bottle, unfurling it for examination. It radiated the scorching narcotic odor of athamine. Clearly the chemical had been used to disable Cecil and Drake for capture.

If Daimos' nonchalance was consistent, the warlord would have no more than a single guard stationed in the dungeons. With the athamine as his weapon, Anubis hoped he wouldn't be required to put up much of a fight. He waved away the stench and stuffed the rag back into his vest pocket.

Anubis briefly augmented his light as the tunnel

widened into an oblong chamber with two carved entrance-ways. One was marked by an "x" scratched in chalk on the wall beside it, supposedly a crude sign to guide the way to the castle. He proceeded through the marked entrance.

Anubis had been here only twice before, the first time on the night he and his herbalist colleagues had been hauled by Daimos' men through the tunnel and into the dungeons. He knew almost nothing about the mysterious passage or how it had originated. In places, the rough wall structure suggested a former use as a mine, but there wasn't much else to uphold the theory. The tunnel looked strangely ancient; no doubt it had existed long before Daimos' time, even Brendan's. If it wasn't once a closely guarded secret, it was a forgotten relic unearthed by the warlord for reasons unknown.

After miles, the tunnel came to an abrupt end and opened to a room of flat stone walls—the castle cellars. A crowd of barrels and grain sacks huddled in a filthy corner, a share of the citadel's smuggled food store. Anubis walked on through the only doorway in sight, into a meandering hall with a low vaulted ceiling. Pitch-black rooms gaped at him as he walked past. The hall terminated at a steel door with a small barred window, which he peered through vigilantly.

The dungeon corridor lay beyond. Since the castle had never originally housed a prison, Daimos had utilized a large part of the cellars to construct his cages of torture. Anubis saw a guard seated languidly on a chair near the door; Cecil and Drake were in a cell farther on. Withdrawing from the door window, Anubis renewed his quaking breath in a vain attempt to stoke his courage. He unscrewed the cap of the athamine bottle with clenched lungs, then produced the rag from his pocket to moisten it with the chemical. He dared to breathe again only once the resealed bottle was set aside and the wet rag tucked in his fist. After a final moment of wrangling his reluctance, he opened the door.

The shrill moan of the hinges seized the guard's attention. The balding square-faced man glared at Anubis with contempt, which then settled into bored expectation. "You again?" he croaked like an inebriated dog.

"I—" Anubis lost his words in the pit of his throat when his eyes met those of his scowling companions in the cell. He turned away and swallowed to speak again. "One of the prisoners had my bag when they were arrested. I came to retrieve it."

"Over there." The guard shrugged toward the heap of coats, backpacks, and weapons on the floor across from him.

Anubis stalled a moment, then stepped ahead and crouched to sift through the confiscated equipment. The guard looked on with aloof impatience until he appeared to be struck by a thought. He tossed a glance in the direction of the door. "Hey, what were you doing back in the tunnel? Didn't I just see you—"

Anubis cut short the guard's sentence when he whipped around to deliver a vicious flash of light from his ring. The dazed guard staggered to his feet in defence, only to be smothered by Anubis' athamine-soaked rag. He barely managed a groan against the cloth before he toppled back, unconscious.

"Now what?" Drake barked from his cell the moment the guard struck the floor. "First you betray us—"

"Quiet!" Anubis pleaded in a whimper. He discarded the rag and kneeled to rummage the pockets of the comatose guard. "I'm breaking you out!"

"If you're looking for the keys, they're not here," Cecil said astutely. "The guard who locked us in made off with them upstairs. Give us our weapons and I should be able to destroy the lock."

Anubis scrambled away from the guard and stole up the prisoners' staff and sword from the pile. Cecil and Drake charily accepted the weapons through the cell bars. While Cecil began to show at least a prudent willingness to cooperate, Drake's resentment was hardly eased. "Where's my brother?" the older Wingheart interrogated.

"I don't know!" Anubis earnestly shook his head. "I saw him last in the forest. I came here because I thought he might have already been captured."

"So now you're our savior?" Drake roared, thrashing the cell bars with a fist.

"Savior or not, we've got nothing to lose," Cecil reminded. He secured the staff's ruby headpiece against the cell lock. Sparks fluttered within the gem as the iron encasement was dappled with a searing-red hue.

"I swear to you, I would never betray any of you by my own will," Anubis vowed in a voice wrenched by remorse. "I'm far from innocent, but this is the only chance you have! Please! I'll explain everything once we're out of here!"

Without letting up his scowl, Drake sighed in compliance. "How do we leave?"

"The same way we came in. If there are any soldiers, we'll have to fight our way through."

Cecil wrested out every ounce of power in the staff until the metal had slumped under the heat, dissolving the lock to a dented wad of molten iron. A finishing blow by the trunk of the weapon broke open the door. The inmates rushed out of their cage, but were halted before they could so much as reach for their equipment.

"Oh, pity. That was a perfectly good cell," a deathly cold drone pierced the corridor. Noctell Knever entered the dungeons from the tunnel, a small mob of soldiers at his back. With the escapees' startled eyes upon him, he jostled forward a disheveled figure—it was Magnus. "Now settle down," said the necromancer, "and we'll try not to hurt anyone."

In the moments that Cecil, Drake, and Anubis idled to weigh their options, the soldiers trod in to surround them. As the prisoners opened their arms in surrender, their weapons struck the floor with a sound that seemed to echo on perpetually until it fused with the throb of footsteps on the dungeon stairwell.

"Visitors!" a voice that could only have belonged to the dead poured out from the shadows. When the creature reached the bottom of the stairs, it stood with the ostentation of a mad king and the appearance of a man cursed by every mortal ill. "All together at last!" Daimos Recett proclaimed, beaming. "Welcome to MorningStar."

24

A Deal with the Devil

MAGNUS COULD NOT HAVE imagined a person more hideous. Daimos was a nightmare in flesh, or, more correctly, skin and bone. Drake seemed no less appalled at the sight. Anubis simply withdrew, head hung in terror-struck disappointment. Cecil met the warlord's sunken eyes dauntlessly, as if confronting an old enemy.

"What an honor," Cecil announced with cutting resentment. "Daimos Recett, I presume."

Not a moment after the warlord's arrival, a second shadow parted from the darkness of the stairs. By its slender contour and five-foot-tall wings, its identity was instantly clear. Magnus and Drake shivered at the dread that skewered their hearts like a crooked arrow. Before them, for the first time unveiled to them in torchlight, stood the wicked chimera that so long ago murdered their mother.

"And I see you are accompanied," Cecil added, "by the oversized bat."

Medeva raised her brow with stoic surprise. "I'm amazed you have the nerve to insult a person at first sight."

"That was how your associate introduced you." Cecil gave a nodding gesture to Noctell, whose lip twitched in amusement.

"I wouldn't listen to someone with an ego larger than their head," the harpie answered flatly, collapsing Noctell's expression.

As Daimos came to stand before Drake, he smiled as if every part of his world had fallen into place. "Wingheart!" he exclaimed. "It's been so many years. I can hardly believe myself in thinking that this chase has finally come to an end."

"Then I trust you have a worthy reason for gathering us here," Cecil interjected. "Unless there really is no method to your madness."

Daimos droned a laugh. He turned to Cecil with half-shut eyes that burned with insanity. "Sixteen years ago, I waged a war for the control of this city. In the heat of the final battle, its council head, Brendan Wingheart, was slain. On his corpse, my men found a singular, most disturbing object." The warlord rasped a feral snarl. "A terrible thing. A stone that blazed with light, like a piece of the sun! I had my men study it, to discover whence it came, to discover how an inferno so bright could have been sealed within a block of crystal.

"Ah, but then...it exploded! And blinded them! Blinded

them! They said it shattered to unleash the light of ten thousand flames! All that remained? Splinters of lucidus so unremarkable that they could have been scrounged out of the dirt." Daimos' languorous smile returned as his fury subsided. "It had already come to my attention that Brendan had acquired a new weapon; I believe that it was this stone. And that is why I have hunted you. That is why I have gathered you here—so that, perhaps, you could lend me some information."

"I apologize, Recett..." Cecil bowed his head solemnly. "...but we are no physicians, and I certainly know of no way to cure the blind."

Daimos murmured another laugh that sounded more like he was trying to dislodge a rock from his throat. With no warning, he lashed up a hand doused in black sparks and grazed Cecil's chest. Cecil cringed and grimaced in restraint of a scream. As his captor withdrew, he embraced himself to stifle the pain that smoldered behind the burn marks on his shirt.

"Your sarcasm is unwelcome, Handel," said Daimos. "Your knowledge is what I require. I would like you to tell me everything you know about this wretched item that Brendan harbored."

Cecil forced a smirk through the ebbing pain. "I'm surprised that you, of all people, would be scared of a glowing pebble."

"You think my caution is for my own sake?" Daimos scoffed. "The shades are the only creatures at risk here. Surely you don't believe that I would fear such a petty thing."

"Surely," Cecil rejoined, "you don't believe such a petty thing could destroy even a shade."

Daimos sobered immediately. "You are hardly in a position to question my purposes. Now are you going to tell me what I wish to know, or will I have to wring it out of your throat?"

"What gives you the idea that we know anything about it?" Cecil retorted. "I wasn't even a member of council."

"After the war," Daimos replied with little attention given to Cecil's argument, "Medeva informed me of an exchange she had observed taking place between you and Brendan Wingheart. Something involving a parcel of mysterious content. A parcel containing research of some sort?" He leaned nearer in anticipation. "Something... about a rock?"

"Is that all you're after?" Cecil widened an eye in feigned surprise. "Then just search us and be done with this. You've already rummaged all our homes, I'm sure."

Anubis and the brothers flinched in shock at Cecil's blatant suggestion. "Empty their bags," Daimos barked to his men. The soldiers stole up each of the prisoners' backpacks and shoveled out their contents by hand. But as the last food can rattled to the floor, it became apparent that the bags contained little more than camping supplies.

"Is this everything?" Daimos returned his frown to the soldiers.

"Yes, milord," Noctell confirmed. He produced a tarnished navy jacket, which he slung into the pile with the rest. "The boy carried nothing but an empty coat."

"What is it you're expecting to find, exactly?" Cecil inquired. "A bundle of papers? A book? Some coded scrawl on the back of a map?"

Daimos tightened his mask of skin to declare his impatience. "My question is not very complicated. I wish to know what was contained in the parcel you were given by Brendan."

"Brendan claimed it contained his research," Cecil answered promptly. "But an error was made, you see. In his haste, Brendan gave us a parcel containing an irrelevant herbology notebook. By the time we'd discovered the mistake, Brendan was dead and the city had fallen." Cecil's smile approached derision. "You've wasted sixteen years hunting us down for something we've never had."

"Do you expect me to believe that?" Daimos didn't seem to even remotely consider that Cecil was telling the truth.

"What would be the point of my lying? Don't you think we would have employed such research by now, if we had it? We've lived all these years in peace; does that not tell you anything?"

"In that case," the warlord replied, "tell me why I shouldn't just kill you all where you stand."

"Why should you?" Cecil countered calmly. "We've done you no harm. If anything, we've put your concerns to rest."

"You've wasted my time." Daimos' voice dropped to a raucous hiss. "Many years of my time. And this I deem punishable by death."

"That seems hardly fair. There isn't anything more we can do."

"You could speak the truth, fool." Daimos brought a half-splayed hand between his and Cecil's faces. His fingers glistened with dark energy like a live wire of deadly voltage. "Because I sense you're leaving out some details."

"Shall I bring the hexed ropes?" Noctell proposed. Magnus could assume the ropes in question were the same ones that had been used to bind him during his interrogation in Markwell. His gut clenched at the thought.

"I'm not interested in fiddling with hemp," Daimos impetuously scorned the idea. "There are blunter methods for extracting the truth." He angled his head as if he were selecting a lamb for slaughter. "Which one of you should I kill first?"

The warlord turned and lunged quicker than any of the prisoners could even think to stop him. A sprawl of black lightning, like monstrous talons, struck Drake and hurled him back against the cell row. "Wait!" Cecil cried on impulse, but without any idea of what else to say.

"Go on," Daimos urged, pulling the half-unconscious Drake to his feet by the front of his shirt. He pinned the older Wingheart to the bars as he raised a hand afire with dark energy. "Tell me all you know, or I'll read the words out of his blood!"

"I'll tell you!" A desperate shout sounded at the warlord's back. Daimos released Drake instantly and turned with fervor in the direction of the cry. There, scowling and shivering, stood Magnus.

"I'll tell you," Magnus reaffirmed his offer. His companions gaped at him with shock and despair, but stayed mute in fear of making an already horrible situation worse. The boy watched Daimos drift toward him with the poise of a phantom.

"What an unlikely candidate." Daimos' expression leapt from a frown to a sneer. "Go on, boy, speak!"

"Will you release us all unharmed if I do?" Magnus asked, voice quavering as he struggled to maintain his stern composure.

"That depends on what I hear," Daimos replied in a ghastly whisper.

Magnus swallowed hard and forced out a reply through half-paralyzed lips: "Cecil is telling the truth. But last night, we discovered that the herbology notebook was a guise, and that the real text was hidden. The hidden text was a journal by my father. That was the research he was talking about."

"Research," Daimos drawled, "on what, pray tell?"

"Something called...the Luminous Rock," Magnus answered, nearly choking on the weight of his words. "The glowing stone you found on my father was a piece of it."

Any trace of hope left on Cecil's face withered away to the deepest sorrow; the same could be said for Drake, and even Anubis. As Magnus poured out the truth like the blood of an animal spilled in sacrifice, it seemed as if an eternity of efforts had been unraveled. But lives were worth more than truth.

"The Luminous Rock..." Daimos said in a manner that tainted the name. "I've never heard of such a thing. Perhaps I could see this research for myself."

"It's gone," Magnus replied. "I burned it when your guards came after me in the forest."

Daimos' brow furled up over his skull with caustic skepticism. "How convenient. I don't suppose you could tell me a little more about this Luminous Rock?"

"It's the core of a meteorite," answered Magnus, "made of lucidus."

"Oh really?" The warlord appeared dangerously unconvinced. "I'm led to believe that the object in question is considerably more powerful than something used to power a streetlamp."

"Highly concentrated lucidus," Magnus amended. "More so than was ever thought to exist."

"You say a lot with very little to substantiate your claims."

"I don't have anything to substantiate them; the book was burned. But I read it all. I could tell you where the Rock is...then you could go there and see for yourself."

Daimos hummed a laugh. "Enlighten me."

"I will if you promise to release us," Magnus staunchly replied.

"I promise to release you," Daimos said with a trivializing smile.

Magnus was suddenly loath to speak further. He realized it foolhardy to think that the warlord would keep any such promise. But when he lingered too long in silence, Daimos whisked his eyes back to his other captives and seized Drake again.

"In the Galem mountains!" Magnus exclaimed on an impulse of panic.

Daimos thrust Drake out of his grasp with twice as much force as before. "Let's not make this more difficult than it has to be." He growled a sigh, which oddly morphed back into laughter. "Where in the mountains, boy?"

"In a crater," Magnus quavered, "five miles northeast of some valley. That was what my father wrote."

"Excellent." Daimos faced the boy to bare a grin like a misshapen gash.

"So you'll release us?"

"Now why would I do that?" the warlord asked almost as if it were an honest question. "I don't even know if such a thing exists."

"Then send your men there and find out," Magnus replied. "Once you're sure I'm telling the truth, you can release us."

"Fascinating proposal..." Daimos gazed to the ceiling in feigned contemplation. "...but I have a better one. If you have faith in your claim, boy, you will journey to Galem yourself and destroy the Luminous Rock."

Silence ensued; each of the prisoners returned stares of astonishment smothered in doubt. "Are you joking?" Cecil exclaimed.

"Why should I risk leading my men into a trap?" said Daimos. "Let the young Wingheart prove his own tale."

"That's ridiculous!" Cecil snapped. "Send that boy alone and you're sending him to his death!"

"Oh, he won't be alone." Daimos shifted about his eyes in their cavernous sockets, then turned in the way of the harpie lurking at the opposite end of the corridor. "Medeva will accompany him."

Cecil lanced a glare at the harpie, whose expression barely flickered with surprise. He looked to Drake and Anubis, who seemed no more confident than he. But Magnus' resolve had not faltered by much.

"Then once we find the Luminous Rock and return," said Magnus, "you will release us?"

"Once you find the Luminous Rock," Daimos corrected, "and destroy it."

When Magnus opened his mouth to speak, he felt as if a knife had been readied at his heart. He knew the consequences of the actions he would be required to take, but he had no better chance at freeing his companions. His reply rolled off his tongue like lead: "I'll do it."

"No..." Drake whimpered, crumpling back against the cell row.

"Spare the boy," Cecil interposed firmly. "I will go in his place."

"I'm afraid not, Handel," Daimos sneered behind an obdurate frown. "You've caused me enough trouble already." He gripped Magnus' shoulder in a rawboned claw. "In a gamble of lives, I choose the most valuable—the soul most treasured by all of you. The boy will be the one to do away with the Luminous Rock; your and the elder Wingheart's freedom will be considered only once his task is complete."

Magnus forcefully shrugged off the warlord's hand. "What about Anubis?"

"This buffoon?" Daimos swiped Anubis' scraggly hair in a fist and hauled the man forward like a ragdoll. "I can hardly imagine why you would want to free your traitor." Magnus gave a look of bewilderment, to which Daimos responded with something of a cackle. "I suppose you were not aware..." said the warlord. "Araiya, you see, has served as my informant since your stay in Markwell. With his aid, I formulated a plan that ultimately led to your capture in the forest tunnel. Stricken with guilt, he scrambled back here to free his friends, only to end up a captive himself."

Magnus maintained an incredulous stare at first, then looked to his companions in question. His brother delivered a resentful nod. "It's true, Magnus," Drake affirmed. "If it wasn't for him, we wouldn't be here."

Magnus turned a suddenly seething scowl to the herbalist, whose eyes shivered with anguish and screamed innocence. "Please, Magnus!" Anubis begged. "I was forced! I'll explain everything... Please don't leave me to die here!"

Magnus drained away his rage in a sigh. "You can explain later. I won't leave anyone behind." He faced Daimos again. "I will destroy the Rock, and in return, you will release all of us, including Anubis."

Daimos beamed with revolting content. "You have my solemn word." But his tone seemed less than solemn. He snapped his sinewy neck in the direction of the stairwell. "Medeva, take the boy upstairs."

The harpie waved a stone-gray hand in a motion to

follow, and Magnus trudged on through the corridor behind her. His step lingered by his despondent companions. "I'll be fine," he muttered. "Trust me."

Cecil's reply was a crestfallen grimace. Drake watched his brother dwindle into the distant stairwell like a wisp of smoke curling off a dead torch. He was too deep in sorrow to even comprehend his own fears. Only in the pit of his mind did he realize the risk of never seeing his brother again.

When Magnus and Medeva had departed, the warlord beckoned over his elite guard. "Noctell," he called. "Get the hexed ropes. You will confirm the boy's tale." He turned ominously to the three remaining prisoners. "...on Cecil."

"Of course, milord." Noctell hastened to the stairs with disturbing enthusiasm.

"Don't look so glum now," Daimos jeered in response to Cecil's glares of contempt. He produced his key ring from his belt and whirled it around a gaunt finger as though he were flaunting a band of priceless jewels. "From the day you left this city, Handel," he said, "you knew this could not have ended any other way."

Magnus was ushered into a chamber that he assumed to be some large storeroom. It was too dark to discern much. After Medeva, Daimos entered, wielding a blazing ancient oil lantern, which he set at the edge of a table. The firelight gave shape to a prodigious barricade of crates that occupied the rest of the room. Staffs, swords, and parchment rolls jutted out from the mass, so smothered in dust that they appeared colorless.

Daimos extracted a parchment roll—one bundled around a pair of three-foot rods, like a scroll—and dropped it onto the surprisingly uncluttered table. "Have a seat, boy," he invited in a melody that might have sounded cordial were it not for his ever-scathing undertone.

Magnus descended onto one of the two chairs at the table. The harpie and the warlord remained standing. With a sweep of his hand, Daimos unfurled the parchment over the table's tapestry of wood scars. It was a badly faded chart of the three southern Arkane provinces: Serenia, Nemus, and Galem.

"The Luminous Rock," muttered Daimos, "is where, you say?"

Under the sputtering firelight, Magnus struggled to make out the broken swirls of ink swimming on the jaundiced parchment. He placed a hesitant finger on a network of ridges that separated Serenia and Galem. "The Galem mountain range," he answered.

"Where in the mountain range?"

"As I said, five miles northeast of..." Magnus tried to distinguish any kind of detail in the evanescent map print, but failed to do so. "...a valley. My father wrote something about Old Galem."

Daimos' features twitched with curiosity. "The valley of Old Galem city. Yes. And your planned route?"

"I don't know." Magnus shook his head weakly. "I don't know anything about traveling on Arkane. I've lived on Earth all my life."

Daimos uttered a scoff at the back of his throat. "Very well." He leaned over the map and knifed a bent fingernail across the short stretch of land west of the mountains. "You will leave MorningStar by Route 5, heading east. Once you reach the town of Flynn at the River Venieres, you will travel off the paved road and through the Venieres Forest. The mountains lie beyond."

"I still don't know any of those places," Magnus insisted. "Can I at least take a map?"

"Never mind. Irrelevant to you." Daimos dismissively waved a hand over the chart. "Medeva will lead the way."

"Milord," Noctell called from the doorway, tearing Magnus' and the warlord's attention off the map. He exhibited the rope coil gathered in the bend of his arm. "I've gotten as much as I could out of Handel. He confirms all the boy's descriptions."

"Does he," Daimos replied in more of a remark than a question.

"The stone found by Brendan was indeed a shard of the Luminous Rock," Noctell continued. "Handel says he knows of no other such shard existing. The parcel he received from Brendan, he says, contained nothing more than the notebook the boy spoke of, and a piece of basalt."

Daimos narrowed his eyes under veinous, paper-thin lids. "Why the devil would Brendan give Handel a piece of basalt?"

"The ropes are nearly infallible," Noctell assured. "I've never known of anyone deceiving them."

"For all our sakes, I hope you're right." Daimos turned an indignant frown back upon the map. "Now I would like you to go and prepare a flask of black acid for our voyager—something to destroy the Rock when it is found."

"Certainly, milord." Noctell bowed his head and sauntered out. As he departed, the doorway was eclipsed by another familiar figure.

"I heard the news," Raven crowed, ducking into the chamber. Gilded by the firelight, he loomed like an apparition of the devil himself. His grin was faintly visible. "Glad to see you've come to your senses and agreed to lend a hand."

Magnus glared at the demon from out of the corner of his eye. "I guess Daimos is short of able men if he's forcing his own prisoners to work for him."

Raven's smile thinned to one of dry amusement. Daimos uttered the first breath of a laugh. "Make yourself useful, Raven. Fetch the boy a new coat and a backpack filled with five days' worth of rations and a waterskin." He turned to Magnus with a motion to the boy's diamond pendant. "I trust that you, Wingheart, are equipped to conjure anything else necessary for survival."

Raven gave a disgruntled drone of agreement and plodded out of the room. Daimos parted the slit of his mouth to speak, but was halted by his captive.

"If you're certain that the Rock exists now," said Magnus, "why don't you just send your own men to destroy it?"

"Because you're useful in more ways than one," replied the warlord. "I don't suppose you know of the Rammeren?" Magnus shook his head, and Daimos continued: "The bandits that lurk in the mountains as the self-proclaimed border guards of Galem. They have a peculiar distaste for us in Serenia. Medeva has a decent chance of flying past, undetected, but they would never allow any of my men passage, and I'm not about to waste my time on a war with cave dwellers. You, boy, they would never think anything of."

"Then send Medeva alone. I've already told you where it is."

"And risk her life in destroying such a volatile object? I think not." Daimos' touch hovered over the mountain range on the chart. "You will rejoin Medeva once you pass the Rammeren. From there, you will need to devise a route to wherever you believe this Luminous Rock to reside."

"I should be able to find it if we go through the valley," Magnus replied. "That was the route my father took."

Daimos' expression suddenly hardened, as if he were offended or even troubled. "There is no need for you to traverse the valley."

Magnus was momentarily speechless. "I don't know if I'd be able to find the crater otherwise."

"You will travel around the valley. Is that understood?"

"Why?"

"Because it is dangerous." Daimos hammered his palms on the table as he buckled forward, impaling his glower deeper into Magnus. "Do you need any better a reason?"

"It can't be that dangerous," Magnus contested. "My father traveled through there."

"I don't know about your father's course, boy," Daimos answered in a tone perhaps more somber than Magnus had ever heard from the warlord. "What I know is that there are some things you'd be wise to avoid, regardless of your strength. Places that crush the sense of what it means to be powerful. The valley is one of those places, and if you insist on treading its roads, I may as well save you your voyage and kill you where you sit."

Magnus was fiercely skeptical of Daimos' warning, but his circumstances didn't allow him to argue. "Fine," he said. "We'll go around the valley."

"I thought so." Daimos rolled shut the map in a single swipe and skewered the bundle back inside the clutter.

Noctell promptly reentered the storeroom. He was carrying a bulbous black flask, which he set on the table under the irascible glow of the lantern. "The black acid, milord."

Daimos seized the vial to scrutinize it, then portentously extended it to Magnus. "Possibly the most corrosive substance known to exist," he described. "A few drops would be enough to burn off your hand. Be wary."

"The amount I've given you should be enough to dissolve a small monolith," Noctell said to the boy. "It evaporates quickly, but use only as much as you require to destroy the object."

Magnus accepted the flask with a cringe. It was burning-cold and heavy. The opaque glass of the container, which had obviously been fortified against the acid in some manner, was so dark that it appeared two-dimensional, as if it devoured light.

"So your course is set," Daimos declared, turning to exit with Noctell. "Come, come."

Magnus rose and followed, trailed by Medeva, whom, in her silent presence, he had nearly forgotten. They proceeded back into the castle corridor from where they had entered. Raven was already advancing toward them through the fiery miasma. As Noctell and Daimos stepped aside, the demon thrust a slovenly folded bundle into Magnus' arms. "Your accoutrements, sir," said Raven in a mordant hiss.

Magnus dissected the heap to find a crude leather backpack and an overcoat of some indefinable murky color. He dropped the coat to slip the black acid flask inside the bag. "What's wrong with my old coat and backpack?"

"Glaringly suspicious," Daimos replied. "If you're going to pass the Rammeren, you need to at least look like you belong to this world."

Magnus heaved on the coat and shouldered the backpack. Daimos motioned him on through the corridor. "I take it that you're ready to leave?" said the warlord.

"Wait." Magnus slowed. "I want to see Cecil and Drake again before I go."

"You will see them again when you return," Daimos snubbed the request. "You've already wasted enough of my time. The sooner you get moving, the sooner they'll be freed."

Magnus grudgingly yielded and resumed his dismal march. Surrounded by his enemies and forced into a sordid mission alongside his mother's murderer, it seemed that his world had been inverted in the most dreadful way conceivable. In his ire, he blamed Anubis, but accepted that the herbalist had likely been no more than a tool. Just as Daimos had now enlisted Magnus as his pawn, no one was to blame but the warlord himself.

The corridor met the entrance hall, where Daimos, Noctell, and Raven withdrew to allow the boy and the harpie passage. Magnus bravely glanced overhead to meet eyes with the corpses above, which returned him eyeless gazes of the deepest despair. But beyond that despair was something else—like the cadavers' ancient wish that those passing beneath would fare better than they had.

Magnus faced the entrance. Medeva thrust open one of the prodigious doors, inciting a chilling whirlwind. With feet that seemed heavy as stone, Magnus followed the harpie out of the castle. Before him, like a shadow-drowned mirage given form by a hundred eyes of flame, the citadel loomed.

Medeva reached behind to unsheathe her halberd from a holster nestled between her wings. Clapping the weapon's blunt end to the stone, she led the boy down through the courtyard and onto the main road. Every guard they passed became roused with interest, angling glares at Magnus in wonder of what business such an inconspicuous youth could have with such a menacing creature. But with the harpie present, they dared not ask.

Magnus eyed the buildings with awe yet strange familiarity. He had seen these grand façades in his dream two nights ago; he had seen these bricks and shingles and glass, and the ash that stained them. The scene became more haunting the longer he looked. He saw very little when he turned skyward, but he reckoned it was for the best—for beyond that darkness was not a night sky, but a storm of bones he wished he would never need to behold.

When he turned back to the road, he was captivated by a glint of metal from the mouth of an alley. He stopped and peered in to see a peculiar mangle of gears and steel framing half-devoured by rust.

"It's a velocipede," Medeva answered the boy's unspoken question. "Move on."

Magnus lingered by the alley a few seconds longer before proceeding. "The velocipedes...why were they destroyed?" he asked, hardly expecting a response.

"Because they alluded to an era that Recett was unwilling to acknowledge," said the harpie. "He shaped his world to the only one he believed would triumph. In the end, this only inhibits him."

"You don't sound very reverent toward your master," Magnus shrewdly remarked.

"Unlike the others here," Medeva replied. "I'm not a follower nor admirer of Recett."

Curiosity lined Magnus' widening eyes. "Then why are you working for him?"

This time, no answer came. Only after some moments, she spoke again. "Don't waste your time with conversation," she said. "Your fate is bound to a promise you would be wise to fulfill quickly."

25

A Pawn No Longer

RAKE PRESSED HIS FACE through the prison bars, which he clenched in the numbing fist of his uninjured arm. His discomfort had grown irrelevant to him; he dwelled in his seething mind, where his environment seemed but a backdrop. Cecil rested against the wall near him, one leg arched, arms folded. In the opposite corner, Anubis was crumpled up, unmoving, his hair wilted over his face.

At the far end of the corridor, their jail guard sat inert on a chair outside the cellar door. The hood of his cloak was draped so low over his face that it was difficult to tell whether or not he was actually keeping watch of the prisoners, let alone whether he was even awake.

"What time is it?" Drake asked in a monotone.

Cecil pushed his sleeve off his wristwatch. "Eight thirty-two."

"Morning or evening?"

"Morning."

Drake's angst subsided for a moment. "Doesn't make a bloody difference." He delivered a vehement kick to the cell gate before turning and slumping against it.

"Please at least try to calm down," Cecil sighed. "There's nothing we can do at this point, so you may as well just save your energy."

"Calm down?" Drake repeated as if it were an absurd suggestion, turning to his former guardian. The torchlight made his features appear as gaunt as those of Daimos' soldiers. "My brother just left to wander in a wasteland with our mother's murderer as his guide! And I don't even know if he'll return!"

Cecil tried to respond, but found himself at a loss for an answer. He could only hope that the boy would be safe in the company of one of Serenia's deadliest fighters, and that the deceptive warlord Daimos wouldn't go back on his promise.

"I'm sorry, Drake." Cecil shrank back against the wall. "This is my fault to begin with. If they'd never found me, we wouldn't be stuck in this ungodly place."

"Cecil, none of this is your fault." Drake shook his head sullenly, then affixed a livid stare on Anubis. "It's yours." But the herbalist did not even show his face in response.

"It's your fault," Drake went on, "that we're imprisoned. It's your fault that my brother's life is on the line, and even if he does make it back, you'll be the one to blame when the

Rock is destroyed and all this world's chances of victory are lost forever!"

Cecil gave no comment. Anubis shuddered, but said nothing.

Drake threw his head aside and growled. "Sickening coward..."

"Just...!" Anubis exclaimed, but lost his words in a guttural whimper. He pressed his fingers against his eyes and respired. "Just let me explain."

Drake returned a silent, impassive glare. Anubis heaved a breath and pulled up his head. "Last week," he said, "I traveled to the MorningStar forest with three of my colleagues, as we do every few months, to gather dried Arkane foliage for our trade. We've been doing it for years...never had any trouble, even though I knew we were tempting fate every time we came near here. That particular evening, our luck betrayed us. For whatever reason, there was a troop of soldiers in the forest that spotted us and hauled us to these dungeons."

Anubis cast a glance across the low ceiling, then shut his eyes as if to sever his vision in disturbance. "Daimos came to harass us. One of my colleagues, Margus, was strangled to death when he rebelled. Then Noctell and Raven entered. By the sound of it, they'd just come back from raiding Cecil's house without much to show. That angered Daimos to the point that he was prepared to murder all of us just to quell his frustration.

"What I did then I now regret terribly...but I told Daimos

that I knew Cecil personally. I thought I might be able to trade a few harmless shreds of information for the release of my remaining colleagues and me. I didn't say a lot, of course, since I didn't even know much more than Daimos already did. But it was enough to settle his rage, it seemed, and he set us all free.

"Sadly, our freedom was limited. Each of us was escorted back home by a pair of Daimos' soldiers with the purpose of recording our addresses. In my case, my house and shop were searched. By some twisted mockery of fate, the soldiers found Cecil's letter when we arrived at the apothecary. They used a strange sort of magic— some teleportation method involving ash rather than any potion—to transport me back to MorningStar.

"After reading the letter, Daimos thought I was perfectly suited for the job of informant. He demanded that I report Cecil's location within the next two days, else he would hunt down me, my colleagues, and all their families, and inflict unthinkable punishment on the lot of us. Should I abide, he promised me freedom and a reward, which I pretended to desire so that he wouldn't hold any suspicion against my loyalties.

"I could have run away then and there, but I couldn't abandon you with your plea. Knowing Daimos' men were in the forest, I was too much of a coward to abandon my task. When I reported to Daimos, he devised a plot to drive you into capture and held on to me as his operative."

"Is that what the attack in Markwell was about?" Cecil interjected temperately.

"Yes," replied Anubis. "Daimos believed that trying to arrest you forcibly would only risk your escaping, or worse, fighting yourselves to the death. The purpose of the Markwell attack was to ensure you'd have no place left to run but MorningStar."

"And the poisoned dagger?"

Anubis shook his head with conviction. "I knew nothing about it. When Drake was wounded, I feared for the worst. I later figured that the shock poison was a diversion to allow Daimos time to set up his trap in MorningStar. My final step in the plot was fulfilled last night, when I notified Medeva that you were in the forest. By that point, the inevitable was fast approaching, and if nothing else, I could try to slow Daimos down.

"Later, I slipped Brendan's satchel inside Magnus' backpack. When we were at the glade, I left Magnus to go last, then sent him away before he could follow you two. I hoped that he would be able to stay hidden in the forest for long enough that I could make it back there, find him, and rescue you. It was a feeble attempt that ultimately failed, of course...but it was the best I could do."

"Why my brother?" Drake asked. It appeared that he had calmed considerably.

"I reckoned he would be the most inclined to abide," Anubis answered. "Luckily, it seems he left his bags behind in the forest, along with Ember, since he wasn't carrying anything when Noctell caught him."

"That was why I goaded Recett to search our things," Cecil added. "With Magnus' bag missing, there was a chance that the satchel wasn't with us, and I needed to be sure. When Recett first approached us, I did my best to steal his attention and orchestrate the conversation in our favor. I vainly thought I could convince him to release us. We can only be thankful for our lives. At least the research was never found."

"Not that it's made any difference." Anubis folded his head back into his hands. "Our last hope is still bound for destruction, and there's no one to blame but me."

Drake was brought to a somber temper after hearing Anubis' account. "No," he sighed. "No one is to blame but Recett. I'm sorry for being so...stubborn. I'm just worried about Magnus."

A leaden silence came and passed. "I fail to see what Daimos hopes to accomplish," Anubis moaned, "by killing every soul that sets foot in this place—by striving for invincibility so maniacally. What's his aim in ruling a barren empire for an eternity?"

"You cannot define the reasons of a madman," said Cecil. "Recett has no interest in the land he rules. His ultimate will is that of his possessor."

"And what would that be?" Drake asked in reply.

Cecil's expression turned mordantly grim. "Pray we find out soon enough."

26

Eyes of the Forest

ITH MORNINGSTAR more than a day's travel behind him, Magnus could almost convince himself that he had never left Earth. Route 5, the road that stretched east of the city, was eerily reminiscent of the highway to Markwell he had traveled with Cecil and his brother. Paved with a substance not unlike asphalt, it speared into the distance, unwavering. Beyond a partially toppled road barrier were planes stippled with dead trees, which hemmed in crumbling farmhouses and fields of withered grain. The only explicit difference between here and the Markwell highway was the prodigious ashen cloud cover. The rising sun was filtered to little more than an indiscernible glow on the horizon.

While Magnus hiked the road, Medeva spent most of her time airborne, hovering in the farthest reaches of the sky like a shadow no more conspicuous than a falcon's. Miles of travel with meager rest were already taking their toll on Magnus; Medeva, conversely, didn't appear the slightest bit worn from her voyage by wing.

By the afternoon of the second day, the road had carried Magnus into Flynn, the town that Daimos had spoken of. Unsurprisingly, the place was derelict. Magnus passed a wistful eye over a row of abandoned homes, a sizable inn, and a strip of shops with shattered windows that gaped like toothy gashes. Even out here, Daimos' ruin was intensely present.

Medeva descended to guide Magnus the rest of the way out of the town. After cutting through a field by the side of the road, they saw the Venieres forest take shape around them. First to emerge was a graveyard of stumps crowned with dagger-like splinters; the trees that followed were not much different than those in MorningStar. An undulating slope marked the mouth of the forest, where Magnus drew to a halt.

"Wait," he called to Medeva, who had already moved far in front. "Shouldn't we rest before we head through?"

"I don't see a need," Medeva answered, barely slowing. "You can still walk, can't you?"

Magnus shed a frown of jaded frustration and staggered down the slope. "And I don't suppose you're too tired or hungry after all these hours of gliding overhead?"

"How could I be?" Medeva replied. "I do not need food, nor do I sleep. Such limits don't affect me as they do you."

"Just what are you?" Magnus shouted over the distance,

mustering a burst of speed to draw even with the harpie. "Some kind of golem created by Daimos?"

Medeva faintly scoffed a laugh, her back still to the boy. "The very suggestion is appalling. I'm of my own immortal race."

"If you're immortal," Magnus said astutely, "then why was Daimos so concerned about sending you to destroy the Rock without me?"

"There's a difference between immortality and invincibility," Medeva retorted. "I do not age, yet I can be killed."

Magnus saw Medeva's form blur as the umbrage thickened. He suddenly found himself in darkness, which suggested that the forest was either impossibly dense or deep as a canyon. Clutching his pendant, he fashioned a sun in his mind's eye and evoked a steadfast glow to the diamond. He raised the jewel as his torch, unveiling a world of ominous splendor.

The trees that towered over him, though dead, were colossal and visibly ancient. Their roots gripped the earth with infallible strength, upholding twisted columns that lurched toward the heavens like the arms of titans. Their branches, which forked and interwove with labyrinthine complexity, clawed at the sunless sky as if ravenous for light.

Magnus hurried to catch up with Medeva, but she veered aside and thrust out a hand at his approach. "Keep that thing away from me," she snapped.

"What, my pendant?" Magnus swept a glance from the jewel to the harpie. "How can you see anything without a light?"

"I see clearest in the dark," said Medeva. "Your light only blinds me."

Magnus complied with Medeva's bizarre suggestion and withdrew to a reasonable distance. The terrain was still steepening, without any end in sight. When his path tapered to an eroded furrow, his foot became snagged under an exposed root. He promptly lost balance and shifted his weight onto a tree for support.

Then a murmur pierced his ears—a shivering moan like the croak of a steel-throated crow—sounding from nowhere in particular. When Magnus recoiled on impulse, the voice slipped away as if he'd only imagined it to begin with. "Did you hear that?" he called to the harpie.

"The whispers?" Medeva answered from far ahead. "They're the arboryn. Stay wary."

"The what?" Magnus sprinted over a mostly bare hillock to catch up.

"Arboryn," Medeva repeated. "Tree spirits. Normally harmless, but in a place like this, they may be dangerous."

Magnus intentionally leaned near to another tree as he passed it; the same whisper resonated, this time shaped to a word of ungraspable intricacy. A much more strident groan of the trunk startled him away. "Dangerous how?" he asked.

"Ask yourself," said Medeva, "what it would be like to have your surroundings turn against you."

Magnus gazed up at the walls of the forest with a new-found sense of terror. It was just as easy to marvel at the trees as it was to reckon them petrified leviathans. "Would they attack us?"

"Maybe," Medeva replied grimly. "The death of the forest has driven them to defending their environment with blind madness."

Magnus refocused his vision uneasily, as if a mob of beasts were suddenly looming around him. From there on, the austere scenery continued with little variation. In every direction that Magnus turned, the lifelessness of the forest prevailed like a plague, as though the Reaper himself had scored every tree with his scythe.

But then, inspiring a jolt of both awe and confusion, a single still-living tree emerged. It was stout, not very tall, but upheld an enormous bushel of leaves. It brandished bark and roots as radiant as those of a sapling, in stunning contrast with the wilderness around it.

Magnus strayed toward the tree with childlike fascination. "Incredible..." he mused aloud. "Of the entire forest, this one tree is still alive." An abrupt tug on his coat restrained him.

"Stay away." Medeva hauled the boy back. "An arboryn is fueling it with life."

Magnus dug in his heels and gaped at the tree from afar. He saw its branches shudder, then come motionless. An indignant creak bellowed from somewhere behind him. The dead forest suddenly seemed far too alive for comfort.

Medeva unsheathed her halberd. As she dropped its blunt end to the dirt, a root twitched at her feet. "We need to hurry," she solemnly advised. "They don't want us here."

Medeva and the boy spurred past the living tree and deeper into the forest. Now the voices were returning—first individually, as no more than sporadic coughs of displeasure, then as a feverish babel in which each word poured into the next. Their language was incomprehensible, almost ethereal, with an inflection like the crackle of tree bark.

Magnus didn't know whether to be amazed or disturbed to encounter so many more lush trees. The withered world that had moments ago encompassed him was rapidly giving way to greenery. Once-dead branches now teeming with leaves crowded his vision, while the ground, earlier strewn with black underbrush, was transformed into a morass of quivering shrubs. In correspondence, the voices multiplied.

Magnus felt as if he were running on the back of a serpent. Even the earth seemed to heave and slump to the rhythm of the voices. But the second he slowed to regain balance, Medeva goaded him on with urgency.

"What are we supposed to do?" Magnus hollered over the bedlam. He received no warning before Medeva leapt and tackled him to the ground. Magnus tried to come upright, but the harpie pinned him to his place as a hefty tree limb came down in a violent slash over their heads.

Magnus scrambled to a stand as the harpie unhanded him. "What—" he blurted out, totally disoriented. "Did a tree just fall?"

Medeva seized the boy by his collar and heaved him onward. "Nothing fell," she barked. "The branch was moving!"

Magnus gawked ahead, hurled back into a furious pace. His surroundings blurred to writhing splashes of foliage;

he had given up trying to distinguish anything. He staggered with each step and kept from falling only by latching onto every tree he collided with.

A swarm of branches lunged in to obstruct the path like a poacher's net. The harpie swept down her halberd blade and cleaved the web deftly. But as she recoiled, the branches' severed ends lashed out and voraciously tangled the weapon.

"It's pointless to fight them," shouted Medeva, wrestling for control of the polearm. She unsheathed her shortsword from her belt holster and hacked at the wooden vines until they shrank away meekly and relinquished their hold. "Run for any open space. I'll try to defend."

Magnus did his best to obey the instruction, though finding open space seemed like an impossibility. He ran with his head pulled between his shoulders to avoid coming within range of the largest branches. As the voices ebbed in their flow, he could hear the forest shivering with wrath.

He and Medeva had scarcely gone twenty feet before a buckled oak swatted at them from the base of a hillside. Medeva raised her halberd to meet the rugged limb, gashing the wood at the impact. The oak flinched and withdrew as a brassy roar of anguish knifed the clamor from some distant place.

Then Magnus felt something take a fierce grip of his ankle. Caught in step, he toppled face-first into the dirt. He tried to stand, but found himself firmly latched to the ground by a root roped about his foot. When Medeva turned back to aid him, a dangling net of ivy snared the tip of her halberd. Again, she drew her shortsword, only for a second vine to grapple her wrist in defense.

Magnus heaved himself onto his palms and pulled away. The root held on and towed him back, then wrenched. He scrambled onto his back and locked his ankle fast in place just in time to save it from being broken. As long as he was near the ground, the branches above could not reach him. But the root was relentless. In the struggle, it abandoned trying to break his ankle and instead grew unbearably tight. He almost failed to notice that a shrub had taken hold of his left arm.

Medeva surrendered her halberd to the vines to be able to draw one of the daggers at her belt. In a perilous maneuver, she stabbed the blade twice to the vine that clutched her wrist, causing the woody manacle to quail and release. Sheathing her dagger, she slashed the remaining vines with her shortsword to free her halberd.

Magnus felt the shrub and root tug in opposite directions, as if with the aim of dismembering him. When the attempt failed, a thread of ivy lunged out from the shrub to coil around his neck. A gasp of agony was all that Magnus could muster before the vine began to throttle him. His pendant's light guttered out, and any vision he had left was crumbling to black stains. His pain was fading, but he knew it was only because he was turning numb.

Relief came with a fierce gust—as if by the swoop of a sword—across the back of his head. His senses surged back to him as he felt the severed ivy lynch trickle off his shoulder. He saw Medeva deliver a final strike with her halberd to the root at his ankle, unbinding him entirely.

Magnus clambered to his feet. As his lungs heaved, his body gushed with needles. Half-blind in the dark, he strove to reignite his pendant, but failed hopelessly. He thought he felt another vine grab hold of his sleeve and tear him forward; thankfully, it was the harpie.

"We're almost out of the grove," Medeva announced, hauling the boy alongside her.

With two more attempts, Magnus managed to conjure a fresh light. Around him, the forest's greenery was waning. Emerald mingled with charcoal as dead obelisks rose in the place of leafy pillars. The voices were disbanding. It seemed as though he and Medeva were leaving the arboryn's domain, but the spirits remained unappeased.

A sonorous crackle, like a stone colossus rising to life, shattered the air. When Magnus saw the wooden monolith emerge, he didn't dare turn his head to face it. He pressed on with reckless speed. He heard a crushing swoop, a second before Medeva bashed him aside. Sprawled over the edge of a hillock, he glanced past his shoulder to see the monstrous tree limb seize the harpie by the end of her wings.

Magnus looked on helplessly. Under what little light his pendant shed, he watched Medeva, suspended some thirty feet above him, swivel the spear of her halberd over her shoulder to stab the limb with merciless repetition. Inevitably, when the branches cringed and retracted, the harpie plummeted to the earth.

Magnus rushed toward her, but Medeva pulled herself to a stand and furiously waved him away. "Go! I'm fine!"

Magnus obeyed with hesitation and faltered onward, well out of breath. Within another minute, the voices evanesced. He found the courage to halt only once the flimsiest tinge of green was far behind him. He crumpled against the side of an evidently inanimate tree and turned to Medeva at his back.

The harpie approached steadfastly, but with a hand clutched to her buckled waist. Her wings were half splayed and torn considerably; one jutted out, warped, like a cracked mast.

"Your wing is broken," Magnus diagnosed with alarm.

"That's not my main concern," Medeva replied. She unlatched her hand from her waist, exposing a tear in her leather armor smeared with ink-black blood. "I've been poisoned."

"What?" Magnus gaped. "How?"

"Two of the daggers on my belt are tipped with tanaxyde poison," she answered, eyeing the mangled set of holsters at her waist. "When the arboryn dropped me, I was cut by one of them."

Magnus opened and shut his mouth at a loss for words. The dire implication that arose in his mind settled in his gut like a lead ember.

"My poison works to stop the heart, and no less," said Medeva. "I have two hours to be cured."

27

Set in Stone

WITH ANOTHER HOUR of travel, the harpie led Magnus to the edge of the river Venieres that coursed through the forest. Here, the trees receded to unveil the clouds and the sun's diffuse veins that struggled through them. Vast banks of gravel lined a languidly coasting waterway that rambled into the haze in both directions.

Medeva folded against an uprooted, prostrate tree by the riverside. Magnus slumped to the ground in front of her. "How much time do you have?" he asked.

"About an hour," she replied. "Longer if I don't move."

"What about your wound?"

"Only a cut. It will heal quickly. The poison is my main concern."

Magnus propped his forehead in his hand. "I'm supposed to find..."

"Taren bark, as I said, will suffice," Medeva answered impatiently. "Head northeast along the river, turn back into the forest where the river forks, and search there. You won't encounter any arboryn."

Magnus pulled himself straight and suspired, stoking his strength with river air. He secured his backpack and came to his feet. "You don't eat or sleep," he muttered, "but you can be poisoned by your own weapon."

"My black blood differs from yours, but I have blood nonetheless," the harpie retorted. "Be grateful it isn't you who's poisoned. Tanaxyde would kill a human in minutes."

Magnus grimaced, turning away. "I'll hurry."

"That would be best," Medeva replied as the boy departed.

On weary legs, Magnus hastened along the river. He held no sympathy toward the harpie, his mother's murderer, but reminded himself of the other lives at stake. Surely, if Medeva perished, Daimos would see to it that Magnus and his imprisoned companions suffered a similar fate.

Reaching the fork in the river, Magnus turned and dove back inside the trees. The rapidly thickening forest forced him to rekindle his pendant. As he opened his grip on the jewel, the light glazed his hands to reveal cuts like those by the slash of a nine-tailed whip—the brutal works of the arboryn, whose thorns and burrs still clung to his coat. He palmed his neck to feel the band of scars left behind by the tree spirits' attempt to strangle him. It was disheartening to think that even the last of life in Serenia had been driven to such insanity.

Magnus picked up his pendant and focused its light to scrutinize the trees. After having leafed through the pages of Cecil's herbology encyclopedia, he well recalled the distinctive chalk-stroked texture of the taren tree. The species was said to be common over most parts of Arkane, but in such gloom, each tree showed hardly any difference from the next.

Magnus fought to curb his gnawing anxiety and to remain thorough in his search. Even with Medeva's assurance that the arboryn were far away, he found himself glancing about with every lurch of his heart, fearing a glimpse of greenery. When he became confident that the trees around him were dead as fire logs, he was consumed by panic over not being able to return to the wounded harpie in time.

A while into his quest, he came across a peculiar squarish object faintly outlined by his pendant's light. He moved up closer to discover a set of decaying wooden planks propped against the foot of a tree. Intrigued, he kneeled and extended his light for closer inspection. The boards were laid overtop each other and feebly held in the form of a cross by a rusted nail. There may have been a thread of text etched into the horizontal plank, though the artifact's ancient age made it impossible to decipher any such writing.

It looks like some kind of grave marker, pondered Magnus. *Who on earth would want to be buried in this awful place?*

He shook his head at his own thoughts. Obviously the forest hadn't always been like this. It was only sixteen years ago that Daimos had cast his shroud of death over

Serenia, and the grave marker was no doubt decades older.

Magnus surveyed the neighboring area. There was a second, equally dilapidated grave marker not far from the first. He clambered up in front of it and swept aside the brushwood to clear his vision. As with the marker before it, the inscription etched into the wood was worn away and illegible.

He pulled himself upright and stared at the marker in a senseless trance. He allowed his eyes to wander off the grave and into space, when he was sharply reminded of his chore—to the immediate left of the marker was a tree whose bark was grazed with streaks of pale white.

Relief washed over Magnus as he leapt to the taren tree. He traced his thumb along the furrows of the trunk until he found an open crevice. Stabbing his nails into the crack, he pried out a shred of the prized bark, which he slipped into his trouser pocket. He swiveled about in an attempt to reassess his direction, when his attention was diverted back to the lopsided grave markers.

There, between the graves, was a vaguely trodden path that tunneled into the shadows—as if carved by the frequent passage of travelers. Magnus succumbed to his curiosity and drifted closer. Aside from Daimos and his men, Serenia was practically deserted, yet this path hardly looked as if it had been abandoned.

Magnus leaned into the path, but his light wasn't nearly strong enough to see far. Assuring himself that he had sufficient time to return to the harpie, he inched further down the path until the two graves slipped into the shadows behind him. Before long, he had strayed far from his original course, and the channel ahead still yawned deeper.

He encountered another two grave markers a bit farther down the trail. These were planted on either side of the path, crumbling under the weight of their years in the overgrown woods.

More graves, Magnus noted. *Maybe there used to be a cemetery here...this path was probably made by people who'd come to visit it.*

He took a second glance at the markers and dismissed his theory. *No*, he concluded. *None of these graves look like they've been visited at all, and these tracks are fresh. There must be something else around here.*

Magnus jostled a tree limb out of his way and peered further onward. A third pair of grave markers lay ahead, nestled within an ivy-smothered plot at the right of the path. Unlike the ones he had discovered before, each of these markers consisted of a solid stone slab.

He approached and lowered himself to eye level with one of the graves. The deceased's name was considerably more legible than the inscriptions he had seen on the wooden stakes:

Lucifere Hade
2757 – 2799

Magnus bit his lip in thought. According to the Arkane calendar, the current year was 3808. That implied that the grave was over a thousand years old.

He angled his head to look past the tombstone. The trail, oddly, coursed into a knot of soaring dead trees with no continuation in sight. Undaunted, Magnus confronted the abrupt blockage and pressed aside the rigid veil of branches that obscured his vision. There was a clearing ahead, but it was a void beyond the range of his light. Striding over a mound of roots, he wedged himself through the fissure between the trunks and reeled into the clearing.

Magnus drew in a gasp, which bit his lungs like broken glass. It felt as if his heart had been throttled to a stop. What lay before him was an image he had seen before—and one that was inerasably burned into his mind.

He was in a clearing, but more distinctly, a ruined cemetery. Rubble piles and rotted grave markers were scattered around him. Only a single headstone stood tall and prominent in his vision. Its foundation was a colossal plinth from which rose a pair of emaciated arms and hands. Within the clasp of the hands, raised as if in an offering to the gaping black heavens, was a giant skull of stone— an immaculate sphere with a broad, notched cylinder of teeth fitted beneath it, and a set of drooping hollows for its eyes and nose.

It was the Saxum Diaboli, the headstone of Sennair Drakathel.

I don't believe it. Magnus gawked at the malefic headstone. *I won't believe it. This can't be real.*

He clawed into his pocket and extracted the taren bark shred. Clutching it under ghostly white fingers, he felt for every rut and knob in its surface. He looked to his palms still scrawled with cuts. He knew he wasn't dreaming this time.

Magnus returned the bark to his pocket and trepidly faced the Saxum Diaboli. The forest cemetery was identical to that from his nightmare. The stone rose as tall as Magnus and was in astoundingly good condition for the age it was said to bear. It was the only grave in the cemetery that had its perimeter swept of woodland debris. Clearly, it was far from forgotten.

Magnus trod up to the side of the kingly monument, careful not to fall within the gaze of the skull as if in fear of being devoured by it. He was strangely terrified, but marveled at seeing his dream manifested as a perfect reality. When he stood close enough to touch the sculpture, he held out his pendant to illuminate every crevice of its deathly features.

In my dream, Eras pierced the top of the stone with a dagger, Magnus recalled. *If it's still there, it could confirm everything.*

He gathered the nerve to cast his light onto the scalp of the granite skull. Three daggers. He was thoroughly shocked at the sight. The hilts of three daggers protruded from the crown of the headstone without the smallest fracture to mar the surface around them. Which one of the daggers was Eras', and to whom could the others belong? When Magnus had first seen the cemetery in his nightmare, Recett was the only one to have impaled his blade into the headstone.

Magnus drew a finger up the hilt of the middle dagger.

The metal was so cold that it numbed his touch. Stamped on the pommel of the hilt was an emblem he had seen before in MorningStar: Daimos' skeletal cult icon.

This has to be Daimos' dagger, he assumed. *It means that my dream was true...that the ghost possessing Daimos is Sennair Drakathel.*

He allowed his hand to glide down the face of the stone skull. It was apparent that Daimos had drawn considerably from Sennair and his cult—the headstone was carved in the likeness of the same skeletal icon.

Magnus locked his stare on the remaining two knives in the Devil's Stone. *But what about the other daggers? If Sennair used one to possess Daimos, then whom else is he controlling?*

He sought an answer to his question in the rightmost dagger. This one was adorned with an iron arabesque that wrapped all corners of its hilt, but, most noticeably, it was inlaid with a flawless marble. He gazed into the marble as if he expected to glimpse the face of the weapon's owner, but saw nothing more than his own distended reflection.

Lastly, Magnus flitted his eyes over to the leftmost hilt. Its appearance was generally nondescript, apart from a silver crest on the dagger's grip. Shimmering in Magnus' diamond light, the crest depicted a kite shield entwined by a helix of ribbon. Its design made it appear the most noble of the three knives, but it just as well lacked anything that could tell Magnus to whom it belonged.

He finally withdrew from the stone. *I need to get back to Medeva,* he reminded himself. *But once this is all over with, I'll come back here with Cecil and Drake. This grave alone could be the key to explaining everything I saw in my dream, and a lot about Daimos' history.*

Magnus' train of thought was choked when he glimpsed a stark-white apparition at the edge of his vision. He lurched around on an impulse of terror, but the object was gone as if it had never existed.

A chill breeze fell over the cemetery. Something in the way the wind soughed, like an irate inquiry, told Magnus he wasn't welcome here. He stood defiant at first, but the dread that began tearing at his heart was unbearable. His blood cooled; his lungs seemed to wither thin. He took to his feet and escaped toward the trodden path. With a parting glare of disdain, the Saxum Diaboli slunk back into the shadows.

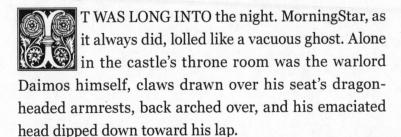

28

Forever Loyal

T WAS LONG INTO the night. MorningStar, as it always did, lolled like a vacuous ghost. Alone in the castle's throne room was the warlord Daimos himself, claws drawn over his seat's dragon-headed armrests, back arched over, and his emaciated head dipped down toward his lap.

Daimos Recett was a powerful man with a nefarious history. He had spent his life as an unswervingly devout member of the New Order, a cause to which he gave all his soul, strength, and wholehearted allegiance. His aim had been to gather every remaining follower of the Order and reestablish the goals that had been set out by its original founder, thereby shaping the cult that he now commanded as a fearsome warlord.

Daimos' reign had ended sharply, however, when his forces were struck down by the Serenian army and the

MorningStar Guard. His hopes shattered and his cult on the verge of collapse, he had turned to his master in a plea to forgive his failure. And thus, the warlord was gifted with a second chance, in the form of his master's own immortal spirit and a deathless army with which to rebuild his cult.

From that day on, Daimos became unstoppable. With a legion of shades behind him, the immortal warlord conquered city after city until all of Serenia had come under his control. Anyone who resisted was killed, while those who wished to live had no option but to join Daimos' forces.

Sixteen years had passed since MorningStar was first seized. By now, the shades' leviathan clouds of ashes had blotted out the sun to such an extent that all of Serenia had withered, forcing animals and people alike to abandon their homes and seek shelter elsewhere on the continent. Even among Daimos' men, most could no longer bear the ashen waste and ultimately succumbed to a lingering death from lack of light and air. Of the followers who still remained, few had managed to retain their sanity.

Daimos was ruling a dead and empty land. But to Recett, it mattered not what land he ruled. What only mattered was the will of the Order, and that those who didn't obey it were destroyed.

And so they were. After slaughtering any of Serenia's remaining population who dared oppose him, Daimos became known as a mad dictator who killed for the glory of his cult, and as a slave driver to anyone beneath him. He was a person to whom all others would bow, yet he would bow to no one—except one man; for Daimos, too, had a master.

Daimos, too, was a servant. He was a servant to the Order, and a puppet to the spirit that had granted him a new life of dominance and immortality. Even with all his power, he was and always would be at the beckon of his lord and master—his master, whom he would put above all else, and for whom he had grown insane with devotion. His master, to whom he was forever loyal.

Daimos' knotted fingers twitched as a chill washed over his body. Suddenly, he felt alive and brimming with strength. The air upon him was instilled with a forceful presence that coursed through his fleshless skeleton and snapped him to his senses.

Daimos picked up his head like a beast spurred from its slumber. He pulled back his hood, setting his eyes on a portentous figure in the center of the throne room. It was swathed in an opulent dark cloak painted with sprawling veins the color of blood, glazed in the shimmer of the encircling torches that cast the figure's shadow in eight directions. It raised a leather-clad hand and, slowly, also drew off the veil of its hood.

A man stood before Daimos. His sheer white hair flowed down on either side of his face and well past his shoulders. His complexion was bloodlessly pale. A pair of tapered eyebrows accented his infernally red eyes; a placid smile honed his narrow jaw.

Daimos' eyes came afire with astonishment and delight. "My lord!" he exclaimed. "Is it truly you?"

Sennair Drakathel opened his arms and bared a hospitable grin. "Eras," he called. "My most trusted disciple."

Daimos hastened from his throne to step down in front of his master. "Forgive me, my lord," he gasped, kneeling in a bow, "for it is you who should be in my seat of power. I cannot rest in this throne with you in my presence."

Drakathel beamed at the warlord's offer. "You are kind, Eras," he said, "but the time is not yet."

Daimos looked up meekly to Sennair. "But have you not returned, my lord? You stand before me now, powerful and in the flesh!"

"I'm afraid that your eyes deceive you." Drakathel frowned. "I am still only but a ghost. With what strength I have gathered, I now project my existence through you. Thanks to you, I have become powerful, yes...but I will need to be freed from the shackles of the nether realm before I can reclaim my body and reenter the world of the living."

Drakathel tipped his head lower, his stare boring into the kneeling Daimos. "Eras..." Sennair's voice descended to a whisper. "With your soul to lend me power, my existence in this realm grows stronger by the day. The moment of my return is ever so near, and there is only one task remaining that stands in the way of my freedom."

"Anything that you require, my lord," Daimos promptly replied. "Speak the word, and I shall act upon it, for I am forever at your command."

"Gather Noctell Knever and Raven Gaunt," answered Drakathel, "and come by my grave along with them. It is the place where I hold most power. All three of you are required to work toward what I intend to achieve, and none of you are to stray from my command."

The warlord nodded zealously. "Of course, my lord! We will set course for your sacred shrine by the morn!"

Sennair appeared to brood over Daimos' response as he turned aside. "No," he surprisingly disagreed. "You will wait. Medeva and the boy Wingheart are to return before any further steps are taken."

"But master, why?" Daimos crooked his head aside. "The boy is no threat to us."

"The boy perhaps not," said Drakathel. "It is the lucidus meteorite that concerns me—what your prisoners have referred to as the Luminous Rock. It is a threat to us all, including the army of the Order. If it is not destroyed, its light could be harnessed and used as a formidable weapon against us. We must abolish everything that could hinder our passage to victory."

"I have made certain that the Rock will be destroyed," Daimos assured. "If Magnus does not succeed in his mission, Cecil Handel and the older Wingheart will face the consequences of the boy's failure. If he values his brother's life, the boy cannot let us down." He tightened his lipless mouth, as if briefly restraining his words. "But you do realize, my lord, that even without the Rock, those who oppose us will do all they can to resist us."

"Then they are fools." Drakathel turned on the warlord to cast his stare down the macabre entrance corridor. "The time of the Order is inevitable and nigh. When it comes, those who oppose us will be struck asunder. It is the destiny of these lands to rise into a golden age of prosperity and power, and our enemies must learn to accept what cannot be stopped."

As Sennair spread out his arms, the flames of the hall-way's torches flared to the peak of the ceiling, scarring the limestone with black talons of soot. "Behold, Eras!" he shouted mightily. "For this is the dawn of a new world! We shall burn away the old, and the new shall be birthed from the ashes!"

He turned to Recett as he lowered his arms and looked down upon the skull mosaic that rolled out across the chamber floor. "And this," he said, "this is the mark of the Order. It is the mark of the alliance that will shatter our rivals and unite the people of Arkane into a single, ever-lasting empire."

Drakathel tilted up his pale countenance and allowed his gaze to roam thoughtfully. "It is the mark of my army," he hissed with barely a twitch of his lip. "An army of the greatest beasts ever to walk in the mortal realm. They have slept for a millennium, and when I return, I will call them forth from the ruins of the old kingdom."

Daimos patiently stayed his tongue until his master had finished speaking. "My lord," he addressed the ghost in a hesitant quaver. "The harpie Medeva—what if she herself can call about the army? The shades obey her as if she were their own summoner. What if she has lied to us?"

"She has too much at stake," Sennair pressed aside Daimos' concern. "Bear in mind, Eras, that we have made a promise to her. She longs for the fulfillment of that promise more than anything else, and with any act she does against us, she risks our abandoning her."

"Yes, my lord, but," Daimos continued, "just as we could break our promise, she could dismiss MorningStar's entire shade legion on a whim. She has much influence over our plans and she could be purposely impeding them. She detests me..." His words lingered. "...and I'm afraid she thinks no better of you."

Drakathel remained indifferent. "I am well aware of what you say, Eras, as I am aware of the limits of her power. When I first gathered my army, the creatures that I brought into this realm were drawn to me; they saw me as their summoner and their master. There were a meager few of the creatures who ignored my command, all of them shades. It seemed as though they'd respond to no one but those of their own kind. These are the beasts that only Medeva can awaken, as she is akin to their race. A creature cannot have two masters, therefore my army obeys me alone."

"What about Noctell?" Daimos cited the name of his elite guard. "He is a necromancer—a skilled one, no doubt. Don't you suppose he could hold power over the army?"

"A necromancer," answered Sennair, "controls an ethereal creature by using its natural element as lure. Indeed Noctell could manipulate the soldiers of my army, but only I, their summoner, have sufficient control to stir them from their slumber. Only in their wakened state can a mage such as Noctell have any power over them."

Daimos' eyes trailed his master as Drakathel paced alongside the tattered rim of the skull mosaic. "Does this mean that anyone with Noctell's abilities could do the very same?" asked the warlord.

"Never," Sennair replied. "These creatures can tell friend from foe. They will not blindly obey an enemy of their true master. When my army is risen, I will make certain that its rule falls under no other man..." he said, drawing to a halt, "...not even Noctell."

Daimos met the ghost's statement with a look of cautious inquiry. "But he is a trusted ally to the Order, is he not?"

"Perhaps once," said Sennair, "but no longer. He and Raven are beginning to doubt themselves and stray from the path, filled with the delusion that they are better off without me and the Order. Their loyalty toward us hangs by a fine thread of desire for their personal benefit, and my trust in them is waning."

"Do you—" Daimos faltered over his words, "do you wish for me to...eliminate...these disloyalists?"

"We cannot." Drakathel turned to the warlord. "Our plans have advanced too far for us to cast away our pawns. We will progress as intended, but I regret to say that their devotion is too weak for them to earn a place in the new army."

Daimos bowed even lower before his master in concurrence. "Very well, my lord. At the time of your return, they will be disposed of in the way you see fit."

"You speak this as if it were an easy task." Sennair smirked. "They are powerful, Eras, Noctell especially. They cannot be eliminated so simply. There will come a day when they will arise to their true nature and place themselves against the Order. But by then..." He uttered a degrading laugh. "...it will be too late.

"Before six days have passed, my soul and my physical form will unite once again. My existences in these realms will merge into one, and I will be complete—body, mind, and soul. After a thousand years of imprisonment, it feels as if it is only a matter of minutes before I can walk out onto the earth of the old kingdom."

The ghost returned his wandering eyes to Recett and lifted a pallid arm. "Rise, Eras." Obediently, Daimos stood upright, head still locked in a bow.

"I thank you always for your adamant faithfulness," Sennair said. "You have proved yourself to be one of the few on whom I can steadfastly rely."

"After all you have given me, my debt to you is eternal, my lord," Daimos replied in an instant. "Shall I spread the news of your arrival to the rest of the Order?"

Drakathel's smile broadened. "That will not be necessary," he said, curtaining his dagger-sharp face with the hood of his cloak, "for when I return, my army will rise with me..."

As Daimos looked on, Sennair became licked with wisps of smoldering black embers, his robes unraveling in flame while his image receded from sight. And just as suddenly as he had first appeared, the ghost glimmered out of existence.

But then, rattling even the warlord, the voice of Sennair Drakathel echoed across the throne room as if from some ethereal void: "...and all Arkane will know!"

Magnus sprinted along the river's edge, fearing every minute would be one too late to save the harpie. In his hand, he clutched the taren bark shard—the antidote for Medeva's poisonous injury—knowing that the fate of his imprisoned companions depended on it.

Magnus neared his destination to find the harpie still sprawled by the fallen tree where he had left her. He was relieved to see her pick up her emerald eyes and fling a bitter scowl at the boy.

"It's about time," she spat.

Magnus skidded to a halt and kneeled beside her. "You said I had an hour." He stared at the bark to consider his next steps, but Medeva didn't let him pause for long. "Crush it and put it in water," she instructed brusquely.

Barely nodding, Magnus leaned aside and raked his hand through the gravel to select a pointed stone, then shrugged his backpack off his shoulders. From under a few scantly touched food rations and the black acid flask, he rummaged out his waterskin, which was weightless and likely near empty.

He opened the waterskin, put his index finger to the lip of the container, and, focusing intently, conjured a steady flow of water from his palm into the empty container. When the skin was a little less than half-full, Magnus broke the flow and shook the moisture off his flesh. He proceeded to use the pointed stone to pummel the taren bark against the flat side of his backpack until he was left with a splintery dust, which he scraped into his fist and deposited through the neck of the waterskin.

He shook the vessel thoroughly and proffered it to Medeva, who snatched the skin without a word of response. After swilling the antidote, she returned the skin and subsided against the tree.

Magnus fitted the skin back inside his bag. "How long will it take before you're cured?"

"The antidote will go straight to my blood," Medeva replied. "If I'm not dead in a few minutes, then you've proved yourself to be competent."

Magnus sighed and frowned, bringing himself to rest against a still-standing tree. He tilted up his head in a dismal reverie. "Ironic, isn't it?" he mused aloud. "I'm saving the life of the one who killed my mother."

"It's not only my life you're saving," said the harpie. "You're saving the lives of those who would die along with me."

"That's what I hope," Magnus snapped. "With Anubis betraying us, this whole thing could have been plotted out from the start. How do I even know if Drake and Cecil are still alive? Daimos has no use for them!"

"Daimos also has no reason to kill them," Medeva replied. "They'll survive. The only question is if you will."

Magnus gave a narrow-eyed grimace. "So you're just going to run me through with your halberd once you heal?"

"I have no interest in harming you, Wingheart," Medeva dismissed the boy's cynicism. "But the mountain bandits may. My wing is broken and as long as I can't fly, evading the Rammeren will be all the more deadly."

29

Trespassage

AGNUS TURNED UP his head. The sky was noticeably brighter than it had been the previous day. The thinning ash clouds told that he and Medeva were not much farther from Serenia's neighboring province of Galem, a place over which Daimos' ruin had not yet spread.

A day and a half after departing their rest stop by the river's edge, Magnus and the harpie had safely navigated the remainder of the forest and made fair headway across the planes beyond. Medeva had been quickly cured after receiving the poison antidote, but her wing remained too damaged for her to fly at all. Magnus feared that they would have no option but to traverse the Galem border together, and from what he had gathered, the mountain bandits—the Rammeren—were not welcoming to anyone who served under Daimos Recett.

Medeva slowed just enough to allow the breathless Magnus to draw beside her. "We'll both be forced to head across on foot," she said. "If the Rammeren are around here, we have no realistic chance of keeping from their sight. They know the mountains exceptionally well, and their fighting abilities are not to be underestimated."

"So is this just it?" Magnus gave a blank shrug. "If we know we have no chance, why are we even trying to head across?"

Medeva glared sidelong at the boy. "Because the mountain range is hundreds of miles long, and those bandits can't possibly be guarding every inch of rock. Luck prevailing, we won't have to face any of the Rammeren."

"And if we do?"

"We have many options, all of which are irrelevant until we know what we're facing." The harpie skillfully gauged the sharpness of her halberd with her thumb, as if in some dark suggestion. "Either way, we're making our passage as swift as possible."

"I hope you're planning on letting me rest before the climb," Magnus said in an aggravated, slightly louder tone. "Unless it makes no difference to you whether I drop dead from exhaustion."

"I don't take concern in your discomfort," Medeva replied. "If you die anywhere near here, it will be by the work of a blade." She looked away. "And not one of mine." She gathered pace and returned to the lead, suggesting that the discussion was over.

As he trod onward, Magnus saw the parched ground

heave and crash in rolling slopes, and the fields crease with gravelly troughs and hillocks. The practically incessant hike had already left him worn and cold to the bone, all while having to haul his backpack containing Noctell's weighty black acid flask. The obstructive change in terrain did nothing but worsen conditions.

Medeva strode far ahead of the boy to where the mountains were beginning to take shape in erratic rocky knolls. Even with a crippled wing, she moved steadfastly and without the slightest trace of exhaustion. When the field narrowed under the rising mountain walls, she halted and turned to the boy far behind her.

Magnus ineptly scrambled another fifty feet across the boulder-strewn plane before reaching the harpie. He gasped to speak, but managed barely a syllable before Medeva flicked up her palm, motioning him to be silent. Magnus could tell by the harpie's darting eyes that she had detected something, presumably something foreboding. He looked in all directions, but failed to make out any imminent threat.

Then a distant figure entered his field of vision, as if from nowhere. Magnus snapped his head toward the approaching figure, a burly man, just as a second man of scrawnier build followed into sight. Magnus stole a step backward and turned fretfully to Medeva, who remained unperturbed. Taking a cautionary glance over his shoulder, he spotted another three figures scattered between the rocks behind him.

Both the approaching men were draped in shabby

gray coats and fitted with leathery vests and gauntlets. The first man was distinguished by a short bristly beard and a furrowed countenance that was painted with scars and brushed over with a rag of dark-blond hair. His belt exhibited a small array of weapon holsters, with at least one blade and handbow. The second man, slightly shorter, had a younger face and tousled black hair. In an acrobatic boast of his skills, he unsheathed a pair of shortswords, flicked them into an airborne spiral, and caught them by their hilts nearly a full second later without a stammer in his poise.

As soon as he reached Magnus and Medeva, the bearded man lifted the corners of his lips and broke into a mocking laugh. "I can hardly believe it," the man cackled with eyes fixed on the harpie. "Of all the outlaws that pass through here, you're the last one I'd expect to meet!"

Magnus was somewhat astonished at the man's remark and was unsure whether to be relieved or alarmed that the harpie was known to the guard. Medeva, meanwhile, held her indifferent stare.

"The Rammeren, I believe," she said, more as a statement than a query.

"Indeed," said the man. "I'm surprised to see you all the way out here, harpie. What brings you to these parts?"

Medeva pulled a crooked frown. "I'm touring the area."

Both the bandits responded with a boisterous chuckle. "Your tongue is as sharp as your blades, I see," the bearded man sneered. "How are things in Serenia? Still under the control of that shriveled sack of bones?"

"Quite so," Medeva hummed. "I'm surprised myself

that you all managed to survive in this barren place for so many years."

The man folded his arms and grinned smugly. "Oh, as long as one province is wiped off the map, thanks to your master, a large part of our guard has been enlisted into the Galem army. The people of Galem appreciate us, you see; they give us what we need to survive, in return for our defending their border."

Medeva met the words of the Rammeren guard with a sardonically cockeyed stare. "You're being paid to defend a mountain range that borders an empty province?"

"On the contrary," replied the man, "you'd be surprised how many fools believe they still have a chance at smuggling their stolen goods in and out of Galem. They come all the way from Nemus thinking they can pass off a few sacks of abylite as a cartload of straw."

The second man wielding the shortswords came forward as his partner finished to speak. "So what about you, harpie?" he began, brandishing the head of one of his two blades at Medeva. "What's your contraband? Gems? Weapons? Animals? By the looks of it, you have some sort of mangled bat dangling off the back of your shoulders."

"By the looks of it," Medeva countered with barely a pause following the guard's quip, "your friend there has the head of a boar perched atop his neck."

The bearded man grimaced, becoming noticeably agitated. "I find it hard not to be amused in your presence, harpie."

Medeva's fingers curled around the trunk of her halberd

in a subtle warning. "You may find it easier with a spear-head in your throat."

The bearded man finally dropped what remained of his smile into a scowl. "Alright now, that's enough out of you," he snarled. "We've seen you with Recett and those ash devils of his at least a dozen times before. Give me one good reason why we shouldn't just kill you here and now."

"Because before you can draw that handbow," replied Medeva, "you'll be lying in a pool of your own blood. And by the time any other of you mountain dwellers manage to strike me down, your fate will be shared by three more of your comrades."

The Rammeren guard's fury was reluctantly settled. He said nothing, though it was obvious that he acknowledged Medeva's gruesome threat.

The man with the shortswords moved out in front of the bearded guard and cast a suspicious eye on Magnus, diverting attention from the uneasy dialogue. "And who's this?" he spat. "Your mountain guide?"

Magnus tried to conceal his fear behind a façade of composure as he watched the guard approach him with his twin blades at the ready.

"Speak, boy," ordered the man. "What's your name?"

Magnus was struck with a shiver in memory of his last interrogation in Markwell. "Magnus," he replied.

"Are you with the harpie?" the man asked again.

Magnus nodded. "Yes."

The guard gave a look of cynical curiosity, scanning the disheveled Magnus from the ground up. "You don't come across like one of Recett's thugs. What are you doing with the likes of her?"

The boy looked past Medeva from out of the corner of his eye. "I..." he stammered, "I found her lying by the river. She didn't tell me who she was or where she was going, but she was wounded and her wing was broken. I thought I could help her on to the other side of the mountains, where she could be treated."

The shortswordsman regarded Medeva's crippled wing, but then smirked as if he were trying to retain his laughter. "And what, pray tell, were you doing in Serenia?"

"I escaped," Magnus answered impulsively. "I escaped from MorningStar. I was trying to reach a relative in Galem, when I found the harpie."

"Look, boy," the bearded man roared, putting a hasty end to the conversation. "Your lies don't make a difference. You both must be fools to think we're going to let either of you into Galem. Our duty is to protect this province from those who would harm it, and I'm not inclined to believe that Recett's own assassin harpie could have come here with peaceful intentions."

"Leave now," said the man with the shortswords, "and we'll spare you the bloodshed. But if either of you comes within fifty feet of the place we now stand, you will not be warned again, and we will not hesitate to kill."

Medeva's impassivity persisted. "Very well."

When Medeva turned to depart the scene, Magnus was surprised that she didn't make a more combative exit. It was only after the harpie had paced well away that Magnus finally abided by the Rammeren's demand and bolted back toward the western planes.

Magnus quickly moved up to the harpie's side. He drew in a breath to speak, but Medeva silenced him with a raised hand. Looking over his shoulder, Magnus could no longer see the five guards, and the rocky slopes were fading to a distant haze.

Medeva slowed her steps and halted as Magnus clambered over a hill of fractured stone and came to a stand close behind her. "Wonderful," he griped. "I suppose we're ruined now, aren't we?"

"Hardly," Medeva replied. "We will proceed. Only a slight change in plan is needed."

Magnus was shocked yet unsurprised by the harpie's persistence. "They already saw us. We'll both be slaughtered if we try to get near there again."

"We needed to know what we're up against," she said. "The next task at hand is to make it through alive. Since we cannot avoid being seen, and we most certainly cannot avoid an attack, the only thing we can avoid is a quick death."

"That's no different than being seen," snapped Magnus. "We were surrounded by men before we made it up the bottom of the mountain, and we'll be killed before we can make it far."

"Not if we have help on our side," Medeva replied, baring her teeth under the crook of her mouth in a surprising grin.

Magnus could only surmise that the harpie's answer held sinister implications. "And how is that?"

Medeva extended a pale gray arm, palm turned upward. "You will see." A coat of black sparks glimmered into existence on the harpie's hand. She cocked her wrist, propelling the sparks into the air, where they dispersed as if spit from a fire. Detecting no change to the area around him, Magnus assumed that whatever Medeva attempted had failed—however, it did not take long for him to be convinced otherwise.

A ghastly scream blazed from high above them. It was like that of a human, only shriller, warped, and with an echo that seemed to linger endlessly. When Magnus gazed skyward, the echo was reinforced by an indistinguishable multitude of the same harsh cries, and a rain of pulsing, fiendish murmurs.

Magnus looked on with growing terror. The clouds themselves appeared to throb in tune to the voices that emanated from them like the pounding of an enormous black heart. Then, suddenly, the dark heavens ruptured open and a waterfall of cinders gushed out from the clouds.

"Shades!" Magnus shrieked at the sight of the ashen smog amassing overhead. "They're going to kill me before those mountain guards do!"

"Not while they're under my control," Medeva assured. "Their will is my own. They will not harm you if I do not wish for them to."

Magnus crooked his neck so as to keep both the clouds and the harpie within his field of vision. "Your control?" he repeated, disbelieving. "You can control the shades?"

"In fact, few others can." Medeva's reply was subtly

laced with pride. "The shades are my kin, Wingheart. They heed my call."

The boy was finding it difficult to speak with his attention fastened to the growing shade horde. "What about Daimos?" he quavered. "Or even Noctell and Raven? It looked like they were the ones controlling the shades that attacked us at the shelter."

Medeva breathed a demeaning cackle. "Recett has about as much control over the shades as you do. As a necromancer, Noctell can control them, but only I can awaken them. Without my command, the shades would fall into a slumber, and they would rise to no one's call but mine."

Magnus' mind stirred with the memories of his conversation with Cecil on the morning after their arrival in Markwell. His former guardian had speculated that Daimos was the one who had first summoned the shades, and therefore the one who controlled them. But if Medeva was truthful, the warlord's powers were more limited than they seemed.

"So does that..." Magnus' voice became momentarily drowned in the wailing of the shades. "...does that make you the summoner? The one who brought them to Arkane to begin with?"

Medeva's smile turned straight and rigid. "I was not the one who summoned the shades."

"Then who did?"

Medeva faced Magnus forbiddingly. "You ask too many questions," she said, "and expect too many answers."

As Magnus stood stiffened by the hostile gleam in Medeva's eyes, he felt the airstream coil into a whirlwind that surged high into the overhanging shade horde. The amorphous cloud began to stir and expand, dispersing to reveal a gruesome entanglement of smoky skulls and talons. Finally, it plummeted toward Magnus and the harpie.

For an instant, Magnus was certain he was going to be prey to the shade horde that cascaded out of the skies. His gaze was dominated by hundreds of the specters' spindly appendages lurching inward and out of the abyssal mass from which they were spawned. He screamed and cowered under the shield of his arms, petrified. But his painful expectations were turned to curiosity when the howl and the lash of the wind came still. He guardedly emerged from his defensive stance.

Looming at the brink of a vast radius, the shades encircled Magnus and Medeva like the inner wall of a tower sculpted from charred bone. The shades themselves had interwoven to form a wreathing barrier against all but those audacious enough to leap into a wall of fervently gnawing claws.

"The shades are capable of gathering into a single, massive entity," said Medeva. "When they attack, they become an unstoppable horde that spreads death like wildfire. When they defend, they become a solidly opaque cloak to their allies that destroys all who would attempt to penetrate it."

Magnus fretfully observed the ashen barrier. "This is how you intend to get past the Rammeren?"

"How else?" replied the harpie. "The shades will surround us as we make our way over the mountains. They will keep our contact with the Rammeren to a minimum, but that doesn't guarantee an entirely harmless climb. Skillful as those guards are, they'll find ways to traverse our defenses, so prepare for a fight."

Magnus tried to restrain his gut-wrenching nervousness, though he was failing to do so. When he had fought alongside Cecil, Drake, and Anubis against Daimos' men a few days earlier, he had, at the least, been confident knowing that he was in the company of his friends and older brother. Now, conversely, he found himself in the company of only his enemies, whether it was Medeva, the shades, or the Rammeren bandits. The fear of a brutal death prevailed in his mind, even with the harpie's ever-ready blade to defend him.

"Alright," Magnus affirmed timidly.

Medeva stared out in the direction of the mountains, halberd steady in her grip. "Then run."

Not a moment later, the encircling shade wall broke from its idleness and picked up the speed of its rotation, accelerating until the specters' nightmarish visages were engulfed in the cyclone. Medeva sprang forward on the toe of her boot, and the shades moved along with her.

Magnus was less than prepared to see the inner edge of the cyclone begin to roar quickly toward him. Just before the shades were practically near enough to slash him by the nape of his neck, Magnus came to his senses and bolted after Medeva into the eye of the twister.

Medeva slowed her pace to let the boy draw level. The banshee-like wails of the shades blared from all directions, stifled by the rush of the wind. His vision already hampered by the cyclone wall, Magnus was forced to shield his eyes to avoid being blinded by the sooty wisps that thrashed his face.

"They should've seen us by now," Medeva said in a voice loud enough to be heard above the clamor. "You can expect a warm welcome at the foot of the mountains."

"How are we supposed to make it there when we can't see anything more than ten feet away?" Magnus hollered back.

"Just follow my lead," instructed the harpie. "You've no choice but to trust me."

30

Whatever the Odds

VER CENTURIES, the Galem mountains had been called home by countless clans of outlaws, bandits, and highwaymen. They stole from those who attempted passage through the Larithian Gorge—one of the few straight roads that led into Galem— and murdered those from whom they found nothing to steal. They knew the mountain range and its labyrinthine complex of caves within and without, and they were notorious for their unrivaled dexterity in battle.

Many of these clans, however, had died out quickly, as one could only survive on the harsh crags of the mountains for so long without sufficient food or shelter. Their names were forgotten, many of their records lost to history. But there was one clan that had prevailed far longer than any other—the clan known as the Rammeren.

From the time the clan had been formed nearly three decades ago, the Rammeren had easily dwarfed any of the mountain's still-surviving bandit clans in both strength and numbers for the simple reason that they were unlike any of their thievish predecessors: rather than stealing from the innocent, the Rammeren understood that they could gain far greater honor and secure their survival by working in tandem with Galem and its army to defend the province's border. Until then, Galem had been a land dominated by the light-fingered merchants of the black market, a smugglers' capital thanks to its scarce roads of trade and seclusion from the rest of Arkane. But with the Rammeren as their new defense, it became far more challenging, not to mention much deadlier, for smugglers to continue hauling their freight of contraband in and out of the province.

However, though well intentioned, the Rammeren were ruthless, and often killed the outlaws whom Galem would have preferred to be jailed, letting live only those from whom the border guards could collect a generous bounty. It was because of this indiscriminate brutality that, despite protecting the Galem province, the Rammeren had attained a terrible reputation across a large part of the continent.

Understandably, in return, the Rammeren had grown hostile and callously indifferent toward anyone outside of Galem—even sixteen years earlier, when Daimos Recett had first begun the war that ultimately decimated the population of their neighboring province. Though the Galem army had dispatched its troops to assist Serenia in its battle against the shades, the Rammeren had remained oblivious to the bloodshed that took place just past the reaches of their border. As far as they were concerned, they had no reason to take part in a war that did not involve Galem to begin with. Daimos had never even seemed interested in expanding his empire into Galem—until now.

The bearded Rammeren guard who had earlier halted Magnus and the harpie, a captain of the clan, stood at the brink of a narrow cliff that jutted out high over the fields beneath him. From here, he could see miles off in every direction, but at the moment, all that he saw was the monstrous cyclone of black ash that crept steadily toward the mountain range. He was concerned for the rest of the clan, but above all, for the province of Galem. It seemed as if Recett had finally made his decision to usurp another corner of the continent.

"Malion!" a voice cried out from behind.

The bearded man turned at the call of his name. A fellow guard hurried toward Malion, winding sideways to slither through the tight corridor of rock that led up to the cliff where the captain stood.

"Malion..." the guard repeated as he emerged from the corridor. It was the shortswordsman who'd been with Malion at the base of the mountains minutes ago. "Did you see—"

"—that?" Malion stole the last word of the swordsman's question, motioning toward the shade swarm. "It's hard to miss."

"Well, what you do think it is?"

"Shades," the captain answered. "I can't think what else. I knew it would only be so long before Recett worked up the nerve to spread his plague into Galem." He sighed through his teeth. "That must've been why he sent the harpie. He wanted to see whether or not we still held any dominance here before giving out the order for the shades to attack."

"But...shades..." the swordsman sputtered in his rising panic, "they would've had to come from nowhere! We were all on watch for the past five hours and we didn't see a thing!"

Malion shook his head somberly. "We wouldn't have. As long as those infernally black clouds hang overhead, those creatures materialize just about anywhere."

The swordsman drew one of his blades with the hiss of sliding steel. "Shall I notify Master Rammeren?"

"You do that," Malion replied. He inattentively stroked the back wrist of the gauntlet on his right hand, where a trio of cut gems was embedded into the hide, interlocked in the shape of an inverted triangle—a bold-green emerald, a scintillating lucidus fragment, and a translucent shard of quartz crystal. "Tell the rest to prepare for battle, and I'll try to send a messenger to alert the Galem army," he continued. "The only element that has any effect on the shades is light. If you see any of Recett's men, they're to be killed without question. If you see the harpie, she must be stopped at all costs, for she is our most dangerous enemy."

"Yes, sir," the shortswordsman gave a fleeting nod before scampering away through the rocky corridor.

"Just above all, be..." Malion tried to speak to his colleague a final time, but as he turned back, the swordsman had already departed. "...careful."

Still running relentlessly in the heart of the shade swarm, Magnus and Medeva neared the foot of the Galem mountains. They had not yet spotted any more of the Rammeren; but then again, the cloak of the shades made it impossible to see clearly.

"Remember, Wingheart, that this is far from safe," said the harpie. "The shades will keep us from being seen too easily, but they will also severely hinder our vision. Our chances of being shot dead are about equal to the chances of our making it through here alive, so stay as alert as you're able."

Magnus felt his throat constrict and his veins clench icily at Medeva's warning. He noticed the terrain becoming progressively steeper and his environment bearing down on him with coarse blankets of rock that flowed past the shades' inscrutable veil behind him. Ahead of him, a hazardously unkempt pathway took shape as it emerged from behind the north edge of the swarm. Moving further, he saw the ground to his left rise into a low wall that cut into the shades' formation, while the ground to his right plummeted into a perilous eighty-degree slope.

Magnus was already in the mountain range. With the rugged path still ascending, he was reluctant to look anywhere that would tell him the extent of his climb so far. Though he wasn't normally afraid of heights, the Rammeren's presence and his inability to see past the cliff alongside him turned his thoughts to the numerous ways he could perish, starting with the likelihood of his stumbling off the precarious walkway.

Then, as if it were a mockery of Magnus' qualms, the path began to narrow. Medeva moved in front, no longer finding enough room to maintain a position beside the boy. By this point, the right-hand slope had already plunged to a perfectly vertical incline, and the wall on the opposite side had swelled to a dizzying height.

Only a few feet more and the path was now barely wide enough for Magnus to stand upright. Not far onward, the left wall jutted out, and the diminishing path tapered to little more than a furrow in the rock face.

Medeva halted to face the boy. "Stay close at my back," she said, "and move quickly." With that, she leapt off the edge of the path.

Magnus froze at watching the harpie vanish beyond the curtain of the swarm. No sooner had the ends of her wings slipped from sight than Magnus saw the shades' sooty veins begin to seep over the ground between his feet. When he glanced past his shoulder, he was taken aback at the sight of an ashen torrent surging down over the mountain wall. The swarm was moving onward in order to keep Medeva in its center, and Magnus' stalling would leave him outside of the shades' protection if he didn't follow fast.

"Jump, fool!" he heard Medeva cry out from the shadows beneath the path. "What are you waiting for?"

Feeling the airstream of the swarm graze his neck, Magnus choked his pressing fears and leapt blindly after Medeva. He let out a gasp of alarm as his feet slammed against a crumbled incline, causing him to trip and hurtle face-first onto a flat stone platform.

Magnus forced up his head with a shudder of pain. He saw Medeva standing nearby, but his surroundings, as before, were concealed behind the wall of the swarm. From what he could make out, he had landed on some nondescript plane beneath the pathway.

Suddenly, the wailing of the shades became intolerably shrill. The disturbance that stole over Medeva's expression told that something was amiss. Magnus pulled himself straight to look up through the opening in the crown of the swarm, when dread plummeted on him.

A full assault of flashes was pounding against the uppermost part of the swarm. The shades in range of the light were caught in a frenzy, struggling to hold their arrangement, and were already beginning to scatter. The mountain guards were clearly using light magic in an attempt to disperse the veil.

"It's the Rammeren," Medeva said urgently. She grabbed Magnus by his arm and wrenched him from his place. As she let go, she darted ahead, and Magnus staggered to a running speed behind her. The swarm moved along with them, but the pulsing rays and the shades' cries of distress were hardly letting up.

Magnus tried to study the rocky plane around him, but his view was severely impeded by the swarm. Then a particularly devastating flash glimmered at the edge of his vision, much lower in height than the others. It seemed that the guards were beginning to target the base of the swarm, where Medeva and the boy were hidden.

There was another flash, this time from the left. When Magnus turned in the direction of the attack, he saw a figure lunge through the section of the shade veil that had been disbanded by the light burst—it was a man clad in the scruffy garb of the Rammeren guards, his sword raised in a double-handed grip. The guard cocked the blade already seething with luminous magic, but even before his legs had completely passed through the swarm, the shades reconverged behind him. A single gaunt, gray claw whipped out from the veil and slashed the guard's back, and Magnus observed in horror as the man instantly fell limp and collapsed dead onto the ground, his dropped sword clanging on the stone.

It was last week that Magnus had first been warned of Daimos' shades. It was only now that he saw them fight, and that he witnessed just how effortlessly a shade could kill.

For a fleet moment, Magnus' eyes were drawn to the guard's abandoned longsword. There was something peculiar about the shape of its hilt. He tried to get a closer inspection, but was restrained by a violent tug on his shoulder.

"He's dead. Keep moving." Medeva pulled the boy backward and shoved him in the other direction. "We're still under attack."

Magnus almost fell forward at the harpie's jostling. Medeva bolted in front and they both resumed their escape through the mountain range, wails and flashes unremitting overhead. As they traveled further, the once-level ground sloped in like a trough, and the mountain walls grew taller on either side to form a roofless corridor.

The swarm warped to fit the shape of the passage, thinning where it touched the rock face and condensing over the crevices where the eye of the twister was exposed. Ash and stone swirled into a dark-gray blur around Magnus and the harpie, rendering any obstacle in their path invisible until they were only footsteps away from meeting it.

Magnus was jolted by the sound of a whipping gust—like that of a projectile streaming through the air. As a sliver of steel clattered against the left mountain wall, Magnus realized that their danger was quickly worsening.

One by one, another trio of crossbow bolts rebounded off the rocks above. The shades were no longer the focal target of the Rammeren's attacks, but rather, it was the two intruders who scampered between them.

"They must have spotted us in here," Medeva warned. "Keep moving. Remember that they can't see us any better than we can see them."

The aimless barrage of steel bolts persisted, now being rejoined by the guards' attempts to breach the veil with formidable light magic. Magnus could tell that the shades were scattering, but as long as he and the harpie upheld their pace, the Rammeren seemed unable to keep a steady aim.

The mountain corridor suddenly veered aside and disappeared behind the edge of the right wall. Medeva grappled onto the rocks for support and nimbly swerved down the path's new direction without a break in her speed. Caught unawares, Magnus lurched to a stop just before another crossbow bolt struck the ground a few feet away from him. He was reminded of his deadly pursuers and slipped around the curve, out from the corridor.

Magnus found himself on a much more slender pathway. It was similar to the serpentine indent that he and Medeva had taken to ascend the foot of the mountains—a profound abyss marked its left edge and a stone wall its right—and was only marginally wider. The boy ran as fast yet as carefully as he could to catch up with the agile harpie, who was already well down the path. He was quick to notice that the Rammeren's onslaught had died off, but he doubted it would stay that way for long.

Malion strode across a rocky islet that soared amidst the lower peaks of the mountain range. A multitude of Rammeren guards flitted past him in every direction, hastening to reposition themselves on the eastern bank of the islet, below which the shade swarm was making its way.

"Malion, sir," a guard raced up to Malion's side. "We've discovered the harpie. She travels with the boy in the eye of the swarm."

"So I hear," the captain replied, walking briskly. "You're doing well. The shades must be dispersed before they can reach Galem." He grimaced. "I just don't understand what that harpie's doing here. If Recett wanted to launch an attack on this province, he would've sent a band of his men, not a lone fighter."

"And that boy..." the other guard pondered. "What in the world is he doing with her? He can't possibly be one of Recett's followers."

"He looks like a fool to me," snapped Malion. "He's probably being used, either by Recett or the harpie. For what purpose, I can't imagine."

The guard glanced at the ground coasting under his feet. "Perhaps Recett isn't trying to attack Galem. What if he's only trying to get them past the border?"

"And what then?" Malion shrugged. "Is he planning to use them as spies? After the Galem army receives my message, the price on that harpie's head will be so high that every bounty hunter in the province will be searching for her."

The guard nodded in concurrence. "Then perhaps they want something from the mountains themselves?"

"What could he possibly want here?" Malion flung up his arm to outline the surrounding area. "The contents of our treasury?"

"What about the valley?"

Malion's brow lifted with interest as his movement lagged. "What about the valley?" he repeated, no longer as dismissive.

"You know those ruins," said his comrade. "They have that defiling mark of the Order scrawled all over the place like it's a shrine to their god. I'd hardly be surprised if they had some dark deed to fulfill there."

"True," Malion replied, "but that still doesn't explain Recett's strange selection of foot soldiers to carry out the task."

They were nearing the end of the islet, where many of the other Rammeren guards were already gathering, crouched, crossbows and handbows mounted on an array of rocky outcrops and aimed off a sheer cliff. "Does it really matter?" said the guard. "Either way, the harpie won't be alive for much longer."

"It matters because Recett could be planning something," answered Malion. "If he is, we need to know what." The captain kneeled by the crossbowmen and gazed down at the ledge at least seventy feet below, where the ashen swarm was heading. "The harpie is far too dangerous to capture and must be killed, but spread word that I want the boy alive. He could do well with answering a few questions in front of Master Rammeren."

"Straight away," the guard agreed before rushing off to inform the others.

Malion stirred through the trove of spare equipment next to the crossbowmen. He took up a leather quiver with a shoulder strap that he slung over his right arm and under his left, and a thick-barreled handbow that he set on the rocks at the cliff's edge. The lucidus gem pressed into his gauntlet blazed faintly and, in tune with it, his weapon glimmered with an identical tinge. Finally, the captain took aim, awaiting the swarm's passage beneath him.

Medeva flicked up her head to peer through the aperture at the top of the swarm. She could distinguish a crowd of figures moving about on the cliffs above. "They're getting ready to attack again," she said. "Hurry!"

Magnus struggled to keep up with the harpie. At the rate he was already moving, the extreme lack of space on the ledge gave him the feeling of treading a tightrope, and he was wary of proceeding any faster. The burden of his backpack often shifted his weight treacherously near to the edge of the precipice. When he tried to speed up, he easily lost his footing, slipped, and clung to the mountain wall to avoid a deadly plunge.

Medeva glanced again between the peaks and the boy. She seemed to waver briefly before she turned around and streaked toward Magnus, skipping across the ledge as if there were not the slightest chance of her falling. She seized the boy, pulled him back, and flattened herself against the mountain wall alongside him.

"The cliff from where the Rammeren are firing is an overhang," she said in a voice so hurried that it was difficult to make out. "Stay as close as you can to the wall, and we'll be too deep under the overhang for them to get a clear shot at us."

"What?" Magnus exclaimed, partly unsure if he'd heard right. "So we're just going to stand here and hope that they won't be able to reach us?"

"What else do you want to try, then?" Medeva barked. "If we continue along this ledge, we cannot even hope to survive. Their accuracy relies on how much room we have to maneuver, so a narrow path means that they'll be a lot less likely to miss."

The first bow was fired. A bolt struck the ground before Magnus with such force that its tip was crooked out of shape and it recoiled nearly a foot into the air before dropping. The lone shot was followed moments later by an incessant rain of sharp steel only inches away from Magnus' face. He shrugged the leather bag off his shoulders and took its straps into his fist, allowing him to drive himself even further back against the wall until the coarse rock stabbed him through his coat.

Then, among the cascade of projectiles, another flash erupted over the swarm. An instant later, a pillar of light blazed into existence before Magnus and the harpie, accompanied by an explosive blow to the ledge like a cannonball. Medeva cried out and winced at the harsh rays discharged from the blast, as if singed by the light. The shade swarm was catapulted into a bedlam. When the scattering swarm had settled, the once-vast cyclone of ashes was reduced to little more than a chaotic web.

"What was that?" Magnus gasped under the perpetual rattle of ammunition.

"An enchanted bolt of some kind," Medeva muttered, face wrung with pain. "Obviously someone here is as good a spellcaster as he is a marksman."

"We're going to get hit if we stay here any longer," Magnus deliberated. "Maybe we could keep moving if we stayed close enough to the wall."

Medeva gave a rigid shake of her head. "No. The overhang recedes further on. We won't be able to stay covered for the entire length of the path." She motioned toward something in the bottom-left direction, taking care not to let her hand become skewered by a bolt in the process. "There's an alcove down there, under the cliff. If we can slip out of the Rammeren's focus for a moment, we can use it to hide until they give up the chase."

"They won't stop firing at us until we're both dead," Magnus reminded.

"Oh, but they can't see us," Medeva noted shrewdly. She outstretched her arm to the right. "What they're firing at are the shades, for they know that we stand between them."

Medeva's raised hand glinted with black sparks— something that Magnus had seen before when she'd first beckoned the shade horde to surround them. The sparks whirled for a second, then glided off the harpie's fingertips and guttered out. With little delay, the shades lurched rightward as if a new course had been established for them.

Magnus instinctively tried to follow the swarm, but Medeva threw out her free arm across the boy's chest and restrained him back against the wall. "Don't move until I tell you to," she commanded. "By separating ourselves from the shades, we can fool the Rammeren into thinking that we're still in the middle of the swarm."

Magnus looked askance; the inner wall of the shade swarm crept closer, churning faster. He buried his head in the bend of his arm as he felt the ashes pass over him. A mortuary chill was cast onto him like a lead blanket; terror in its purest form seemed to permeate him. Within seconds, the sensations subsided. Magnus picked up his head and, for the first time, observed the frenzied shade swarm from an outside perspective as it reeled down the path, trailing soot in its wake. At last he was allowed an unobstructed view of the mountain range and a better grasp on their less-than-optimal situation.

Close ahead, across from the ledge and the chasm, was another impassible mountain wall. It was thoroughly rutted, carved with many recesses and walkways— apparently the area in which Medeva hoped to find shelter from the Rammeren.

"Get ready to act." Medeva signaled the boy.

Magnus balked, seeing no immediate change in the guards' attacks. "I don't think so...we're still under fire."

"Not for long," said the harpie. And with that, the bolts lessened.

The Rammeren's target was shifting. The projectiles were taking a new, oblique course, pelting the still-moving ashen swarm. The bolts in front of Magnus and Medeva became increasingly scarce until they dissipated entirely.

Medeva stepped out onto the ledge in plain view and threaded her halberd through the holster between her wings. "We'll have to climb down from here if we want to get low enough to reach the alcove. It won't be long before the Rammeren realize we've deceived them, so you'd better move quickly." She slipped one leg over the cliff, turned her back to the chasm, and dropped off the path, upholding herself by a firm clutch on the cliff's edge.

Unsafe as the harpie's maneuvering appeared to be, Magnus knew that he'd have to do the same. He kneeled and, clinging securely onto an indent in the rocks, slumped off the ledge like Medeva. As he did, the downward jolt of his body weight made his hands burn with the strain of holding on. He kicked aimlessly, desperate to find as much as a small protrusion in the cliffside on which he could support himself. When he finally established a foothold, he caught his breath and turned to face Medeva beside him, who seized the stone wall on all fours with perfect poise. Knowing that he was likely suspended a couple of hundred feet above ground, Magnus was loath to let his eyes wander anywhere below and glimpse the mortal depth of the chasm.

Medeva began her descent, fluently maintaining a hold on the cliffside with both her hands and boots as she climbed. Magnus strove to do the same at an ever-cautious pace. He faltered often, each time pausing to recover his grip while his heart throbbed against the rock face. He could hardly concentrate, knowing that the Rammeren may be only seconds away from finding them again.

Once they had made it low enough, Medeva pulled the toes of her boots free from the cliffside and released her grasp. She dropped to a stand on another roughly horizontal ledge that jutted out over the chasm. With great difficulty, Magnus followed down to the platform, letting go only when his feet had already met the floor.

He looked around to find that they had hit a dead end. The ledge was barely wider than he was tall, and only half as deep. The chasm seemed to close in on them like the ocean on a desert island, while below them, the rock face fell impossibly sheer. The opposing mountain wall stood as the sole object in his vision, and he saw nothing in their imminent range that could be considered much of an alcove. "Where now?" Magnus cast a troubled glance off the ledge.

"It's still further down," answered Medeva. When she paused, as if to listen, the crackle of footsteps on gravel sounded faintly from somewhere above. "They're coming back for us. We have no choice but to jump."

The harpie paced to the rim of the ledge, where the ground was thinnest. She stared down a short stretch below at a rubble-obscured recess in the opposing wall. "That's the alcove," she indicated. She crouched, then propelled herself off the ledge in a mighty bound. "Now jump!"

The harpie lunged through the air and dropped to a stand on the ground of the alcove. Magnus was dizzied at the thought of following her. He hovered at the edge of the platform, gazing downward, and the bouldery chasm floor returned his stare with a reminder of how certain his death would be, should he fall.

The commotion above was loudening. Magnus was doubtful of whether he'd be able to vault the chasm, but he hadn't much of a choice other than waiting to be shot by the Rammeren like a wounded fowl. So he wrung his hands into fists, recoiled a step, and leapt with all of his strength.

After a hasty scramble down the cliffside, Malion and a pair of the Rammeren guards arrived on the ledge beneath the pathway on which they had last spotted Magnus and the harpie. Malion sank his brow and studied the mountainscape, embittered. The two trespassers were nowhere in sight.

"Are you sure you saw them come down here?" the captain asked the others.

"I thought I did," one of the men replied, perplexed. "I was too far to say for sure."

"Well, there's no one here." Malion sighed. "And if there was, they'll be long gone by now."

"So is that all?" said the other guard. "Have we lost them for good?"

"Difficult to say," answered Malion. "With the shades gone, they might just ditch their plan, whatever it was. They could have already fled back toward Serenia. If not, of course, they're heading someplace else." He gazed to the outlying peaks of the mountains. "If only we knew where."

Malion exchanged looks with his colleagues. "We must

keep searching nonetheless. Recett is a menace to all of us, and the reason he sent his scouts to Galem could never be a good one."

Magnus glanced past Medeva, shivering. He sat crumpled behind a rockslide, next to the harpie, deep within the alcove. They could make out a host of voices echoing somewhere from the cliffside on the other side of the chasm.

Medeva peered over the top of the rockslide and slithered back down, halberd readied in her grasp. "They can't see us from here," she whispered. "Keep still until they leave and we'll be safe."

Magnus did as he was told while continuing to eavesdrop. It was difficult to discern exactly what the guards were saying, but their tones were noticeably disgruntled. It took some time before the voices started to diminish; a few minutes later, all had come quiet. Even afterward, the silence lingered on ominously.

Medeva flung another indirect look over the rockslide and turned away. She waited a while longer before finally motioning to Magnus. "They've gone for now," she said. "It should be clear to move on."

"Wait," Magnus stopped the harpie before she could rise. "Can't you call the shades back first? In case they see us again?"

"With the shades back, they *will* see us again," Medeva

argued, "and that's not what we want to happen. Now that they've lost us, we've got to stay out of view." She gripped the rockslide and came upright—only to freeze in her place.

A wiry man clambered up over the edge of the alcove. It was a Rammeren soldier, specifically the shortswordsman of the five guards who had stopped Magnus and Medeva at the foot of the mountains. He unsheathed both his weapons as soon as he was able to stand. "Clever trick of yours, that was," he sneered. "Thought you could pull the wool over our eyes, did you?"

Medeva didn't waste a second before lunging toward the guard, halberd extended to his chest. Unwary of such a prompt assault, the swordsman ducked aside to avoid being speared, losing much of his stability in the process. The harpie swept her polearm back up again, but her blow was deflected by one from the guard. Magnus gawked from the sidelines without knowing how, or even if, he was expected to help in the fight.

"I wasn't as blind as the others," the guard continued to brag even as he wrestled to thwart Medeva's strikes. "I wasn't so blind as to bother reporting you. Instead, I followed you all the way here, so that I may return with your head as a hunting trophy!"

Medeva couldn't have paid less attention to the guard's conceited boasting. She brought her halberd sidelong and shoved it forward, repelling another blow and sending the swordsman lurching back a few paces nearer to the cliff. When the guard raised one of his blades again, a bash by Medeva's weapon almost knocked it from his grasp.

The guard fortified his stance and delivered an unsuccessful counterattack. "It seems that we're evenly matched, harpie!" he crowed, as if to convince himself that he had any chance against his opponent.

Medeva once more thrust out the trunk of her halberd, and the swordsman was driven back further toward the alcove's edge, his left foot already half off the cliff. The guard made an inept twist of his neck so as to determine how much more room he had behind himself, which turned out to be his worst mistake. In the instant the swordsman took his eyes off Medeva, she speared her polearm at him too swiftly for him to defend. She slit the front of his throat in a motion so deft that not even the slightest fleck of blood could tarnish her halberd blade. The guard drew in a choked gasp and spilled his weapons onto the floor. He toppled backward, and his body plummeted off the alcove.

The harpie's gaze fell after the guard into the chasm. "Fool," she spat. "Moved his mouth more than his swords." She stood there a moment, then turned away from the cliff to find Magnus kneeling over one of the guard's former weapons, examining it intently. He came upright with the shortsword in his hand, using his thumb to trace the pattern embossed in its hilt, then flipped it over twice, onto its other side and back.

"You're only going to slow yourself down if you lug that thing all the way to the valley," the harpie woke Magnus from his trance.

"I wasn't planning on keeping it," he muttered slowly, still in a muse, and set the blade on the ground. "Just looking at it." He suddenly picked up his head at realizing what Medeva had said to him. "Wait—the valley? I thought Daimos didn't want us to go anywhere near there."

"Circumstances have changed," replied Medeva. "They'll be hunting us all across the mountains. The valley is the only place where the Rammeren would never dare to search for us."

"Why?" Magnus inquired keenly.

"For both our sakes," said Medeva as she re-holstered her polearm behind her, "it would be best if you didn't find out."

31

The Old Kingdom

S THE HOURS OF THE DAY dwindled, so did the light of the sun's ash-blurred sphere that hovered over the mountains' western summits. Magnus and Medeva made most of their progress traveling in the higher reaches of the mountain range, where the ground was roughly level and paths were consistent. Fortunately for them, the slain shortswordsman was the last they had seen of the Rammeren guards.

After a steady hike over flat land, they began a descent down an enormous slope with seemingly limitless span and depth. Far below, the slope progressively evened before plunging into hazy darkness. The harpie led Magnus down the slope on a series of outcrops that tilted into one another like a broken staircase. She found no difficulty in leaping across the stone ledges; the boy took far more caution in following.

Magnus slid off the first outcrop, dangling from its rim by both his hands. Medeva waited impatiently several feet beneath him. He unhooked his grasp and landed on a lower platform, beside the harpie.

"You sure know these mountains well," Magnus commented, curious for Medeva's response.

Medeva swiveled around and gracefully dropped onto the next step in the mountain staircase. "I used to spend a lot of time around here."

"Really?" Magnus scrambled down to Medeva's level. "Even with all the Rammeren guards?"

"Ha!" Medeva scoffed. "I was here long before any of those arrogant outlaws could claim this land for themselves."

Magnus followed her onto another outcrop. "And how long ago was that?"

The boy's query caused Medeva to halt suddenly. "Too long ago," she whispered, as if she were replying to herself.

Magnus saw Medeva's sudden somberness and refrained from questioning her further. He trailed her onto the next platform, where a pair of jagged rock mounds rose up behind the cliff's edge in a formation that resembled a set of upturned claws. He strode beside one of the mounds, palming its gritty stone, and peered downward.

The bottom of the slope was in sight—a final incline merging into a level plane, dotted with gnarled, leafless trees and painted with black earth. But most prominent of all was the labyrinth of shadows that extended as far as Magnus could see, meeting every angle of his vision. It was the valley, and the ancient city of Old Galem.

Crammed, meandering streets and alleys wreathed between angular masses of buildings in a convoluted black-and-gray sprawl. No structure appeared significantly taller than the next, aside from a particularly impressive construction atop a hill in the utmost east. Ascending the hill was a dilapidated fortification of walls stretched between soaring towers. And within the walls, adorning the hill's crest, was a grand castle whose spires climbed to the ashen skies, basking in the gloom that enveloped them.

Magnus was riveted by the valley's awesome sight. Even as Medeva ambled ahead of the boy, Magnus was too deep in his pensive trance to follow her. Never in his life had he witnessed something this extraordinary—Galem's old mountain empire, and supposedly one of the greatest cities ever to have been built on Arkane.

"This..." Magnus said solemnly, "...is the valley?"

"Correct," Medeva answered, and resumed her descent as if the city were no more spectacular than a trench of rubble in the landscape.

Magnus snapped himself out of his pondering and clambered past the rock mounds. "What could possibly be so dangerous about this place that Daimos didn't want us to come here? It looks totally deserted."

"Looks can be deceiving, Wingheart," Medeva called from below. "As you saw with the arboryn in the forest, a place does not need to be inhabited in order for it to carry a threat."

"But what *is* so dangerous, then?" Magnus rejoined, growing irritated. He climbed down after the harpie.

"And why are you so secretive? If we're going to encounter this threat anyway, then isn't it in my best interest that you tell me what it is?"

"This threat is not unavoidable," said Medeva, turning on the boy, "therefore it is merely a risk. Follow in my tracks, and the both of us will be safe."

Many more minutes of arduous climbing passed before Magnus and Medeva arrived at the base of the slope. Immediately, Magnus glanced back to see the distance they had traveled from the slope's peak, which was barely visible from the depth of the valley. Medeva, meanwhile, trod on with little interest in her environment. Once Magnus followed her, they left the mountain slope to crumble into the dusk as the valley took shape before them.

The scattering of gnarled trees that Magnus had first observed from the mountainside made up the only notable detail in the scenery. Blacker than soot, these trees were beyond dead and practically charcoal. Some leaned out from their place, barely clinging to the earth. Others had been torn out entirely, baring roots like the withered necks of a hydra's corpse.

Magnus dragged himself over a rather large one of the fallen trees to catch up with Medeva, far in the lead. He sprinted ahead, when his foot snagged a protrusion in the ground and caused him to trip. Recovering his stance, Magnus found himself within the remains of an ancient structure outlined by strips of dirt-encrusted rubble that hardly jutted above the ground.

Even more such ruins came into view the farther

Magnus pursued Medeva. These were at least partially built up, comprised of a few disjointed walls spilling bricks and mangled scraps of metal like broken bones. But as his gaze wandered down from the rubble, he discovered something far stranger.

The earth was flooded with black ash. A gentle kick was all Magnus needed to send up a whirl of the fine dust into the air, where it lingered like a haze. Ever since he and the harpie had left MorningStar, the ashes that bled from Daimos' fortress had vanished from the ground over the course of their journey; it was odd indeed that these ruins so far from Serenia's capital overflowed with the very same ashes.

Magnus saw Medeva disappear behind the brink of a hill and scampered after her. He couldn't afford to get lost after nightfall, and it didn't seem as though the harpie were paying much attention to him or to how much he had fallen behind. The ash beneath his feet was making him lose traction, but steadily, Magnus scaled the hillside to arrive at the outskirts of the ancient city.

A slender side street welcomed Magnus into the sinister complex. Closely constructed against it were some of the oldest, most ramshackle buildings that Magnus had ever seen. Their frames were engorged by rot, and their stone foundations were barely discernible amidst the debris. Their rooftops, or what remained of them, had most of their shingles dispersed on the ground as fractured clay splinters.

Magnus drifted into the city, down the side street, and

after Medeva, whose features had by now been blackened to a silhouette in the darkness. Night was upon them, so Magnus conjured a light to his pendant. At that very instant, Medeva spun her head around and glared at the boy, but then turned away without a word.

Magnus extended his neckpiece as a makeshift torch while he walked. It seemed unnaturally challenging for him to keep the gem aglow as its light wavered like a feeble flame. He recalled what Anubis had told him about the difficulty of conjuring light in darkness, but this seemed strangely different—it was impossible to even steady the glow of his pendant, let alone make it strong enough. He sensed that there was an opposing force trying to keep his light extinguished, but he regarded the feeling as a mere trick of his mind.

Turning past a corner, Magnus strayed from the path to better examine one of the ruined buildings. This one was reasonably large, with a jetty extending over the first floor. Cut into its half-timbered façade was a row of small square window openings set above a collapsed doorframe. He waded through the ashes to approach the building, halted at the three-step staircase that led up to the doorway, and leaned inside. His pendant cast light on the disheveled interior—it was practically gutted, the only fixture still standing being a ruined brick hearth. The floor, just like the streets of the city, was drowned in ash.

Magnus had seen enough to notice just how eerily similar this place was to MorningStar. The almost limitless ashes seemed to indicate that Old Galem had met the same fate as Serenia's capital, but, considering that the kingdom of Galem had fallen over a millennium ago, it couldn't have been possible...or could it? A barrage of memories cascaded through Magnus' mind—from his nightmare to Cecil's tales of Galem's history, Daimos Recett, and the Saxum Diaboli—and he wove them together to develop an ominous tapestry:

A thousand years ago, the warlord who led the cult known as the New Order, Sennair Drakathel, usurped the Galem throne and claimed the kingdom for his own. History stated that in his years as king, Sennair recruited an army of thousands, most of whom were not even human, but chimerical beasts that no living being could ever have fathomed to exist. Among those beasts were the shades— the shades that, a thousand years later, Sennair would bequeath to his most loyal follower, Eras Recett, the man who would continue his master's work and seize the province of Serenia.

The shades had indeed been in Galem. But that gave rise to another question: If Medeva was really the shades' puppeteer as she had claimed, then was the harpie just as ancient as Old Galem? Had Medeva once also been a pawn at the hand of Sennair Drakathel?

"What are you standing there gawking at?" Medeva's voice suddenly rang from afar.

Magnus heeded the harpie's call and rushed up behind her. She stopped and glared at him forbiddingly. "This valley is not a safe place to be, Wingheart, remember that," Medeva spat, stressing every word. "We come here by lack of other options and not willingly, so our passage should be as brief and direct as possible."

Magnus only nodded, knowing it was best not to disagree and anger Medeva further. Now walking faster and following the harpie more closely, he found himself heading deeper into the valley by an extensive downhill lane. Magnus avidly scanned each disintegrated frontage he passed. There was something more than just age that had destroyed these buildings—they had been scorched, with burn marks splattered on their walls like the inerasable shadows of the blaze that had defiled them.

Magnus caught sight of something else as he came rather close to one of the ruins. Etched into a still-standing wall was quite a distinct marking, however partially effaced by a scorch mark. From what he could make out, it was a circle mounted on some squarish shape. The rest had been gnawed away by the scorch. He reached out to trace the marking, when Medeva's voice shook him again.

"What now?" Medeva growled to the boy. "Must you halt at every rubble pile? For your own sake, get a move on!"

Magnus withdrew from the wall in compliance, only after playing with the thought of ignoring her. Medeva noticeably sped her pace, either in aggravation or with the intention of forcing Magnus to travel quicker if he'd want to keep up. Before they had made it much farther, Medeva rounded a corner so abruptly that Magnus could have sworn she had passed straight through the walls of the buildings. He stopped by the place where the harpie had changed course and saw that an alleyway tunneled between the charred houses. He darted in just as the harpie left the radius of Magnus' light and dissolved into the dark.

Magnus hastened until Medeva was back inside his field of vision. She had her halberd in hand now. Taking a large stride over a mound of debris, she moved faster still. When the boy passed the same mound, he looked up to see a procession of collapsed arches fitted between the alley walls overhead. Each one was demolished at its peak, with the resulting rubble spilled into the ashes on the floor beneath. Lowering his eyes, Magnus' attention became snagged by a crude scrawling on the wall to his left. He needed only glance at it once to become enthralled by it: it was the skull icon that could be seen all across MorningStar, and the unmistakable likeness of the Saxum Diaboli. The charred etching that Magnus had spotted earlier must have been the same symbol.

Magnus turned away and saw that Medeva had also halted. She glowered at the boy, but Magnus was sure to speak first before Medeva could have a chance to scold him again. "That symbol..." he said, gesturing to the icon. "That's Daimos' symbol, isn't it?"

Medeva looked away and carried on down the alley at a much slower rate. "It is an ancient symbol," she replied impassively, "one that signifies strength in death. It has been used throughout history by many factions and people."

Magnus proceeded behind her. "People like..." He paused dramatically. "...Sennair Drakathel?"

Medeva remained emotionless. "You know your history well," she said with a shadow of sarcasm.

"I read about this city," said Magnus. Exiting the alley, he wandered by the remains of an old tavern eclipsed by scorch marks. "It was usurped by Sennair about a thousand years ago. He must have been the one associated with the symbol." He waited for a reaction from Medeva, but continued when she stayed silent. "It's incredible, actually," he muttered, "how much similarity there is between this city and MorningStar."

Again, Magnus failed to get the harpie's attention, and so he persisted with his rhetorical statements. "The symbol, the ruins, the ashes," he said. "It's almost like Daimos himself used to be here."

"Whatever it is you're trying to allude to, you're failing at it," Medeva finally snapped. "Recett is a follower of the Order; that is why he adopted its icon for his army. And these ruins are a millennium old. You have no way of knowing how the ashes first appeared here."

"It was said that Sennair had a legion of shades fighting on his side." Magnus put on a shrewd smile. "The ashes must be those that were left behind by them." He paused again. "Seems familiar, doesn't it?"

"Sennair's army would have had to be vastly different from Recett's," Medeva answered in a voice more maddened.

"Many of Daimos' followers don't seem to think so."

"Then they are fools."

Magnus shrugged in an almost sarcastic manner. "I guess I don't know then...It's just all strangely ironic, considering—"

"You're getting very tiring to listen to, Wingheart,"

the harpie barged in. "Conjure up your own pointless conspiracies in your head if you must, but if I were you, I'd rather spend my concentration on navigating the city." She swiveled around and seized Magnus by the front of his shirt. He gasped and locked his breath in his throat as Medeva leaned closer. "Now shut your mouth," she hissed, "and keep moving." With that, she hauled Magnus aside and let go, throwing him face-first onto the ground in an explosion of soot.

Magnus raised his upper body on the support of his hands and spit the bitter ash from his mouth. By the time he had brought himself to a stand, Medeva was already close to vanishing in the gloom beyond.

There must be some truth behind all this, Magnus insisted to himself. *Her anger confirms it.* He shouldered his pack and scurried in her footsteps, sweeping the ash off his clothes. *She's hiding something, and she acts as if my knowing it could be even more of a threat than the Luminous Rock.*

The next hours passed tediously. Magnus hadn't rested since long before they had left the mountains, and fatigue was catching up with him. Not making his trek any more enjoyable was the biting, stagnant cold that lingered in the air. At night especially, the valley sustained a frigid temperature. Magnus folded his hands under his arms for warmth, but he couldn't even convince himself that it made much of a difference. In the mountains and on the planes, dead trees and brushwood were common enough for him to gather and ignite, should he need the heat. In the city, alas, any kindling of the sort was scarce, and the trees were so withered that fire would devour their wood in seconds.

Turning a corner, he came across another skeletal icon, engraved into the first wall of a terrace of houses. So many of the same markings had crossed his path over the last hour that he had already lost count. It was unsurprising, of course, seeing how the valley had once been the heart of the empire ruled by Sennair Drakathel, to whom the icon clearly belonged.

Again, Magnus' thoughts turned to Daimos' unsubstantiated warnings about the valley. The warlord, quite like Medeva, had claimed that Old Galem was a place of mortal danger. But after spending much of an evening in the valley itself, Magnus could be assured that this was a blatant lie. That begged the question of why else Daimos could have wanted to keep Magnus from this place. Taking into account that Daimos' possessor was Sennair himself, perhaps Daimos knew something about the abandoned kingdom that others did not—something that both he and Medeva did not want Magnus to discover.

Magnus and the harpie emerged from the houses and stepped out into an open court. It appeared to be a town square, stared upon by the two dozen gaping carcasses of the encircling storefronts. A multi-floored construction—possibly an inn—stood slumped in the near south. The rest of the buildings were too devastated to permit any guess as to what purpose they used to serve.

Medeva proceeded into the square, but Magnus slowed his steps. "Hold it," he called. "Wouldn't this be a good place to rest before we move on?"

The harpie stopped walking and answered with her back still to Magnus. "No," she bluntly refused. "You can rest once we've left the city."

Magnus gave an indignant frown. "And how long is that going to be? I've been hiking for hours nonstop!"

"You should be glad that you're still alive after all we've been through," snapped Medeva. "You'll also find that you'll move faster if you stop protesting."

"Fifteen minutes," Magnus sighed acrimoniously and collapsed to a seat against a patch of wall. "Even if I'm your and Daimos' slave, you still need me to reach the Rock alive." He braced himself for the harpie's rebuke, but none came. Medeva drifted into the center of the court and halted, silent.

Magnus opened his eyes after some time. He wasn't sure how long he'd been resting, though he didn't feel much less fatigued. For a second, he thought Medeva had abandoned him; then he saw her, at a distance, by the mouth of the road that led east out of the court.

She stood still as the ruin around her, as if she were carved of the same ancient stone. She was gazing out at what seemed like something impossibly far away. Her appearance was almost wistful, but Magnus doubted she could be touched by such an emotion. As he got up and approached her, she brusquely veered south and began pacing away.

"What's out there?" Magnus asked with an upward nod to the east road.

"The castle." Medeva halted, but scarcely looked back. "We're going around."

"Castle?" Magnus wondered aloud. "Sennair's castle?"

"Correct," the harpie said tonelessly.

"Why go around?"

"Because we can cover more ground faster than if we have to scale that mountain of a hill."

Magnus dwelled a moment on Medeva's answers. He wasn't prepared to pass on an opportunity to explore a site so portentous as Sennair Drakathel's old castle. "I saw it from the mountain slope," said Magnus. "The hill's just as wide as it is high. It would be a lot quicker just to cut through the castle."

"The castle is a heap of rubble with no straight path through," Medeva asserted. "Traveling around is our only clear route."

"But all the castle walls are demolished," Magnus countered. "There won't be any clearer a path up there than there is across this labyrinth." He paused a moment, slanting his eyes dubiously. "And when's the last time you've been up there?"

With her back still turned, Medeva clenched tighter the ebony trunk of her halberd as if stirred with some profound resentment. "As I said before, Wingheart, I used to spend a lot of time here, so it would be best for you to trust me as your guide."

"I'm not sure about that," Magnus replied, scoffing.

"What about all that nonsense you told me about the valley being dangerous? If that wasn't an outright lie..."

"You've hardly seen enough of this place to judge it," the harpie snapped, mortally stern.

"It's the castle, isn't it?" asked Magnus.

Medeva finally turned around, fury simmering. "It's the castle *what?*"

"I get it by now." Magnus' lip crept to a smirk. "There's nothing dangerous in the valley. You and Daimos were just trying to hide something from me. If that something isn't in the city, it must be in the castle."

Medeva's stare turned blank with disbelief. "You're more of a fool than I could ever have expected. You think this is all some plot we concocted to keep you in secrecy? That castle is just as void as anything else in the valley!"

"Then what makes you so reluctant to go there?" Magnus drilled her further. "It will take just as long to go over that hill as it would to go around it."

"I beg to differ." Medeva turned on Magnus as if she were about to storm off, but remained with her heels locked on the sooty stone.

"I know it's in the castle," Magnus persisted. He feigned conviction for the sake of the harpie's response. "It makes no difference which way you lead me. I'll come back here someday and find that secret of yours."

"Kill yourself if you wish." A baritone murmur of laughter twisted Medeva's voice. "It's no responsibility of mine what folly you commit on your own time."

Magnus returned the laugh with irony. "So now you tell me that this 'void' castle is a threat to my life?"

Medeva faced Magnus again. By the look of her expression, her anger had turned to what seemed like cynical amusement. "Look, boy—you want to go up there? I've no qualms about it; you're the one who's been griping for rest. If you want to waste your strength at the expense of your jailed brother, let it be your own loss."

Magnus shed an offhand glance in the direction of the castle. With a contented curl of his lip, he began to saunter down the eastern path. Before he'd made it ten feet, Medeva bustled past him and took the lead.

32

Pinnacle

HE PATH TO OLD GALEM'S CASTLE was a long and wearisome one. It not only climbed a steep hill, but also ducked and wove harshly to maneuver the jagged terrain. It led out from the densest parts of the city and into new fields, where buildings were reduced to the same sparse number that Magnus had seen earlier in the valley's outskirts. The blackened trees, on the other hand, were more common here, though they seemed to lessen farther up on the hill.

Magnus tried futilely to glimpse the peak of the hill while he ascended the path. The castle, even at its leviathan size, was but a shadow against the night sky. It was identifiable only by the contours of its four towers, one enormously tall and the other three only half the size. The nearer that Magnus and the harpie came, the larger the shadow swelled and, eventually, it took on traces of color and detail. And the more of the fortress that emerged into sight, the more Magnus' mind seethed with notions of what Daimos and Medeva could be trying to hide from him.

He was almost certain that the castle was of some significance, but that still failed to answer just why. By the look on Daimos' face when Magnus had spoken of crossing the valley, the reason would have to be terribly important. Was it a source of great power? Or, conversely, a source of great danger? Magnus was disinclined to believe the latter, since he couldn't think of any logical explanation for it.

Then, of course, there was always the possibility that the castle was just as barren as Medeva claimed. Her willingness to head through suggested that she and Daimos had, in fact, very little to hide. According to his journal, even Brendan Wingheart had been here, yet his writings stated nothing specific about the valley nor the castle. Either the harpie was right, or there had simply been too little time for Brendan to completely explore Sennair's old kingdom.

But if it wasn't the castle, then what was it that made the valley such a portentous location? What was it that made Daimos warn of a danger that would "crush the sense of what it means to be powerful"? Could it be that Daimos had another weakness here aside from the Luminous Rock?

After Medeva and Magnus passed the demolished outer defenses, the castle's inner wall was now close in sight. Any signs of buildings or trees were gone at this height on the hill. Already from afar, Magnus could see that the entrance gate had long collapsed. Only its imposing arch remained, lining a great stone doorway that opened into the castle grounds. Twin towers stood against the walls at either side with the poise of petrified guardsmen. As the gloom beyond the entrance wafted away at the light of Magnus' pendant, a disheartening black smear emerged on the narrow horizon—the castle moat.

In short sequence, Medeva and the boy came still upon reaching the moat. It was, predictably, dry and tremendously deep. As Magnus shuffled his foot forward, ash and soil crumbled from the moat's eroded outer rim and faded into the pit. Aside from trying to scramble through the seemingly bottomless ditch, the only other way across was by the lowered castle drawbridge at his left. It was intact, but its wood was profoundly rotted. Only one of its suspension chains remained, passed through a slot high on the wall beside the archway and hooked tautly to the bridge's front end about twenty feet away. Many of its boards, especially down its centre, were fractured or missing.

"We take the bridge." Medeva motioned the boy aside.

Magnus reluctantly surveyed the disintegrating walkway. "Will it hold?"

"I'm not sure," Medeva replied with ironic inflection. "It was your clever idea to come here." She turned away, came before the drawbridge, and stared through the fallen gate on the other end. The chain that suspended the bridge's right side was still attached; the leftmost one had been cleaved by centuries worth of rust. "Walk the right edge," she instructed. Bringing down her halberd's pole, she rapped the bridge twice to verify its strength, then took a single step forward.

Magnus stood behind the harpie and waited for her to move farther down the bridge, allowing him enough room to follow. Medeva leaned her halberd forward again to test another segment of the drawbridge. When she was sure it was safe, she advanced, and continued in this manner along the bridge's length. Magnus was able to proceed now and did so with caution, taking care to trace the harpie's footsteps exactly. Striding over a gap in the final stretch of the bridge, Medeva arrived under the gateway arch. The moment that Magnus reached her, she trampled over the prostrate entrance gate and hastened off through the mouth of the castle.

Magnus eagerly proceeded after her. Observing the arch, he noticed Sennair's skeletal icon again, this time as a raised stone carving on the peak of the gateway. He turned ahead when, suddenly, his pendant's light flickered more madly than ever before. He cupped the jewel into his hand and renewed his focus on it, steadying the light. His magic truly was being oppressed by another force—it seemed too strange for him to believe anything else. All throughout his passage through the valley, he had found it unusually difficult to keep his pendant lit, and the castle only seemed to amplify that difficulty. Whatever the cause of this was, it had to be decidedly powerful to subdue a spell from such distance.

Magnus made his way, along with Medeva, toward the castle's inner passage while keeping half a stare fastened on his dim light source. He entered a desolate roofless corridor that was as wide as it was deep, closed within four bare stone walls. Two rows of confined window openings dotted the walls on the east and west sides; a second gateway was cut into the farthermost wall ahead.

Medeva lingered by the doorway at the back of the passage until Magnus had caught up, then continued through it with the boy. They entered a short hall that appeared to separate the inner passage from the rest of the castle. It was shaped by a vaulted ceiling and terminated at an august entranceway beyond which nothing was perceivable. Magnus walked with his head tilted to the ceiling in fascination, readjusting his gaze only once he had reached the corridor's end. He and the harpie emerged from the hall and, to his surprise, ended up back in the open.

Magnus could have reckoned that this section of the castle had been destroyed entirely, leaving behind no remnants to prove its past existence. An open hallway encircled the vast plane, rowed with pillars that supported a mostly demolished canopy along the outer castle walls. There was little to distinguish this place from any other bleak field in the valley, but its site within the castle suggested that this had once been an inner courtyard.

Magnus paced charily and watched his environment keenly. It was eerie here, and perhaps not made any more auspicious by the ashes that carpeted the ground. Eventually he came to a wide circular recess that marked the center of the courtyard, and stepped down into it. Before him was a great stone basin with a smaller plinth nested inside of it. Whatever had rested on the plinth—possibly the upper half of what used to be a fountain—was now cleaved into ornately carved boulders strewn around a smashed portion of the basin. He lifted his head and tried to locate Medeva, realizing that she had halted farther on. Magnus moved up beside her, eyes set onward in the same direction she faced.

There was a gate ahead, but unlike others they had encountered so far, this one was shut securely. It was barred with crossed strips of iron and sealed by the wreckage of a collapsed passage behind it. It looked as though Magnus and the harpie had hit a dead end.

Medeva did nothing but gaze, as if unsurprised. Magnus approached the gate and locked his palm against its blistered iron. "Is there any way around?" he asked.

"No," replied Medeva, "as I said from the beginning."

All Magnus' hopes of discovering the castle's secrets withered instantly. He slammed a fist to the gate. "What's on the other side?"

"How should I know?" Medeva answered without a fleck of emotion.

"By the way you've been talking, I assumed you used to live here," Magnus replied. He half closed an eye, provocatively dubious. "Did you?"

"Never," she droned with loathing, turning to depart.

Magnus dogged her. "Then why was it you used to spend so much time around here?" He was already certain of an indignant reaction and recoiled a step in defense.

But Medeva walked on, unmoved. "Why do you ask so many questions, Wingheart?" she said with surprising composure. "Even if you knew the answers...what would you hope to do with them?"

Magnus dropped his head in deliberation of whether to respond. It was then that he caught sight of something strange. "Wait..." He came still, pointing to the ground at his feet. "What's that?"

Medeva turned to see what the boy was indicating. The ashes on the floor appeared to be moving, steadily shifting along a fixed stream. Her brow twitched; she faced Magnus. "It's the wind," she said, then trod away. "Come on."

Magnus lifted his doubtful face to feel the air. "There's no wind." He refocused on the ashes and began to follow the stream. It was very broad at first, but soon split into several thinner paths that each carved the black dust like serpents.

"Where are you going?" Medeva barked. "I said come! You're wasting time!"

But Magnus ignored her, entranced. The trail took him northward until it reached the open hallway that surrounded the courtyard, where it wound between the pillars and into the shadows. He stopped when he met the hall and leaned inside, hand rested on a headless column. Under his wan light, he was just able to recognize the shape of a doorway in the castle wall through which the trail flowed. A gate of spear-headed poles barred the door, but, on closer inspection, it seemed that a pair of the poles had been pried apart by force. There was just enough space to fit through.

"I think there's another doorway here," Magnus alerted the harpie to the newfound entrance and crept toward it.

"It's a dead-end extension of the courtyard," Medeva

replied. "You saw the only route through the castle and it's blocked, so come!"

Magnus walked to the mangled gate, peering beyond it. "The ashes are coming out from here...or moving inside..." His sentence trailed off. "There must be something down here..." Giving no other warning, he turned sideways and wedged himself through the bars, vanishing from Medeva's sight.

"Wait, no!" Medeva hollered back. "Wingheart!" Soot splashing in her tracks, she raced for the open hall and toward the gateway.

Magnus emerged on the other side of the gate. He found himself standing at the back edge of a much smaller court-yard. The western tower's wall was close to his left, and the highest point of the castle, the keep tower, soared over him from the opposite side. The flowing ashen trail was densest here, but its end was not yet visible. It snaked all the way into a distant region of the courtyard, where a nebulous blur loomed on the horizon.

Magnus cringed and shivered. There was something profoundly disturbing about this place. He was nevertheless determined to unveil the source of the shifting ashes and walked out into the courtyard, down the trail. The blur took shape—it was an isolated stone pavilion with a single doorway, fashioned in the same lordly appearance as the other parts of the castle. Most curious was that the ash trail poured in through the doorway, then bled back out from it in a sprawl of veins that throbbed and rippled as if the earth itself were breathing. This was the source of the trail: a sinister edifice nested in the heart of Sennair Drakathel's old empire.

"Magnus, stop!" Medeva suddenly burst from the courtyard gate. She tried to charge after the boy, but staggered to a halt before she could get anywhere near him. Magnus spun around to see Medeva step back, her teeth gritted and her breathing heavy, as if she were in pain. "Don't you dare go any farther," she demanded in her hoarsest voice. "Come back now!"

Magnus stopped, but refused to return. "Why?" he asked suspiciously, angling his head toward the stone building. "What is that thing?"

"It's doesn't matter," Medeva said breathlessly. "Just get away from it, and come here."

Magnus looked sidelong at the harpie, who remained far from his reach by the courtyard gate. He paused to weigh his options, but remained adamantly in position. "This is the place," he determined. "This is what you and Daimos were trying to hide from me." He took another stride toward the building. The ashen trail was getting so turbulent that he could feel it brushing past his ankles.

"You shouldn't care what it is!" rasped Medeva. "If you had any wit left, you'd listen to me! This isn't about Recett, this is about us making it out of here alive!"

Magnus scarcely heard her. He had finally uncovered Daimos' secret, sealed within the walls of Sennair's castle, and he wouldn't lose this opportunity to glimpse it with his own eyes. Captivated by the pavilion's almost bestial maw, he walked further into the courtyard.

"You're going to kill us both if you don't stop! Listen to me, Wingheart!" Medeva's cries grew more urgent. "This is dangerous!"

Magnus sighed acrimoniously. "Then tell me why!" he shouted with his back to the harpie. "You said that you had nothing to hide in the castle. Tell me why this is so dangerous."

"It won't even make a difference," Medeva hissed, "when your broken, bloody bones will be all that remains of you."

Magnus' mind reeled as his heart pounded. *She's lying,* he convinced himself. *She and Daimos already fooled me once about the valley. Now is my chance to see just what they were hiding.* He clenched his pallid fists and approached the pavilion. He could clearly make out its carvings from such close distance. One in particular, perched at the apex of the doorway, was of the infamous skull icon upheld by an arch of bone-thin hands and arms. It was practically a depiction of the Saxum Diaboli, and only greater indication that the chamber beyond this doorway was of considerable importance to Sennair Drakathel and his cult.

Peering in, Magnus saw that the pavilion housed a staircase. The ashen trail poured down it and was eventually swallowed by an abyss at the bottom of the steps. Magnus lifted a foot over the first stair, but was interrupted by a strident clash of metal on the ground only inches away.

A sooty gust whirled into his face, just as he spotted a small metallic object clatter down the staircase and fade into the abyss.

Magnus flung a look over his shoulder. Medeva, now far behind him, appeared to be wielding a knife. She had the blade cocked and raised as if she were ready to hurl it directly at Magnus. "Take one more step," she threatened, "and the next knife I throw will impale you."

Magnus spent a moment in thought, then replied calmly, "You wouldn't kill me."

"I don't need to kill you," she retorted. "I only need to wound you in order to drag you out of here."

Magnus hesitated at first, but shortly responded. "If you could drag me away, then why didn't you do it from the start? By the looks of it, you're too scared to even get near here."

Two seconds crept past in silence. Surprisingly, Medeva lowered her weapon. "Very well," she spat. "Go ahead and kill yourself."

When Magnus turned back to the staircase, he heard the harpie's voice again: "Just remember," said Medeva, "the ones who will perish along with you."

Magnus froze immediately, remembering Drake, Cecil, and Anubis in the MorningStar dungeons. He would willingly take any risk to himself if it meant discovering the valley's secret, but couldn't say the same with his life tied to those locked away in Daimos' citadel. If he couldn't make it to the Luminous Rock, then all three would be killed.

I can't take any chances, he thought, *but I need to find out what's down there. If only I could see clearer...* He raised his lit pendant. The most he could do was brighten his light enough to illuminate the staircase. He summoned all his concentration to the jewel, whose light flared threefold.

"No!" Medeva exclaimed. "No, you fool, not the light!"

A warbled hiss flickered in the air, lunging from afar and into the stone structure as if in some backward reverberation. With the aid of his light, Magnus was able to glimpse the base of the stairs—a confined chamber with an expansive tiling embedded in its farthermost wall. The tiling was a mosaic of Sennair's skull icon, larger than any he had seen, and perfectly intact. And the entire chamber, from ceiling to floor, was enmeshed in tendrils of ashes that seeped from behind the mosaic through a slit around its edge. Was this what Daimos had been trying to keep secret? Magnus had only seconds to think before circumstances took an abrupt and unpleasant turn.

The hiss loudened, then broke into a wraithlike snarl. A furious squall exploded from the staircase, and Magnus' pendant was extinguished in an instant.

"Run, Wingheart!" Medeva cried at the top of her lungs. "Run this way! Hurry!"

Magnus was paralyzed in his disarray. Blinded by the dark, he heard only the wind surging against his ears, broken by a multitude of horrific screams like those of beasts, but hollow, mangled, and almost ethereal. It seemed that something beyond terrible had been stirred to life.

33

Ashes Awakened

MAGNUS TRIED FRANTICALLY to reignite his pendant, but all his attempts were in vain. The force that had subdued his light from the time he had set foot in the valley was at its strongest, and no magic of his could hope to oppose it.

"Don't just stand there!" the harpie cried even louder. "Run!"

Magnus leapt to his feet and sprinted blindly toward Medeva. Once he had gotten far enough away from the pavilion, he was finally able to light his pendant. Through the limited beam that shone from it, he saw the ash on the ground whirl as if it had been spurred by a hurricane. He shielded his eyes while he ran, tackled by the sooty billows that grayed out everything in sight. The wind raged faster and the ethereal cries multiplied before reaching a ghastly climax.

A deafening roar bellowed over the courtyard and drowned out any other audible noise. Magnus slowed to a crawl and winced, his palms pressed against his ears. As the roar diminished, he was taken aback by a powerful upsurge of ashes at his feet. He leapt away and observed as the erupted ash clung to the air and weaved a menacing shadow. The shadow swelled to at least twice Magnus' height, then solidified to form a beast, or rather, an abomination.

It was a creature shaped from ash, and one that shouldn't have existed beyond the world of a nightmare. Its body was that of an emaciated stallion, with four hooves thick as boulders and legs high as small trees. At the end of its whiplike tail were fastened twin curved spines as long and broad as dirks. A pair of arms extended from the front of its body, lank and lithe, each with a single claw like the blade of a scythe. Its neck was long and slender, snaking up to meet the head of a monstrous horned serpent, fangs unsheathed and beady eyes staring downward.

"Get away, quick!" Medeva shrieked.

Magnus ducked aside and spurred around the stallion beast. When he heard it roar again, he cast a fleeting look behind himself to see it galloping toward him madly. He reached the exit, sped past Medeva, and wove through the bars of the gate that led back into the main courtyard. If he was right, the beast was too large to follow him through the narrow gateway.

He stalled at the other side of the gate until Medeva had also made it through, then resumed his frantic retreat.

Magnus had almost reached the shattered fountain in the courtyard's center when he realized that Medeva was nowhere near him. He stopped at once to look back, only to find the harpie still standing by the mangled gate.

Magnus thought to shout for her attention, but he was rendered speechless when a surge of ashes lunged through the gateway and toward Medeva. In an instant, the ashes converged to regain the form of the serpent-headed stallion beast. It smashed its hooves onto the ground and bared its fangs and claws, ready to strike the harpie.

"Medeva!" Magnus exclaimed in shock.

Medeva didn't even bother to meet eyes with the boy. Instead, she fortified her stance, halberd in hand, prepared to combat the stallion. By the looks of the beast, Magnus was unsure if she even had any chance against it, but she was swift to demonstrate her skill. A spectral gray aura sparked from the tip of Medeva's halberd and flared down its length, catching the polearm like fire. She thrust out the weapon's spearhead and vigorously impaled the beast's chest. The stallion beast reared with a wail of agony, then shattered into a smog of the ashes that formed it, leaving behind no trace of its former existence.

Medeva darted from the gate and drew beside the boy. Magnus turned to her, slowing his run. "That was incredible," he said blankly. "What kind of magic was that?"

"I do not use any sort of your petty spells," Medeva dismissed his notion. "The ash plays tricks on your eyes."

"You destroyed it somehow," Magnus persisted. "Your

halberd glowed...and how else would that creature have just burst—"

"Now isn't the time to discuss your delusions," the harpie cut in. "We're still far from safety."

Medeva's warning was affirmed by another two eruptions from the ashes around them. Though Magnus expected to see the stallion beast rise again, the freshly spewed clouds slumped back to the ground, each into its own amorphous shadow. They slithered rapidly across the floor and accelerated until they came up to speed with Magnus and Medeva, where they maintained their positions on either side.

Magnus tried to run faster, but the shadows adjusted to his new pace effortlessly. Medeva, strangely, was falling behind, and Magnus was forced to slow down in order to keep the harpie beside him. Medeva had always been the faster one by far—in the castle, however, it seemed quite the opposite.

They streaked inside the hall before the inner passage, trailed by the two shadows. Magnus kept his sights fastened on the exit gateway straight ahead, when he saw the shadows race in front and come to a halt by the gate. Then, in the same way that the stallion beast had appeared, the shadows rose and gained shape in the blink of an eye.

These creatures were not as large as the stallion, but still considerably taller than Magnus and Medeva. A single pair of hooves was their foundation, attached to legs and an upright body that resembled a human skeleton.

Their arms were equally fleshless, with oversized claws in place of fingers. Mounted on crumpled vertebrae were heads like rams' skulls: two gnarled horns set behind crooked eyeholes, and a snout with long, blunt teeth.

Magnus was inclined to stop, but Medeva had opposite thoughts. "Keep down and go as fast as you as can," she instructed, picking up speed. "They're slower than they appear."

Uneasily, Magnus did as he was told. The skeletal horrors sluggishly heaved their claws and hunched forward while the two escapees ducked between them. Magnus and the harpie stumbled through the gate into the inner passage just as the skeletons brought down their claws and barely missed their targets.

Magnus tossed up his head. "This is madness..." he said. "What were all those things, those creatures?"

"Enough questions!" Medeva snarled in reply. "Run! Your life depends on it!"

Magnus nodded quickly and obeyed. Though he had doubted her before, Magnus knew now that Medeva was, and had been, warning him of a very real threat. Could Daimos have been doing the same when he forbid Magnus' passage through the valley? Was it really the danger itself that concerned Daimos, or rather the secret that resided at its source?

Clearly, it was something within the structure in the side courtyard that gave life to the beasts. And since Daimos and Medeva had both refused to tell the reason for their warnings, clearly that something was not meant for Magnus to know. Perhaps it wasn't for danger alone that they had been told not to pass through here. Daimos' warnings, echoed by the harpie, were merely a cloak over a much greater secret that resided in Sennair Drakathel's castle.

Magnus and Medeva were close to the entrance gate when a roar shattered the rush of the wind. Magnus knew by the sound what was coming their way and stole a backward glance to confirm it. Another stallion beast stood at the back end of the inner passage, razor-toothed jaws unhinged. It was flanked by two other creatures that were the smallest of any Magnus had seen so far. They were like wolves, with thick fur blacker than soot that flowed like a shawl of smoke over their bodies. A snout jutted from beneath their practically invisible dark eyes; they bared fangs like a gamut of daggers as they growled.

"No..." Medeva said under her breath. "We have to move faster or they're going to catch up with us!"

Magnus struggled to gain speed. He heard the stallion's hooves and the croaking snarls of the wolves as the beasts charged behind them. His body shivered with fatigue from his tiring hike to the castle, and he knew that he was too worn to go much farther without falling prey to the beasts. Even Medeva wasn't moving much quicker than he.

Medeva ceased her run at the foot of the drawbridge and gave a hasty motion to Magnus to do the same. "There's no way we can make it. We'll have to jump into the moat."

Magnus looked behind again. The stallion and wolves were already halfway through the inner passage. He turned to the bridge's edge, where he could see the eroded slope that plunged into the moat. Medeva leapt off the draw-bridge, landing on the slope, where she skidded down on the inside of her boot.

The beasts were almost at the castle gateway. Magnus' only chance to survive was to follow Medeva. He jumped from the bridge and threw himself against the wall of the pit. By clawing his hands into the dirt, he was just able to keep from slipping into the moat's depths. Medeva was a few feet beneath him, back pressed to the slope and heels dug in.

The brief thunder of hooves resounded from above as the stallion crossed the drawbridge. It was miraculous that the rickety bridge itself did not collapse; the beasts must have been far lighter than they appeared. As soon as the rattle had faded, Magnus slumped down to Medeva's side and pressed on with his questioning.

"Medeva, please!" he begged. "What are these creatures? There's no sense in hiding this from me anymore! I need to know how I can fight them!"

Medeva's eyes suddenly burned with indignation. "How *you* can *fight* them? Do you have any idea how powerful those creatures are? You cannot even begin to grasp it! Your magic won't do any more than stun them, and they're impervious to any physical weapon."

"That's a lie," said Magnus. "You speared one and destroyed it yourself! I saw you!"

"You saw nothing." Medeva spoke as if it were an order.

"We have to defeat them somehow!" Magnus rejoined irately. "How else are we going to escape?"

"The same way that we escaped the Rammeren." The

harpie extended her hand, which once again scintillated with flecks of shadow. "Except now, the shades won't only be protecting us—they'll be fighting for us."

The sparks on Medeva's palm dissipated as she fisted her hand. "The shades won't afflict much damage on the beasts as a whole," she said, "but their effect will be great enough to fend the beasts off while we flee."

Magnus waited patiently for a result of Medeva's summoning, until the ashes below his feet began to stir. But instead of the shades, a black, clawed hand of bone snapped into existence from the bottom of the moat and clamped onto the slope. Behind the claw, as Magnus had feared, emerged a horned ram's skull.

"It's them again," Magnus alerted, voice shuddering with urgency. "The creatures that attacked us in the hallway."

"I'm not blind," snapped the harpie, her eyes fixed on the clouds. "The shades will take care of them."

The skeleton made its way up the slope by a lumbering climb. Promptly, another pair of identical beasts emerged from behind it and followed suite. Even at their ponderous pace, they would reach Magnus and Medeva in seconds if they weren't stopped.

Magnus shuffled to a higher place on the slope, charged the glow of his pendant, and flashed it before himself in defense. The skeletons recoiled with a moaning bray, but were not affected beyond a stutter in their movement. *Nothing can stop these creatures,* Magnus thought, *except Medeva. I know what I saw. She can destroy them, so why isn't she fighting?*

Magnus stared skyward in hope of a rescue by the shades. Lo and behold, a fracture divided the clouds, giving way to shades' ashes that gushed forth and descended in a formless, spectral mass. As the ashes fell low enough, Magnus dropped his head into folded arms and felt the unearthly multitude wash over him. Finally, the ashes diverged, carried off in plumes that each developed the deathly mask and spindly arms of a shade.

Magnus lifted his head and looked upon Medeva's horde. The shades took to the skies and the ground in droves and devoured the scene immediately. They swarmed the skeletons, tearing at them mercilessly until the beasts wailed in surrender and lost their grip on the slope. Two of the beasts toppled backward into the moat; the third became overwhelmed by a trio of shades and was slashed apart to leave nothing but a mist in its place.

"Now, quickly," Medeva signaled. She turned and began a nimble climb back out of the moat on her hands and feet. Magnus followed her until they both reached the eroded strip of land by the main gateway. With reckless speed, they raced across the chained edge of the drawbridge and into the castle grounds.

Here, the shades were ubiquitous, darting without direction, deluging the air with their bloodcurdling shrieks. But they were not alone—they were accompanied by a foursome of the skeleton beasts that flailed at the specters with the poise of buckling birch trees. Fighting alongside the beasts were the wolves that had chased Magnus and the harpie through the inner passage, but even they were too occupied with battling the shades to pay any attention to their true targets.

Magnus and Medeva plunged into the chaos. They skirted the reach of the skeleton beasts, trusting that the shades would protect them. They came dangerously close to a wolf, which gnashed and pounced toward Medeva, but a shade swooped in and bashed the creature aside before it could assault the harpie.

Magnus felt in worse danger than ever before. He would rather have been back among the Rammeren, where at least the threat that he had faced was human. These beasts could hardly be considered animals, let alone mortal.

As he and Medeva broke through the crowd of skeletons, Magnus prematurely assumed that they were safe from the beasts. He was proven wrong when a second wolf leapt from the shadows with its claws drawn. Medeva clutched the boy by his arm and wrested him away from the hound, which skidded to a halt nearby. Before the beast had a chance to reestablish its focus, a passing shade lunged and grappled onto the wolf's mane. Blinded and berserk, the wolf gave a sonorous howl and thrashed about senselessly.

Magnus and Medeva seized the opportunity to flee onward. The hound vanished in the distance, but the rest of the beasts were not diminishing. In fact, they were multiplying as if from nowhere. Skeletons, wolves, and yet another stallion flickered past as Magnus and the harpie ran. The unrelenting horde of shades was the only thing that kept the beasts from maiming the intruders on sight.

Then Magnus heard a shrill crowing from above.

He raised his attention to the sky, where the shades' flitting silhouettes crowded his vision. He couldn't determine from where exactly the crowing had sounded—instead, he noticed two shades beginning to circle one another. He thought nothing of it at first, until one of the circling shades tackled the other, slashing it violently. The attacked shade writhed, shrieked, and lashed out its claws in rebellion, but a second blow destroyed it entirely.

Magnus' eyes plummeted back to Medeva, still on the run. "The shades!" he alerted. "They're fighting each other! What's happening?"

"It's not each other that they're fighting," said Medeva. "They're protecting us from the shades that would otherwise harm us."

"Harm us?" Magnus exclaimed. "I thought you controlled the shades!"

"Not all of them," replied the harpie. "There are some that would rather obey another master."

"What other master?"

Medeva shoved the boy aside as a skeleton beast suddenly drove its claws toward Magnus from the right. "Keep your mouth shut and your eyes open!" she scolded. "How many times do you have to brush against death before you realize what kind of threat you're facing?"

Magnus was distracted from their dialogue by the same crow-like warble that he'd picked up earlier on. He looked again to the sky and saw nothing much different than before, though it was hard to tell for sure while moving at such speed. Only when he was about to turn away, one of the shadows gliding overhead unfurled a pair of long, webbed limbs, like wings. This couldn't possibly be one of the shades.

The crowing sounded again and the winged shadow lowered its altitude. It tilted inward, flying in an idle circle above Magnus and Medeva like an expectant vulture. A second, identical shadow joined it, followed closely by a third. As a shade approached them, the trio piled down on the specter and beat their wings at it in unison, destroying it instantly.

Another leftward jostle by Medeva sent Magnus stumbling off his course. A stallion beast stampeded past them, then whipped around and bit its hooves into the dust. It settled its flat black eyes on the fleeing boy and harpie, and galloped after them. The beast would have caught up within seconds if it weren't for the flock of shades that assailed it, immobilizing it in a wild struggle.

Now, the crowing noise sounded louder and clearer than ever, prompting Magnus to glance behind. It was, as he had feared, one of the three winged beasts that he had seen before only as a shadow, rapidly descending on him and the harpie. Its head was a raven's, obsidian-black and with a beak like the curved blade of a sickle. Its wings were eerily identical to Medeva's, only smaller, and served doubly as the creature's arms, with a clawed hand fastened at their ends. Below its coif of feathers, scales encrusted its reptilian body and its stubby, taloned legs.

Magnus ducked in anticipation of the raven's attack. which was intercepted when a shade hurled itself against the raven in flight and knocked it into a spiraling fall. Magnus straightened his running posture only to be confronted by the second of the three beasts as it also dropped from the air, talons bared. He knew that he wouldn't be fast enough to elude it, so he tucked his lit pendant into his palm and empowered it with his floundering concentration.

The raven beast plunged and parted its bladed beak. Magnus pulled his hand away from his pendant, and, with the jewel's glow still burning inside of it, expelled the light over his head with as much force as he could muster. Caught in the outburst, the raven croaked as it recoiled and pushed itself up, away from the intruders, on a desperate flapping of its wings.

Magnus remained wary of another attack; as expected, the last of the three raven beasts hovered directly above him. But rather than assaulting him, the beast took toward the castle in the opposite direction. Even when Magnus waited for it to return, it did not.

The ravens' pursuit wasn't the only thing that had ended—the monstrous cries had ceased as a whole. All had turned to immaculate silence. The beasts had vanished, leaving Medeva's shades to flee back to their haven in the clouds. It seemed as if the battle had come to an abrupt end.

Magnus dragged his feet until coming to a halt. He stood someplace in the middle of the desolate hillside that he and the harpie had climbed to reach the castle. The ancient Galem city lay submerged in shadow at the base of the hill, while Sennair's fortress marred the opposite horizon.

Placing all his attention on the beasts' disappearance, Magnus failed to notice that Medeva was already treading much farther down the hill. He hastened after her.

"Medeva," he called. "I think they've stopped chasing us. They're all gone." He was sure that the harpie had heard him, but she stayed mute and unresponsive. "You've got to tell me what those creatures were!" Magnus demanded an answer for the third time. "And why did they all just vanish like that?"

Medeva did not even bother to slow down. If anything, she was moving faster. "Medeva, wait!" hollered the boy. He put the last of his strength into a sprint that brought him close behind the harpie. "Medeva!"

Medeva whipped around with her halberd extended, violently smashing the blunt side of her polearm against Magnus' shoulder. The boy was instantly hurled to the ground into a pool of ash.

"Enough!" Medeva roared so loudly that her voice pierced the distance and echoed across the hill for seconds after. She nailed her hard leather boot on Magnus' chest and swiveled her weapon so that its blade sat vertically by his throat. "I've had it with you!" she bellowed. "I've had it with your questions! I've had it with your blind and mindless curiosity that nearly got us both killed!"

Magnus could barely find the air to speak, his breathing restrained by the harpie's boot that felt heavy enough to crush his ribs. Cold steel burned his neck. He had never seen her like this—so devoured by fury that it seethed from her eyes like hellfire. Nothing stood in her way of cleaving the boy apart, and by her temper, it didn't look as if she were prepared to pass up the opportunity.

"How can you be such a fool," Medeva went on, pressing her halberd blade even closer against Magnus' flesh, "that when I plead for you to listen to my warning, you cannot think of anything more than how I'm trying to deceive you! You thought that this was all some ploy I crafted in my mind in order to keep you in ignorance!" Her berating speech was interrupted by a pause, in which her anger only consumed her further. "I should have let you die at the claws of those beasts," she hissed in a lower volume. "But I'll kill you either way, Wingheart. Here and now."

Magnus cringed at the pain of the blade already cutting into his skin. He found himself unable to move a muscle, let alone attempt an escape. "Daimos wouldn't...like it if you killed me," he stammered weakly.

"I don't care about you, or Recett," spat the harpie. "As far as I'm concerned, that conceited corpse can die where he stands!" She lowered her voice further until it droned under shuddering breaths. "I've had it with Recett as I've had it with you, and I'd kill him myself if I could."

Magnus was astounded not only by her rage, but also by her words. He had seen before that she was less than reverent toward Daimos, but never to the extent of her harboring a death wish against him.

Even Medeva appeared to reconsider her comments and hesitate to deliver her strike. Magnus shut his eyes and gritted his teeth, shivering, until he felt the icy blade lift away from his throat. When he dared to look again, he saw that Medeva had retracted her weapon.

She withdrew, removing the burden of her boot from Magnus' chest. "Get up," she demanded. The anger in her tone was subtler, yet still present. Magnus did as he was ordered, shaken by the harpie's threat, but relieved that she had changed her mind.

"We're going to find the Rock and end this journey by tomorrow morning," said Medeva. "I don't want to hear another word from you until we do. You will do as I say and ask no questions."

Medeva turned on Magnus and stormed away. Muted, the boy had no option but to follow her and immerse himself in his thoughts. He pressed his coat collar against the bleeding wound that had been carved by Medeva's halberd. *I suppose it's my fault that we were attacked,* he mused. *She took me up to the castle probably just so I wouldn't stay suspicious. Then I ignored her when she warned me and called me to return. But it's also just as much her fault that she lied from the beginning and never told me anything about those creatures. Why didn't she?*

Because she and Daimos were hiding them from me, he replied to himself. It was evident—the castle's danger and its secret were one and the same. *It seemed like the beasts were guarding the mosaic's chamber, since they vanished by the time we got far enough away from the castle...but how could that old tiling alone be so important?*

His question was answered by his memories. *It wasn't*

the mosaic...the trail I followed came from behind it. The mosaic is a doorway, and whatever it leads to was what caused those creatures to attack us.

If there was anything on the other side of the mosaic, entombed beneath the earth of Sennair's stronghold, then certainly, it was of tremendous power. *The closer I got to it, the harder it was to use my magic,* he thought. *Even Medeva acted as if she was too scared, or even unable to get near it, and she seemed much weaker through the entire castle.*

How could she have been weaker, he questioned his own statement, *when she destroyed that stallion in a single blow, using magic that I'd never seen her conjure elsewhere? And when I question her about it, she denies it like I've seen a hallucination! Not even her shades could last long enough against those beasts!*

And not even she could control all of them, Magnus reminded himself. He had seen the shades fight each other, even destroy one another, and certainly not under Medeva's direction. Had the shades simply gone mad from the same force that had weakened her and his magic? Or were some of them really under the command of another master, as Medeva had claimed?

The answer was given to him through his memory of Cecil's tale about the history behind the ancient Galem city: *Sennair Drakathel,* he concluded. The shades were originally Sennair's. The horde that Medeva leads was by some means passed on from him to his most loyal follower, Daimos. Could it be that the opposing shades were, in fact, from a faction still obedient to Sennair? And where would that leave the rest of the attacking creatures?

According to Cecil, Sennair's forces were comprised of not only the shades, but also of many other nightmarish chimeras. *Could it be that what I've just seen,* Magnus wondered, *were the beasts of Sennair Drakathel's old army?*

34

Luminous Rock

MAGNUS AND MEDEVA walked the remainder of the valley in silence. With the beasts gone, the ancient Galem city resumed its sepulchral ambience. Upon reaching the valley's edge, Medeva allowed the boy to rest a while before they would travel back up into the mountain range. Though not very long, the respite was enough for Magnus to gather his strength and prepare for the final stretch of their mission to find the Rock.

The sun had set soon after they entered the valley, suggesting that it was now close to midnight. Magnus had proposed to rest until dawn, but Medeva had insisted on ending their mission before morning. They would make way through the mountains in the dark of night, with no torch to guide Magnus other than his radiant diamond pendant.

From here, the terrain began to steepen. A narrow, straggling pathway formed over it, around which rose banks of rock. It wasn't much longer before Magnus once again found himself in mountainous terrain. Medeva had assured him that there would be few of the Rammeren guards wandering in such a deep region of the mountains, but that didn't stop Magnus from being concerned.

They reached a considerable altitude within the first few hours of their climb. Magnus knew that they were close, very close, to the crater where the Luminous Rock lay. *Five miles northeast of the valley*, Brendan Wingheart's journal had instructed. After four days and nights, their goal was finally near.

Magnus hiked this road knowing that he was tracing his father's footsteps. Sixteen years ago, Brendan had embarked across these fields, forests, and mountains in search of the Rock; now Magnus was doing the same. Magnus was reliving Brendan's journey, only days after which Daimos had seized the city of MorningStar. But Magnus strongly suspected that there was one location his father had not visited: Sennair Drakathel's castle.

If he had, he would have never lived to make it to the Rock, thought Magnus. Certainly, if Brendan had witnessed and survived the onslaught of the mysterious beasts, he would have written much about the ordeal in his journal. Instead, he merely spoke of taking route through the valley, with no mention whatsoever of the castle.

Two more hours crawled past on the rocky peaks before Magnus and Medeva arrived at an immense, level plane. Boulders dotted the horizon like pale buoys in a dead sea of stone. Magnus wrapped his arms around himself for warmth, for the wind here was more frigid than any place he had yet ventured during his voyage.

The ashen smog in the sky had waned thin, now that Magnus and the harpie were far enough away from Serenia. With the pallid orb of the moon now visible, Magnus recognized that the clouds would no longer be dense enough to hold back the sunlight after dawn—Medeva's bane, and yet another reason why they would need to end their journey by daybreak.

Magnus was beginning to drag his steps, impaired by the cold. His senses numbed, he was left feeling only the excruciating soreness of his muscles. There was an unexpected drop in the landscape, along with an increase in the rubble that blanketed it. Magnus was finding it hard to keep a foothold on the coarse incline, which seemed to steepen progressively. Medeva adeptly made her way down on the support of her polearm, landing her steps on the flattest patches of the slope.

When the incline became too sheer, a stone rolled out from under Magnus' foot, causing him to stagger and lose his balance entirely. He fell limp as he collapsed to the cold gravel and hurtled down the slope on his side. His surroundings churned behind half-closed eyes, his enfeebled frame beaten as it tumbled over the rocks. Only when the ground came level was he finally brought to a halt.

Magnus allowed fatigue to overcome him; he remained unmoving where he lay. His pendant's light faded to nothing, leaving him sightless and bruised at the bottom of the slope. In all his ire, frustration, and exhaustion, he could have wished that Medeva had killed him when she had threatened to, and spared him his suffering. But he kept strong in his mind the reminder that the harsh road he endured was not for Daimos' sake, nor his own, but for the lives of his brother, Cecil, and Anubis. He had no choice but to go on.

He heard Medeva glide off the bottom of the incline, followed by the dull tap of her halberd on the ground in front of his face. "We're here," she droned.

Magnus faintly picked up his head. "What..." he muttered. "Where's here?"

"The crater," Medeva replied.

Magnus scrambled to his feet in astonishment. He gripped his pendant and infused it with light to give shape to the ditch where he stood. At every angle around him, the rocks seemed to dip sharply inward to form a rugged dent in the mountain terrain. The location was true to Brendan's journal—this was the crater of the Luminous Rock. For a fleeting moment, Magnus forgot his tiredness, aches, and wounds altogether. At long last, they had reached their destination.

Medeva, conversely, appeared less than thrilled. "Now start talking," she ordered. "Where is the Rock?"

Magnus was too caught up in his excitement to pay much attention to the harpie. "It's hidden somewhere around here...in a cavern," he said without facing her. "But my father cloaked the entrance. Wherever it is, it would be invisible from the outside."

Medeva trudged deeper into the crater as she eyed

it. Its walls were buried under sheets of rubble, and its erosion showed its ancient age. The ground was mostly flat, save for a few stray boulders. "Cloaking..." she said, "...the manipulation of light patterns, designed to trick the eye into believing something is there when it is not. Correct?"

Magnus nodded and Medeva continued: "So revealing this cloak is merely a question of passing a physical object through it."

Magnus nodded again. Medeva smashed her halberd's rod to the ground, and a splatter of dust resulted. "Then start searching. I'll take the west, you take the east." She trod off toward the far end of the crater. Magnus lingered briefly, then turned in the opposite direction and stooped down. He began groping between the rocks, feeling the solidness of each patch of stone as he clambered along the crater's perimeter.

Once the Rock is found and all this is done with, Magnus thought to himself, *I'll be able to see Drake and Cecil again.* Then he added a nervous doubt: *I hope.* He didn't know just what Daimos would decide to do once Magnus and Medeva returned. Having the Rock destroyed and his goal attained, there would be nothing to stop the warlord from going back on his word and murdering his captives, as well as Magnus. Daimos was an undisputed madman, and he needed little to justify the impetuous slaughter of those who displeased him.

Magnus' thoughts were cut short when an oddity snagged his attention: a stone, no larger than a pebble, crumbled out from beneath his palm and vanished on impact with the lowermost rocks. He extended an arm to touch the surface of the rocks. As he had expected, his fingertips passed through as if the stone slope were no more solid than a reflection cast by water.

Magnus retracted his hand immediately, then paused. He reached out a second time for confirmation, and once again, his hand slipped through the rocks with ease. He froze at the sight of his forearm half-sunk into stone, when he saw Medeva come to stand beside him. "Found it, did you?" she asked rhetorically.

Magnus turned to Medeva and pulled himself upright. The harpie shouldered him aside and speared her halberd through the cloaked opening. "Convincing," she remarked, drawing her polearm in and out of the false rocks. She crouched to collect a fist-sized stone from the slope and lobbed it through the cloak. Close to a second after the stone vanished, it audibly struck solid ground. She snapped her head to Magnus, then back to the cloaked entrance. "You head in first."

Magnus gave no reaction and mutely abided. He kneeled, his back to the cloak, and lowered his legs down through it. Securing his feet and hands on the rocks below, he ducked under the cloak and watched Medeva, along with the mountain crater, slip behind the inner side of the cloak's veil. He released his grip, dropping to the ground immediately beneath him.

He found himself in a confined cavern. The floor here was even more rutted than much of the mountain's terrain, vaulted over by a ceiling that threatened to collapse at the slightest disturbance. The air was as dry as the enclosing stone walls, and almost colder than the wind outside. But it was not dark, far from it. It was as if the sun had risen in the cavern, its rays blazing against Magnus' back like a celestial inferno. He knew there was only one thing that could deliver such illumination, and so, with ardor, he turned around to behold it.

Before Magnus lay an enormous boulder, six feet high and half as wide. It bore an elongated shape and a jagged, crystalline surface, rooted upright in a bed of rocks. It was swathed in radiant gold, burning with light that glowed from within, penetrated its glassy exterior, and flooded the cavern with its unparalleled brilliance. It was the vision of a lifetime—the greatest source of brightness throughout all of Serenia and the Galem border. It was the Luminous Rock.

Magnus was rapt at the Rock's glorious sight. But he hadn't time to admire it for long before Medeva nimbly slumped through the cloak and landed close beside him. Caught in the Rock's rays, she recoiled and turned away, grimacing. "This is it, Wingheart," she announced in a spiteful hiss. "Now destroy that foul thing."

Medeva was prepared to exit the cavern, but her curiosity was drawn by a peculiar translucent beam that stood vertically behind the corner of her eye. She traced it to its destination, which was none other than the cloak that masked the cavern entrance, then to its source, a crevice by the rocks at her feet. She levered aside the rocks with her polearm to discover a minuscule glass prism nestled inside the crevice, cleverly positioned to catch the light of the Rock. It was the projector of the magical cloak, placed by Brendan upon his discovery of the cavern sixteen years ago. The harpie swiveled her halberd's spearhead to the floor and thrust it down on the prism. Glassy shrapnel gushed over of the ground as the crystal shattered, and the cloak guttered out of existence. Gripping the cavern wall with all fours, Medeva heaved herself up and slithered back out through the entrance.

Magnus returned his stare to the Rock. He realized sorrowfully what would have to be done if he wished to secure the lives of Daimos' captives. He would need to destroy the Luminous Rock. It had been difficult enough to agree to the task, but it was now that he would be held to his word. He had made a promise to the warlord and had no option but to fulfill it.

Magnus slipped his backpack off his shoulder, catching the strap into his hand. He groped through the bag, pressing aside food rations and an empty waterskin before finding what he needed: the sleek bulb that was Noctell's black acid flask. Setting down the backpack, Magnus took the flask in his hands. He could've sworn it wasn't his imagination when a potent burning sensation came over his palms on contact with the glass container.

He clamped a hand onto the flask and struggled to unscrew its cap, which was sealed too securely for him to move it the slightest at first try. As he wrenched it harder, its serrated edge knifed into his skin as if in violent protest. When the cap finally came loose, it tumbled from Magnus' cut, sprained hand to bare the nightmarish brew it had confined.

Magnus peered into the flask: it was filled near to the brim with a thin, black liquid that hissed, spat, and writhed fiercely. Magnus immediately grew watery-eyed and was forced to extend the flask far from his face. The acid seemed to emit an odorless vapor that wasn't much less corrosive than the substance itself.

Flask in hand, Magnus prepared to carry out his task. He admired the Rock forlornly, the way one might look upon an innocent prisoner before he is sent to the gallows. Magnus was about to destroy a possibly millennia-old artifact of nature with a flask of liquid darkness crafted by one of Daimos' men. He could only continue reminding himself that he did this not out of persuasion, fear, or loyalty, nor for a reward of riches, but for the prisoners whose fate, if the Rock weren't destroyed, could be far worse than the gallows.

Magnus raised the flask above the Luminous Rock. The radiance was tremendous, blinding, yet magnificent. He looked up at the flask in his trembling hand, heat rising at the back of his throat and his touch numbed with hesitation. He couldn't bring himself to pour the acid.

He retracted the flask, breathing heavily. Time seemed to slow to a crawl while his mind raced faster than ever. *There has to be another way*, he hoped. *I can't do this.*

Magnus scanned the cavern desperately in search of an answer. Medeva didn't appear to be observing him from above. The boy entertained the notion of concealing the Rock somehow, but he knew that the idea was totally impractical—the cavern's only cloaking prism lay in pieces, not to say that Magnus would even have had a clue how to use it.

And if I refused? the prospect arose in his mind. *What if I refused to destroy the Rock?*

Then Cecil and your brother will perish, the answer came to him quickly. *What do you value more? Their lives or the Rock? You can't let Drake and Cecil die!*

He sighed. *I know I can't.* And with that, he tilted the flask. A threadlike stream of black acid slithered out from the container, sizzling as it seared the air. When it touched the peak of the Rock, a flare of steam and a resonant hiss erupted. Magnus withdrew the flask and watched as the black acid pooled into a watery film and ravenously began to devour every inch of the Luminous Rock. Little by little, the light in the cavern diminished, as did the Rock's great stature.

The more that the acid consumed of the Rock, the deeper Magnus' heart sank into the pit of his stomach. His mournful gaze was inert. By now, the Rock had been dissolved to a height not much above his waist. Every shred of zeal that had amassed in him upon discovering the crater now melted away with the lucidus boulder. The cavern grew dimmer still. After many long seconds, the Rock's foundation was all that remained. It, too, succumbed to the acid and gradually crumbled to nothing. Then the cavern, once brimming with resplendent light, fell dark like an abyss.

Magnus blinked a tear from his eye. He brought a soft glow to his pendant, revealing a coarse pit where the Rock had once stood. His mission was complete. The Luminous Rock had been destroyed.

"Pathetic." Medeva's voice suddenly shook the boy. Magnus twisted his head to set one eye on the harpie, who had come up behind without his noticing at all.

"Sixteen years," she continued, "for this one simple task. The incompetence of Recett and his men is unbelievable." She motioned to the black acid flask in Magnus' hand. "Put that thing down."

With utmost care, Magnus laid the half-empty flask upright on a flat patch of ground. Not a moment later, Medeva took a ruthless hold of Magnus' backpack and tore it off his shoulders. As she lobbed the backpack against the cavern wall, its contents were spilled into the gravel.

"Thought I'd try hiding something?" Magnus asked with annoyance.

"I've learned not to underestimate your foolishness." Medeva studied the discarded waterskin and food rations, then paced to the Rock's former location and scanned it also.

Magnus lifted his brow ironically. "If I'd taken a piece from the Rock, I wouldn't have been so stupid to put it right in the bag anyhow."

"So you're suggesting that I should rummage through your pockets?" the harpie retorted. "If you were keeping any part of that stone on your person, it would be glowing too brightly for you to conceal it."

"And what about the return trip?" questioned Magnus. "I don't suppose we're going to retrace our steps all the way back to MorningStar? Or were you planning to just kill me now that this is all done with?"

Medeva glanced at him indifferently. "We'll be teleporting back to MorningStar."

"By what means, exactly?" Magnus pointed to his battered backpack. "We don't have anything to teleport with."

Medeva selected a fine cord that was strung around her neck and pulled it out from under her leather breastplate. The cord was fastened to a miniature gray pendant carved in the likeness of the New Order's skull icon used by Daimos and his guard. "This," she spat, "is another of my *gifts* to Recett." The sardonic loathing in her voice was evident. "The combination of the shades' ashes with an alchemist's magic. It will transport us to MorningStar, the place bearing the largest concentration of my shade horde."

Magnus eyed the pendant. It was an exact replica of one he had seen on Noctell. "How will it work?"

"Stand by me," she instructed. "The ashes will engulf us."

Magnus placed himself next to the harpie. Medeva gripped the teeth of the skull pendant, twisting the cylinder repeatedly until she was able to wrest it out like a cork. Like an unleashed legion, ashes gushed from the open cavity.

The ash pooled at Magnus and Medeva's feet, whirling like black fire that ensnared their legs and climbed to engulf them. Magnus shut his eyes and embraced himself as he felt the ashes reach past his waist. It was as if he were being cocooned by the shades—he could sense their malevolent presence descend on him, chilling him terribly. When the sooty tongues crept up over his face, he was overcome by a violent dizziness. His body lost all feeling as his senses crumbled and the void devoured him.

35

Path Once Trodden

RAKE OPENED HIS EYES to the sight of Cecil slumped beside him peacefully. But as his vision sharpened, the bars of their cell grew strong in the foreground, reminding him that he would spend yet another day in the tomblike MorningStar dungeons.

Anubis sat against the opposite wall. His head was tipped down toward his lap in his typical posture, his black hair shrouding his face completely. He seemed to be awake, though it was hard to tell for sure. Cecil was soon roused from his dozing as well. He turned over to Drake and offered a half-smile, which he straightened after seeing the older Wingheart's solemnity. "How are you, Drake?" he asked, only for the sake of breaking the silence.

"The best I've ever been," Drake replied mordantly.

Cecil grimaced in commiseration. "It's the fifth day already, isn't it? Magnus should be back soon."

"I don't know what day it is." Drake shook his head. "I don't know whether it's night or morning. All I want is to see my brother."

Cecil gripped Drake's shoulder in a feeble attempt to comfort him. "Try not to drown yourself in worry. Daimos won't let anything happen to Magnus or us until the Rock is destroyed as he wishes."

"And when it *is* destroyed?" Drake barked in reply. "What makes you think he's going to release us?"

"I know," Cecil acknowledged despondently. "But it's the only chance we have at escaping this place."

Drake sighed to calm himself. "Supposing that we do all make it out of here alive, where will we go? What are we going to do once the Rock is gone?"

"I'm not sure," answered Cecil. "Depending on the damage Recett's scouts inflicted, I imagine your bookshop may need some repair. Hopefully there wasn't too much harm done to the books if the intruders gave up their search quickly enough."

Drake was sickened at Cecil's mention of the bookshop. He wasn't even sure if he'd want to see it again after what Daimos' men could have done to it. But he knew that the damage sustained by the shop would be incomparable to all that Arkane would yet have to endure. "And what about the city?" he asked again. "What will become of MorningStar and the rest of this world?"

"I..." Cecil shuddered. "I don't know, Drake."

An abrupt pounding of steps on the dungeon stairs drew the attention of the two captives. Cecil pulled himself up against the cell door and set sight on the back end of the hall, where a dark-robed shadow sauntered down the stairwell and stopped to reveal itself in the torchlight. It was the warlord himself, Daimos Recett.

"Morning, Wingheart. Morning, Handel," Daimos sneered, his grin sharply illuminated. He paced toward the cell that housed his captives. "And, of course, our good friend Araiya." Receiving no response from Anubis, he redirected his attention to the others.

Cecil hunched away from the cell door. "Want something, Recett?"

Daimos' eyes shifted to lock with Drake's. "Why, just to be in the presence of Drake, son of the glorious Brendan Wingheart!" he derided. "Son of the man whose hope for the fate of his city rode on a pitiable, glowing mound of rock." He uttered a chuckle, then his expression fell flat. "You have a visitor."

Cecil and Drake looked back toward the stairwell when more steps sounded. They could hear at least two people this time. First to emerge was the unmistakable silhouette of Medeva. The harpie's impassive stare wandered about the corridor before settling on the three captives in the cell ahead of her. Drake and Cecil were unsure of what to think in reaction, until a second figure darkened the staircase. It limped past Medeva, out into the fiery light.

"Magnus!" Drake leapt against the cell door and called to his brother standing at the end of the hall. Magnus met eyes with his companions, returning an ear-to-ear smile. From his face to his hands, he was plastered with scrapes and bruises; his shirt and jeans were torn and stained with ash, dust, blood, and sweat. By his looks, he had gone to hell and back, but any distress that he suffered was masked by the joy that radiated from his face.

Daimos had already selected the spindly dungeon key from his key ring. He thrust it into the cell lock and wrenched it counterclockwise. As the gate clicked open, Drake and Cecil bolted out into the hall to greet Magnus.

Magnus staggered forward, into his brother's arms. Drake embraced him closely, then leaned away with his hands on Magnus' shoulders, beaming brightly, teary-eyed. "You have no idea how glad I am to see you," he said through a mild whimper. "I thought you might never return."

"I know..." Magnus' grin became mixed with a sympathetic frown. "I didn't even know if you'd still be alive by the time I made it back."

Cecil came beside the younger brother and enfolded him in his arms as well. "Don't worry about what could have been, Magnus." He smiled. "As long as you're back here with us."

As Cecil pulled away from the boy, Magnus was given a clear view of the dungeon corridor, where he saw Anubis standing at a distance. Magnus cast the herbalist an impartial stare; Anubis did nothing but look askance to the ground in an attempt to avoid eye contact.

"Perhaps you'd best all continue your reunion outside," suggested Daimos scathingly. "Since the young Wingheart was kind enough to destroy the Rock, I will stay true to my word and set the four of you free." He bared his crooked teeth in a grin. "If I were you, I'd be sure to take advantage of the opportunity."

Drake brought an arm behind his brother's back and urged him toward the dungeon stairwell. "Come on, Magnus."

"Oh no, not through there." Daimos cocked his head in the direction of the cellar door at the opposite end of the hall. "You're going back the way you came in."

Medeva stepped out from the shadows and hastily escorted Cecil and the brothers down the corridor, flames and steel flickering by. She passed Anubis as if he were invisible, or simply of no concern whatsoever to anyone in the chamber. The herbalist waited until Medeva and the three former captives were positioned in front of the door before he padded along in their steps.

Medeva was about to lead the foursome out into the cellars when Cecil caught sight of their coats and empty backpacks that were scraped into a pile nearby. Cecil stooped to collect them, but saw Medeva's halberd blade plunge next to his hand in refusal.

Surprisingly, Daimos waved her aside and laughed amusedly. "Please, Medeva!" he jeered. "Let them have their playthings. They are of no use to us! And besides..." he drew next to the kneeling Cecil, towering over him. "...what could you possibly hope to do to me?"

Cecil rose with the staff, sword, and ring in hand and his eyes nailed to the warlord. He distributed the equipment to Drake and Anubis while Medeva hauled ajar the steel door to the cellars.

"Leave this place, Winghearts," Daimos continued haughtily. "That Rock of your father's is gone forever. You have nothing here anymore!"

Drake and Magnus were first to proceed. They were followed by Cecil, who conjured a glow to his sword to illuminate the forbidding chambers ahead. Anubis trudged on behind.

"Now back to your own world, all of you!" hollered Daimos as the former prisoners tunneled their way through shadows that fogged the cellar corridor. "But return here someday," his voice loudened in victorious pride, "and witness the rise of a new era on Arkane!" Letting his words cascade through the tunnel, the warlord slammed shut the dungeon door.

Cecil, Anubis, and the brothers ventured through the rock-hewn tunnel with Cecil's lucidus sword as their light. The last time any of them had walked this path, it was after being betrayed by the herbalist into the hands of Daimos Recett. The memory of the incident seemed to make the traitor mortally unsettled. But when the silence was finally broken, it was, surprisingly, Anubis who uttered the first words.

"It's good to see you again, Magnus." Anubis spoke for the first time in what was likely hours.

Magnus offered Anubis a meager twitch of his lip that seemed like a halfhearted attempt at a smile. He glanced in question to Cecil and his brother.

"Anubis didn't want any of this to happen," Cecil said solemnly. "He was forced by Daimos to serve as his spy."

Magnus' stare settled to the floor passing under his feet. "Forced how?"

"A couple of weeks ago," Cecil replied, "Anubis, along with three of his colleagues, was captured in the MorningStar forest by Daimos' men. One of them was killed. After Recett learned of Anubis' association with us, Anubis was offered a deal in which he and his remaining colleagues would be spared from a gruesome death...if he would serve as a pawn in Recett's plot to capture us. You were in the same situation when you agreed to destroy the Rock, Magnus—we can't blame Anubis for what he's done."

Magnus looked again to the herbalist, who returned a frown that was wilted with melancholy. "I'm sorry for everything I've done," said Anubis, dropping his eyes. "I've betrayed my friends and sealed the fate of Arkane with no excuse but cowardice."

"You're forgiven," Magnus said with a resolute nod. "I know what it feels like to face Daimos and stare up at death itself. If there was anyone with the courage to defy him... they'd be long dead."

"Thank you, Magnus..." Anubis mustered a quivering smile. "Though I have nevertheless done a terrible thing to all of you. If I'd just slipped away from Daimos when I had the opportunity, we'd still have a chance at finding the Rock to defeat him."

"I'm not sure about that," replied Magnus. "Things might have ultimately turned out for the best. After traveling to Galem, I doubt we would've survived without someone like Medeva to protect us like she did me."

Drake, Cecil, and Anubis seemed momentarily alarmed. "Goodness!" exclaimed Cecil. "I knew that the road would be harsh, but I never expected it to be deadly. Did the Rammeren give you any trouble at the border?"

"This isn't the place to talk," said Magnus. "Let's head back to the forest first. I left Ember there before we were captured." He smirked discreetly. "...and something else."

"Ember," Anubis repeated. "Is he alright?"

Magnus nodded. "He should be. His leg was still injured, but hopefully it will have healed by now."

Anubis bowed his head graciously. "I can't thank you enough, Magnus. We'll head out at once."

As the party entered a chamber where the tunnel forked, Anubis steered the others through a passage whose entrance was scored with chalk. Cecil especially seemed to take in every detail of his surroundings. "I remember Brendan mentioning these tunnels," he said. "Never seen them myself until now."

"I had no idea such a place existed," Anubis replied. "Was this once some sort of siege tunnel?"

Cecil's eyes leapt to scan a strip of seemingly primordial bricks. "That may have been only its most recent use. When

Brendan became council head, the tunnels had already been sealed for decades, if not longer; they've got to be a few centuries old, at the least."

"Built for what purpose?" Drake pondered aloud.

"I'd love to know," Cecil hummed. "The length is certainly astounding. The most Brendan said they ever discovered down here were a few shoddy burial vaults. What Recett expected to find by unearthing this place, I can't imagine."

"His men must have found the entrance while skulking the forest," Anubis surmised. "If nothing else, it's a route to the castle that suits his medieval tastes."

The conversation dwindled to quiet observation. Time droned on until the party finally reached the grotto at the end of the tunnel. Beginning with Drake, they each hauled themselves up on the rocks, ducked through the narrow opening, and entered the MorningStar forest. They found themselves in the glade to which Anubis had led them prior to their capture last week. Steadfastly, they advanced through the glade and into the dead knotting of trees around them.

"I'll lead." Magnus gestured the others to follow him. "I left Ember and our other things near here."

"After we retrieve Ember," said Anubis, "what then?"

Cecil shrugged dejectedly. "Take the rift out of here, I suppose. Anubis, since your house is in Markwell, it should be simple enough for you to get back home. Drake, Magnus, and I can travel back to the bookshop to assess the damage." After fully realizing what he had just said, he buried his face in his palm. "I can't believe this is happening," he lamented. "Sixteen years of hoping and hiding, all for nothing. I never thought it would come to this."

"But things will be better now," Drake tried to console his former guardian. "We won't need to hide anymore."

"We'd be selfish and blind to think that," Cecil persisted. "Things may be better for us, but they're only going to get worse for the people of Arkane. You heard Daimos boasting; he thinks he's invincible now, and he's probably right. What's there to stop him from spreading his ruin even further in the years to come?"

"He said that Arkane would rise into a new era..." added Anubis cautiously. "What do you suppose that means?"

Cecil seemed reluctant to respond. "I don't know," he replied, "and I'm not sure I want to know."

The party advanced in silence. The dead woodland was beginning to thicken. Drake kept his hand rested on his brother's shoulder while Cecil and the herbalist traveled close behind. Though Cecil, Drake, and Anubis lugged grief with every step, they were forever thankful for Magnus' safety and their freedom from Daimos' clutches. Magnus, however, behaved indifferently. His expression was surprisingly unreadable, as were his emotions. Among all of them, Magnus appeared to be the least affected by the loss of the Rock—a strange thing, considering that he was the one to have destroyed it.

Magnus also appeared to have an impressive sense of direction. He burrowed through the black-green snarl with eyes that grappled onto every distinguishable landmark.

The area where he eventually stopped was impossible to distinguish from any other part of the forest. But Magnus seemed confident in his navigation.

"Here," he announced, splashing the surroundings with his pendant's light.

Anubis moved ahead of the brothers. "Where's Ember?" was the first thing he asked.

His answer came from inside a hollowed tree stump, where the head of a small creature emerged from behind the splintered rim. It scampered from its hiding place and took a soaring leap, landing in the arms of the herbalist.

"Ember!" exclaimed Anubis, beaming down at the salamander. "Thank goodness, you're alright." Ember returned his master's joyous look with a gleeful luster in his eyes. The creature was in perfect health, and its agility suggested that its leg had healed significantly.

"He's not wearing his cast anymore," Drake commented, inspecting Ember's once-injured leg.

Anubis caressed the salamander's spined back. "He clawed it off, probably. Once his sprain got better, the splint would only have impaired him."

In a momentary pause, the three exchanged glances to see where Magnus had gone. Cecil scanned the premises with his illuminated sword until its rays fell on the boy, who kneeled over the stump from where Ember had leapt, rummaging inside of it.

"Magnus?" Drake called. "Are you looking for something?"

Magnus did not answer, but persisted with his search,

now beginning to pull out bundles of dried leaves and brushwood from inside the rotted hollow.

"What's all this now?" asked Cecil. He drew beside Magnus just as the boy wrested out his dirty backpack from the stump.

Already there was a peculiar luster to the bag, as if something were smouldering within it. When Magnus opened the backpack, it breathed a subtle but vibrant glow. From inside, he withdrew the source of the light— a fist-sized object, which he held out for all to see.

It was a hunk of uncut crystal, golden in hue and tremendously radiant. Repelling the darkness, it gilded every blackened tree that bowed overhead, and turned Cecil's sword as dim as a candle in comparison.

Drake, Cecil, and Anubis were turned rigid with shock. It seemed a long time before anyone could gather just what to say in reaction. "Is that..." Cecil finally spoke, restrained by great hesitation, "...what I think it is?"

"Yes," Magnus replied. A sly grin stole across his face. "It's a shard from the Luminous Rock."

36

A New Hope

ECIL, DRAKE, AND ANUBIS gaped, rooted in their places. While Magnus beamed uncontrollably, all the others, even Ember, had their eyes fastened on the radiant stone in the boy's cupped hand.

"Hide it quickly, before the light gives us away!" Cecil suddenly urged, swiping the stone to bury it back inside the bag. "Magnus," he whispered, "is this really a shard from the Rock?"

Magnus gave a slow, smiling nod. "I should know. I took it myself."

"But the Rock is destroyed," Cecil answered, then added a doubt: "...is it not?"

"It is," Magnus confirmed more solemnly, sealing the backpack. "But this was removed before I destroyed it."

Cecil shook his head with disbelief. "This is incredible..." he muttered. "What am I saying, this is impossible!

How on earth did you manage to steal a shard with that harpie breathing down your neck?"

"I didn't," the boy replied, and returned a grin to his face. "I'll tell you everything."

Drake and Anubis sat near without letting their attention stray from Magnus. Ember remained still in the arms of the herbalist. Cecil crouched and laid down his effulgent sword to serve as a lantern in the absolute dark.

"It was five days ago, when we fled to the grotto after being attacked here," Magnus began, lowering himself to a seat in front of his former guardian. "After both of you had gone inside the cave, Anubis urged me to turn back instead of following you, then went in himself. I thought something had gone wrong, so I waited by the edge of the glade. A while later, I saw a group of Daimos' guards come out from the grotto. I ran for cover, but I knew I wouldn't be able to hide for long before they'd find me. There was only one way I could think to escape."

Magnus peered in all directions, then began to grope through the brambly blackness until he hauled out Anubis' potions bag from under a concealing net of branches. "I had Anubis' bag with me, as well as my own," he said. "I remembered how Anubis had used that vial to blind Medeva in smoke after she attacked the campsite. I hoped I'd be able to do the same to make a getaway." He leaned in to rummage through the bag. "I couldn't find any more of the smoke vials..." A clatter resounded with each bottle he pressed aside, until he came upright, clutching a bulbous flask entwined in wire mesh. "Instead, I found this."

He set the flask before him. "It's the teleportation potion you first showed me in the shelter. I thought I'd be able to use it to teleport to a safer location."

"Goodness, Magnus, don't you know how dangerous those concoctions are?" Cecil asked with concern.

Magnus nodded, then dropped his head. "I know. But it was either that or losing my father's research to Daimos. It was the only thing I had besides running or fighting back." He reopened his backpack just wide enough to search inside. "If I wanted to teleport, I knew I'd need something that originated from the place I'd want to go. And if it wasn't an object straight from nature, there was no telling where I could end up. At first I thought to use one of Anubis' potion ingredients...but then I remembered something else."

From deep inside the bag, Magnus withdrew an object that was similar in shape to the Luminous Rock shard, only without the shard's lustrous glow. It was a plain piece of basalt. "This is the stone that you showed me on our first day in the shelter," he said to Cecil, "the one that you said my father gave you, along with the notebook. It was in the satchel, which I was lucky to have ended up with. Supposing it came from a cave or somewhere else far away, I thought it might be perfect for teleporting me out of the forest.

"I broke off a branch from a tree and put it in my bag so that I could transport myself back to the forest once I'd given the guards enough time to lose me. Then I held out the stone, and poured a bit of the potion onto it." He suspired sharply. "It felt horrible," he said. "There was a jolt like I was being electrocuted, then everything went black. It felt like I was being torn apart. Seconds later, I was lying on gravel. I was in a small cavern, not much higher than my head. In front of me..." he said, beaming, "...was the Luminous Rock."

"I'll be..." Cecil gaped again. "You're telling me that this stone is from the cave of the Luminous Rock?"

"I guess so." Magnus weighed the stone in his hand. "Why else would it have been in the satchel?"

"Of course," said Cecil. "It makes perfect sense... Brendan must have taken the stone from the cave of the Rock once he'd found it, so that he could transport himself back there should he need to, just as you did without knowing."

"Then why didn't he mention anything about it in his journal?"

"For what purpose?" Cecil replied rhetorically. "As I said, your father did not expect to die. He wrote the journal with the intention of tracking his research, not as posthumous instructions to his descendants."

Magnus pinned a bitterly regretful stare on the stone in his hand, then softened his expression. "With all of us safe, I suppose there's no sense in thinking what should have been," he said. "The Rock is destroyed, but that's our only loss."

"Is it really gone?" asked Drake. "All of it?"

Magnus nodded grievously. "All of it, except for the shard. I had no other choice, else Daimos would've killed every one of you. Noctell had given me a vial of black acid;

I used it to dissolve the entire Rock in seconds. Even though I knew I'd hidden a piece of it, it wasn't any easier to destroy it."

"That's understandable," Cecil remarked drearily. "And what about removing the shard? Was the explosion like your father described?"

"Absolutely," said Magnus. "I used my shirt to blindfold myself, closed my eyes, and turned away. I hammered the Rock with a stone until a shard broke off. The light was incredible...brighter than anything I'd ever seen. If that same blast were to happen anywhere near Daimos, it would be bound to affect him somehow."

"We can only hope," Cecil concurred. "Considering that you're here in one piece, I also assume that you didn't have any trouble teleporting back to the forest."

Magnus nodded affirmatively. "After waiting long enough in the mountains, I poured out a bit more of the potion onto the tree branch I'd taken earlier. I ended up exactly where I'd been before, in the forest. The guards were gone. They'd either given up their search for me or headed elsewhere. I retrieved Ember, then found that stump, where I left him, my bags, and the shard. When I headed back to the glade, I did everything I could to remember my route, so that I'd be able to find this place again."

Cecil's smile was weighed on by the unease in his eyes. "You're luckier than you might think. Your teleporting could have taken you much farther away than you'd have wanted, or worse. While that branch took you to its parent tree, it could have just as well sent you to the place where the tree's seed had originated. The true origin of an object is never certain."

"And if the stone had been part of the meteorite," Magnus added, "I could've been choked to death in outer space. But it was the best I could do to escape. I thought it would only be logical to take a chance of being killed over surely being caught."

"So you never did burn the notebook," Cecil presumed.

"No," Magnus confirmed, resting a hand on his backpack. "It's in here. Still, I spent all the time I could while I was in the mountains to read every page of it. That was how I knew where to find the crater when I traveled there with Medeva."

There was a long silence, in which everyone's attention became focused on the lambent backpack that held the Luminous Rock shard. Drake was first to speak again. "So what now?" he asked. "We've obtained a shard. What do we do with it?"

"I think we all know," said Cecil forebodingly. "We must use it to defeat Daimos Recett."

A grim frown shadowed Drake's face. "How exactly? We barge in there and hurl the shard at Daimos?"

"The shard must be shattered, not thrown," Cecil corrected. "Brendan wrote that overcharging the shard with a surge of conjured light would cause it to explode. And if we want to get anywhere near Recett, our reentry into the castle will have to be far more discreet."

"That's easier said than done," noted Anubis. "We can't defeat Daimos with wit and stealth alone. We have to gather people to fight on our side. If we head back to Markwell, both you and I have many friends who would be willing to join us."

"That's a great idea," Drake approved. "We could rally the people who fled from MorningStar. Once they see the shard, they'll realize that we still have a chance at victory."

Cecil weighed the suggestion for a moment, but then cast it aside with a shake of his head. "No. If we start spreading word of the shard's existence, Daimos will be sure to find out about it." He faced Anubis regretfully. "I don't mean to blame you, Anubis, but you have taught me that even a close friend cannot always be trusted. We just don't know how many of Markwell's people have fallen to Daimos' side, willingly or not. We need to strike now. Daimos doesn't suspect a thing. As far as he's concerned, we're already halfway back to the shelter."

"Cecil, there's only four of us!" Drake balked at the notion. "We can't just throw all our lives to the wind for the sake of the shard. We'll be facing his entire army! We need more people!"

"What we need," Cecil amended on the tail of Drake's sentence, "is a plan."

Cecil drew circles in the dirt with a gnarled twig. "We cannot look at this as an ambush," he said. "This is an assassination. While we may not be able to avoid being seen, we won't be fighting our way through, either. We have to get in, kill Daimos, and escape, all without facing too many of his guards or shades at once." He threw a questioning glance at Anubis. "I assume you're a little more familiar with the revamped citadel and castle?"

"Somewhat," replied Anubis. "The council chambers were demolished and a throne room built in their place. Of course, part of the cellars was converted into dungeons. Aside from that, I don't think too much of the castle has changed since Brendan's time. In terms of construction, the citadel looks about the same."

"Excellent," Cecil pulled his twig along a straight line on the ground, ending at the circle he had drawn in the dirt. "We'll make our way through the city until we reach the gates of the citadel. We must stay relatively hidden by traveling along side streets and through buildings." He used his twig to sketch a smaller circle within the larger one. "Once inside the citadel, we must enter the castle. Anubis, what do you suggest?"

"Well, the front door seems never to be locked," Anubis answered promptly. "My only concern with that entrance is that it's in plain sight, and I've seen that harpie skulking near it too often. The only other door I'm aware of being in use is the back door to the armory. The third, and arguably our best chance at getting into the castle, is the dungeon tunnel, especially since it leads straight into the throne room."

Cecil brooded over their choices, inattentively rapping his twig on the ground. "Even if the tunnel is the most convenient route, it's by no means the safest. Such a narrow corridor would yield no escape if we end up flanked by guards."

"But don't you think that the chances we take in scrambling all the way through the citadel outweigh those of taking the tunnel?" argued Anubis. "That tunnel is never patrolled. And we'll be facing far more guards by going above ground."

"By going above ground, we'll also be traveling through open ground," Cecil countered. "If any guards catch sight of us in the city, we'll have plenty of room to run and hide from view. In the tunnel, this is quite the opposite. However slim the odds of someone seeing us in the tunnel, it is still a chance. We cannot take any chances. We have only one shot at victory."

Anubis dipped his head in agreement. "Alright. In that case, our next best option is the armory door. Our only problem will be that the surrounding area seems to draw a lot of guards."

"But if the door was being guarded," Magnus interjected, "why would they leave it unlocked?"

"Because they're not guarding it," Anubis answered ironically. "None of Daimos' guards are guarding anything at all. MorningStar has remained uninhabited for sixteen years, and an attack is the last thing they'd expect. The guards have gone from defending their master's fortress to simply loitering the streets in boredom. The back of the castle court seems to be a popular haunt."

"Then what's our last option?" asked Cecil.

"The front door," said Anubis.

Cecil grimaced at their limited choices of entrance. "The armory is still our best bet. All we need is something to draw the lounging guards away from the back of the castle."

"A diversion?" Drake proposed.

"Exactly," said Cecil. He thrust his twig back to the ground, scoring the southernmost border of the circle that depicted the citadel. "We'll need to split up. Drake and I can head off to the eastern wall and try to pull the guards in our direction." He scratched the twig across the dirt, marking a broad, curving path that ended at the circle's right edge. "We need to attract them somehow."

"What about...a fire?" Magnus warily suggested.

"Quite what I was thinking. We'll set flame to one of the abandoned buildings at the far east end of the citadel. The guards are bound to come racing to find the source of the inferno, lessening the number of eyes around the castle."

Anubis cast a doubtful glance over the sketch in the soil. "That sounds incredibly dangerous. And we still need to get into the castle, not just lure the guards away from it."

"Indeed," said Cecil plainly. "Refresh my memory, Anubis; where exactly is the armory located?"

The herbalist reached into the inner circle of the citadel diagram and marked the armory door with a touch of his finger.

"Thank you." Cecil brought the tip of his twig back to the citadel gate in his drawing, then traced another curving path to the left to meet the point that Anubis had indicated. "Anubis, Magnus, perhaps in the meantime the two of you could proceed in the opposite direction." He shifted the twig so that it hovered a short distance away from the armory. "You both will need to remain hidden until you see the guards around the castle starting to scatter toward the east. If you think it's safe enough, make for the armory door. Come to think of it...it would probably be best for me to be with you two in case we have to deal with any leftover guards."

"I may be able to take out a couple of men without too much of a fight," said Anubis, gesturing to his potions bag. "An athamine bomb, perhaps. It would be safest."

Cecil returned a troubled stare at first, then nodded. "If you're comfortable with that idea, it would be best, yes. But if there are too many men left, hold your ground and wait for Drake and me to meet up with you. We may end up having to flee if the opposition is too strong." He repositioned his twig at the rightmost curving path and continued along it, arching around the castle and ending at the armory door. "Provided things go as planned, you'll have to make sure that the way to the door is cleared, and that the entrance itself is unlocked. By this point, Drake and I are to have circled the castle, arriving at your position. The guards will surely be trailing us, so we'll have to hurry into the armory as quickly as we can. Once inside the citadel, we lock the door behind us, sealing out the guards."

"Sounds like a decent plan," Drake observed.

"So we're inside the castle," Magnus hypothesized. "What now?"

"We find Recett," said Cecil, "and kill him. I would

recommend that from here on, I head alone. We need only one person to break the shard, and that will be me. None of you have to be put at risk."

"Cecil, never!" Drake vehemently opposed. "We all risk ourselves in this; we have no reason to abandon you at the end. If nothing else, we can serve as a distraction."

Cecil gave a slight frown, but no objection. "We'll see how things stand once we're inside the castle. Our final battle will depend on where we face Recett and how many others we face with him."

"I don't think he wanders far from his throne room," said Anubis. "And wherever he is, it would be unusual to find any guards nearby. He seems to think that he doesn't have any need for protection."

"All the better for us, then," said Cecil. "Now let's suppose we've found our target. There stands Recett, a man who can most likely kill any of us effortlessly. Our only usable weapon is the shard."

"We'll have to overcharge it with light to shatter it, like my father wrote," Magnus reminded. "And we probably have to be close enough for the light to affect Daimos."

"I know," Cecil replied somberly. "This could well be the deadliest aspect of our plan, and we'll have to execute it as swiftly as possible. The least we can do is bombard him with light magic until we get in range. Then I'll overcharge the shard. All of us must shut our eyes at once to avoid being blinded by the explosion. If it works—and I say *if* it works—the light will kill Daimos."

"Not quite," Anubis suddenly warned. "You said before

that the shard is only meant to revert Daimos to his mortal form. We'll still have to kill him."

"Maybe," Cecil amended firmly. "After seeing Recett again, I have doubts as to whether that walking corpse could sustain any life without his possessor. But there's no telling either way; we have to come prepared."

"We're entering the castle by the armory," Magnus interjected as if struck by an answer. "We can take any weapons we need from there."

"Good thinking," Cecil exclaimed. "We'll swipe ourselves some handbows on our way through the armory. After we blast Recett with the shard, we open fire. Luck prevailing, he'll be destroyed for good."

Anubis and the brothers swallowed their strategy with difficulty, knowing that it was the best chance they had at defeating the warlord. "And what of our escape route?" Anubis asked.

"Well, our first task after having killed Recett will be to lock the main entrance and any nearby doors from the inside," said Cecil. "Naturally, we will do this sooner if we don't see Recett when we first enter the throne room. This will prevent the entry of any guards that might have hurried to the front of the castle after discovering the armory door to be locked."

"Surely the guards will break the armory door down before trying another way in," said Anubis. "We'll be cornered by them if we don't get out fast enough."

"Which is why we'll be escaping by way of the dungeon tunnel," Cecil replied. "Not an ideal route by any means, but our safest choice with all the chaos in the citadel by that point. At least we'll be heading for open ground."

The unsettled party exchanged glances. "And that's that," Cecil said in grim conclusion. "Any questions?"

"What if the guards try to get into the castle through the tunnel after we lock the doors?" supposed Drake. "They could run into us while we're making our exit."

"The forest end of the tunnel is too far from the citadel," Anubis countered. "The guards aren't going to make any effort to run all the way to the forest when they can force their way in much quicker."

"Ramming a door off its hinges will always be easier for them than taking a route so cumbersome as the tunnel," Cecil concurred. "That doesn't mean we won't have to escape the citadel swiftly. There's no doubt they'll get in eventually."

Magnus mentally hastened through every step in their plan. "What about Noctell, Raven, and Medeva?" he asked. "If we bump into any of them, there's no telling what could go wrong."

Cecil shifted a worried eye sidelong to Anubis. "Too true," he said. "We ought not to forget about Daimos' strongest fighters."

"Raven hopefully isn't too great a threat," said Anubis. "He's dangerous to face alone, but I doubt he'd try his luck against the four of us at once. Medeva, on the other hand..."

"She's a one-man army," Magnus finished Anubis' sentence. "I've seen her fight. She's inhumanly fast, and she'll dodge any attack you throw at her."

Cecil grimaced. "I don't find that hard to believe. Let's just hope she'll be part of the guard troop that we lock outside of the citadel."

"And Noctell?" Drake raised the name of the last elite guard.

Cecil rubbed his arms as if suddenly noticing the cold of the forest. "Noctell," he said, "is incredibly powerful. I wouldn't be surprised if he's second in strength to the warlord himself. He's certainly the most skilled calimancer I've ever confronted."

"Then what are we going to do about him, or even Medeva?" Magnus' tone became more frantic.

"Not much." Cecil shrugged, but his concern was clear to see. "It's difficult to say where either of them could turn up." He laid down the twig in his hand and allowed his eyes to wind along the lines he had scrawled in the dust. "On that note, I think it's only fair that I ask everyone here a crucial question," he began. "We are about to venture into the heart of enemy territory. We are about to dive straight into an inferno where death is an ever-present possibility." He lifted his sullen stare to Anubis and the brothers. "We are about to face Daimos and his army. There is a very real risk that not all of us will return with our lives, and I need to be sure that everyone is ready to take that risk. Anubis?"

Anubis heaved a tremulous breath. "I'm tired of cowering. It's time that I redeemed myself for your capture and the mess I made."

Cecil set a boring stare on the older Wingheart. "Drake?"

"My father gave us his research in hope that we'd finish

his work," Drake replied without delay, "and bring an end to Daimos. We've come so far, and I'm not about to let his wish go unfulfilled, whatever the risks."

Lastly, Cecil's focus fell onto the younger brother. "Magnus? Remember, if even one of us has any hesitation whatsoever, we're not going to do this."

"No," Magnus said with valiance strengthening his voice. "Drake is right. We have to do this for the sake of our father, and everyone else who perished in this horrible place." He paused. "But what about you, Cecil?"

Cecil delivered a single, firm nod. "For Brendan," he declared, "and for MorningStar." He took up his sword, sealing its hilt in a fist resolute as if he were gripping his own soul. "Let us go and reclaim our city."

37

Into the Fray

EDEVA'S FOOTSTEPS throbbed through the corridor. Ashes stirred from the soiled carpet at the pounding of her boots and clung to the air in her trail. Ushered by torches and darkened archways, she advanced with her focus set directly before her. Terminating the corridor was a set of double doors slathered with strips of peeling gold paint. Upon reaching the doors, Medeva clutched them both by their handles and heaved them open.

A sizable chamber filled the harpie's view, along with a vast round table. Perched in the farthermost and stateliest chair of the table's ten seats was the warlord Daimos. Seated close at his right was Noctell, and Raven at his left. The light of half a dozen torches fell over the trio from high upon the walls, casting a tortuous network of shadows.

Daimos smiled at the sight of the harpie. "Ah, Medeva," he greeted. "We were just about to begin our discussions."

Medeva descended a pair of stone steps at the foot of the doorway. "Don't let me stop you," she icily replied.

"Come!" invited the warlord. "Sit with us, if you please."

Medeva hardened her distant gaze. "I'm fine where I am."

Daimos turned to his minions beside him, splaying his hands over the prodigiously mangled table. "Today is a great day," he began. "Today we celebrate an accomplishment that took nearly two decades to achieve—the Luminous Rock is at long last gone from the face of this world. Well done to all of you."

Noctell and Raven bowed their heads appreciatively. "Thank you, milord," said the necromancer. "I only regret that it has taken us this long."

"No need for regret, Noctell," his master replied, "for things seem to have fallen into place perfectly. Today marks not only the end of the Rock, but also the beginning of a new chapter in the rebirth of the Order." He let his voice linger and stoke the anticipation of his minions. "Two nights ago, I received word from our master."

Raven's eyes widened eagerly, as did Noctell's. "What does he say?" the demon asked.

"I have waited until the Rock's destruction to tell you this, as it was our master's wish," said Daimos with zeal. "Our master appeared before my throne at night's darkest hour. He said that he had gathered strength enough. He said that the time has come for him to reenter the world of the living, and all that he needs is one final task from us in order to do so."

"Very well, then," the necromancer readily agreed. "What is it that he asks?"

Daimos folded his hands under his chin as he turned his pensive gaze into space. "Our master requests that we gather by his sacred grave to receive his further instructions." He tilted up his head until it was bathed in the torchlight, then closed his eyes and filled his lungs with the sultry air. "We are to free him," he said, his voice beginning to rasp. "The shackles of the nether realm that bind him are strong, but he has grown stronger. His raw power bleeds into my soul—I feel it."

As the warlord dropped his head, Noctell spoke again. "When do we leave?" he asked.

"As soon as possible," Daimos answered, snapping open his eyes. "Our master cannot wait any longer. We will depart for the grave at dawn."

"Is this really it?" said Raven. "Is our master...returning at last?"

Daimos' smile broadened while his stare hovered ahead of him. "Indeed, Raven. He spoke to me this: *'Before six days have passed, my soul and my physical form will unite once again.'* The age of the New Order is upon us!" The warlord cast his arms out to his side, his hands clenched and his speech impeded by his fervent breathing. "Can you imagine? We are the ones chosen to aid in the rise of our future empire!"

"I hope that you're not forgetting something in all your

celebration." Medeva gave an unexpected call for the room's attention. "Your promise to me, perhaps?"

Daimos regained his presence of mind and brought his unblinking eyes to the harpie. "Why, no, Medeva," he said in a suddenly calm and hospitable melody. "Of course not. After all that you have done for the Order, I would do anything I can to repay you."

"What I have done is not for the Order," she hissed through her teeth. "It is for my own sake, and for the sake of your elusive promise."

Daimos scraped his chair back and rose from his seat at the table. He smiled and sighed. "Medeva," he said, "I'll never understand you. You possess such incredible skill, such mastery with your blades, yet you make yourself an enemy of the Order. Why?" The warlord unfolded his arms in welcome. "Join us, Medeva. Do not stray from us. Your presence in our master's new army is invaluable."

Deep scorn set over the harpie's face. "I'd rather not sell my soul to the devil like you three did."

Noctell and Raven made their expressions frigid, as if they'd been offended. Daimos cocked his neck and brow, laughing amusedly. "What makes you think I sold my soul to the devil?"

"You're a puppet with no will of your own," Medeva spat. "You've given everything you own to a mad ghost whom you worship like a god. And just look at you—you're an abomination, a living corpse."

"Appearance means nothing," the warlord said through an unsightly grin. "It's the power within that matters. Don't you want it, Medeva? Don't you want this power to course through your veins, fill you with everlasting strength, as it does me?"

"My power is enough," the harpie declared with no hesitation. "All I need is the fulfillment of your promise."

"Then you shall have it." Daimos smiled indifferently. "I only wish that you'd be wiser in your decisions."

"Wise or not," Medeva rejoined. "It's my decision."

Daimos eased back into his regal chair at the head of the table, rolling his claws over the armrests. "Then I suppose we'd best be getting back to the matters at hand. Noctell, Raven, we will prepare to leave by dawn."

"Hold it." Medeva's bitter voice interrupted the warlord again. "I'm coming as well."

Daimos' look turned to an obviously forced expression of regret. "I'm so sorry, Medeva...but I'm afraid our master has requested that only the three of us attend."

A piercing cold anger seethed from Medeva's stare. "If your *master* has requested it," she mocked, "then your *master* will have as he wishes. Very well. Go and worship your Saxum Diaboli without me."

Medeva's mordant response seemed to transfer her wrath onto the face of the warlord. Daimos sank the fleshless folds of his brow and snarled. "Don't you dare speak of our master's grave by that wretched name."

"And don't you," Medeva retorted immediately, "dare break your promise."

The harpie turned her back to Daimos and proceeded up the steps before the entranceway. She stormed out of the room, shoving ajar its massive doors and slamming them indignantly behind her.

The MorningStar citadel was the heart of Daimos' empire. It was the warlord's blackened crown jewel and the most tainted part of all Serenia. Ashes gushed like the forks of a river over streets enclosed by scarred, battered brick and littered with knots of broken metal. The wind flowed thick with soot, ever shifting the clouds that churned with the carcasses of the shades against the sky's unending void.

Cecil, Drake, Magnus, and Anubis stood close against the wall of an alley. The salamander Ember lay alertly on the ground by their feet. The citadel's torch-hemmed main road was directly to their left—an unswerving bridge between the nearby entrance gate and the castle that soared in the distance. The foursome hadn't much difficulty in entering the citadel itself, but breaching the castle doors would put each of their lives on the line.

"This is it," Cecil whispered to his companions. "Does everyone know what they're supposed to do?" His question was met with a nod from Anubis and the brothers. "Good," he continued. "Magnus, Anubis, remember not to approach the armory door until you're sure that all, or at least most, of the guards have gone. If anything goes wrong, flee back deeper into the citadel and wait for us to find you. Ready?"

"Wait," said Magnus, slipping off his backpack. "You need to take the shard."

"No, Magnus," Cecil stopped the boy. "Not now. Keep it with your things until we get inside the castle. With Drake and me as the ones who'll be working in the open, it will be safer with you for the time being."

Magnus signaled his agreement and re-shouldered the bag. Cecil swallowed hard, clasping the hilt of his weapon tighter. "Alright," he concluded. "Let's go."

Drake and Cecil streaked toward the other side of the road, staff and sword in hand. Drake stole a glance over his shoulder to see his brother, Anubis, and Ember vanish behind him. He sighed uneasily.

It seemed to Drake as if he had done this before, sixteen years ago on the night that Daimos usurped the city. He could still recall the experience entirely, his bolting through blazing streets while the wails of the shades and the clamor of war rang on endlessly. But his most disturbing memory of all was his strongest—that fleeting moment in which it felt as if his heart were crushed inside him and his mother was killed by the inevasible arrow of the harpie Medeva.

Only a few short weeks after Magnus' discovery of their father's book, Drake found himself scurrying through the same battlefield that he had escaped so long ago. With Cecil's warning in mind that their safe return wasn't certain, he only hoped that he would not have to see another loved one die at the hands of the warlord.

Once Drake and his former guardian had passed beyond the light of the road torches, Cecil pulled the older brother back against another building wall. "Hold it," Cecil said in a curt whisper. Listening keenly, Drake heard a pair of muffled voices emerge. As they loudened, two guardsmen in the midst of a conversation slouched past the mouth of the alley. They sauntered into the distance, oblivious to the intruders in the shadows, and their voices faded.

Drake respired heavily. Only after having absolute certainty that the guards had moved on, Cecil took the older brother by his arm and hurried him out of the side street. Another torchlit road crossed their path—leftward, it meandered into an open plaza; rightward, it met the citadel's inner wall, though it offered a narrow fork that slipped behind another row of buildings. Cecil flung a glance in both directions, then sprinted rightward across the road with Drake.

They ducked into the road fork and followed it swiftly. Near its end, the road passed an exceptionally decrepit building by the citadel wall. Cecil led Drake over a toppled streetlamp and around to the side of the ramshackle building, where they halted to scan the area.

"All clear?" Cecil whispered, peering down the road they had just crossed.

Drake checked all neighboring pathways and gave an affirmative nod. Cecil turned back to the building to confront a stale brown door. "Do you remember this place, Drake?" asked Cecil, clutching the doorknob.

"I can't say so. No," Drake answered.

Cecil wrenched the rust-stiffened knob and forced the door open, discharging over a decade's worth of dust into his face. He coughed into his fist and fanned apart the dust cloud. "This is a citadel storage shed," he rasped, then cleared his throat, "and one of the easternmost buildings in the complex. It will be our perfect choice for the fire."

Cecil and Drake cagily proceeded inside. They were overwhelmed by a sudden pitch-darkness and a profound lack of air. Cecil shut the door halfway so as to prevent their being detected by a passing guard. Drake refrained from moving at all, in fear of colliding with the colorless contours of sacks, crates, and other indistinct materials that enclosed them.

Cecil paced deeper inside the shed. The floorboards moaned raucously even under his careful step. "Grain sacks, firewood, rags..." he listed as he brushed his hand along the neatly stacked trove of supplies. "This place will go up in flames in no time." He looked over his shoulder to Drake for approval. "Are you ready for this?"

Drake panned his eyes around the shed, only to have the same indistinguishable blackness fill his vision. "Alright," he said, stealing a final glance out the door. "Go for it."

"Your staff, please," Cecil requested and blindly swapped weapons with Drake. He crept back and raised the staff in one hand. A fiery luster overcame the ruby headpiece, as if it were growing hotter. When the jewel appeared to climax in its effulgence, Cecil took a double grip on the trunk, and the staff burst into flame.

He swept down the head of the burning staff without as much as singeing his flesh. A great ribbon of fire lashed out from before him and seized every mound of burlap, wood, and cloth in its reach. As he drew back the extinguished staff, he watched the fire expand gluttonously to the deepest corners of the shed and lick the highest timbers of the ceiling.

Drake gawked at the blazing heaps. Within seconds, the rising heat became intolerable and oxygen grew scarce. Cecil pulled his shirt up over his mouth and nose to guard against the smoke and darted for the exit, motioning for Drake to follow him.

Together they streaked out the door and back into the fortress while the fire crackled madly behind them. Cecil steered Drake in the direction of the citadel wall, alongside which ran another discreet alleyway. "We'll circle the citadel and meet up with Anubis and Magnus at the armory door," Cecil reviewed their plan aloud. The torrid breath and glow of the fire abated at their backs as they slipped inside the alley.

"How long do you think it'll take the guards to put out the fire?" asked Drake.

"I doubt that those guards carry much around with them besides their abylite weapons," Cecil replied. "If I'm right, they won't be equipped to readily extinguish the fire. By the time they manage to get the blaze under control..." He smiled thinly. "...we'll already be inside the castle."

"We will reach the forest within two nights," said Daimos, ascending the steps at the foot of the entranceway. "Pack yourselves some supplies for the journey, and we'll leave the city on the hour."

Noctell and Raven proceeded around the enormous table and followed the warlord up to the door. The demon fell behind when he briefly halted to question his master. "What about Medeva?" he asked. "Are you sure we should be excluding her like this? She'll be furious with you."

"Then let her be." Daimos flicked up a hand in an apathetic gesture. "Don't concern yourself with her, Raven. We have more important matters to deal with at the moment."

"But milord," the demon persisted, "we'll have to fulfill our promise to her sooner or later anyhow."

"Our Master's revival comes before all else," Daimos staunchly retorted. "The fulfillment of our promise to the harpie will be an afterthought." He paused. "And I'd rather we not commit ourselves."

Without another word, Daimos delivered a vigorous thrust to the double doors, shoving them open. To everyone's prompt surprise, the first thing to fall into view was a guard bolting toward them through the corridor ahead.

"Milord!" cried the guard. He moved at such speed that his sagging hood was blown off to reveal his sallow, mottled face. "Milord, there's a fire in the citadel!"

"What?" Daimos furrowed his brow.

The guard stooped before his master. "Milord there's a fire—"

"I heard you the first time," snapped Daimos irritably. "What are you running to me for? Can't you handle it yourselves?"

"Of course, milord," answered the guard, bowing lower. "But I thought I should inform you that we've seen a pair of intruders flee from the burning building. We think that they may have started the fire."

Daimos' face became lined with curiosity rather than any sort of alarm. He turned around to Noctell and Raven, whose reactions were unreadable.

"Do you think it's Handel and the Winghearts?" the necromancer asked in a casual slur.

A smirk touched Daimos' lips. "I'd draw no conclusions," he said, "but I would not be surprised. They must be more foolish than I'd thought to try incinerating my citadel as a revenge scheme." His stare shifted to the demon. "Raven, why don't you head down and see about all the commotion? If this really is the work of the Winghearts and the others, send word that I want every one of them killed on sight."

"Yes, milord." Raven nodded and headed out of the door, past the kneeling guard.

"We've already given those four ingrates a chance at survival," sneered Daimos. "We cannot help them if they refuse to take it."

Magnus embraced the chill of the bricks beneath his downturned palms. With his back to a wall and Anubis beside him, he lurked behind the edge of a strip of buildings just outside the castle court. The herbalist leaned ever so slightly past the lip of the wall, allowing him an unobstructed view of their precarious goal—the armory door, a hefty steel shield fitted over an entrance at the back wall of the castle.

"Can you see anything?" whispered Magnus. He looked down at his feet to ensure that Ember was still with them.

"Yes," Anubis affirmed in an equally soft volume. "The door is straight ahead."

"Are there any guards?"

Anubis frowned at the question. He could count at least nine of the warlord's cloaked minions scattered along the castle wall ahead. They appeared fervently occupied, blaring unintelligible arguments and commands to each other from afar.

"Unfortunately, yes..." answered Anubis, "...but they don't seem to be very much at ease. Something's going on, no doubt."

"It's the fire." Magnus' face lit up. "Cecil and Drake must have—"

"Shush!" Anubis suddenly silenced the boy. He gestured to Magnus to come by the wall's edge, then slunk behind in line. Looking out, Magnus noticed a rather enormous figure pacing into the crowd. As the giant turned its head, the glow of a nearby torch made the figure instantly recognizable by the crimson sheen of its face.

"It's Raven," the herbalist muttered in Magnus' ear. "Listen."

The guards appeared to compose themselves upon seeing the demon approach. "Well, what is it?" Raven's growl boomed over the sudden silence. "What's this about a fire?"

"Someone said they saw smoke and flames near the east

wall," the guard replied, raising an arm to indicate the said direction, "and that two people were spotted fleeing from it. They weren't in our robes and were obviously intruders. They must have started the fire."

"Did anyone see what they looked like?"

"No one told me. Maybe it was too difficult to say."

Raven idled a second before delivering his orders. "Spread out," he commanded. "Some of you come with me to deal with the fire. The rest, start searching for the arsonists. If you find them, Daimos wants them killed on sight." He extended a clawed finger to single out a pair of guards from the crowd. "You two stay here and keep watch."

Magnus felt the stone at his back grow scalding cold in his unease. "They saw Drake and Cecil," he whispered urgently.

"I heard everything," Anubis sighed. "Let's hope they'll make it here safely."

Magnus observed Raven give a signal to depart and lead the guards away. The party trod off briskly and scattered as they crossed the court. But not all had abandoned the armory entrance—just as the demon had instructed, a pair of the guards still lingered in their places.

"Raven left two of them behind," Magnus reported. The remaining men had their arms folded in a leisurely fashion as they babbled to one another about the situation.

Anubis glimpsed the scene over Magnus' shoulder. "This isn't good," he said, withdrawing. "But we can't wait much longer. We have to clear the way to the armory before Cecil and Drake arrive."

Magnus was disinclined to speak his thoughts, in fear that he'd regret it. "Do you think we could take on both the guards?" he finally suggested.

Anubis faced the boy through the drape of his hair. "That might be our best choice." From his vest pocket, he fished out a corked vial containing what looked like milky water—the concoction that Magnus had watched him prepare a few hours earlier. "An athamine smoke bomb," Anubis recapped. "Similar to what I used when we were fleeing from Medeva four nights ago, except infused with a knockout chemical. You stay hidden; I'll lure the guards here and cast the bomb. The smog will be vast and impossible to disperse, and we must not breathe the fumes. Understood?"

Magnus nodded rapidly. Anubis stole down the street, hustling the boy along. They passed four mutilated storefronts before reaching a vaulted alley that bridged the street and the castle courtyard beyond. Anubis leaned into the corridor to ensure he was still in view of the guardsmen, then withdrew and heaved a steadying breath.

"Your necklace, please," Anubis requested with an outstretched hand to Magnus, who readily removed his pendant and passed it over. Slipping on the diamond neckpiece, Anubis stepped into the mouth of the alley. He conjured to his ring a light as obtrusive as a scream in a mausoleum. When the guards' heads spun in his direction, he made a show of inept furtiveness and stumbled back behind the buildings.

"Run! Run!" Anubis spurred Magnus away from the

alley in a whisper. He retreated to the shadow of a veranda, where he summoned a spark from Magnus' pendant to the cork of his vial and tossed the bottle ahead. The clink of the glass on the road sounded a second before the two guards stormed through the alley and into the street. The first and last thing they spotted was the smoldering bottle on the floor. Glass shattered in a tempest of white smoke.

Anubis and Magnus fled the billowing smog, Ember following. Behind them, a duet of breathless, guttural coughing dwindled to silence. "They won't be unconscious for long," Anubis warned. He swept Magnus' pendant off his neck and returned it to its owner. "We'll make sure the door's open, then take cover until Cecil and Drake get here."

Magnus pulled the necklace back over his head and raced on. Torchflames spat contemptuously in his ears while he tore through the castle courtyard and to the armory entrance. He had just reached the door when he was jarred by a sudden shriek let off by Ember.

Magnus whipped his head around. What he saw was worse than he could ever have predicted or imagined to go wrong. Standing only yards away, directly behind Anubis, was Medeva, her halberd raised high and ready to strike. Before Magnus could even part his lips to utter a warning, the harpie swept down her blade at full force. Anubis scrambled to escape the weapon's trajectory, but was nowhere near fast enough. Slashed across his back, he collapsed to the paving stones with a gasp of agony.

Magnus had hardly seconds to think after the attack. Medeva's blazing-green eyes flickered toward him as if the angel of death had chosen its next target. Magnus felt his mind turn numb as terror seized control of him. He lunged, ramming open the armory door, then shut it behind him with the weight of his shoulder. He was rattled a moment later by a violent blow against the door from outside. Clearly, Medeva was trying to break in.

By fortifying his sideways stance, Magnus was just able to prevent the barrier from being forced open. He jabbed the edge of his foot to the door and braced himself in anticipation of another blow by Medeva. He wouldn't be able to hold the harpie back for long. He shifted his eyes aside to find a sliding crossbar mounted at the left of the doorframe.

Another, even more ferocious, assault on the door nearly sent him reeling forward. But the instant that Medeva seemed to withdraw in preparation for a new strike, Magnus whirled around and grappled onto the crossbar. He drew it over the face of the door in a single sweep, securing it in a mount on the opposite side, just as the harpie delivered a third attempt and pounded futilely on the now-locked entrance.

Magnus recoiled from the doorway and turned to study the room he found himself in. The armory was in profound disarray, obviously not having seen much use in years. Under the glow of two lit torches shone the contours of crates, chests, and metal stands, banked in chaotic rows and columns like the building blocks of a labyrinth wall. Weapons of all sorts—longswords, poleaxes, and handbows—were mounted on the walls in impressive quantities. A gamut of jeweled staffs stood upright in an expansive, rectangular rack that lined the north end of the chamber.

Another jolt from Medeva shook the sealed door. Thankfully, the crossbar showed no sign of weakening. *She doesn't know it's locked,* thought Magnus, *but she'll realize it eventually. When she does, she'll gather all the guards to break it down. I have to find a safe way out of here.*

His wavering was cut short by Medeva's final attempt to force open the armory door. His heart racing ever faster in his panic, Magnus haphazardly pinned his attention on a wrought-iron spiral staircase behind a fence of crates near the wall at his right.

Wherever it will take me, at the least, it will give me a chance to think about what to do next, he decided. *As things stand, I'm trapped in here...and everyone else is locked outside with Medeva.*

With his mind made up, Magnus hastened for the stairs.

Medeva receded from the door. It seemed that the boy had been smart enough to draw the crossbar. A raucous cough prompted her to turn around. There lay the gravely wounded Anubis, arched over the ground on his knees and hands, scarred by a bloodied gash across his back. As the harpie neared him in measured paces, the herbalist slumped to the floor at a loss for strength.

Medeva stared down at Anubis' pain-contorted frame. Her expression was an enigma, marked by neither remorse nor cruelty. Her eyes traced the sinuous splashes of blood on the paving stones, then leapt up to a distant light emerging from the citadel buildings. Without turning away from the light, she leisurely placed her halberd's spear at the back of Anubis' head.

Cecil and Drake hurried inside the courtyard. The moment they became aware of the mangled figure lying beneath the harpie's blade, Cecil extinguished the light of his sword and sheathed the weapon, leaving the torches to shine on their own.

"Please," Cecil said in an earnest, dismal quaver. "Please spare him."

"Why did you come back here?" Medeva inquired with no acknowledgment of Cecil's request.

Drake scanned the courtyard vehemently. "Magnus!" he exclaimed.

"Where's Magnus?" Cecil asked the harpie in turn.

"Why did you come back here?" Medeva repeated her question in a tone that was surprisingly resolute.

Cecil hesitated, but delivered a blunt answer. "To kill Daimos Recett," he said, then raised his hands to his sides. "But his death is not worth Anubis' life. Please."

Still, Medeva did not shift her halberd from its threatening position. "The boy locked himself in the armory," she barked, then shook her head, as if in disbelief. "You know you have no chance against Recett. For what purpose could you have come here other than suicide?"

Cecil hardly imagined that Medeva would uphold a dialogue in such a situation. He replied when he realized that the harpie actually expected a response. "It's irrelevant," he said. "We came to fight, but we end in surrender. If you plan on sparing us, then please—release Anubis or he'll sooner die of his wounds."

"Do you think I care?" Medeva retorted, pressing her polearm closer against her victim's skull. Anubis uttered a convulsing whimper. "Recett already freed you," she continued. "What fools trade freedom for death?"

"Our demise was not certain," Cecil answered staunchly. "We took the only chance we had, no matter how slim. But we've failed. Let us have Anubis and Magnus, and we will leave this place. We have no purpose to stay here any longer."

There was absolute silence. Then Medeva replied: "Neither do I." In a maneuver too deft to follow, she sheathed her halberd at her back and removed a composite bow that had been hooped crosswise over her body. Not a second later, she had an arrow readied in the bowstring and aimed precisely at Cecil. "You're in the hands of that madman, not mine," she said. "I've more important matters to attend to."

Steadily, Medeva withdrew to the distant end of the courtyard. She fired her arrow. Cecil ducked and dove away, lashing out his sword. But the projectile struck the ground so far from its target that it could never have landed a hit. When Cecil refocused on the courtyard's edge, Medeva was nowhere in sight.

Cecil spent a moment in unmoving shock. The sight of the frantically pacing Ember pulled him back to his senses, and along with Drake, he rushed to the wounded herbalist.

A grievously deep gash crossed Anubis' shoulder and ran slantways down the length of his back, through his blood-sodden leather vest. Cecil lifted Anubis onto his side with care and was grateful to find him still breathing.

"Anubis," Cecil called as Drake leaned in from behind. "Anubis, can you hear me?"

Anubis pried open his eyes to slits. "Cecil, Drake...no...." he struggled to say.

Drake, meanwhile, leapt for the armory door, nearly tripping over Ember on his way. He rattled the door by its handle, but it was fastened shut, as Medeva had claimed. "Magnus!" he panicked, hammering an icy fist on the metal. "Magnus, it's Drake!"

Cecil pressed his palm to the deeper, upper part of Anubis' wound. "Anubis, we have to get you out of here. You're losing too much blood."

"No, Cecil!" said the herbalist under a cough. "Leave me and save Magnus! The guards could arrive any minute!"

Cecil took up Anubis' shivering left arm and draped it over his shoulders. "We're not going to let you die," he replied steadfastly. "Come on, Drake."

Drake allowed his hand to slip off the armory door. Knowing that his brother was trapped beyond it, he drew away with great difficulty. He sprinted to Anubis' aid, taking the herbalist's other arm. "What about Magnus?" he fretted.

"First we've got to carry Anubis to safety," answered Cecil, lifting Anubis off the ground as he came to a stand with Drake. "Then we'll focus on devising a plan. As long as we're out here, we're in blatant view of the guards."

They ran for the shelter of the buildings, Anubis suspended between them and Ember scurrying in their tracks. "If things continue as they are now," Cecil said grimly, "our odds of escaping this place alive are growing slimmer by the second."

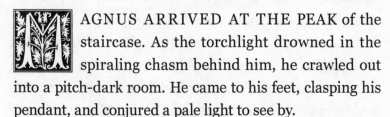

38

Entrapment

AGNUS ARRIVED AT THE PEAK of the staircase. As the torchlight drowned in the spiraling chasm behind him, he crawled out into a pitch-dark room. He came to his feet, clasping his pendant, and conjured a pale light to see by.

At first glance, the room did not appear to bear much difference from the armory except for its more confined size—crates and chests were similarly abundant here, as well as some discarded pieces of weaponry, suggesting it was some kind of storage chamber. A lone, arched window hung in the perfect center of the right wall; a closed door sat plainly ahead.

Magnus didn't waste any time scrutinizing his new environment and instead walked directly over to the window. He laid an unsteady hand on the pane, straining to peer through it, but the glass was dirtied and scraped beyond repair. No matter how hard he tried to see, the image of the citadel grounds behind it was filtered to an indistinct, monochrome blur.

I must be on the second floor, Magnus assessed his situation to himself. *Anubis is lying somewhere down there, probably dead, and Drake and Cecil are running straight for Medeva. Every last thing's gone wrong.*

He eased his palm off the glass, stricken with despair. The one chance they'd had at ending Daimos' reign had been lost to a plan turned awry, and it seemed as if any effort to undo the damage would be in vain. *What were we thinking?* he lamented. *Four people can't take on an entire army. Now we've already lost a life...and the rest of us are going to die if we don't leave this place fast.*

Magnus fell back against the wall with his bag left dangling from a single shoulder. He clawed a trembling hand over his face. Their plan had fallen to pieces, Anubis had been slaughtered by the harpie, and Magnus himself had been cornered inside the castle. Yet again, Daimos had bettered them.

His grieving was disrupted when his backpack slipped off his arm and hit the floor with a muted thud. He retrieved it, remembering the Luminous Rock shard that he carried inside it. *All's not lost,* an encouraging voice then came to him. *Anubis may be gone, but I have the shard. If I can find a way out of here and meet up with Cecil and Drake, we still have a chance to escape.*

Fueled by new hope, Magnus shouldered his backpack and turned his mind away from misery. *Anubis mentioned three ways in and out of the castle,* he recalled. *The front door, the armory, and the dungeon tunnel. With Medeva out there, the armory is out of the question...and I can't risk facing Daimos alone by taking the main entrance. And the grounds outside ought to be swarmed with guards by now. The tunnel is my last option.*

Then I'll be taking the same risk, he argued to himself. *The only access to the dungeons is through the throne room—right where we'd planned to confront Daimos.*

Magnus felt close to abandoning all hope again upon realizing his every exit to be blocked. But if he stayed where he was, surely his only way out of the castle would be his death. *I have no choice,* he thought. *I'll have to take the dungeon tunnel, risk or not. With enough luck, Daimos will be in another part of the castle.*

He came in front of the only door in sight and swiveled down its handle, opening it a few inches to let the light from the hallway seep in. *I just need to find another way back to the first floor. There must be another staircase aside from the one in the armory.*

Magnus shouldered the door ajar. He entered into an unfamiliar corridor and closed the storage room door behind him. Here, many entranceways lined the walls, trimmed with lofty arches and lit by torches that made everything appear as if it were burning. Far ahead, the hall met a spacious, circular chamber similar in construction to the throne room on the lower level. Behind him, the corridor terminated at a stark stone-slab wall.

Magnus began to wander guardedly, footsteps deadened

by the carpeting. His attention was drawn to a distinct doorway in the back wall of the chamber ahead of him— beyond it glinted the wiry frame of a second spiral staircase.

Magnus hurried his pace. The crackle of fire dimmed and sharpened at every torch that he passed, until he arrived at the mouth of the grandiose chamber. Four elaborately sculpted pillars of marble upheld the ceiling here, curling into an ornamental circlet at their peaks. A painted replica of the throne room's skull mosaic coated the floor, drowned in the haze of the firelight.

The boy had only just set foot in the chamber when the sudden slam of a door resonated from afar. He lurched backward and came to a halt to be able to listen for any more signs of activity. Then the echo of voices reached his ears.

A dire panic engulfed Magnus. The conversing voices were rapidly approaching. Fleeing back into the open hall would put him in danger of being seen, and he likely wouldn't have enough time to return to the storage room. With few alternatives, Magnus saw the chamber's pillars as his best choice for a spontaneous shelter. He ducked under the colossal shadow of the pillar close by his right and narrowed his frame against the marble.

"But don't you at least want to find out who the intruders are?" the first voice clearly sounded, joined by the dim clapping of footsteps on the chamber floor. Aside from the fact that the voice was recognizable as a man's, the speaker was otherwise impossible to identify.

"It makes no difference at this point," a second person

retorted. "We can't spend all morning here. Our master is waiting for us!" Doubtlessly, this harrowing voice was none other than that of Daimos himself.

The footsteps came silent near the center of the chamber. Magnus folded his arms around his body and slumped lower to avoid being spotted. "Very well, milord," replied the other man.

"Head down and get Raven," Daimos instructed. "Leave the rest of the guards to deal with the fire."

"And what of the intruders?" the man queried.

"Forget them," snapped the warlord. "Whoever they are, they are to be killed without question. I don't need any more rebelling buffoons to take up room in my dungeon."

"What if they're the Winghearts and the others? The four people I believe we've just released?"

Daimos cackled derisively. "All the better."

"If they are, that means the rest of them are missing," said the other man. "They've only spotted two intruders fleeing from the fire. No doubt the other two will be with them."

Magnus was given temporary relief in knowing that his and his companions' identities had not yet become known to Daimos. After listening long enough, Magnus was almost certain that the man to whom the warlord spoke was the dreaded calimancer Noctell.

"Oh, I'll bet it's all part of their ruse," scoffed the warlord. "The fire is just a petty distraction for whatever they're planning. Before long, they'll try infiltrating the castle or do something else equally foolish."

"Shall we fortify our defenses?" Noctell proposed.

"Hardly," spat Daimos. "Send a few guards to the tunnel. That should ensure the intruders' deaths or, at the least, their failure."

"At once, milord."

"I'll be waiting for you on the tower roof," said Daimos. "I'd like to get a view of the fray. Perhaps I'll be able to catch a glimpse of the culprits from above."

"Of course, milord, go right ahead."

Footsteps faded to a distant echo as Daimos made his way to the second-floor staircase and ascended its iron spiral. Noctell could be heard following him moments later. When the murmuring crackle of the torches was the only sound that remained, Magnus scouted the chamber from behind the edge of the pillar. Noctell and the warlord had left from sight.

Magnus brought himself back against the marble pillar, numbed and trembling. With his arms wrapped from shoulder to shoulder and his knees doubled to his chest, his thoughts droned despondently: *Once Noctell sends the guards to the tunnel, my only exit will be blocked. I'll have no way left to escape.*

In the same way as the Luminous Rock had melted to nothing before his eyes, every last sliver of hope and vigor that Magnus gripped within him ebbed away painfully, only to be replaced twofold by fear. *I have to find another way out*, he persisted. But he knew that he was being impossibly optimistic. Of the castle's three known exits, each one would land him directly into the arms of Daimos' guards.

Anubis is dead, he listed, *Medeva is waiting right outside the castle doors, and Noctell is heading down to join her. Drake and Cecil have barely a chance to survive if they get anywhere near here, and my chances inside this place are even worse. I don't know what to do anymore... all this...everything is ruined. We've failed.*

Magnus lifted an unsteady hand over his eyes. *I can't fight back,* he thought, *but I can't just give up, either. If I'm killed, Daimos will find and destroy the shard, and all that's left of the Luminous Rock will be gone.*

Which means I'll have to kill him first, he answered himself. *Whatever the risks.*

The boy turned his side to the pillar and looked out again. He eyed the entranceway at the back of the chamber that opened to the second-floor staircase—the one he had seen on his way from the storage room. *Noctell and Daimos went through there. Those must be the main stairs,* he presumed. *Now's an opportunity I'll never get again: while Noctell is heading down to the grounds, Daimos will be alone on the tower roof. All I need to do is take the stairs, find Daimos, kill him with the shard, and make my escape.*

He held his posture stiffly for a moment before hunching back against the pillar in despair. *Who am I kidding? I don't have any way of escaping, and I don't stand a chance against Daimos. Even if I manage to use the shard, he would only have been rendered mortal. Afterwards, he'll kill me on a whim.*

He sighed, placing his distraught gaze ahead of him. *What happens to me isn't the point. My fate is already sealed. But if I'm going to die...then at least I'll die having won the battle.*

At last, Magnus rose to a stand. He clenched his fists with newfound courage and stepped out from behind the pillar. *For Brendan,* he recalled Cecil's valiant words before their departure from the forest, *and for MorningStar. We came here to finish my father's work. If ridding Daimos of his immortality is all I can do, then it's what I'll do.*

Magnus strode into the center of the chamber, coming to a stop between the eyeholes of the skeletal floor mural, and unshouldered his backpack. *Whatever happens to me,* he concluded, *my death won't be in vain.*

He kneeled and struggled to open his bag with a quivering grip. But before he could, his thoughts and actions were arrested by a heart-stopping assault—a conjured blast of dark energy to his side. He was cast like a rag across the chamber floor until he skidded to a stop on his stomach several feet away.

"Hello, Wingheart," a familiarly suave voice greeted him. Magnus turned up his head from the ground. Staring down at him was the manifestation of his fears, the calimancer Noctell Knever.

"You did a sorry job trying to hide behind that pillar," Noctell sneered with a darkly glowing hand outstretched to the boy. "You're lucky that Daimos had his back to you. Else you might have been killed on the spot."

Magnus scrambled upright and tried desperately to sprint past the necromancer. Noctell's eyes pursued the boy like those of a preying snake, then he whirled around, expelling another bolt of dark energy in Magnus' way. Again, Magnus was propelled to the floor.

Noctell swaggered closer. "I didn't want Daimos to have to exert any effort in dealing with the likes of you. Besides, I'd take far more pleasure in doing so myself."

A helix of smoky veins coiled around the necromancer's arm and converged in the center of his palm. After rising again, Magnus backed against the wall with no conceivable escape. At this rate, he was unsure if he would live to make it anywhere near the warlord.

"Now tell me..." Noctell curled up his fingertips and the veins slithered into the cup of his hand. "What kind of fool sends a boy like you to infiltrate a castle?" He jabbed his fist forward and opened it, causing a single vein to reappear and lash out at Magnus in the form of a menacing black whip. As if by its own accord, the whip flicked itself around Magnus' legs and grew taut, binding him in his place. Finally, Noctell drew back the whip still clasped in his hand and swept it to the opposite end of the chamber, heaving Magnus against the side of a pillar.

With a cry of pain, Magnus collided against the marble column and dropped to its base as the whip relaxed his hold. Noctell retracted the whip, cracking it at the

highest point of the ceiling before he allowed it to slacken
and sprawl around his feet. "But it's no matter," he said
through a nonchalant smile. "Because I'll kill you at last,
Wingheart. Oh yes, I'll kill you slowly." Again he raised his
whip. His glare was murderous, affixed on the boy before
him who still fought to recover his stance from the impact.
"Death by a thousand cuts!" the necromancer roared and
scarred Magnus' arm with a mighty slash of his whip that
struck the boy back to the floor. "One for every moment of
suffering that you and that wretched brother of yours ever
caused me!"

Magnus cringed and clutched his burning wound.
Before he could as much as pull himself to his knees, he
again felt the necromancer's whip ensnare him by his waist.

"Let's begin with the sixteen years of my life that
I wasted in search of you two." Noctell's derisions leapt
off his tongue like flames as he cast Magnus against the
wall with another thrash of his whip. "Sixteen years spent
scouring Earth and Arkane with no avail. Do you know
how many times my master strangled me when I returned
empty-handed? How many times I've been choked by his
withered claw wrapped around my throat? Feel my pain,
Wingheart! Feel it!"

Under leadened eyelids, Magnus saw the necromancer
pace toward him. He tried to raise his upper body off
the floor by the support of his hands, but then, as if in
submission, simply collapsed back into a lifeless slump.
He shuddered in agony as a second slash of Noctell's whip
stung his back, tearing his shirt.

"And then, when finally you are just within my reach," Noctell lowered his voice to a near-whisper, "you escape... not once, not twice, but three times! Whether it was your own home, those barren campgrounds, or even the MorningStar forest, you always seemed to just slip away without a trace."

Turning his palm upward, Noctell relaxed his hold on the whip. "But not anymore." With startling haste, the whip began to extend and meander across the floor. From its tip curled wisps of smoke, which glided overtop the boy, clinging to him like smoldering embers. When the whip slithered over Magnus' body, the smoke hardened to a coil of sinewy black tendons.

Noctell beamed smugly. "Remember that night in Markwell, Wingheart?" He wrenched back his whip, now bound to the tendons. The coil that enfolded Magnus contracted in response, causing him to writhe and gasp for air in alarm. "Remember my ropes that bound you so? Remember the bonds that you somehow miraculously escaped, humiliating me to no end?" The necromancer tugged on the whip until his hand was pulled behind his head. "Remember, *Mark Emburn?*"

Another sharp contraction of the tendons limited Magnus' breathing even further. His legs bound and his chest wrung by the vines of dark energy, his heart was thrown into a frenzy as if in a struggle to fuel him with life.

"Escape this, boy!" Noctell bellowed, drawing the whip like the strings of a marionette. Magnus' limp body was pried off the ground by the grip of the tendons and heaved upright against the wall. Now Magnus was growing light-headed; Noctell was strangling him.

Fighting the tendons' powerful hold, Magnus only just managed to curl his fingertips around his iridescent pendant. But no matter how hard he tried, he couldn't possibly muster enough focus to break Noctell's magic. His arms had long gone numb and he found himself at an almost complete loss of air.

Noctell broadened his smile as he pulled his whip tighter. To see the boy suffering at his hand satiated him, like a retribution for every time that Noctell had experienced the same breathlessness in his master's grasp. Only just when Magnus was clearly on the verge of succumbing to the tendons did Noctell lower his arms, dispelling his magic.

The whip and the tendons alike collapsed to smoke. Magnus gasped and crumpled forward with his face to the floor and his hand still tensed in a fist under his chest. Noctell fanned away the smoke and grinned with pride.

"How does it feel, Wingheart?" the necromancer scoffed. "How does it feel to have the life wrung out of you?" He paced around Magnus, casting his unremorseful stare upon him from every angle. "How does it feel to suffer?"

Magnus showed no reaction to Noctell's mocking. Unmoving he lay, his breathing muffled against the floor and his limbs sprawled out, aside from his right arm, which remained tucked beneath him.

"Have you given up already?" Noctell relentlessly taunted. "After all you've done to get here, you're not even going to try and fight me? Rise, boy!" He threw his foot to Magnus' side in a vigorous kick. "Rise and face your opponent!"

The bash of the necromancer's heavy sole knocked Magnus onto his back. But as the boy turned up his face, Noctell was met with a sudden, impressive counterattack—a dazzling light burst that exploded from the pendant still clutched fast in Magnus' hand.

Taken unawares, Noctell staggered away with the full force of the flash still throbbing in his eyes. Grasping a split-second opportunity, Magnus pressed his weight to his shoulder and delivered a sweeping kick to the necromancer's heels.

Noctell, already caught in an unsound stance, was knocked off his feet. He plunged backward, brutally striking the back of his head against the stone floor.

Magnus' assault had succeeded, and he knew he hadn't a moment to lose. He battled the excruciating soreness of his body as he rose and raced with a limp toward his backpack slumped in the center of the chamber. But when he snatched up the bag and made for the staircase, he glanced past his shoulder to see that Noctell had not yet risen.

Magnus halted—Noctell wasn't moving and didn't appear to be feigning. The blow must have been enough to render the necromancer unconscious. *Even if I did manage to knock him out, it can't be for long*, thought Magnus. *I'll have just enough time to run up the tower and find Daimos.*

He reached inside his backpack and withdrew the blazingly bright Luminous Rock shard. Magnus needed only set his eyes on it to be filled once more with the courage to confront the warlord. Leaving the burden of his bag behind, rested against the wall, he cast a final, confirmative look at the unconscious Noctell. *This is it*, he prepared himself and sighed heavily, turning to face the doorway that preceded the staircase. *It's now or never.*

39

Manhunt

RAKE SURVEYED the deserted citadel streets from behind the crack of a narrowly opened door. The building he found himself in was the long-abandoned ruin of an apothecary, one that he remembered well from his childhood years in MorningStar. The shelf units beside him were dusted with glass splinters and otherwise bare save for a few tin boxes that had been mostly looted of their contents.

Behind the older brother, hunched against the battered store counter, was the wounded Anubis. Cecil kneeled over him with his palm clamped over the gash still dripping with blood, and his other hand coiled around the herbalist's ice-cold wrist. Anubis' face was bent with pain while he stared lifelessly ahead. His breaths were growing sharply irregular. Nestled close beside him, his salamander, Ember, tilted its spined head up to its master in anxious wait.

"All clear?" Cecil asked Drake quietly.

Drake pulled away from the door. "I think so. But it's impossible to say for sure in this light."

"R-Raven sent..." Anubis pried open his quivering lips to speak, "...Raven sent the guards to...search for you. They... they're scouring the whole citadel. They're going to find you if you don't keep moving!"

"We can't go anywhere with you like this!" Cecil protested. "And we need to plan a way into the citadel to rescue Magnus. Fleeing aimlessly won't do any good!"

"Cecil..." Anubis lamely raised the arm of his uninjured side to clutch Cecil's shoulder. "I'm dying. T-there's no way you can help me. The longer you stay here with me, the more danger you'll be in." His terrified eyes bored into Cecil's. "But you can still s-save Magnus. Leave me here, Cecil! Anyone who betrays his friends to the gallows like I've done deserves no better."

"This isn't a matter of what you've done, Anubis!" snapped Cecil. "We're not leaving you here to die!"

Anubis shook his head rigidly. "No, Cecil. T-this is my punishment." He cringed, drawing his hand away from Cecil. "Now go! There's nothing you can do for me anymore!"

Cecil's determined expression was unshaken. "We can suppress the bleeding," he said and released his grip on Anubis' wound. He pulled his shirt off over his head, exposing his bare torso to the frigid air. "See anything that can help, Drake?" he asked, feeling the hem of the shirt's collar. "Anything solid enough to tie down against the wound." He stopped his finger over a small slit in the collar, then wrenched it with all his strength, tearing the fabric halfway down the middle.

Drake turned away from the door. The ground was strewn with litter, including the rubble from a crumbled portion of the wall by a shelf unit against which were propped his and Cecil's weapons. He culled a flat stone from the rubble pile and offered it to his former guardian. "How's this?"

"No, no..." Cecil muttered hastily. He finished tearing apart his shirt, to be left with a separated sleeve. "I need something thinner, sturdier..." His sentence trailed off as he scouted the dark room. "There." He indicated a demolished wooden shelf in the unit beside Drake. "Hand me that plank."

Drake reached for the shattered piece of timber to withdraw it from its rusted shelving mounts. At least half of the wood snapped off as he pulled it away. He passed the splintery plank to Cecil after shaking it free of glass and ash.

Cecil placed the plank beside himself, along with the torn shirt. "We've got to find some way of getting inside the castle," he said to Drake as he began, with care, to remove Anubis' bloodied leather vest. "Or at least anticipate how Magnus might try to escape." Ember picked up its head and scurried aside as Cecil laid down the herbalist's slashed garment.

"He wouldn't try his luck through the front entrance, that's for sure," answered Drake, resuming his watch of the streets outside. "The armory door and the tunnel would be his only exits...and probably our only ways in."

Cecil tore open the herbalist's shirt to expose the wounded flesh. "True," he remarked. "If I were him, of course, I'd choose the dungeon tunnel. But that doesn't mean he wouldn't still try to leave through the armory."

Drake paused to deliberate. "We can't be in both places at once. What if we were to at least head to the tunnel? It would be our best chance at finding him."

"And what if he chooses the armory?" Cecil supposed. "At least if he takes the tunnel, he'll have entered into the safety of the forest. If, for whatever reason, he escapes back into the citadel, he'll have to deal with a lot more guards...and he'll most certainly need our help." Cecil took up the ragged sleeve he had torn from his shirt and bundled it to the size of a large fist. He compressed the bundle against Anubis' wound, dousing the fabric red with blood.

"Then we might already be too late," said Drake. "With the time it took us to carry Anubis out here, Magnus could've made his escape through the armory long ago."

Still holding the bundled cloth, Cecil retrieved the broken plank from the ground at his side. "That's a risk we take no matter which way we head. Magnus could just as well be halfway through the tunnel by now, and we have no way of catching up with him. But as I already told you, your brother will be in far more danger if he leaves through the armory door. Unless we're there as his defense, he'll have little chance to survive in the guards' manhunt." He laid the plank on top of the bloody cloth, aligning it vertically over the deepest length of the wound.

Drake curled his hand around the edge of the door as his focus faded. His vision rose to the dominating monolith of the castle tower in the distance. "Do you think our chances are any better?" he asked as if he were already certain of a negative answer. "How are we supposed to help Magnus if we can't even leave this building without being spotted?"

Cecil shrugged despondently. "We can only try our best, Drake." He swept up the massacred remains of his shirt and wrung them with his free hand, crafting them into a makeshift fabric cord. Looping the cord around Anubis' shoulder, he secured the plank and the cloth bundle in place with a firm knot. "We said from the start that this would be dangerous," he sighed. "We said from the start that not all of us may return." He tied the cord a second time to ensure its strength. "At least the pressure of the wood will restrict Anubis' bleeding enough for now. Only until we can find something more permanent."

"Thank..." Anubis stammered and shivered. "T-thank you, Cecil."

Drake's attention dropped from the tower. But as he laid eyes on the citadel streets, he flinched at the sight of two darkened figures roaming between the houses afar. "Guards!" he exclaimed in a raucous whisper.

Cecil turned alertly at Drake's warning. He slunk toward the doorway to peer outside for himself. The distant sentries moved listlessly from building to building, throwing open every door and leaning their hunched frames into the mouths of every alley. They worked sluggishly, but were heading in Cecil and Drake's direction.

"It doesn't look like they've seen us," Cecil noted in a hushed volume.

"It doesn't matter," said Drake. "They're coming straight for us. What are we supposed to do?"

Cecil cast a first glance at Anubis and a second glance back out the doorway. He seized their sword and staff propped against the shelves. "This place doesn't have any other exits." He passed the staff to Drake. "We'll either have to hide or fight."

"Then we hide," Drake replied immediately. "Behind the counter!"

"Drake..." Anubis called feebly. "Take my ring to defend yourself. The guards are sensitive to light."

Giving a nod, Drake slipped the lucidus ring off Anubis' finger and onto his own. He helped Cecil lift the wounded herbalist off the floor. Together with Ember, the three of them hurdled the countertop and ducked behind it.

Less than a minute later, a crushing blow to the front door hurled it wide open. The two guards darkened the entranceway with their crooked, robed figures. After one of the sentries' black-rimmed eyes had flickered across the empty room, the guard looked away to indolently resume his search of the citadel. But before he took more than a single step ahead, he stopped suddenly, leaning back into the apothecary for another glance.

The second guard turned in the direction of his lingering partner. "What is it?" he barked.

"Look." The first guard gestured inside the apothecary.

The floor was smeared with tracks imprinted in the ashes. "Someone was here."

The other guard picked up his head in curiosity as he and his partner headed in through the door. "The intruders?"

"It better be," murmured the first guard. He scanned the premises, lumbering forward. When he reached the store counter, he kneeled to examine a glistening dark splatter across the counter's front. He felt the substance, then brought his wetted fingertips under the visor of his hood. "Blood," he slurred through a barely open mouth. "It's fresh. Whosever it is, they couldn't have made it far from here."

The guard dried off his hand in the dust and stood up. His eyes followed the trickle of blood down to a thin pool soaked into the filth at his feet, then up to another darkened smear on the countertop. Giving his sole attention to the bloody markings, he paced ahead, only to be halted before he could look beyond the back edge of the counter.

A ferocious blaze of light erupted from behind the counter, stunning the guard. Cecil promptly pounced up from his hiding place and thrust out the hilt of his sword, violently bashing the guard's jaw. The guard was knocked cold by the blow and slumped into the dust.

The second guard by the doorway, from his palm swathed in blackness, launched a dark energy bolt in retaliation. A clever swipe of Cecil's lit blade deflected the strike, just as Drake leapt up to return the assault with a blast of luminous force from Anubis' ring. The guard took the full strength of the blast to his chest and was knocked against the wall behind him in a daze. Before he could counteract, Cecil fired off a subsequent light burst that hammered into the guard's stomach. With a groan of agony, the guard doubled over and crumpled face-first into the ashes.

Cecil hauled himself back over the counter to approach the second guard still twitching about his arms in a pitiable attempt to get up. By the time the guard had managed to pry his upper body out of the ashes, a deft strike of Cecil's sword hilt to the nape of his neck knocked him back to the floor, unconscious.

Drake clambered over the counter to join his former guardian; Ember came bounding in his tracks. "Do you think we're safe for now?"

"Not by a long shot," Cecil replied. "We have to take Anubis to another building far from here before the guards wake up, and we still have no clue how to rescue Magnus." His thoughts appeared to roam before causing him to look back on the guard that lay in front of him. "Drake...I have an idea."

Cecil crouched and tugged at the guard's abyss-black cloak. He heaved up the comatose man and rolled him onto his back. The guard's hood was cast off to expose his deathly pale, almost vampiric complexion. "This is perfect," Cecil quietly exclaimed. "These robes—they're the ultimate disguise. If we put these on, no one will recognize us."

Drake kneeled by the first of the guards. Slowly, he dropped his head into a nod. "We can go straight into the castle with those hoods pulled over our faces, and no one will suspect a thing." He paused. "But what about Anubis?"

"It will only look more suspicious if two guards are seen lugging a wounded man about," answered Cecil, lifting one of the guard's arms out of its sleeve. "We'll have to find a safe place to leave Anubis. Preferably one of the buildings around this area of the citadel."

"What if he's found?"

"His best chances are that he won't be. If the guards were assigned to spread out across the citadel's quadrants, then the two charged with keeping watch of these parts are lying unconscious in the dirt."

"And what happens when they come to?"

Cecil pulled away the last sleeve of the cloak and dragged the garment out from under its owner, leaving the guard with only his ragged leather body armor and leggins. "Let's hope they'll be too humiliated to come running back to Daimos, saying they've been beaten and robbed by intruders. When they regain consciousness, they'll be scrambling to find another set of robes if they don't want to be mistaken for intruders themselves."

Cecil took up the sinister robe and slipped his arms through its sleeves. As the rest of the cloak draped over him, he drew down the hem of the hood past his eyes, lending him the indistinguishable likeness of a MorningStar guard. "After we get Anubis out of here, we'll make for the armory door and rescue Magnus, wherever he is."

40

Facing the Skull

AGNUS' FOOTSTEPS CLATTERED on the iron staircase. By the glow of the Luminous Rock shard in his hand, the boy ascended the precarious spiral of footholds, never looking down to measure his progress. Walls of colossal bricks encircled him; above and below him, darkness loomed like a thirstily gaping maw.

There were no torches here, and no light. To Magnus, each stair along the way was one that he'd never again set foot on. This was his point of no return. Without anywhere else to run, he had chosen to walk the path directly to his executioner and seize the only opportunity he'd get to complete his father's work. Whether he would escape with his life or not, he would have done all he could, facing the fleshless skull of death that was Daimos Recett.

Magnus had already climbed through two floors of the tower, both crate-filled storage chambers plastered with a layer of dust for every year they had remained untouched. The tower roof was bound to be close. With the shard as his only weapon against the warlord, he prepared himself for a battle that was unlikely to end in his survival, even if in his victory. He shielded his mind from fear, doubt, and any lingering memory of his old life in Drake's bookshop, and filled it only with the thought of his father, and with a vengeance against the warlord who had killed him.

A pale light emerged from above. The chilling wind that fell against Magnus' face warned that the tower peak was nigh. He was immediately overcome by terror that rooted him in his place, but he persisted, lifting his foot onto the next step of the spiral to resume his ascent.

At last, a confined opening at the top of the stairs parted the darkness. The gray light that filtered through seemed almost heavenly, but Magnus knew that what awaited him on the other side was far from benevolent, and would be the greatest danger he'd yet faced. He silenced his steps on the metal and mustered the nerve to press on up the final stretch of the staircase. With a long and quivering breath, he arrived on the roof of the tower.

Magnus flicked his eyes around him. A parapet of eight enormous stone-slab merlons encircled a bare arena. The air roiled with a deathly breeze. The ash clouds were so low above him that he could distinguish the carcasses of the shades that formed them—an entwinement of bones, claws, and skulls, like a catacomb set in the sky. And far at the opposite end of the roof, standing with his back to the boy, was the cloaked figure of Daimos Recett.

The warlord cast his unblinking stare over the citadel below him. The wind slithered through the tears of his robes, soughing. With his hood pulled back onto jagged shoulders, his eyeholes were darkened by his sunken brow; his stony expression accented the lines that drew out every detail of his skull.

From this altitude, the city of MorningStar lay before Daimos as if it were his chess board, and its buildings his game pieces. He held great satisfaction in observing the extent of his ruin, each plane and building he had seized and scored with ash. But while this blackened empire was his, it would soon rise to the order of a new king, his master, Sennair Drakathel.

Indeed, Daimos watched over his land and possessions as never his own, but rather as the treasures of the lich whom he served. Since the day that Drakathel had bestowed his gift of immortality upon him, Daimos had made it his unswerving mission to prepare the ground of Serenia for his master's arrival. How he longed to see the banners of the Order ride on the winds of Galem's highest mountains, hailed by the myriad rejoicing cries of Lord Drakathel's army. But the wait was approaching its end—the day was near, so very near, on which the master of the New Order would walk once more in the flesh upon the earth of Arkane.

The almost silent scrape of footsteps disturbed the air. Something was amiss. Daimos blinked his eyes sidewise, then swiveled around and blindly discharged a sprawl of black lightning from his palm. At the clap of a thunderbolt, the lightning struck a dim figure standing by the tower stairs and instantly knocked it forward to the floor.

The warlord stayed his raised hand, prepared for the figure to return the attack. But upon taking a second glance at the person who had just been scorched by his magic, he dropped his arm back to his side. Then Daimos lifted the corners of his open mouth and spoke through a snide laugh. "Incredible," he jeered. "The boy Wingheart. I have to admit, you're the last person I'd have expected to see here."

Magnus fought to pry his head off the stone floor, his body coursing with pain. He saw Daimos grin at him scornfully under the shadow of the ashen tempest that raged above them.

"I'm amazed that you've made it this far, Wingheart," said Daimos, taking two steps forward. "But where's the rest of your troop of court jesters? Have they abandoned you?" As he curved back his hand, a slender trail of smoke materialized from the ground beside Magnus. "Or were they all too cowardly to climb up here themselves?"

The smoke trail multiplied and devoured Magnus like fire set to brushwood. A dark haze eclipsed his vision while an unpliable force ensnared his chest and legs. Within seconds, he found himself unable to move or speak at all.

Daimos extended a hand to the boy, who lay cocooned in the impenetrable smoke. "Now come to me, Wingheart," he whispered hoarsely, "and join your father in death!"

Mute, lame, and nearly blind, Magnus felt the smoke

begin to tow him forward. Terror resumed its icy grip on him. The ground rasped against his tattered cloths hard enough to bruise his flesh, while he was drawn dangerously closer to the warlord, as if into his own grave.

Daimos boasted a haughty smile, scoffing under his breath when Magnus reached his feet. To kill the son of his nemesis Brendan—how Daimos relished the thought. Though the boy was almost powerless, his death would be a retribution for every year wasted in search of his brother.

Magnus was brought to a halt under Daimos' spiring shadow. Still bound by shackles of smoke, his upper body was raised off the ground and suspended in midair. He felt the warlord's knobbed, skeletal claw coil around his throat, scalding him with a touch colder than that of a corpse. As the claw constricted, he was lifted up until his feet could only graze the floor.

Daimos' deep-set eyes smoldered with contempt, though a broad smile remained on his lips. He swept back his free hand, conjuring around it a black glow that came ablaze as Magnus' smoke shawl collapsed and faded. With his vision restored, Magnus arrested his breath in horror at the sight of the warlord's impending death strike.

"What...!" Daimos suddenly stammered and widened his eyes. He thrust out his grip impulsively, casting Magnus back onto the floor away from him, and recoiled as if he were trying to retreat from the boy whom he had nearly killed only a moment ago.

Magnus scurried to his feet and stayed fast in place, fearful and at a loss as to how he should react. Daimos himself was clearly in a state of shock, eyes riveted on Magnus' clenched hands. It wasn't until Magnus glanced down for himself that he realized what had alarmed the warlord: the radiant Luminous Rock shard, still in his grasp. Immediately, he extended the shard in a threatening pose, causing Daimos to shrink away even further.

Daimos stopped against the wall of a merlon, where he held his stance defensively. "So this is why you've come," he said somberly. He recognized the incandescent stone beyond a doubt—it was identical to the one his men had discovered in Brendan Wingheart's dagger holster so many years ago. It was a shard of the Luminous Rock he had thought to be destroyed. For the first time since Daimos had been gifted with his master's power, he was confronted with a weapon that could potentially rid him of his immortality. He hadn't a sense of how suddenly Magnus could explode the shard, so he was given no option but to stand and set his mind searching for a way to retaliate.

"You'd best not do anything rash, Wingheart," Daimos warned. His left hand crept behind his back discreetly. "Your brother was found and captured in the citadel. If anything happens to me, he will die at the hands of my guards. If you put down that stone, I'll spare you both your lives." A dark glower twisted his face. "Choose what matters to you most, boy—the mere loss of my immortality, or your own brother's life."

Magnus was taken aback and almost withdrew the shard. Had Drake really been caught by the warlord's men? It was a likely possibility, but, on second thought, much likelier a lie. *When I heard Daimos speak with Noctell, neither one was even sure of our identities,* he considered through a racing mind. *He has no way of knowing Drake's fate. He's lying.*

After only a second of hesitation, Magnus extended the shard again. His pendant's light flickered as he channeled a surge of energy into his grip, intensifying the glow of the shard. Its fierce radiance sustained, the crystal burned before the warlord like a loaded cannon.

Daimos recoiled further and tensed. His ruse had clearly failed. Into his palm still concealed behind his back, he conjured an amorphous black glow. He would need to kill Magnus as suddenly and swiftly as possible to avoid a counterattack.

"Be wise with your decisions," the warlord hissed, inconspicuously magnifying the strength of his spell. "You've already lost both your parents in this city. Are you prepared to lose your only brother as well?" He folded his fingertips over the palm in which he garnered his power, shaping a seething orb of dark energy behind his back.

Magnus clenched the shard to brace his trembling arm. *What if he's telling the truth?* the thought suddenly struck him. *While I was facing Noctell, Daimos could have seen Drake from the tower. I don't even know what's happened to Cecil and Anubis since I left the citadel...Medeva and the guards could have captured all of them at the armory.*

Magnus stalled in his confusion. Though the glimmering shard was at the brink of explosion, he could no longer gather the nerve to attack, knowing that he could be endangering Drake and the others. Daimos, however, took on a victorious air as the orb nestled in his palm flared, abounding with power. He prepared to release the deadly force of his magic and bring an end to the standoff— but not before his vision detected a sudden movement in the distance.

Daimos shifted his focus away from Magnus to glimpse the background. He observed a scraggy man emerge from the mouth of the tower stairs; it was Noctell Knever.

The boy, however, remained oblivious to the presence of the necromancer. Daimos dispelled the dark orb and drew out his hand from behind his back to place himself in a more cavalier stance. Allowing Noctell to attack from the rear would make for a far better strategy.

"I suppose I can't blame you for not caring about your brother's fate," the warlord said in a lighter tone, disrupting Magnus' concentration again. Daimos lifted another glance in the way of the tower stairs to see Noctell staring vacantly at the conflict taking stage. "After all," he continued, "he was the one who sent you here to your death to begin with, was he not?" A third time, Daimos' eyes flickered to the necromancer, who didn't appear to be taking the slightest action, his face unreadable.

"But no matter what happens to me," Daimos added, an anxious rasp touching his voice, "it is certain that you won't leave this place alive. Light alone cannot kill me, and as long as you're too weak to fight me to the death, you'll achieve nothing."

As his ease faded, Daimos could only wonder why

Noctell was refusing to act. Every passing second was another chance for Magnus to unleash the power of the shard, yet the necromancer idled even in the face of the opportunity to kill the boy unawares. The warlord's anxiety had grown to the point that it could no longer stay hidden behind his mask of indifference. He was at too much of a distance to kill Magnus in a single hit, but was at risk of being attacked first if he did anything less.

Time slowed to a crawl. Three people, each with the ability to alter the others' fate, stood immobilized by their racing minds and hesitation. But of them all, Noctell's indecisiveness was the most surprising.

Noctell observed the scene before him as if it were in a state of suspended animation. The wind shattered against his ears, laced with the shades' unearthly presence. He saw the resplendent beacon that was the Luminous Rock shard readied in Magnus' fist, and his horrified master Daimos driven up against the merlon wall. He saw the warlord glare at him as if in an explicit order to take action, but Noctell had other thoughts.

"I've been fooling myself." Noctell recalled the words that had filled his mind many days ago in the Markwell campgrounds. *"I obey Daimos out of fear over his rage and threats, and barely out of loyalty."*

If Noctell heeded the warlord's wish to kill the boy, he would be doing nothing different than what he had done for the past two decades, playing servant while strung by the leash of his master's fury. It was Daimos who had always been the necromancer's puppeteer, but now, the tables had been turned—the fate of the warlord was in Noctell's hands alone.

"Do you know how many times my master has strangled me when I returned empty-handed?" Noctell recalled his own words from only minutes ago during his fight with Magnus. *"How many times I've been choked by his withered claw wrapped around my throat?"*

Too many times, he replied to himself. He would often spend sleepless nights questioning his loyalties, his reasons for having any respect toward a man who commanded him like a slave and punished him as if he were a convict in the MorningStar citadel dungeons. And almost just as often, he would find himself without answers.

I don't have to endure this any longer, the necromancer thought. *I have, right before me, the only opportunity I will ever get to set myself free. If I don't seize it, I'll forever spend my life in this ashen hell with my jail keeper.*

Noctell turned his sights back to Magnus and the Luminous Rock shard. By the looks of it, it could only be moments before the crystal would shatter. All that Noctell had to do was stand steadfast with his decision and wait for the boy to act first.

"Light alone cannot kill me." It was now Daimos' own warnings that echoed to the necromancer. What if the warlord survived? Noctell's punishment for disloyalty would be too horrid to fathom. *But if the boy cannot kill him*, the thought then arose to Noctell, *perhaps I can lend a hand.*

Arrogant fool! A deafening roar suddenly rattled the

necromancer from inside his mind, seething with anger. *Your thoughts are poisoned with treason! How dare you abandon your master, let alone contemplate killing him!*

Noctell's blood turned cold at the sound of the wrathful voice, for it was not his own. *You are the one who is poisoning my thoughts,* he retorted. *I've made up my mind. Daimos has enslaved me long enough.*

No! The voice swelled in both fury and volume. *You cannot! Listen to me, you fool!*

Once this is over with, the necromancer continued, *I will be rid of you both. I will be free of the Order.*

You will never be free! the voice bellowed in return. *Heed me! If you betray us, you will forever be a sworn enemy of the Order! Every man who bears the mark of my army will carry a sword to stain with your blood! You will be hunted—forever hunted as the traitor who alone is responsible for the death of the great Daimos Recett!*

A crushing nervousness descended on Noctell. His thoughts were mute. As his determination withered to timidity, the voice grew dominant in his mind.

Traitor! shouted the voice, now painfully strident. *Die, traitor! Your throat shall be slit by the shades twice for every time that you disobeyed me!*

Noctell could not tolerate the voice's unrelenting rage any longer. He could already feel the deathly frigid claws of the shades come upon his neck like a guillotine blade.

Traitor! the voice chanted. *Traitor of the Order!*

Trembling immensely, Noctell brought a hand underneath the hem of his coat. With a blind touch, he grasped the cold hilt of a dagger from its holster on his belt, and took aim at the boy ahead of him.

Magnus' concentration was weakening. He would need to decide hastily about his actions or risk taking another blast from Daimos. Consumed by distress, however, Magnus almost failed to notice that Daimos was no longer looking at him—the warlord's eyes were focused heatedly on something or someone behind the boy.

A terrible chill fell over Magnus. He became aware that he and Daimos were no longer alone on the tower. On an impulse, he spun himself around on his heels.

Noctell. Magnus gasped as dread's hammer pounded on him. His death was made certain with the necromancer's arrival. He couldn't as much as blink before an explosive blaze of dark energy was discharged from Noctell's raised hand, fronted by a glint of steel. Instantly, Magnus was struck by an agonizing, piercing blow to his side.

Magnus lurched and doubled over. He saw a short-bladed dagger clatter to the floor, painted with flecks of fresh blood. Dizzied by the pain, he folded backward and collapsed onto the support of his left hand, allowing the Luminous Rock shard to roll out of his grip and fall to his feet.

Magnus' heart rate became frantic; an iciness overcame him. His right side had been slashed open by the necromancer's dagger, which would have impaled him had he not turned around at the last second. Blood darkened his shirt and pooled beneath him, saturating the stone floor in splashes of deep red.

Daimos' eyes leapt toward the shard the instant that it dropped. Relieved that it did not shatter on impact, he refocused on Noctell with a frown bent by sheer rage.

"Fool!" scolded the warlord, still recoiled against the merlon. "What took you so long?" He turned to the injured boy, who kneeled feebly in the stains of his own blood. "And no less of a fool are you," he spat. "We've not captured your brother yet, but we will. He'll be hanged by a noose of thorns and mounted in the entrance hall before noon!"

Noctell practically ignored his master's reproach out of the shame that weighed his mouth shut. He came forward and crouched to steal the Luminous Rock shard. The crystal had lost much of its radiance after being released, but still shone brightly enough to keep Daimos in angst.

Noctell raised the shard to his face. He twirled it in his fingertips, leaving no side unscrutinized, then held it high above Magnus as if it were the boy's unattainable treasure. A taunting smile eased across his face.

"You amaze me, Wingheart," the necromancer finally spoke. "By some miracle, you've managed to acquire a piece of the Rock itself. Yet you come here actually believing that, with it alone, you have a chance at victory."

Magnus' breaths were rapid and hoarse. Pain wrung his face. But even in his wounded state, hunched over sideways at a loss for strength, his pendant flickered desperately as if he were still trying to invoke the limited power of his magic.

"You've made it this far," continued the necromancer, "yet here you die." He paused to admire the shard mounted victoriously in his hand, then turned to Magnus with a look of scornfully insincere remorse. "How I pity you," he said. "A lifetime spent in hiding...so much bloodshed, so many battles fought, yet, in the end, the result is the same. No more of a victory would have been achieved if you had simply sat in your bookshop and let yourself be crushed under the rubble heap that it is now." He scoffed and grinned. "How terrible it must feel—such a young life all lived for naught."

Magnus' pendant took on a sudden brightness before again falling dim. The hand that he had laid on his wound was pulled back and fisted, rested against his chest where the diamond dangled by its cord.

"And just what are you trying to do now?" Noctell laughed at the boy's struggle to charge his pendant. "Still trying to fight? Go on, then! Go on! Blind me with your dying candlelight!"

"Enough of your taunting!" Daimos' voice suddenly cracked like thunder over the tower roof. "You're wasting time! Destroy that wretched stone and kill the boy!"

Noctell was snapped from his arrogance by his master's roar, swallowing hard. "Of course, milord."

Almost completely unnoticed by the necromancer and the warlord, the light of Magnus' pendant had became fierce and sustained, no longer wavering. From within his fist emerged a pale glow that leaked through his clenched fingertips and glazed his seeping blood.

"Get downstairs and prepare another flask of black acid," Daimos nervously commanded Noctell. "Dissolve the stone and don't leave a grain of it behind." He swept up his hand, casting his ragged sleeve off the bony stalk of his arm. "But first the boy." A black aura condensed around the warlord's palm, then burst into voracious flames of dark energy. "We'll kill him together!"

At his master's command, Noctell raised his other arm high until it was lifted nearly in reach of the shades' claws overhead. But in an abrupt turn of events, it was not Noctell nor Daimos, but rather Magnus, who was first to act.

The boy extended his fist and opened it wide in the face of the necromancer. From his palm gushed out a light beam of startling intensity—a spell driven and magnified by immovable determination—that targeted not Noctell, but the Luminous Rock shard in Noctell's grasp. The shard caught the light rays like wildfire, suddenly swelling to a brilliance unmatched by any of Magnus' former attempts to empower it.

"No!" Daimos uttered a frantic scream.

Terror-stricken, Noctell could scarcely breathe at the sight of the effulgent shard that grew brighter by the second. He found himself doing nothing more than grip the crystal with such force that his flesh was scalded with the power that exuded from it. When he finally snapped to his senses, he acted on impulse and threw up his hands, casting the shard out into the center of the tower roof.

The shard clattered to the floor. Daimos recoiled for his life. Like a bomb whose wick was quickly burning, the shard, his one bane, lay flickering, brimming with energy before him. With claws and shoulders dug into the merlon, he raised his hand a second time and revived the black fire that he had conjured moments ago.

Shutting his eyes, Magnus ducked his head to the floor to shield from the shard's rising intensity. Noctell, too, turned away and buried his face in the bend of his arm, willfully oblivious to the danger that threatened his master.

Daimos whipped forth his shadow-swathed hand, launching a dart of dark energy in a frantic attempt to knock the shard off the tower.

But barely before the shard was struck by the warlord's magic, it burst and shattered.

An explosion of unparalleled radiance swept the tower roof. Light rays sevenfold those of the sun broke the surrounding clouds. Even behind Magnus' shut eyes, the brightness was close to intolerable. The shades' agonized wails pulsed from every imaginable direction. But then, above all other sounds, rose a single strident cry—that of Daimos Recett.

Within seconds, the light subsided; soon after, so did the clamor brought on by the shades, leaving Daimos' bloodcurdling scream to ring out, lone and unbroken. It was only after the cry had faded that Magnus dared to open his eyes.

At the tower's edge, Daimos stood. His head was crooked down and gripped in his hands, while his back was arched to the point that the knobs of his spine protruded through his cloak. He writhed and trembled as if in horrendous pain, then threw up his head, emitting a shrill roar that seemed to echo within his own voice.

His face, bared in all its withered horror, still burned with the shard's radiance from inside his skull. Light of blinding strength beamed through the hollows of his eyes; lambent white rays poured from his open mouth and lit his skin to a hue as pale as bone.

With a second, even more vehement roar, the warlord flung his head aside. He brutally clawed his nails into his face, driven mad by the insufferable pain of the light. He folded forward, then wrenched himself upright as a shivering glow stole over his chest, the light of the shard smoldering inside of him. For a mere moment, he stood as if suspended by idle strings, but then tossed back his skeletal frame and let out a last, dying cry into the black heavens of MorningStar.

There was a flash, followed by a sound like a thunder clap. A violent shock wave of dark energy erupted from Daimos' body and blazed across the tower roof, powerful enough to drive a sprawling crack through the merlon behind the warlord. Magnus was able to prevent being thrown back by the blast by holding himself fast against the ground, but Noctell, even at such distance, was hurled to the floor as if he weighed no more than the air itself.

Once the shockwave had abated, Magnus feebly picked up his head. This time, Daimos was no longer standing, but slumped against the demolished merlon, lifeless. There appeared to be an aura surrounding him; one that flickered as if wavering in and out of existence. Magnus narrowed his already heavy eyes, but it was no less difficult to tell if the aura was simply a delusion—for as his blood continued to spill on the floor, Magnus could feel his mind growing fainter.

There was the sound of grinding stone. The demolished merlon was breaking off of its shattered mortar seam. Daimos had not regained consciousness, still lying over the rubble. Magnus could perceive the aura with more sharpness now: it hung like a cast around the warlord, curling wisps of ethereal light over his limbs and body. It possessed detail, features like those of another man—the features of Eras Recett, the mortal form that Daimos had once owned, as Magnus had witnessed in his nightmare. But at the mere blink of Magnus' eyes, the aura returned to its amorphous state, only to disperse and evanesce.

The demolished merlon leaned back, pulling the unconscious Daimos with it. It began to fall backward, dragged down by its own colossal weight. A final crackling of stone resounded before, at last, Daimos and the crumbled merlon hurtled off the edge of the tower roof.

Magnus' eyes remained locked on the gritty patch of mortar where the merlon and the warlord had once stood. He refused to blink, just as he refused to believe all that he had witnessed, until a bellowing collision sent tremors up from the castle far beneath him. The fallen merlon had crashed.

A silence rose out of the chaos as the tremors receded. With quivering legs and hands, Noctell pulled himself up to his feet. His expression was warped by horror, eyes pried open under the arch of his brow. Through parted lips that trembled at his slightest breath, he struggled to speak. "N-no..." He shook his head in near hysteria. "No!" Without further words, the necromancer clapped his hands to his ears and streaked to the tower stairs, leaving the boy behind.

Magnus winced and enfolded himself in his arms. As his heart throbbed faster, so did the pain of his wound. The fear of death was stronger than it had ever been in him, but death was something for which he had readied himself long before he had first set foot on the tower stairs. His fate mattered not. Daimos Recett was dead.

41

Fallen Empire

"DID YOU SEE THAT?" Drake cried out to Cecil behind him. "The light! The light from the top of the tower!"

"Of course I saw it!" Cecil replied zealously, peering out from under the hood of his disguising cloak. From amidst the northern citadel streets, he looked up to the castle tower that hung prodigiously against the sky. After having left Anubis and Ember in an abandoned residence neighboring the apothecary, Cecil and Drake had donned the guards' baleful garb and set out for the castle to rescue Magnus. Only minutes into their journey, they were halted by a glaring flash from the distant tower roof—and with it, hope's flame flickered back to life.

Cecil turned to the older brother, whose expression was mixed with both apprehension and excitement. "Do you think...?" asked Cecil cautiously.

"The shard?" Drake inferred. He drew back the hood of his cloak just enough for him to see clearly. "That means Magnus could still be alive!"

"The chances are decent," Cecil agreed. "With enough luck, that light was Magnus' doing."

Drake looked back to the tower, consumed by racing thought. "Then what about Daimos?"

Cecil's stare remained somber. "We can't know at this point. We don't know Magnus' fate alone."

Giving no reply, Drake suddenly threw up his hand in the direction of the tower. "Look!"

The grind of heavy stone boomed across the citadel. Cecil and Drake observed as a colossal mass hurtled down from the castle tower's peak and promptly struck the roof of the castle below it. An earth-rattling blast resounded as the ceiling caved in under the impact and boulder crushed and hammered upon boulder.

"What on...?" Cecil exclaimed, bewildered. Dust billowed from the castle in gargantuan clouds that mingled with the blanket of ashes above it. "What could that possibly have been?"

"Some kind of massive stone block," Drake surmised. "I can't imagine what could have moved something so huge."

Cecil shook his head as if in disagreement with his own thoughts. "It couldn't have been the shard—its explosion couldn't have given off nearly such force."

"Whatever it was, Magnus could be up there with it." Drake's tone grew distraught. "We have to hurry!"

Drake resumed his fervent race down the street toward

the castle. Cecil followed, cloak rippling behind him like a tail of sooty flames. They hadn't made it far, however, before the rasp of shifting stone echoed again from the tower.

Cecil skidded to a halt at the sound. He returned his gaze to the castle, causing Drake to stop in his tracks and do the same. The fallen stone block was not the end of the castle's destruction. Along with the ceiling, the tower's eastern foundation had been demolished. Stripped of its support, the tower wall was failing rapidly.

"No..." Cecil's voice was softened to a murmur by his disbelief, but then rose to a frantic cry. "The tower is collapsing!"

Magnus lay flat on the roof of the castle tower. A crimson carpet of blood stained the ground beneath him. Under heavy eyelids, he watched the roof's gray plane waft into a haze of stone and ash; he felt numb save for the cold sting of the floor against his skin and a gnawing pain that sent fire coursing through every nerve in his body.

He allowed his focus to dissipate and his strength to drain. His persistent agony was a sign that he had life left in him yet, even while he felt as if death had already taken its hold. Slowly, his grasp on reality was waning, leaving the miasma of delusion to descend on him.

The blackness that enveloped Magnus began to shift and shimmer with the shades' gruesome masks and claws. It was carried, as if by the wind, in a mesmerizing ripple across the sky beyond the tower's edge. Then from deep within its void emerged shadows of a new form—a thickly built fence of tall, knobbed stalks, each sprouting twenty spindly limbs.

Magnus could feel his body growing weightless as his eyelids became heavier. Reality had abandoned him. When he opened his eyes, he found himself no longer on the castle tower, but surrounded by a veil of ethereal, drifting dead trees. His environment was dark, and its details were scarce. He could not tell from one moment to the next where he lay, or what he was observing, as fragments of charred walls, doorways, and faces glimmered amidst the indistinct trees. He tried to move, but was incapable of more than curling his fingertips over the ground, which was carpeted in ash.

Before long, the forest scene had disintegrated, leaving his broken hallucinations to flash rampantly. He glimpsed the deathly visage of Daimos Recett only moments before it wavered and reformed to become that of the calimancer Noctell. When his vision was not crowded by faces, it became filled with the ever-shifting images of rooms and hallways whose fabric pulsed in sync to the throb of his wound.

Magnus longed for the chaotic phantasm to cease. He could not turn his eyes away, nor could he close them. The Galem mountains, the MorningStar citadel, the Saxum Diaboli—a thousand memories were manifested before him. But then, in his mind's disarray, a single figure took shape in the foreground. Unlike the fluttering curtain of the other images in his hallucination, the figure was stably formed. As it advanced toward him, it became distinguishable as a man with fair skin and a shag of brown hair. His expression was somber, marked by fierce concern.

Magnus struggled to see the man with more clarity, but failed to do so. The man stood in resolute silence at first, then suddenly parted his lips to speak.

"*Magnus!*" the man cried out urgently. His voice seemed to echo off the ethereal walls and amplify at each reverberation. Magnus was shaken to his senses as the call of his name sent his dark world spiraling and crumbling back into the haze from which it was formed. He crooked his head under the bend of his arm, shielding his eyes in fear of what he would see, should he look again. But when he emerged from his cowering pose, he was touched with a wary relief at finding that he was still lying on the deserted tower roof.

Magnus gasped as his vision returned to him. It took him only seconds to realize the identity of the figure in his hallucination, for it carried the air of the same man who had spurred him from his nightmare the week before—his father, Brendan.

Another collapse of stone roared from beneath the tower. Unthinkingly, Magnus tried to stand, only to be crumpled back to the floor by a stabbing pain from his injured side. He drew in a sharp breath and looked down at his hands and chest. His ragged sleeves were soiled red with the blood that he had spilled on the ground. He was reminded of the severity of his wound, and of how his death had already been certain from the moment that the necromancer's dagger had gashed him.

It will all be over soon, he thought, restraining tears through a wretched grimace. *The battle is won. I have nothing left to fear but my death.*

You're giving up, Magnus' own voice seemed to answer. *It was determination alone that brought you this far. How can you lie here, proclaiming your own death, when you still live, think, and breathe?*

Because I have no way of escaping this place as I am, he argued against his dogged state of mind.

Not even the strongest person could escape this place if they didn't try, his will persisted. *You've fought and fled beasts and warriors that no one else would dare to face. You've single-handedly defeated Daimos Recett, yet you're prepared to let yourself bleed to death on this miserable crow's nest? Get up! Get up and save yourself!*

Magnus fisted his icy hands, his determination rekindled. *If I die here,* he thought to himself adamantly, *then at least I die trying to survive.*

He summoned every ounce of his strength in an attempt to lift his body off the ground. His wound throbbed more than ever before, but he endured the pain long enough for him to rise onto a folded right knee. He clutched the gash through his blood-sodden shirt, and finally raised himself to a bent-over stance.

As he came to his feet, vertigo sent him reeling from side to side and his view of the tower's edge rocking fiercely.

Even when he managed to steady his balance, however, he felt as if the ground were not as stable as it seemed.

For the second time since the merlon's collapse, a sonorous rumble bellowed from the base of the tower. A subsequent tremor nearly made the boy lose his footing, and upon subsiding, left the tower roof tilted. Magnus planted his feet farther apart to stabilize himself. He realized then that his injury may not be his greatest hindrance to his escape from the castle.

With his forearm pressed against his wound, Magnus hobbled toward the gritty mortar layer that spanned the gap where the fallen merlon had once stood. Locking his soles on the ancient mortar, he leaned to gaze over the tower's unbarred edge.

It was as if he were looking down from a mountain cliff, one with a face so sheer and a height so great that a pebble could fall for several seconds before striking solid ground. The haze that enveloped the castle was like a raging sea whose water flowed thick with soot, and Magnus was but stranded on the crown of a pole that rose up from the heart of the storm.

As the wind drove an opening through the dust clouds, Magnus was allowed a clearer view of the brutal aftermath of his fight with the warlord—a hole, nearly the diameter of the tower itself, that had been torn through the castle roof by the fall of the merlon. More concerning yet, the wreckage extended far into the tower's base to the point that the tower wall itself had been damaged. With each passing minute, increasingly larger amounts of rubble folded into the mouth of the pit. The castle was caving in on itself, and taking its leviathan tower along with it.

Another of the tower's stone blocks broke from its demolished foundation and dissolved into the murk. As it struck the mounds of already-spilled debris below it, the stone shattered as if under the blow of a sledgehammer. Magnus knew that if the loss of support had already caused the tower to tilt, it wouldn't take much more for it to collapse entirely.

Magnus withdrew from the mortar patch at the tower's edge. Shifting his weight onto his right side, he turned and limped past his bloody trail and in the direction of the tower staircase. His every step spurred his wound like a sword through his ribs. He stopped before the tower stairs and plunged his gaze down the dizzying helix of steps; the sight only further drained his hopes.

"You've made it this far," Noctell's derisions echoed back to Magnus, *"yet here you die."*

No, Magnus thought in reply and shook his quivering head. He staggered forth and planted his feet on the first iron stair. *I made it this far—but I'll go as far as I need to escape this place alive.*

It wasn't long before Cecil and Drake neared the castle. At their frenetic pace, ash and gravel were kicked up in their tracks and deflected off the fluttering tails of their cloaks. They were no longer racing only against Daimos' men, but against the quickly disintegrating castle that speared the sky ahead.

Past the citadel buildings, the street pooled into the castle courtyard. Dozens of the warlord's guards were here, gathered in teeming mobs around the fortress. Many were shouting anxiously as if to no one in particular; others were darting from person from person to spread their own murmured notions and reports.

Drake and Cecil sprinted into the heat of the commotion. Swaddled in their robes, they were indistinguishable among the guards. To any other eyes, they were no more than another pair of the city's faceless sentries running to witness the unexplainable collapse of their master's fortress.

Coming to a stop, Drake lowered the hem of his hood until it fell just past eye level. His former guardian did the same to ensure their identities remained undiscovered amidst the scuttling soldiers. They exchanged glances, then looked around to find themselves drowned in a churning horde of dark-cloaked figures.

"What now?" Drake asked Cecil under the guards' riotous, incoherent growling.

"We need to find a way inside to rescue Magnus," replied Cecil. "Supposing he was in the tower at the time of the explosion, he wouldn't have had much of a chance to escape yet."

Drake delivered a tentative nod. "Then we'll head for the armory."

"As planned," Cecil confirmed, motioning leftward with a tilt of his head.

They turned and briskly proceeded through the crowd. They could see the castle's west wall and the armory entrance approach from behind a dense cluster of guards. The entrance itself was swarmed and voraciously drawing commotion.

"Are you sure?" the concerned shout of a single guard suddenly swelled above the noise. "Are you sure it was him?"

Cecil drifted toward the armory, signaling Drake to follow him. After forcing his way through the thick of the crowd, he found himself standing before a quarrelling company of men outside the warped-hinged, open entranceway to the armory. It appeared that the door had been torn off its frame by the guards upon being found locked from the opposite side.

"Of course I'm sure!" one of the gathering guards snapped at the man who had questioned him. "I saw it with my own eyes! He's dead, I tell you!"

Drake caught up with Cecil. As soon as the word of death touched his ear, he blinked his eyes toward Cecil, burned by unease and concern for his brother. Less than seconds later, he was rattled out of his fears when another guard bolted past him.

"Hear!" the arriving guard cried at the top of his lungs. "Hear! Our master Daimos is dead!" He dove into the crowd, where he was seized by the guard who had last spoken, the tallest and burliest of the men.

"*I hear!*" the tall guard roared, clutching the other man's shoulders. "I found his corpse lying in the ruin! Enough of you people's ceaseless shouting!"

The seized guard trembled and writhed, breaking free. "But how? How did our immortal master die?"

"I don't know!" bellowed the tall guard. "A great boulder came crashing through the roof, and I saw our master's body lying lifeless in the rubble. I don't know what to think! If our master was truly immortal, he wouldn't have suffered such fate!"

"I saw a blinding flash from the top of the tower," a neighboring guard remarked. "The boulder fell shortly after. The light was what seemed to be the start of it all!"

As the argument drew on heatedly, Cecil turned a rigid smile to Drake, who appeared too shocked to even pry his stare away from the guards.

"Daimos is dead..." Drake recited the news to himself as if to help him believe it. He snapped his eyes toward Cecil, nearly casting back his hood. "This is unbelievable!"

"It seems what we saw was indeed the shard's light," Cecil affirmed. "We can only assume it was Magnus who caused it."

Solemnity bled into Drake's excitement. "That means Magnus could still be in the tower."

"Wherever he is, he'll either need to escape or be rescued fast," Cecil added. "If the latter, then it's we who need to act."

Drake stole a second glance at the armory entrance. The guards had hardly let up their dispute. Another three men raced out from the armory, barely with enough room to press past the mangled doorframe and through the staunch crowd of guards that refused to budge at the expense of their quarrel.

"We can't access the armory at this rate," said Cecil. "Too many people are escaping at once. None of those guards is going to believe that anyone wants to head inside that castle as it is."

Another layer of the tower's bricks seemed to crumble and shatter. The thunderous echo that followed spurred every guard in earshot into an even greater frenzy.

"Then we tell them we need to rescue a trapped guard," Drake countered, his speech becoming slurred.

"That only risks other guards joining to help us," Cecil argued.

"Then we'll just head through the front door, where there's more open space!" Drake's frustration brought his voice to a volume that could have jeopardized their safety.

"That will make us look more suspicious than ever!" snapped Cecil in a harsh whisper, motioning Drake to be silent with a fleeting finger to his lips. "We can't—"

"We don't have time for this!" Drake barged into Cecil's sentence. "Magnus is trapped in there! And if he doesn't make it outside or to the tunnel in the next five minutes, that tower is going to crush the castle and everyone inside it! We can't just stand here discussing what risks we can or cannot take!"

Cecil tried to retort, but found that he had nothing to say. Minutes were passing swiftly. Daimos' castle teetered on the verge of collapse.

"Last time we fled from this place, we left without either

of my parents," Drake continued in a softer yet graver tone. "This time, I'm not leaving without my brother."

Cecil set a boring stare through the shadow of Drake's hood. The look that the older brother returned him was one of a staunch and unmatched determination—the same kind that Cecil had received from Brendan on the night that Daimos usurped the city. But though it was that very determination that had ultimately cost Brendan his life, here and now, they would surely lose another life if they didn't choose to throw caution to the wind.

"You're right," Cecil said resolutely, turning away without a second thought. "Come on."

With fierce speed, jostling aside every guard in their path, Drake and Cecil took for the castle's main entrance.

The downward spiral of the tower stairs was quickly taking its toll on Magnus. As his feet lurched from one step to the next, agony's barbed blade plunged deeper into his wound. He had grown sick from the pain. His stomach churned; his vision throbbed with stains of black. Though he was cold to the bone, his bloodied skin was doused in sweat. With his head crooked down and his quivering hands wrung around the stairs' low banister for support, layer after layer of the metal footholds passed across his eyes under his pendant's dim light.

At long last, Magnus was nearing the end of the stairs. A faltering, golden glow wafted through an opening in the wall far beneath him—the doorway that led back onto the second floor. Rapt by the sight of the approaching exit, he almost failed to notice the arctic chill that had settled on his shoulders.

Magnus turned up his head. He found that he was standing at the very height of the stairs where the fallen merlon had struck, where the castle roof met the wall of the tower. Through a vast archway of crumbled stone, he could gaze out across the partly shattered castle roof that was burdened with a smog of dust set against an ocean of blackness. By this point, the damage, which had begun as a crushing blow to the castle roof, had stolen away close to half of the tower's foundation.

Another enormous slab of the tower wall broke from its century-old film of crude mortar. Magnus' eyes clung to the slab as it plunged down along the length of the staircase and into the tower's sheer abyss. The tower quivered at the impact far below.

Magnus hadn't much more time until gravity would wrench the tower off what remained of its foundation. He dropped his head back toward the beacon of the second-floor doorway and resumed his staggered descent down the staircase. As the furor of the collapsing tower rang again in his ears, an avalanche of rock dust and crumbled stone cascaded down the walls that enclosed him. Magnus' heart flinched at every sound; he half-mindedly anticipated the jagged face of a boulder to strike his back any second.

When he finally approached his destination, he stalled on the steps. The fortress' second level was marked by a platform that was heavily damaged. It served as a bridge, albeit a ruined one, to the torchlit chamber where Magnus had first combatted Noctell. An opening in the center of the platform allowed for the staircase to continue down to the first and basement levels.

The only access to the dungeon tunnel is through the throne room, Magnus contemplated quickly. *Which means I'll have to go lower.*

His deliberation was cut short when another rush of dust drenched him from above. He ducked impulsively to see the residue filter through the platform's gaping cracks beneath him. *No*, he thought again. *I can't stay another minute in this tower. And continuing down these stairs could get me buried in rubble if the platform collapses.*

He hobbled over the remaining steps, taking a large stride onto the broken platform. He lifted his head just enough for the exit archway to half fill his vision; the torch-light that poured through it stung his eyes. Blinking away his irritation to the bright-orange rays, he advanced.

The second level was virtually unrecognizable from the time that Magnus had last visited it. Mounds of crushed brick were piled about him, most notably one mammoth heap that had flattened the chamber's northwestern pillar. Magnus buckled over and cast his bloodied grip onto the archway, when another jabbing pain set his nerves afire. Drawing a breath through his teeth, he let his hand slip off the doorframe and stray back over his wound. With a debilitating limp, he struggled on through the ruined chamber.

He turned his head slightly to eye the largest rubble heap as he passed it—this was undoubtedly the site of the fallen merlon. Somewhere beneath the innumerable sheets of limestone and marble lay the remains of Serenia's mighty usurper. Though Magnus was unable to straighten himself to look high enough, the frigid air that fell upon the chamber made it evident that there was little left of the ceiling.

My backpack! Magnus suddenly recalled and whisked his eyes toward the gravelly bundle of his bag that he had earlier abandoned by the tower entrance. Leaving the bag behind would mean the loss of all of Brendan's research, but Magnus knew that burdening himself would only hinder his chances of escape. He would be forced to relinquish the bag and all its contents to the inevitable collapse of the tower.

Again, a harrowing roar bellowed from high above him. But when its distant echo returned from across the cavernous halls at either side of the chamber, it caught the muted pounding of footsteps. *Noctell.* The calimancer came to Magnus' mind instinctively. Magnus reeled behind the nearest rubble heap to escape from view, his head folded to his blood-soaked waist. When the frenzied pacing approached, it was not Noctell, but a pair of citadel guards, who dove into the chamber from the eastern hallway. Without even glancing in Magnus' direction, they rounded a corner and sped down the main hall ahead.

Magnus angled his stance to be able to look out from behind his rocky shield. He saw the guards' rippling shadows drift into a blur under the rise and fall of the torchlight. Upon reaching the corridor's end, the guards swerved through a doorway at their left and vanished faster than Magnus' eyes could follow them.

The storage room. Magnus immediately presumed the men to be headed there, at the same moment realizing his only route left to take. *The staircase in the storage room will lead me back to the armory. If I can't escape through there, then at least I'll be back at ground level to find another way out.*

Lamely, he shuffled back into the center of the chamber, drawing a crooked path through the dust in his tracks. He raised his eyes to the mouth of the main hall and dragged himself onward, the tower's thunder raging overhead.

As Magnus trudged deeper into the corridor, he felt the heat of the torches scald his hunched back. He tried to move aside, away from the flames, but his feeble legs sent him reeling against the opposite wall. The abrupt maneuver incited another bout of pain that flared up through his spine. He gritted his teeth and faltered back into the center of the hall, flinching at the sound of an explosive collision somewhere in the chamber behind him.

Magnus finally spotted the last doorway of the corridor as it emerged at his side. Pulling left, he veered through the open door and entered the storage chamber. The lambent rays of the torches instantly fell dim, overtaken by shadow. The only light here was that which struggled up through the plummeting shaft of the armory staircase.

Magnus paced to the shaft and gazed down, blurring the stairs out of focus to peer beyond them. He could clearly distinguish the armory from here—he saw at least two more guards as they fled toward the armory exit beneath him. After their footsteps had diminished, more clamor arose. Voices quarreling, a babel of shouting, a vehement commotion could be heard from outside.

There are too many guards, Magnus assessed quickly. The uproar was suddenly stifled by the collapse of more rubble from the tower. *I'll be trampled and caught in seconds if I go down there.*

Once again, Magnus found himself flanked by peril. Proceeding into the armory was out of the question, but as long as the stones of the tower did not cease their barrage upon the castle, death was a perpetual risk. In whatever way possible, Magnus had to escape immediately.

He twisted his neck with difficulty to glance behind himself, back to the doorway from where the collisions bellowed. Prodded by the sudden sting of his wound, he stooped lower in agony and whipped his head straight. But when he rose again, his pain subsiding, he found himself turned to face the narrow castle window on the chamber's eastern wall.

Magnus took a single step and heaved his bent frame up to the window. He flattened his palm against the glass, just as he had done when he had first entered the storage room from the armory. This was his last remaining escape from the fortress. *Break the glass and climb out*, he thought in desperation. *It's my best chance to get out of here before I end up crushed in the rubble, like Daimos.*

The window remained as hopelessly dirtied and inscrutable as he had left it. If his directions didn't fail him, Magnus was looking out over the courtyard that encircled the castle. There were certain to be throngs of the citadel's guards gathered outside, as could vaguely be heard from the stairs to the armory. But even so, of whatever dangers that awaited Magnus in the open, none would be as dire as the ones he now faced inside the castle.

Magnus shifted his throbbing eyes from side to side, unable to turn his head without aggravating the pain of his injury. The room was stocked copiously with crates, upon which was strewn an array of scabbards, picks, and handbows. Many of the weapons here would be more than strong enough to shatter the pane, but much too heavy for Magnus to wield in his current state. He would need something other than brawn to break his way through.

The answer came to him in the midst of his panic. He wouldn't need much more than his own magic. Magnus fastened his hand against the glass once more, fingers splayed out over dark patches of grime. He let his eyes fall closed, shielding his mind from any thought of the bedlam around him. He embraced the chill of the pane untouched for years by sun or heat, and drew in its burning cold through his bloodless flesh. As he inhaled, locking his shortened breath at the back of his lungs, he sensed the same chill flare up through his chest, and saw it steal his diamond pendant into a pall of blue and white that smoldered behind his shut eyelids. Then he released his breath, expelling the glacial magic held within his pendant out through his palm.

At once, veins of frost began to leach from beneath Magnus' hand and devour the glass surface. Inch by inch, the windowpane became glazed in ice until it was entirely coated from its sill to its arched peak. Magnus lifted his hand away. It didn't take much longer for the glass to give in under the clamp of the ice. With a sudden snap, an almost perfectly diagonal crack burst across the face of the frozen window. Seconds later, the pane shattered into a hundred icy splinters, as if struck by the head of a mace.

Magnus recoiled to dodge the shrapnel discharged from the explosion. Now cleared of its soiled pane, the window allowed a perfect lookout to the castle grounds and the decrepit structures that enclosed them.

Magnus crept toward the window, minding his footsteps on the slick of shattered glass beneath it. With the brush of a sleeve-swathed hand, he swept the sill free of leftover slivers before leaning against the ledge. The frigid outside air gnashed at Magnus' eyes and face. He winced a second, then looked downward. As he had expected, the grounds were speckled with the guards' scuttling figures, miniscule as game pieces. But they were not nearing the castle—they were retreating, eyes lifted to gawk at the crashing monolith as if it were moments away from falling on them.

Magnus backed away as he fought to maintain his composure. His veins swelled and contracted in rhythm with the erratic throb of his heart, sorely tightening their clamp against his skull. He pulled his blood-smeared hand away from his wound to grip the sill and hauled himself up in a slow and painful rise. A hundred double-ended spines pierced him from within, but he shed his agony through an ironhard grimace.

With his heels raised off the ground and his weight balanced over the window ledge, his eyes fell perpendicular to the front wall of the castle. The sheer plunge from here to the ground was at least forty feet, but was softened by the thicket of scraggly bushes that flanked the main doorway below. Filling his lungs, Magnus heaved his right leg over the window frame and pulled his left leg onto the sill in a kneel. He could feel his palms knifed by the frame's jutting razor of broken glass, but the sting was insignificant compared to that of his wound now burning unremittingly.

He could see from first glance that there were few footholds across the wall—not enough to even be considered safe for a climb all the way to ground level. But as he drove his pain-stricken mind to weigh his options, the tower's rumbling momentarily receded to allow in the sudden sound of footsteps from the outside hall.

Magnus froze in his place on the sill. Without thinking, he spun his head around just as the steps came to an abrupt halt. In the mouth of the storeroom's open doorway loomed the silhouette of a citadel guard, black and featureless against the torchlight. The guard's vacant stillness made him seem stunned to have discovered the boy; for Magnus, the guard was the last thing that he saw.

Magnus' turning caused his hand to slip off the edge of the window frame. His heart lurched as he lost his balance and gravity took its hold. The sooty sky turned upward; wind rushed into his ears. He screamed, and plummeted backward off the wall of the castle.

"Retreat!" a guard's mortally anxious cry soared over the noise. "It's collapsing! Retreat, all of you!"

Drake was shoved back by each guard that passed him. He was battling a crowd blinded by panic. While every other man fled in terror, Drake pressed onward with fervor seething behind the mask of his hood. His former guardian at his side, at last, he saw the castle's double doors emerge from behind the rapidly dispersing soldiers.

Like Drake, Cecil had his sights fixed on an unswerving path ahead. He was averse to turn anywhere around him, chiefly fearful of laying eyes on the crumbling tower. He knew by his ears alone that they were running in a direction where being mauled by debris was all too likely. But they could not turn back on what might be their only hope of finding Magnus alive.

By the time they reached the main entrance, the grounds were close to bare, long abandoned by the guards. The tower's tempestuous rumbling was like the roar of a monstrous dying beast. Drake, though already short of breath, gathered speed and streaked ahead of Cecil. He staggered up the stairs at the foot of the ivy-enfolded double doors and seized the right of the door handles. He hauled the enormous wooden panel ajar—only to be arrested by a scream from almost straight above him.

Drake and Cecil turned their heads immediately. They witnessed a figure plunge out of a second-floor window, limp and spiraling backward. It hurtled into the net of dead shrubs alongside the main entrance, spraying shards of black twigs on the ground around it. Sprawled over the thicket and under the shrubs' brittle talons, it now lay lifeless.

Drake became gripped by distress. "What..." He could not muster any further words as his thoughts overtook his speech.

"Is it a guard?" Cecil called as he drew behind the older brother.

"No..." answered Drake, eyes widening. "He's not wearing any robes!" His own words triggering a realization, he leapt off the side of the stairs and made for the fallen figure in the thicket. When he approached, he froze in devastation.

The figure was a young man. His flesh was scrawled with cuts, his palms slashed and impaled by glass splinters. His clothes, clawed by the brambles, were deluged in blood from an open wound across his side. His sere lips parted, he stared up at Drake through the blur of his lashes before shutting his eyes entirely.

"Magnus!" Drake cried with a quivering frown, tears welling in his eyelids. He drew his arms underneath his brother and stole the boy out from the clutch of the branches. Magnus' limbs simply wilted as his head fell aside.

Cecil rushed to Drake's aid. His steps were carried by a cold dread that had flooded him from the moment he'd heard Drake utter the boy's name. As he came between the two brothers, he took Magnus' bloodied neck into the cup of his hand and felt for the throb of his veins.

"He's alive." Cecil's verdict instilled a glimmer of hope

into Drake. "We can still save him if we get him back to Markwell in time."

Drake blinked the tears from his eyes and threaded a still-trembling arm under Magnus' right shoulder. "Then we won't make it," he sobbed, speech muted by the overhead crushing of stone. "The rift is too far away."

"I'll tie his wound once we reach the building where we left Anubis," Cecil said as he took hold of Magnus' opposite side. "He'll make it, but none of us will if we don't get away from that tower."

Drake returned a shivering nod and lifted Magnus upright with Cecil's help. They trudged on toward the citadel buildings, Magnus hoisted securely on the shoulders of his brother and former guardian. Their every step was a toil, heavy with exhaustion and the weight of the injured boy. But no matter their wear, their bloodshed, their strife and misfortune, they had done it—they had destroyed the warlord who had struck his ashen ruin across Arkane; they had brought an end to his inconquerable empire. They had avenged Brendan's army, and the city of MorningStar.

Less than a minute had passed after the trio had cleared the courtyard. Not a single guard had lingered to behold the fall of his master's fortress. Then to the witness of only the barren streets below and the shades' maelstrom that eclipsed its peak, the tower succumbed, shattering at its base, and came down upon the castle in a mighty cascade of rubble.

42

Dawn Break

A DARK HAZE SHADOWED Magnus' vision. It shifted, glistened with static, but refused to part. He felt strange—as if afloat in the midst of a dream. Then, steadily, from the void emerged a sparkling of light. It allured him. As it expanded its glow to consume the darkness around it, a sense of tranquility overcame him. But its blur suddenly contracted and sharpened to develop a spherical shape, and along with it, the haze lifted.

The ceiling Magnus stared at was one of solid wood beams. The orb was a lantern suspended above him, clasping a piece of refulgent lucidus. He blinked repeatedly to ensure the permanence of his environment, then rolled his throbbing head sideways to extend his view. A familiar face consoled him.

Back against the wall and legs drawn over the floor, Cecil sat opposite the boy. His head was tipped to his folded arms in a doze, but as Magnus awoke, he too was roused. He turned up his face, a smile spreading under tired eyes.

"Good morning, Magnus," Cecil said in a gentle greeting.

Magnus wetted his parched lips and strained to respond. "Cecil..." He hesitated, skimming the walls of the almost bare yet crowded enclosure. A sleeping bag was slovenly folded beside him; a desk and chair were tucked in a corner of the room. Next to his former guardian was a door that was opened to a crack. "Where am I?" was all he could ask.

"Safe in the shelter," Cecil replied. He came to kneel at Magnus' side and rested a weightless hand on the boy's shoulder, his smile still unbending. "You're back in Markwell," he said. "The battle is behind us."

"Battle..." Magnus muttered in an attempt to restore his absent memories. He tried to rise, but did so too quickly, evoking a familiar, grievous jab from his waist. A gasp was forced from his lungs, which clenched at the pain. He buckled forward before easing into an upright position, discovering himself nestled under the covers of his old sleeping bag. "I fell and..." He spoke slowly as he pieced together his fragmented thoughts. Then a sudden urgency spread over his face. "Daimos is dead." His most prominent memory sparked to mind. At that moment, every thought, image, and feeling of the citadel and the affray within its walls rushed back to him. He turned to Cecil, as if in shock. "I killed him."

"Then it's you," replied Cecil, "to whom Arkane owes its thanks."

"But what about—" Magnus was jarred by his own words before he had even spoken them. "Drake and Anubis!" he exclaimed, realizing the absence of his brother and the herbalist. "Are they alright?"

"Very much so," the voice of another man resounded. Magnus turned to the now-open doorway, where stood Anubis himself. The herbalist's usual fearful mask was lifted, baring a joy that Magnus had never seen before. His unkempt curtain of dark hair spilled onto his densely bandaged left shoulder, which was raised on the crutch of Cecil's ruby staff. With a limp in his gait, he cleared from the doorway to allow a second person to enter.

Drake Wingheart rushed into the room. Eyes afire with irrepressible bliss, he fell to his knees at the boy's side and drew him close in a longing embrace. "I was so worried about you," he sighed against Magnus' shoulder.

Magnus' stunned expression became drowned in joyous relief as he turned between Drake and Anubis. Drake leaned away to face his brother, beaming profusely, eyes glazed by tears. He tried to speak further, but found that he could not, as he had no words for his emotions.

"After I was trapped inside the castle," said Magnus with fleeting solemnity, "I knew I'd die. I knew I'd never escape to see any of you again." Then his smile returned tenfold. "But I was wrong."

Magnus enveloped his brother in his arms once more.

He cherished every breath of the shelter's stale air, knowing that it was the actions of his companions alone that had saved his life. As he pulled away, his stare fell to his palms, which were swathed in cloth. He found himself to be dressed in fresh clothing with what felt like a bandage roped around his waist. "How long was I asleep for?" he asked.

Cecil tilted his head in thought. "A little more than a day, I believe. How are you feeling?"

"Surprisingly well," answered Magnus, flexing his shoulders to break the stiffness of his bones.

"That should be largely thanks to Anubis." Cecil's eyes drifted sidelong to the herbalist. "Drake and I used his healing salve on the two of you once we'd retrieved the potions bag from the forest. After Anubis recovered enough from his wounds, he treated you extensively."

Cecil's reply reverted Magnus' attention to Anubis, who met the look with a thin smile weighed on heavily by remorse. Magnus motioned to his brother. "Help me up," he said, threading an arm behind Drake's back for support. As Drake rose, Magnus struggled to his feet alongside him. He lifted an unsteady hand to clutch Anubis' free shoulder, offering a wholehearted smile. "I'm glad to see you're well," he said under heavy breath.

"Likewise, Magnus," Anubis answered quietly, beaming. "You have endured more in your battle than I ever would, that's for certain."

"I doubt I would have done much better against Medeva

than you did," Magnus replied in a somber jest. "It's a miracle that you survived."

Anubis' smile flickered brighter. "I likely wouldn't have, if it wasn't for the help of another small companion."

A distinct patter of claws on wood turned Magnus to the open doorway. With a widening grin, Magnus watched the crimson blur of a lithe reptile as it scampered up the side of the doorframe and leapt down with remarkable agility. Catching Anubis' outstretched arm in mid-air, it whipped around to face the boy.

"It seemed that Ember had caught sight of Medeva the moment before she attacked us," said Anubis, folding his arm, the salamander's roost, to his chest. "He cried out in alert. Had I not moved as a result, that harpie would have cleaved me apart."

"That's amazing," Magnus said in a murmur, returning Ember's pointed gaze. "Thank you...Ember."

The salamander's emerald-green irises glimmered. One could almost believe that a smile had curled about his lips. More than ever before, his air shone with an intelligence no less than that of a human being. He leapt off the herbalist's forearm and bared his claws against the floor as he landed, then blinked his eyes onto a book that lay near where Cecil had been sitting. After scurrying to the tome, the salamander flattened his front paws over its cover as if to lift himself high enough to inspect it.

Cecil noted Ember's scrutiny and reached for the book— one that everyone in the room had seen many times before.

"Just something I've been reading over while Magnus was resting," said Cecil with a contorted smile. He displayed the book's cover and its flawlessly embedded lettering: *Galem: The Rise and Fall of Arkane's Most Powerful Nation.*

Galem—the very sight of the name had grown harrowing to Magnus after his journey. Not only was it Galem's border where he had endured the unrelenting fire of the Rammeren guards, but it was also the province of the mountain valley that harbored the darkest and deathliest beasts conceivable.

"Or what I think we all know as a chronicle of Sennair Drakathel's conquests," Cecil amended. "I believe I've come across some more details that you all may find interesting."

"So have I..." Magnus mused to himself, his stare suspended above the floor. He only half-realized he had spoken aloud until Cecil replied.

"Ah." Cecil gave an acknowledging nod. A glint of apprehension passed over his face. "You yourself were in Galem."

"I was," said Magnus simply, and turned back to his former guardian.

Cecil grimaced, hearing the solemn warning that Magnus conveyed by his mere expression. "Well, in that case, we certainly have a lot to discuss," he said as he stood up and fitted the tome inside the bend of his arm. "First things first—you must be starving and thirsty. Drake, stay here with your brother, and I'll get us all some breakfast." As he made his exit, he turned back to reveal a grin that curtained the somber mood. "Then we'll talk. No doubt,

Magnus, that we'll all want to hear the tale of Daimos Recett's slayer."

It was close to two hours after Magnus had awoken. As the boy stepped into the clearing outside the shelter, the woodland breeze fell cold against his face. He savored the air that for days he had not tasted without a lining of ashes to bitter it. While the sky above was cast in pallid blue, dotted by the remnant of a lingering moon, the horizon was set alight with fiery hues of red and gold that shimmered through the trees' ever-swaying boughs.

Drake walked closely at his brother's side, lending his frame as a crutch over which Magnus draped his arm. Cecil and Anubis proceeded in front, the salamander Ember scuttling behind them. As the brothers followed, Cecil lowered himself to a seat on the earth that was wrought with amber by its dried carpet of leaves. He reclined against the trunk of an ample oak and lifted his gaze in admiration.

"Dawn," proclaimed Cecil, folding his arms over the book he held. "No matter how many times you see it, that radiant glow rising up over the edge of the world like heaven itself, the sight is never anything less than magnificent."

With the ruby staff to support his weight, Anubis descended against a prostrate tree not far from Cecil, and the salamander scurried into the bed of his lap. "Certainly after spending almost a week on Arkane," Magnus remarked. He came to a seat next to Drake against the same fallen trunk.

"Indeed!" Cecil pulled a smile and laid his book beside him. He drilled a keen stare through the boy. "And on that note, I'm sure we're all eager to hear your side of our great victory."

"First," replied Magnus, "I want to hear yours. How did you find me? How did you manage to escape Medeva? I thought you'd have all been killed if you crossed her path."

"By some bizarre miracle, she was courteous enough to spare us," Cecil said ironically. "Although I'm not sure *courteous* is the right word. We talked in peace...she seemed very indignant, but not necessarily toward us. Then she simply took off with some remark about having more important things to do."

"Didn't she call Daimos a madman?" Drake asked, sounding skeptical of his own account.

"That's what I thought I heard," Cecil dubiously confirmed. "She acted as if she suddenly couldn't care less about defending the city or her master."

"If she ever cared," Magnus interjected. "Out of every-one serving Daimos, she's definitely the least reverent. And she doesn't hide it—she told me she isn't a follower."

"Then what was she doing in MorningStar?"

"I think I know why Daimos wanted her on his side," replied Magnus, "but that's beside the point now. How did Anubis survive?"

"Well, we took shelter in the ruined citadel apothecary," Cecil continued, "where we were able to dress Anubis' wound. Afterwards, Drake and I raced back towards the castle in search of you, when we saw a great flash erupt from the castle tower. We immediately suspected the shard. We could only hope that you were the one who had shattered it."

"Then we saw something fall," Drake recalled. "Some kind of boulder. It hurtled off the tower and smashed into the roof. The damage started a cave-in at the base of the tower that ultimately caused the whole castle to collapse."

"Not that we ever saw it collapse," Cecil added. "We escaped before it did, after we found Magnus in the shrubs outside the entrance. At any rate, I can't imagine that much would be left of that place after being assailed by rubble like it was."

Magnus nodded slowly. "The light you saw was from the shard," he said. "The boulder was one of the stone blocks from the battlements on the tower roof. It broke off by a shockwave that was released from Daimos' body when the light struck him."

Cecil arched his brow, intrigued. "So Recett did fall victim to the shard. How on earth did you do it? Not to mention that you're unfathomably lucky to have made it out of that place alive."

"Too often I almost didn't," said Magnus. "A staircase in the armory took me to the second floor. That's where I overheard a conversation between Daimos and Noctell—apparently they were still searching for the intruders who'd started the fire in the citadel. When Daimos ordered Noctell to put the dungeon tunnel under guard...all my exits had been blocked. With nowhere left to run, I realized that my best chances were in facing Daimos, whether I lived or not. I heard them both leave; Daimos said he was heading up the tower to watch the citadel from above. But when I tried to follow him, Noctell came out of hiding and attacked me."

A stunned somberness swept the glade. It was as if the others were rapt by the suspense of not knowing whether Magnus had survived the encounter. "Luckily," Magnus ended the brief silence, "he seemed more focused on bragging rather than on killing me. He hurled me across the room twice and nearly strangled me to death, but I managed to catch him off guard and knock him to the ground. While he was out cold, I ran up the tower stairs."

He continued after a slow breath: "Daimos assaulted me the moment I arrived on the roof. But when he saw the shard, he recoiled like he was scared to fight back. He started calling out threats—that Drake had been captured and would be killed unless I put down the shard. I was sure he was lying, but I still couldn't concentrate enough to charge an attack.

"Then Noctell returned. He'd regained consciousness, obviously, and climbed the tower in search of me. He threw a dagger and slashed my side; if I hadn't turned around at the last second, he probably would've killed me right then. I dropped the shard, and Noctell stole it. Again, I only survived because of his boasting. As he was holding up the shard to taunt me, I had just enough of a chance to gather my wits and fire off a blast of light into it. Noctell was startled and dropped the shard, which shattered in a few seconds. I shut my eyes from the light. When I heard Daimos scream, I knew I'd finally won."

The gapes of Magnus' companions were bent by utter disbelief. "I'm not sure whether you're the luckiest," said Cecil, "or the unluckiest person alive. In spite of everything turning awry in the worst way possible, you still managed to defeat Recett."

A passing smirk lifted the corner of Magnus' lips. "I'll go with luckiest, considering that I *am* alive."

"And what of Recett?" asked Anubis. "He is dead, is he not? Was it the shard alone that killed him?"

"It was hard to tell," said Magnus. "After Daimos was struck by the light, there was an explosion, like a shock wave burst out of him. Noctell and I were too far to be hurt by it, but the stone block behind him was smashed off its foundation. Daimos fell unconscious and plummeted off the tower, along with the stone. He was crushed in the rubble before the tower ever collapsed. Noctell ran away, horrified. I managed to escape back to the second floor once I'd gathered my strength."

"I suppose the shockwave could be indicative of exorcism," Cecil replied. "But strong enough to shatter stone? Whatever was inside him must have been vastly more powerful than we'd imagined."

"That's not all," Magnus said without lifting his eyes from the mesmerizing garnet hues of the fallen leaves. "Just before the stone collapsed, I saw...some kind of aura surrounding Daimos, almost like a ghost. It looked exactly like the man I'd seen in my dream—Eras."

"You mean Daimos before he was possessed?" Cecil inquired, and received a nod from the boy. He appeared to lose himself in his musings before muttering, "No, that can't be right...the exorcism would have removed his possessing ghost, not his own."

"Unless the two souls were bound together?" Anubis suggested.

"Perhaps," Cecil replied, deliberating. "Yes. If the possessor's hold is powerful enough, it would naturally bear a great risk of pulling the body's original soul out with it as it is exorcised. What you saw, Magnus, could have well been Daimos'—or should I say Eras'—own ghost."

"Then that means the shard alone could have killed him," Magnus inferred.

"Not in the way of tearing out one's own soul," Cecil explained. "Such a separation of soul and body would be temporary. The bond between the two would still remain strong. It would be only a question of time before the soul returns to its original vessel."

"But what if that vessel is destroyed?" asked Magnus. "Would the soul just...move on?"

Cecil furrowed his brow as if unwilling to say what was on his mind. "Not often," he answered. "These cases are what we know as interrupted deaths. The thought is unsavory that Daimos' body may have been crushed before the repossession of its original soul. Without a body to return to, it isn't uncommon for an abandoned soul—provided it is willing—to develop a stronger physical existence in order to continue surviving in the physical realm."

Dark curiosity trickled over Magnus' eyes. "What does that mean?"

"Revenants, liches, shades," said Cecil, "these are all examples of spirits that have partially regenerated the physical form that they lack. Most become visible to the naked eye, and their capability to manipulate and interact with material objects becomes much greater."

"So you're saying that Daimos...could still be alive? As a ghost?"

"Anything, of course, *could* be," Cecil said flatly. "Don't take my word—I know too little about the subject to presume anything about Daimos' fate. We must focus on the threats that are near and imminent, if any, and not on those conjured by speculation."

"Well, what about the shades, then?" said Drake. "Supposing that their summoner is truly dead, will they just disperse back into their home dimension?"

An odd, dry smile cracked Cecil's solemnity. He retrieved the history book from beside him and waved it suggestively. "If my suspicions are correct, the man who summoned the shades has been dead for a thousand years."

Anubis winced at Cecil's peculiar suggestion. "That's impossible. Daimos controls the shades."

"No," Magnus cut in to deliver a jarring statement, "Medeva does."

The others' attention was whisked in the direction of the boy who had barely lifted his eyes above the ground. "What—" Cecil stammered. "How could that be?"

"She told me," Magnus answered. "She said that Daimos

has about as much control over the shades as I do. Even someone like Noctell can't do any more than command them, and only Medeva can awaken them."

"But that means that Medeva must be their summoner," said Cecil. "And that doesn't even make any sense!"

"She said that she was not the one who summoned the shades," Magnus continued. "I asked her who was, but she never answered."

"How could she control the shades when someone else summoned them?" Anubis mused doubtfully.

"And why would she even tell you the truth?" added Cecil.

Magnus sighed, consumed by the intractable swarm of recollections that remained from his journey. "I know that things don't make much sense now. I have a lot to tell you, and I'm not sure if this all will be any less confusing by the end of it. All I can say for now is that Daimos and the shades...weren't the worst of what we're facing."

Cecil was touched by a grim shiver. A stiffness swelled across the hand in which he clutched the Galem history book. "Then you'd best start from the beginning. Tell us all you've seen and heard."

Magnus scanned his memories, returning in his mind to the hour of his departure from the MorningStar citadel. "Before we set out, I had to tell Daimos my father's route to the crater," he began. "For some strange reason, he was totally averse to me and Medeva traveling through the valley, but refused to say why—I only found out for myself later. Noctell and Raven supplied me with food rations, a waterskin, and a flask of black acid to destroy the Luminous Rock.

"We left MorningStar a few hours later. After a day and a half of hiking across empty road, we reached the Venieres forest. There, I was nearly strangled to death when we were attacked by a mob of arboryn." Magnus found himself coiling a hand around his throat where the arboryn's vine had wrung him. "We survived, but Medeva was wounded and poisoned."

"Poisoned?" Anubis exclaimed. "I've never heard of an arboryn that could poison."

"No." Magnus shook his head. "An arboryn grabbed her and broke her wing. She was cut by one of her own poison-tipped knives when she fell and landed on her dagger holsters. She said that a harpie's blood can withstand poison better than a human's and that I had two hours to find a cure. I returned to the forest and managed to get hold of a shred of taren bark for the antidote...but I ended up finding something else as well." He left his audience in suspense as he gathered the nerve to utter his conclusion: "The Saxum Diaboli."

The breath in which Magnus spoke the forbidding name fell upon the clearing in a wave of dread and silence. "Just like in my dream," said Magnus. "The graveyard of Sennair Drakathel's headstone."

"You *saw* it?" Cecil cried, his expression warped in a disarray of emotions. "That's almost as if your dream was foreseeing the future."

"I know," Magnus answered. "I followed a trail that led

to it. The whole path was cleared through. It looked like people had been there—recently."

"That would make sense, considering that New Order followers would continue to pay homage to their master's grave," said Cecil. "Just as Eras had done, according to your dream."

"Yeah..." Magnus replied, sifting through the rest of his nightmarish reflections, "...and he left something behind." He turned back to his former guardian. "The dagger. The one I saw Eras impale into the headstone in my dream. It was in the Saxum Diaboli."

"Then he truly was possessed by Sennair Drakathel," Cecil affirmed thoughtfully. "It all makes sense, without a doubt. All our suspicions about the New Order's undead master may not be far from reality."

"Except," Magnus added, "there wasn't just one dagger in the stone. There were three."

"Three?" Drake exclaimed incredulously.

"Then Daimos wasn't the only one possessed by Sennair!" Cecil inferred. "That is a disturbing thought indeed."

"Unless they all belonged to Eras," said Anubis. "Perhaps his bond to Sennair was something that had to be renewed over time."

"I don't think so," Magnus replied. "They were each different. One had the Order's skull icon imprinted on the hilt, so it might have been his. Another had a black stone embossed in it, and the last one...wasn't very distinct. It only had some kind of eroded crest on it."

Cecil frowned in deliberation. "Well, I would logically assume the black stone to be a piece of abylite. In that case, the weapon must belong to a calimancer—a diviner of dark magic. I can't see why that dagger would be any different than the one bearing the skull icon. Either one, if not both, could have belonged to Daimos."

"But that's not all," Magnus continued. "When Noctell attacked me on the tower, I saw the weapon he'd thrown. It was identical to the abylite dagger in the headstone."

All eyes widened at the thought of the elite guard's involvement. "Noctell?" Cecil repeated pensively. "As intriguing a thought as that is, it hardly makes sense. We saw what became of Daimos after being possessed by Sennair. Surely Noctell would have been cursed with a similar form."

"And considering that an abylite dagger isn't a particularly uncommon weapon," added Anubis, "it would be difficult to say for sure if the one in the stone is even his. The Order's following is, after all, comprised of those who favor dark magic."

"But then whose is it?" the younger Wingheart persisted. "They can't all belong to Daimos. And what about the third dagger? I saw the same hilts on the swords of the Rammeren guards."

"The Rammeren!" Cecil cried, baffled. "How could you have seen that?"

"I saw it twice," said Magnus, "on the weapons of two dead guards when..." He trailed off in the middle of his sentence and brought his forehead into the prop of his hand.

"I'll explain," he assured his thoroughly perplexed company. "The point is that the third dagger belongs to a Rammeren guard. Their weapons' hilts were exactly the same as the one of the dagger in the stone. I'm sure of it."

Cecil seemed less dismissive of this suggestion, though no less confused. "The Rammeren's crest," he said, "a shield and ribbon, is it not?"

"Yeah," Magnus answered fervently.

"Then you may be right. The Rammeren's equipment is branded with their own insignia to set the clan apart from the rest of Galem's military. It just seems impossibly ironic—the Rammeren are vehement enemies of the Order. To think that one of their own men betrayed them for Drakathel's sake."

"Unless it wasn't a Rammeren guard," Drake supposed, "and the dagger was stolen."

"Why would anyone go through the trouble of stealing someone else's dagger to impale it in place of their own?" Cecil asked with a shrug. "Not to mention that a dagger isn't exactly an object of significant value."

"Then maybe it was someone who had only some kind of affiliation with the Rammeren," said Anubis, "like a Galem soldier."

"Then who?" Cecil replied. "We have absolutely no way of knowing to whom either of those two daggers belongs. Even if one of them were from a soldier of the Rammeren, certainly that person wouldn't be fighting alongside them now. It's extremely unnerving to think that Daimos may not have been Sennair Drakathel's only vessel, but as long as we have no lead, we can't worry about something that we're not even sure of."

"Now what was that about the Rammeren?" Anubis queried the younger brother. "Did you have any trouble making it past the border?"

Magnus did not respond directly, but his leaden expression spoke for itself. "With Medeva's wing broken, we were both forced to cross on foot," he said. "She planned to sneak through, but we were unlucky enough to cross a part of the mountains that was under the Rammeren's guard. They turned us back, threatening to kill us if we came near again. Once we were far enough away, Medeva summoned shades to surround us for protection. Then we stormed the mountains and fought our way through."

"That was certainly an audacious move." Cecil gave a troubled nod. "So I assume this is what you were referring to in saying that Medeva was the shades' commander."

"Yes," confirmed Magnus. "It looked like she conjured some flicker of dark energy from her palm. After that, the shades swarmed us and followed her as we ran."

"And you progressed like this all the way through the mountains?"

"Only until we were able to break from the Rammeren's sight. After that, we—" Magnus stammered as if his own words were wringing his throat. "We escaped into the valley. Medeva said that it was the only place where the Rammeren wouldn't follow us."

Cecil angled his brow over a display of somber curiosity. "And why is that?"

"Even Daimos didn't want us to travel anywhere near it," Magnus answered slowly. "Neither he nor Medeva ever told me why. But I found out soon enough."

A bout of wary silence ensued. The attention of Drake and the herbalist swayed between Cecil and Magnus, whose eyes locked in a silent exchange of emotions. The stillness ceased only when Cecil reached to take the history book he had left by his side. He riffled keenly through its yellowed papers, stopping on a page near the end of the book, then read aloud:

"Still, for nearly a millennium after the revolt that followed Drakathel's death, the kingdom of Galem's decrepit state endured. From an eagle's lofty gaze, the city now appears to lie, festering, like a still-beating heart waiting to be exhumed from the sea of ashes in which it had been drowned. From the eyes of one who walks its deathly still roads, it is clear that an ill-boding presence shrouds the valley as a whole.

Over the course of nine years, the province of Galem has dispatched a total of six parties in exploration of its ancient kingdom's most ominous reaches. All six of these parties, each consisting of eight to twelve armed men, have never returned. After the disappearance of the sixth party, the province declared the valley forbidden grounds, fearing the lives of those who should dare tread its soil again."

Cecil eased the book shut, renewing his breath under the weight of the silence. "What, Magnus—what did you see in the valley?"

Cecil's question was not one that could be answered in a few words. Once he had fashioned his response in his mind, Magnus recounted his journey: "We reached the valley by sundown," he began. "It was incredible—an entire city built in the middle of the mountains. There were thousands of buildings, and one enormous castle that stood on a hilltop. Everything was at least partially destroyed, and there was even more black ash on the ground than in MorningStar. When we got farther into the city, almost every wall I'd turn to had the same symbol scratched into it..."

"The skull icon," Cecil reckoned.

"The same one that Daimos took on for his cult," Magnus affirmed. "It was everywhere. It must have been spawned from Drakathel—even the Saxum Diaboli was carved to look like it. Medeva said it was an ancient symbol, and that it had been adopted by many other factions and people throughout the ages."

Cecil was already feverishly leafing through the book. He stopped, then bared the pages for all to see. Magnus felt his heart stagger into the pit of his chest as his vision became scalded by an immaculate sketch of the skull icon printed on the book's open page.

"This icon is indeed one that has found use by Sennair Drakathel and the Order," said Cecil. "It is an icon that represents strength in death, and the power of the immortal undead. It is known as the *Valeos Moryae*."

"So the icon predates the Order," Drake presumed.

Cecil tipped his head in a nod. "It does. The book states that its first recorded use was, surprisingly, in one of the oldest known texts on Arkane: the *Biblio Necromanica*, a primeval grimoire—possibly millennia old—detailing some of the darkest of necromantic practices."

"The Grimoire..." Anubis mused aloud. "The Necromancer's Grimoire, they call it. I heard of it some years ago. Do you suppose Sennair would have adopted the icon from it?"

"Possibly," said Cecil. "Though it's unlikely that he had gotten a hold of it for himself, as I can't see how it could have survived the rebellion after his death."

"You mean it still exists?" asked Magnus, having at first assumed otherwise.

"Unaccounted for, actually, for the past twenty years or so," said Cecil. "It was stolen from the Zephyrian Archives and hasn't been found since."

"Then what exactly is in it?" Magnus queried implicatively. "Anything about...summoning?"

"The summoning of the dead, I'd imagine," replied Cecil. "Are you thinking that Drakathel used the Grimoire to summon the shades?"

"The shades," Magnus added gradually, "among other creatures."

It seemed clear to Cecil what Magnus' statement entailed. "Go on," he urged with concern.

"Eventually we reached a market square," continued Magnus. "The path forked, one leading farther into the city, and the other to Sennair Drakathel's old castle. I argued that we should travel through the castle, but Medeva wanted to head around it. I didn't give up—I argued that she and Daimos were hiding something from me. Eventually she gave in and agreed to travel though the castle, even though she insisted I was wasting my strength.

"She led me up the hill and inside the castle, where she took me only as far as the courtyard before stopping because of a blocked entrance. She tried to coax me into leaving, but then I saw something strange...like a trail across the ground where the ashes seemed to flow by their own accord. I went after the trail; she kept trying to draw me away from it. I followed it all the way through a bent gate and into another courtyard.

"This was the source of the ashes. The trail led all the way into a stone pavilion in the center of the court. I started walking toward it, when Medeva ran in through the gate behind me. She was more anxious than I'd ever seen her... like she was either scared or unable to come anywhere near me and the pavilion. She kept hollering for me to come back, but I didn't listen. I still thought she was only trying to hide something from me that was perfectly harmless. When I got close enough to the pavilion, I saw that the trail flowed down a staircase going deep underground, but it was too dark to see where it led. I brightened my pendant; I heard Medeva scream for me to stop. There was a horrible cry from the chamber at the bottom of the stairs. Then everything went dark."

Magnus fell into a pause, as if his tale had come to an end. He continued seconds later in a much more distraught tone. "I still doubt myself over whether or not it was just another nightmare," he said. "But then I know what I saw, and I swear, Cecil, I swear I wasn't dreaming. Things rose from the ashes—enormous beasts, fusions of every creature imaginable. There was a horse...a horse with the head of a snake and arms with blades for hands, a skeleton with the head of a ram, and a bird with the body of a lizard and the wings of a bat. They all appeared and attacked us.

"I tried to fight them, but my magic was useless. Light wouldn't do anything but stun them. Medeva and I ran for our lives until we reached the hillside, where she called the shades to protect us while we escaped. In just a few minutes, it was all over. Every single one of the beasts vanished as soon as we got far enough away from the castle."

Magnus' audience stayed mute at a loss for words. Anubis and the older Wingheart leaned tight-lipped glances toward Cecil, who brought an end to the silence with another daunting paragraph from the Galem history book:

"But perhaps most appalling of all were the chimerical monstrosities that now joined him in battle. From the cockatrice and wraithlike specters that eclipsed the sky in myriad hordes, to the phantasmal quadrupeds that broke and cast aside the bodies of the mightiest soldiers, it was certain that Sennair Drakathel had acquired an army of the most fearsome beasts ever to exist on Arkane."

Magnus shuddered at the uncanny resemblance between the book's description and the beasts he had encountered in the valley. "So you're saying," he replied, "that the creatures I saw really were of Drakathel's old army?"

"And still are." Cecil raised his eyes back to Magnus. "It seems that the beasts of the Order's army never simply vanished back into their home dimension, as people once believed—they slumber in Drakathel's old kingdom. Your story suggests that the six Galem exploration parties mentioned in the book likely fell prey to the creatures."

"And our father didn't?" Magnus retorted. "I read in his journal that he traveled through the valley...yet he still lived to find the Rock, and he wrote nothing about the creatures or the castle."

"Interesting," said Cecil. "Perhaps he just chose an alternate route. Medeva obviously believed that the valley's dangers could be evaded by traveling around the castle. Brendan was pressured to reach his destination as quickly as he could, so he wouldn't have had much of a chance to explore anything beyond the city streets." He paused in reconsideration. "And perhaps he knew. Not about the creatures, of course, but he must have had some sort of idea about the perils of his chosen route. Whether or not he knew what those perils were exactly, he was wise enough to keep to the city streets. Had he entered the castle, it's doubtful he would have ever finished his journey to the Rock. Heavens, Magnus...you're lucky to be alive."

"I wouldn't be if it wasn't for Medeva," replied Magnus. "It looked like she knew the creatures well enough to evade them. She even killed one using magic."

"That sounds like quite a feat, given how invincible those beasts were said to be," Cecil remarked. "What kind of elements do you reckon she conjured?"

"It was hard to tell," Magnus answered. "Her halberd glowed, she impaled it into the creature's chest, and the thing just...burst back into ashes. She denied that she did it, though. She insisted that she didn't use magic and that the ash was playing tricks on my eyes. But I know what I saw. She destroyed the beast somehow, magic or not."

"But why would she want to hide that?" Drake pondered in return.

"I think the most dire question is why Recett and Medeva were so averse to telling you any of this," said Cecil. "I can't help but suspect that a greater secret was at stake besides the mere existence of the beasts."

Magnus strayed into a trance at hearing Cecil's conception, revisiting in his mind the courtyard in the moments before he and Medeva were attacked. He could feel the weight of his foot as it leaned off the peak of the precipitous staircase that poured beneath the pavilion. He felt the serpentine current of the ashes at his feet that marred his ankles with soot.

But most of all, he saw the Valeos Moryae, the icon of the Order, in the form of a grandiose mosaic tiling on the back wall of the chamber below him. Though it was a sight on which he had laid his eyes for no longer than a second, it was one that had ineffaceably scarred his memories. It was the source of the ashes. It was what Daimos and Medeva had been hiding from him.

"There was something," said Magnus, straining to weave his thoughts into words, "under the pavilion. At the bottom of the staircase, where the trail flowed in. It was a mosaic of the skull icon...but there was something behind it, like it was some kind of door. The ashes poured in and out from it through a slit around its edge. I don't know where it led to, but the ashes were drawn to it—the same ashes that formed the creatures."

Cecil kneaded his brow, brooding. "So you believe this is the valley's true secret?" he said, his fingers wandering back into the pages of his book. "You may not be far from the truth." He read:

"By 2795, a rumor had strayed to the ears of the Order's lesser followers—that Sennair Drakathel had begun construction on an elaborate subterranean edifice beneath the confines of his castle. Fueling the myth, droves of the warlord's servants could be seen day after day, burdened with cartloads of granite, gold, and abylite that they hauled up the arduous bank on which Drakathel's fortress was perched, only to return with their wagons voided. Even the servants themselves remained unknowing of what purpose their delivered cargo was to serve.

It was said that only the Order's staunchest devotees were privileged to hear of, let alone *see, their master's monumental construction. Which such secrecy abound, those in ignorance could not help but conspire about what marvels could lie entombed beneath the soaring hilltop of Drakathel's stronghold. Some believed it to be a colossal treasury, or perhaps the stone prison of an insatiable beast that feasted on jewels and precious metals. Some believed it to be the source of the warlord's immortality and power; others deemed it to be all of the above."*

Cecil shut the tome portentously. "As I highly doubt that Drakathel would have been keeping such a monstrous treasury or be imprisoning a rock-eating behemoth, I think it's fair to say that the pavilion you stumbled upon lends some truth to the rumor of this subterranean edifice."

"You think that's what's behind the mosaic?" Magnus asked with a shadow of apprehension. "Then what is it? And why would it have such an affinity with the ashes?"

"The source of the warlord's immortality and power?" Drake recited the book's curious suggestion. "What do you make of that?"

"Intriguing, certainly," said Cecil. "But quite vague without further explanation. If we're to speculate any sense out of this, it would have to involve something to which the ashes would have a natural attraction."

"A power that resonates with them," Anubis drew off the tail of Cecil's statement. "An immense, live power."

"Like..." Cecil's words faded abruptly, as if he had arrived at a new realization. "...a rift."

"A rift?" Magnus questioned the word.

"It's a logical assumption," Cecil continued. "Clearly, Drakathel's beasts did not originate on Arkane—they were summoned from a separate dimension. But in order for any summoned entity to exist permanently in its new plane, it needs to have departed fully from its former dimension by means of a rift, as opposed to a temporary gate brought about by a summoning ritual."

Magnus struggled to comprehend Cecil's intricate proposal. "Then the rift is what lies beyond the mosaic?"

"What other power source could the ashes be so drawn to than the gateway to the world from which they came?" replied Cecil. "Rifts are vastly powerful, especially one that would have managed to remain active since Drakathel's time."

"That means Daimos' shades were summoned from the same rift," Drake deduced. "And then where does Medeva fit into all this? She's supposed to be the one who controls the shades."

"She said it was because they were her kin," Magnus recalled the harpie's words. "But that makes no sense... Drakathel could control an entire army of those beasts, including shades, and he can't be related to them in any way. And if Medeva is kin to the shades, then why couldn't she control any of the other creatures that attacked us in the valley?"

"Because the loyalty of a summoned entity can belong to only one master," answered Cecil. "The beasts have already fallen under the control of Sennair Drakathel. How, I cannot say."

"Regardless of the harpie," said Anubis, "what do you make of the idea that such a massive rift could exist beneath the valley? Is it safe for it to be left as it is?"

"Rift or not, it's a power that obviously hasn't affected much of anything outside of the valley," Cecil replied. "And there isn't a lot we can do, anyhow, unless any of us are foolhardy enough to take our chances with those beasts and investigate the mosaic for ourselves." A scant smile came about his lips. "Alas, too many questions remain unanswered for now. We can only wait and see how things continue to unfold. All that seems certain at this point is that our journey does not end here."

A reflective silence descended on the clearing. At least an hour had flitted past over Magnus' harrowing recounts of his voyage and the debates that had arisen from them. The sun had climbed to a low height against the still-golden horizon as morning continued its ascent.

"Then what's next?" Drake suddenly asked. "For MorningStar, for Arkane...for all of us?"

Cecil let his head fall against the oak's trunk at his back. His hopeful gaze meandered into the vivid rays of the sun. "Much, I suppose," he answered. "At last, Daimos' death has given Arkane a chance to reclaim its stolen province, and for its former inhabitants to return."

"Daimos is one matter," said Drake. "What about his followers? Considering that Medeva controls the shades, we haven't done much to dent the power of his army as a whole."

"I think we have," Cecil confidently rejoined. "It's unlikely that many of Daimos' followers would return after witnessing their master's graceless death and defeat. And for whatever reason that Medeva was serving Daimos, I doubt she has much of a reason to return. With the aid of our neighboring provinces, we will ensure that Serenia is defended until all ash has dispersed from its fields and skies. The task at hand is to spread word of our victory, help rebuild Serenia from its ruin, and usher people back into the land from which they fled so many years ago. MorningStar will need a new council..." He looked to the brothers and the herbalist. "...and a new city guard. Together, the four of us will found the city's rise."

"No, Cecil." Anubis shook his head, returning a smile. "I will assist with everything I can, but it is you three alone who are worthy of taking Brendan's place as the city's leaders. My work is as a herbalist—not as a defender of MorningStar."

"We will see in due time." Cecil gave a contented nod. "But know that, even as a herbalist, you will be remembered as one of Serenia's liberators."

"As will you, Cecil," Anubis graciously replied, drawing his hand back over Ember's coiled frame in his lap. "As will all of you."

"So when do we head back?" Magnus beamed zealously. "When do we return to Arkane?"

"Soon indeed," affirmed Cecil. "A new life awaits—for us all!" He turned up his grin to bask in the sun's resplendence. "Just as Serenia, soon, will see dawn once again."

43

Only the Beginning

OCTELL KNEVER WALKED OUT onto the court of the MorningStar castle. His feet dragged over the sooty stone as if they had been shackled with a ball and chain, until he halted, unmoving. The silence was agonizing; it seemed as if all time had stopped. The buckled frames of the citadel buildings encircled the court like a mourning host that stood in solemn witness of the deceased—the ruins of Daimos' castle.

Gone was the soaring, black tower that had once scarred MorningStar's heavens. Gone was the limestone stronghold whose sight every soul had learned to fear. Gone was the warlord who had once sat high in his malefic throne, commanding the wasteland that lay beneath him.

Noctell feasted his eyes on the wreckage. The rubble of the fallen tower extended across the length of the castle, dividing the structure with a channel of crumbled rock and stone slabs. The once-grandiose ivied front entrance had been buried in the ruin, as had much of the castle's eastern wall. Even the shades had departed from this place, leaving in their wake only shattered clouds of ash through which the morning's light filtered in celestial rays.

The scene was no less than devastating. Noctell felt his limbs swell with shivers as he drifted nearer until the ruin filled his vision entirely. A crushing sensation permeated him, as if he were beholding the remains of his one and only home. It was as if a void had been carved within him, with only dread to fill it.

His life in Daimos' empire was no more. The streets once flocked by ashen specters and patrolled by the sickly, hunched shadows of the warlord's guards now lay barren in every direction around him. Eighteen years of Noctell's service to Daimos had been cast away in a matter of hours— but along with them, eighteen years of imprisonment had been lifted off his shoulders.

Whether it was caused by the sight of the once-insuperable construct that had been so pitifully toppled, or the resentment that had too long been stifled inside of him, Noctell sensed a shift overcome his mind. He felt no emptiness, dread, nor melancholy, no—his fetters had been broken, and never had he felt so unbound. At long, long last, Noctell was free of his master.

A narrow smile crept about Noctell's face. He could not hold back his trembling by much, but as he filled his lungs, a newfound sense of supremacy flooded him.

With religious pacing, he advanced toward the ruin, summoning more courage with every step. Finally he stopped, and stood, undaunted, in the face of his old master's demolished fortress.

Never again would Noctell feel the clutch of Daimos' knotted claws around his throat. Never again would he tread the castle's corpse-hemmed entrance hall as he had done every day. Never again would he lay eyes on his master's spitefully grinning, skeletal visage, whose sight had grown so revolting to him.

Never again! Noctell rejoiced in his mind. *If my old life in this wretched netherworld is to be my sacrifice, then I'll gladly take it! I'm free of Recett, and that alone is worth more than every coin of gold that living corpse ever hoarded!*

Noctell scornfully lunged the heavy heel of his boot at a small rubble pile by his feet, shattering an already fractured hunk of stone. His grin broadened. *What power do you hold now, Recett?* he derided. *What power do you hold when you lie crushed under a hundred tons of boulders? Writhe in hell, Recett! Writhe like I did so many times in your strangling grasp!*

By his mocking, Noctell was satiated. *I'm the powerful one now, Recett,* he went on, sobering his tone. *You are my master no longer.*

As Noctell's vivid words trailed from his mind, a peculiar, biting coldness descended on the court through a hoarse breath of wind. Upon snapping back to his senses, he found that he was turned in the way of the castle's demolished east wall. His vision was set on a curious aperture high above him—a breach in the rubble opened by a rare arrangement of fallen slabs. It was, perhaps, only just wide enough to wedge through.

The necromancer gave a wry nod to himself. He could not pass on an opportunity to tour the castle's morbid halls one final time. *One final time*, he thought, *so that I may gaze upon this forsaken ruin from within!*

Driven by audacity, Noctell planted his first step in the rubble slope and heaved himself up toward the aperture. He ascended the stones with ease, pulling his lank frame higher on every jutting slab until he reached the opening. He swivelled up his legs, dropped them through the aperture, and slipped into the castle's interior.

The opposite face of the slope was much sheerer, though it still had an array of footholds to secure his descent. After a precipitous scramble, he arrived on the dirtied tiles of the castle's main level. An oppressive darkness and a sense of claustrophobia weighed down on him; even air seemed scarcer than normal. The place where Noctell found himself was a corridor that lined the castle's inner wall, branching off through a procession of archways in front of him.

Having no light besides that which bled in from the overhead aperture, Noctell stole a nearby torch off its mount and effortlessly conjured a blaze to its iron head. He lashed about the flames to illuminate his surroundings. It was strange, certainly, to observe such a familiar passageway in this destructed state. The castle wall against which the corridor ran had been replaced largely by rubble, while the floor was painted with rock dust and littered copiously with stone shards that had seeped in through the network of cracks in the ceiling.

Noctell passed another glance across the hall before hastening through one of the archways. His strident footfall echoed while he dauntlessly penetrated the gloom of the corridor, then dove through a second arch on his left about midway through the passage. He proceeded into an ample hallway, where he slackened his pace and came still.

This was the entrance hall—a sweep of Noctell's torch confirmed it, painting a harsh glow onto the manacled corpses that glared down on him from either side. Of all places in his master's castle, this corridor was, without a doubt, the most haunting. It was the path to the throne of Daimos Recett, and one that Noctell had walked more times than he could count, often with a mood no lighter than that surrounding a march to the scaffold.

But not today. Today, Noctell would tread this hall in triumph, and without a shadow of fear to taint his emotions. In a slow and savoring gait, he advanced down the corridor, parting the darkness with the solitary beacon of his torch. As the chain of corpses drew to an end, the hall opened into the capacious chamber of the throne room.

To behold the vacant throne of his master! The thought was beyond gratifying. Noctell watched the macabre tiling of Daimos' skull icon emerge from under the light of his torch and pass beneath his feet, before at last, he picked up his head toward the throne of MorningStar's slain usurper.

But there was someone seated on the throne. It was an emaciated figure, hunched over grotesquely in its seat. It was draped in tattered black cloth in the form of a hood and robe, its face shadowed entirely, its knobbed hands protruding from ill-fitting sleeves and constricted around the yawning ebony jaws of the throne's draconic armrests.

Noctell's hands and eyes were pried open as his every muscle turned rigid in shock. His torch fell from his paralyzed grasp and struck the floor with a hollow clatter, its flames still sharply alight. Every ounce of dread he had suppressed was now revived tenfold, as if the entire weight of the crumbled castle had come down upon him in an instant. Through the unwavering blaze of his dropped torch, Noctell could do no more than gape at the deathly still figure that occupied his old master's throne.

"M-my..." Noctell's lips quivered in an attempt to muster out a single phrase. "...my lord?"

The figure did not stir, but its response was prompt: "How can you let your master die," a harsh, guttural voice echoed back to the necromancer, "and still call him your *lord?*"

At the figure's last word, all torches that lined the walls of the entrance corridor and throne room simultaneously caught fire in a deafening hiss of flame. Noctell's torch, however, had been extinguished, as had all courage left within him. His heart churned as he watched the figure come upright in its seat like a corpse suddenly imbued with life. Under the glare of the freshly ignited flames, the cloaked figure rose from the throne and advanced toward the shuddering necromancer.

Noctell saw the figure draw near and halt mere steps away from him. He held his stance timidly, leaning at the verge of a backward step as he stared into the hooded void that was the figure's face. "M-my lord," he repeated, stammering as if he had no control of his lips. "My lord, f-forgive..."

But Noctell's sentence was lost when the figure picked up its scabrous claws and pulled back the hood of its cloak. As its mask of shadows was lifted, a curtain of ghostly white hair poured out over its shoulders. This was not Daimos.

Much of Noctell's terror was suddenly converted to vehement abhorrence. He recoiled in trembling paces from the man who now stared at him impassively. His ire heightened with each step, bringing him to pick up speed until he was halted by a rise of the man's now-gauntleted hand.

"Calm yourself, Knever," said Sennair Drakathel in an irreproachably benign tone. He allowed his arm to drop before continuing to speak. "You have no need to fear me."

Though Noctell had stopped retreating, Drakathel's suggestion did not settle him. He remained tenaciously in place, making no sound but the drone of his wrathful, convulsing breaths.

"Daimos is dead," Sennair declared bluntly. Neither his voice nor his expression carried any discernible emotion. "Without Daimos to lend me his power, my existence in this realm dwindles. I employ the very last of my strength to manifest myself before you now and speak with you one final time."

An air of interest descended on Noctell's scowl. He adjusted his posture to make it clear that he was listening.

"I am weak, Knever," Drakathel continued, almost as if in sorrow. "An eternity of garnering my power has been rendered vain. All I have yearned for, and all I have achieved...it is gone, I am regretful to say."

Noctell still did not speak, but his fury was fading. Never had Drakathel appeared so helpless, so pitiable in his lament for power. Certainly, the lich was being truthful.

Drakathel dropped his head against the rim of his leather breastplate in a despondent bow, folding his arms behind him. "My time here draws to an end, as does your service to the Order," he said as he picked up his solemn stare to rest it on the necromancer. "Thus, Noctell Knever, I relieve you of our bond."

Noctell narrowed his eyes dubiously. "What are you saying?"

"I am saying that you will never see or hear of me again," answered Sennair. "You will be free of all ties with the Order. You may continue to live your life as you see fit, if you believe you are better off without my guidance." His hand vanished beneath the shadows of his robe, then reappeared clutching the hilt of a weapon whose sight had grown sickening to Noctell—the necromancer's abylite dagger once impaled in Drakathel's headstone.

Instinctively upon seeing the blade, Noctell felt his rage

rekindle. But he was lured back into calmness by the lich's candid tenor. "You have served me loyally for many years, Knever," said Drakathel. "Thus, I will give you a choice." He proffered the dagger in an outstretched hand, its ornate hilt and pommel turned in Noctell's way. "This blade is my sole bridge to you. It is what unites our minds. Take it from me now, and my hold upon you will be relinquished; our bond will be forever broken."

As the echo of his voice faded off the walls of the chamber, Drakathel crooked up his wrist, half-concealing the dagger behind his lifted palm. "However, should you allow me to preserve this blade, our bond will remain. And perhaps one day, when time has replenished my strength sufficiently, I will call on your aid once again." He lowered his hand back to its original, outspread position, returning the dagger to Noctell's view. "It is your choice alone, Knever; I will influence you neither way. Accept the dagger, or leave it for me to keep."

Noctell was taken aback by Sennair's offer. He could never have conceived that the lich would allow their bond to be severed. After almost two decades of enduring the torment of his controller's unremitting persuasions, visions, and nightmares, Noctell was now handed the choice to end it all and free himself of the Order's clutch. But as tempted as he was, he could not help but suspect Drakathel's intentions.

"What would become of you," Noctell pointedly questioned the lich, "if this bond were to be broken?"

"My remaining power will diminish further, surely,"

answered Drakathel, his speech declining to a forlorn pause. "I will be forced to seek a new vessel, as well as a new gathering of devotees to aid me, if there is any hope left for my return."

Noctell hesitated to respond, remaining doubtful. "Why are you doing this?" he muttered through the barely open slit of his mouth. "Why are you offering me this if it could mean your downfall?"

"Because you are loyal to me, Knever," Sennair drawled in reply, "and it is time I returned the favor. I would not wish to keep you waiting until I have fully strengthened. If it is your desire, you may free yourself from our bond, here and now."

With reluctance, Noctell wrenched himself from his skepticism and thirstily affixed his eyes on the dagger in Drakathel's palm. He had asked enough questions. He would not risk losing his possibly sole chance of escaping Sennair Drakathel and the Order forever, and he risked nothing by simply accepting an offer that was handed to him.

Staunchly mute, Noctell advanced toward Drakathel. Not once did his sights stray from the prized blade until he halted, coming face-to-face with the lich's daunting figure. He extended his hand to grasp the hilt of the dagger, but his fingertips never made contact with the weapon.

Sennair dexterously spun the dagger upward. The tip of the blade grazed Noctell's right upper arm, slashing through his shirt and his flesh. At once, Noctell clenched his raw wound and reeled back, voiding his lungs in a scream that pierced his own ears like knives. The pain of his lesion was unbearable, perhaps worse than any he had ever experienced. Worse yet, the agony did not fade, continuing to smolder parasitically beneath his flesh, prying his eyes wider as it resonated through his nerves.

Noctell turned his pained grimace back to Drakathel, who raised the head of the dagger tauntingly. The lich's expression was stagnant, but his glare lashed out flames of merciless scorn. "Even with all I've said," Sennair whispered harshly, "your lust for freedom still prevails."

Noctell was struck immobile by the undying burn of his wound. He saw the flecks of his blood on the dagger blade—gradually, they appeared to soak into the metal itself, leaving the weapon unsullied. As his pain died away along with the blood, Noctell bored his rage through the lich in a hellish scowl. "You deceiver!" he cried out. "What was that for?"

"For betrayal, Knever!" Drakathel roared, slipping the dagger back under the veil of his cloak. "For betrayal of the Order! For the murder of Daimos Recett!"

"It was the boy who killed Recett!" Noctell retorted. "I tried to save him! I had no part in his death!"

"Lies!" Sennair lunged out, his hair and robes thrashing. "If it were not for your treachery, Daimos would still be alive! Traitor!" He speared a condemning hand at the necromancer. "Traitor of the Order!"

As if Drakathel's wrath had spurred his wound, Noctell felt the same pain return to him in a stabbing blow to his arm. He writhed and shuddered, even tighter constricting his grip on the lesion as he withdrew in backward paces.

"First," Drakathel bellowed, inciting the flames of every torch to draw their tongues, "for your arrogance! That boy could have been dead long before he scaled the tower— yet you believed it was more worthy of your time to taunt him, rather than killing him! You allowed yourself to be bested by a weakling for the sake of your own arrogance! *Conceited coward!*"

Noctell gasped as a second stab emanated from his wound. Though he continued to retreat, Sennair was swifter in his approach. "Then," the lich snarled as the flames leapt again, "for your disloyalty! At a time when Daimos stood before you in mortal peril, your mind flowed thick with deceit! You could only conceive ways of how you may aid the boy in his heinous act and allow your own master to die! *Murderous traitor!*"

A third stab sent Noctell faltering over his heels and buckling forward. The torch flames billowed more mightily than ever as Drakathel persisted in his rebuke. "Finally," he said, "for your foolishness! Even when you had that wretched stone in your grasp, you did nothing but boast it in the face of that half-dead boy until he actually gathered the strength to shatter it! I cannot fathom how many opportunities you had to thwart your master's slaying, yet you failed in every one! *Mindless fool!*"

A fourth and final stab from his wound drove Noctell to his knees in submission. As the pain this time did not remit, he hardened his grasp on the lesion to the point that his flesh bled under the clamp of his own fingernails. "*Traitor!*" the lich's thunderous cries rang on. "Murderer of Daimos Recett! Feel the pain of the light that destroyed him! Feel his pain, Knever! Feel his pain!"

Tortured, Noctell hunched even lower until his hair draped over the tiles of the skull mosaic. Silence devoured the chamber as Sennair loomed over the necromancer with an expression untouched by the slightest remorse. When Noctell's pain subsided at last, he spoke no louder than a whisper. "Go ahead," he said under his breath. "I'm not afraid to die." Then he threw up his head to bare an irate scowl. "Kill me now! No life under the Order is worth living!"

Drakathel scoffed, his lips curling. "You wish I would kill you," he spat. "But that would be foolish of me. I could not possibly allow such power as great as yours to go untapped."

"You said I was weak!" Noctell retorted. "You said it was you who lent me power!"

"Ha!" the lich sneered, beginning to pace circles around the skull icon at his feet. "I lend you no power. What I give you is the ability to employ the power you would otherwise be too cowardly to use." He halted by Noctell, eyeing him sidewise. "You are immensely powerful, Knever—far more than you ever believed yourself to be. With my mind bound to yours, I bestowed upon you nothing but a lie, and the courage to realize your full strength."

"It doesn't make a difference." Noctell staggered to his feet and lurched away from Sennair. "Powerful or not, I'll serve you no longer! No matter your persuasions, I won't hear you!"

"You needn't hear me, Knever," Drakathel hissed, his sanguine eyes locking with the necromancer's. "You will feel me."

With only Sennair's words as a forewarning, Noctell felt the sting of his lesion suddenly steal over his arm in a fleeting but vehement blaze. Returning his grip over his wound, he screamed and folded to his knees from the intolerable pain. He whipped up his maddened glare to set it back on the lich. "What've you done to me?" he rasped.

"The very same that you did to my headstone," Drakathel answered wryly. "The daggers have grown to become a bridge through which I project my ethereal existence. By scarring you with your own blade, I form a bridge to your body—a bridge through which I may manipulate you on a level beyond that of the mind. Should you ever again resent my command or disobey me, I will cause your wound to echo the pain of the blade that first inflicted it, and I will augment that pain whenever needed."

A growing terror settled over Noctell's already-warped expression. His head shook—or more so, trembled—from side to side as he withdrew even further from the lich.

"Yes, Knever," Sennair continued, his tone nearly mocking. "With a willpower as strong as yours, a heavier shackle is required. If you will not obey me voluntarily, you will obey me out of necessity, if you wish not to grow insane by your suffering. In the tasks that will soon follow for you, I can no longer allow such disloyalty as I have seen in your failure to save Daimos."

"Tasks!" Noctell shakily scoffed at the word. "What tasks could you have besides prying Recett's carcass out from these ruins? You said it yourself, you're weak without Daimos! Powerless!" His exclamations were brusque and unsteady, as if he were trying to evade what he feared to be the truth. "There's no hope for your return!"

"Is there not?" Drakathel crowed, cocking his head. "I am far from powerless, and nowhere near weak. Your foolishness is only fortified by gullibility if you truly believed anything of what I just told you. I have gathered strength enough, and that will never change. All that is left to wait for now is for Eras to return to the Order's service and aid in carrying out my final wishes."

"Daimos is *dead*." The necromancer darkened his glower.

"Daimos is dead," Sennair repeated. "Eras, however, is not."

Noctell returned an adamant shake of his head, eyes gripping the lich. "You're mad," he barked. "That's what you are, you're mad! No matter his name, Recett is dead! Dead as every other corpse in this castle!"

"Daimos is the name that Eras acquired upon receiving my gift of an immortal form," Drakathel replied with little attention given to Noctell's obstinate rejections. "It is that immortal form that has been destroyed, but it is a form that is merely material. You will soon discover that a powerful soul such as Eras is not confined to sustaining existence in a corporal vessel."

"If you're so sure he's alive, then what do you need me for?" Noctell snapped. "Let him kneel at your feet and carry out every one of your tasks! Why should you keep me strung by a leash of thorns when you have the mighty Eras Recett at your beck and call!"

"Because every pawn has its place," replied Sennair. "And three places cannot be filled by one man, no matter how powerful. I needed you then..." Gliding a hand across his belt, the lich produced Noctell's abylite dagger and flaunted the blade. "...and even now, I will not abandon my hold on you so hastily."

"Three places." Noctell tightened his jaw. "Eras, Raven... and I."

"Three daggers," Drakathel added, twirling the weapon by its hilt, its sheer steel catching the torchlight.

"Why?" the necromancer asked. "You have thousands of followers—hundreds visit and pray by your grave as I once did, yet you select only three to be your doomed prisoners. Why me? Why any of us?"

Drakathel's mind appeared to roam as he re-sheathed the blade. "It was not my definite plan," he said. "It seemed as if fate played a notable role in delivering you three to my grave with such immaculate timing." He turned away from Noctell, drawing his gaze across the throne and the fiery walls that enclosed it. "First came loyal Eras, a defeated, repentant warlord abandoned by his followers. I tore from him a fragment of his soul, bestowing in return a fragment of my own. He grew immortal, and he was pleased.

"Then came Raven, a young man exiled by his brother, for whom he yearned to recognize his strength. I gleaned from him a sliver of his material existence, bestowing in return a sliver of my own and fashioning him into a demonic manifestation of the wrathful vigor that imbued him. He grew mighty, and he was pleased."

Drakathel's eyes drifted back onto the necromancer, where they settled like a pair of idle flames. "Lastly came you. You were abandoned, heartbroken, and scarcely an adult, yet your skill as a conjurer of dark energy was already far beyond most others'. You asked for power—power that you already possessed! You were a coward, Knever, and what you required was the mere courage to embrace the deadly strength of your magic. I laid within your mind a seed through which I leeched your thoughts, devouring them and tainting them with my influence. I gave you courage..." He smiled. "...and you were pleased."

"But why?" Noctell persisted in a biting slur. "Why us?"

"Do you not see?" Sennair arched his brow and flattened his lips. "The three of you were ushered to me each by your own respective troubles and desires. In fulfilling those desires, I seized from each of you a part that I required to complete my existence."

Noctell stayed his speech to muse Sennair's response. "Eras' soul," he said, "Raven's body, and my mind."

"Body, mind, and soul." Drakathel gave a condescending half-nod. "The Treus Aetherae. A lich is an entity whose power is shared equally in all three realms—the material, the ethereal, and the spiritual. This is the power I have garnered, and it is the power I must wield if I am to return into the world of the living with my full strength."

"This is what you gain," Noctell replied with still-seething ire, "by torturing us."

"Control does not bring about torture," said Drakathel sardonically. "It is those who resist control who torture themselves."

"Freedom is painless," Noctell retorted.

"Freedom is fickle," Sennair rejoined, "and fickleness leads to infidelity. Indeed, Eras has shown himself to be trustworthy, but you and Raven have too often strayed from my will. Whenever I slackened my grasp on either of you the slightest, you returned the favor by committing a foolish act or by dwelling on notions of betrayal. I was forced to coax my way into your nightmares and lead you to grip the ethereal mirror of your dagger, allowing me to renew the strength of our bond. But to you, Knever, that will not happen again." He grinned, his glare suddenly maniacal. "For you are my puppet," he jeered, "now and forever!"

Noctell reeled and gasped again at the sudden tide of pain that rushed from his wound. He cast his gaping eyes back onto Drakathel, his wrath still swelling within him. "I will not play puppet to a phantasm!"

"A phantasm? Is that what I am?" Sennair cackled amusedly. "I project my existence through you, but that does not make me a hallucination. I am as real as you are and more powerful than you will ever be!"

Noctell whelmed himself with rage to stifle his agony. He lunged at Sennair repeatedly, struggling against the pain, but was repelled each time by the same stabbing blow that grew harsher at every occurrence.

"Pitiable puppet!" Drakathel resounded under mocking laughter. "Feeble marionette! Relinquish your will to my strings and kneel before me!"

Noctell finally halted, recoiling. "To you I relinquish nothing!" he roared, and charged at the lich. Only meters away from Sennair, he was again torn off his foundation by a debilitating surge of pain. He staggered away, enfolding himself in shivering arms. "Coward! You claim you're so mighty, yet you defend yourself by cursing me with the godforsaken scar of a dagger!"

A snide smirk warped Drakathel's bloodless face. "You are one to call me a coward," he said, then converted his tone to a searing hiss: "Approach me, Knever!" He turned out his palms and lashed open his cloak. "If you believe yourself to possess such power, then confront your master! Confront me as the wretched fool you are!"

Noctell allowed the fire of his wrath to permeate him, scalding him from within, fueling him with vigor unlike any he had ever felt before. He wrung his fists as his skeletal pendant donned a vicious blaze of shadow, his buckled spine coursing with the power that deluged him like poison through his blood. He screamed and expelled from his hands and chest a tempestuous barrage of dark energy.

Without a glimmer of concern, Drakathel unsheathed his abyss-black longsword and cleaved its blade through the air before him, deftly meeting Noctell's assault. With a crackle and flare, the dark barrage was deflected upward and swelled over the lich as if he were veiled behind an impenetrable shield. The barrage was dispelled to a haze, which collapsed and clung to Sennair's weapon in a dense mantle. Then Drakathel swept down the blade, black embers curling off the mantle like the smoke of a torch, and heaved it out in front of himself in a tremendous, conflagrant arc.

Noctell could not afford to blink in the split second that his own magic was sent cascading back to him with double its force. Though he conjured a murky barrier for protection, the lich's monstrous counterattack struck him as would the hooves of a stampeding stallion. An instant darkness engulfed him; as a pulverizing blow broke against his chest, he felt as if every tendon in his body were being rent apart. He went numb, his surroundings churning in shadows. When at last he came still, sprawled over the icy tiles of the skull mosaic, his senses abandoned him.

All had reverted to silence. Even his own breathing seemed to carry no sound. His vision was a caliginous blur, throbbing with the fiery eyes of the torches that loomed over him. He felt no pain—only a growing sense of terror and unrest. Before long, Sennair Drakathel's venomous whispers returned to him, this time as an echo within his mind:

And so now I leave you, said the lich. *But know that when the time approaches, you will once again be summoned to the aid of the Order. Your services will be required more than ever to fulfill my final missions.*

Noctell found that his rage had not been alleviated in the slightest. *You may force me to do your bidding*, he spat, *you may command me like your listless puppet. But I swear on my life...I will never again be loyal to the Order.*

I do not need your loyalty! Drakathel bellowed. *When I return, every living soul on Arkane will bow before me, and those who do not will fall drowned in their own blood at the merciless swords of my army!*

You're insane, the necromancer condemned. *You're nothing but a ghost driven mad by a delusion of power! Your army is nonexistent, Eras is dead, and your millennia-old empire lies in festering ruins! You're finished, Sennair! This is the end for you and the Order as one!*

Drakathel's response was shadowed by grim laughter. *This is far from the end, Knever*, he hissed. *This is only the beginning.*

Glossary of Arkane Terms

GEOGRAPHY AND LOCATIONS

- **Anmer:** city in Serenia
- **East Arkane:** the eastern continent of Arkane; encompasses all six provinces and almost all human inhabitancy
- **Galem** ('ga-ləm): one of the six Arkane provinces; occupies the southeast region of East Arkane
- **Galem mountains:** mountain range that marks the Galem border
- **Larithian Gorge:** a mountain pass that cuts through the Galem mountains; one of the few straight roads that lead into Galem
- **MorningStar:** capital city of Serenia
- **Nemus** ('ne-məs): one of the six Arkane provinces; occupies the region north of Serenia and Galem
- **Old Galem:** ruins of the ancient Kingdom of Galem that fell at the turn of the 28th century (Arkane calendar); located in a valley in the Galem mountains

- **River Venieres:** river that begins in Galem and flows west across Serenia, through the Venieres Forest and through MorningStar
- **Serenia:** one of the six Arkane provinces; occupies the southwest region of East Arkane
- **Venieres** (ve-'nē-rəs): city in Serenia
- **Venieres Forest:** one of Arkane's oldest forests; located in Serenia
- **West Arkane:** the western continent of Arkane; has almost no human inhabitancy; is dominated by wildlife, allowing for an abundance of rifts and interdimensional entities; used almost exclusively for interdimensional studies
- **Zephyr:** one of the six Arkane provinces; occupies the northwest region of East Arkane
- **Zephyrian Archives:** Arkane's largest archives; located in Zephyr

CHARACTERS

- **Anubis Araiya** (ə-'rī-yə): herbalist; friend of Cecil Handel
- **Brendan Wingheart:** former council head of MorningStar; husband of Myra Wingheart; father of Magnus and Drake
- **Cecil Handel** ('se-səl): book collector; close friend of Brendan and Myra Wingheart and former guardian of Magnus and Drake; once employed in the MorningStar Guard

- **Drake Wingheart:** son of Brendan and Myra Wingheart; older brother of Magnus Wingheart; 25 years of age
- **Eras "Daimos" Recett:** former councillor of Anmer; leader of the New Order uprising in Anmer that established him as a Serenian warlord; later assumed the name *Daimos* ('dī-mȯs)
- **Magnus Wingheart:** son of Brendan and Myra Wingheart; younger brother of Drake Wingheart; 16 years of age
- **Malion Pendrick** ('ma-lē-ən): a captain of the Rammeren clan
- **Medeva** (me-'dē-və): harpie; skilled wielder of all manner of blades and bows
- **Myra Wingheart:** wife of Brendan Wingheart; mother of Magnus and Drake
- **Noctell Knever** ('ne-vər): necromancer, master calimancer; elite guard of Daimos Recett's army
- **Raven Gaunt:** demon/warped human; pyromancer; elite guard of Daimos Recett's army
- **Sennair Drakathel:** lich; calimancer, necromancer, summoner; master of the New Order

ARMIES, CLANS, AND FACTIONS

- **Indigo Magistrate:** aka "the Magistrate," or "the Indigo Magis"; name derived from "<u>In</u>ter-<u>D</u>imensional <u>G</u>uard <u>of</u> <u>M</u>agic <u>S</u>ecurity"; powerful organization entrusted with guarding and monitoring traffic through

all Earth/Arkane rifts; entrusted with the records and locations of all known Arkane rifts
- **New Order:** massive, ancient cult that worships its founder, Sennair Drakathel; violently advocates calimancy and anarchy
- **Rammeren:** bandit clan that dominates the Galem mountains; commissioned by the Galem army to guard Galem's border

SCIENCE AND TECHNOLOGY

- **Abylite:** rare, highly prized gemstone; only gemstone capable of being enchanted for the manipulation of dark energy
- **Athamine:** potent inhalation anesthetic
- **Cloaking prism:** crystal prism of various shapes capable of storing a photographic light pattern and projecting it elsewhere, "cloaking" a specified area under an illusion
- **Dark energy*:** partially stabilized form of antimatter; can only be conjured using abylite
- **Imrynic acid:** mild solvent
- **Junet:** black herbal dye
- **Light energy:** ethereal force conjured in luminomancy
- **Lucidus:** common crystal that captures and exudes light; can be enchanted for increased potency, as well as for luminomancy

- **Lucidus photosphorite:** alchemically crafted photo-sensitive crystal; used to make photographic slides
- **Occula:** mechanical camera employing photographic slides made with lucidus photosphorite
- **Tanaxyde:** deadly poison
- **Taren tree:** bark is a potent anti-poison; scientific classification: "Acer Tarensis"
- **Teleportation potion:** one of the few known methods of teletransportation of matter; product of highly advanced alchemical herbology; extremely volatile; illegal to trade across all six Arkane provinces

MAGICAL ARTS

- **Aeromancy:** magical manipulation of air
- **Alchemy:** art of enchantment and amalgamation/transformation of matter
- **Aquamancy:** magical manipulation of water
- **Calimancy:** magical manipulation of dark energy
- **Luminomancy:** magical manipulation of light and light energy
- **Necromancy:** study and conjuring of the dead and undead
- **Pyromancy:** magical manipulation of fire
- **Summoning:** art of conjuring elementals and extra-dimensional entities
- **Terramancy:** magical manipulation of earth

BESTIARY

- **Arboryn:** tree spirits; possess no form of their own; inhabit plant life, mainly trees; exist in colonies
- **Dead elemental:** an elemental harboring no soul, given form purely by energy
- **Elemental:** any spirit that is spawned from nature itself without inhabiting a human or bestial body (e.g., arboryn)
- **Shade:**
  * **Natural shade:** a deceased's ghost that exists in the physical realm, lingering around an object or place of importance to the deceased
  * **Daimos' shades:** skeletal wraithlike creatures; formed of black ash
- **Zephyrian Salamander:** a rare and exceptionally intelligent breed of reptile

SYMBOLS

 Shield and Ribbon: emblem of the Rammeren clan of the Galem Mountains

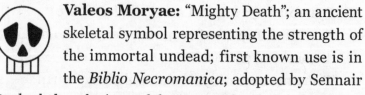 **Valeos Moryae:** "Mighty Death"; an ancient skeletal symbol representing the strength of the immortal undead; first known use is in the *Biblio Necromanica*; adopted by Sennair Drakathel as the icon of the New Order; later adopted by Daimos Recett for the icon of his own cult and guard

MISCELLANEOUS

- *Biblio Necromanica:* aka "The Necromancer's Grimoire"; oldest known Arkane text about the art of necromancy; was once stored in the vaults of the Zephyrian Archives until it was stolen in 3865
- **Saxum Diaboli:** "Stone of the Devil"; derogatory name given to Sennair Drakathel's unmarked headstone in the Venieres Forest
- **Treus Aetherae:** "Three Realms"; term describing the three realms of existence: the physical realm, the ethereal realm (or nether realm), and the spiritual realm

---

*Dark energy:** Not to be mistaken for Earth's cosmological conception of "dark energy," which is thought to make up 70 percent of the observable energy in the universe

ABOUT THE AUTHOR

Photo by Jeff Bloom

Building on an idea sparked in his imagination when he was just seven years old, Benjamin Gabbay developed the story line for the Wingheart trilogy over a decade, working on several drafts of the first book as his writing style evolved and matured. .

When he is not busy writing, Benjamin enjoys music, photography, and other forms of art, including digital art and Web design. He is the creator of an online game, the challenging Web riddle *Cipher: Crack the Code* (www.cipherriddle.com), which has fans in several countries, including China and the Philippines. Benjamin is also a passionate student of classical piano and composition, currently pursuing studies at the Royal Conservatory of Music in Toronto. Benjamin enjoys attending a teen writers' group at a Toronto library and is a member of the Toronto Public Library's Editorial Youth Advisory Group.

Visit Benjamin's website at www.benjamingabbay.com